Things fall apart; the centre cannot hold;
Mere anarchy is loosed upon the world,
The blood-dimmed tide is loosed, and everywhere
The ceremony of innocence is drowned;
The best lack all conviction, while the worst
Are full of passionate intensity.

—W.B. Yeats, "The Second Coming"

CHAPTER ONE

"**A**RE YOU READY TO TALK about the shooting?" Dr. Shue gazes at me from behind her chic rimless glasses and rebalances her notepad on her lap.

The ticking clock on the wall behind her is almost, but not quite, half a second off from the ticking of my watch. We have seven minutes until the fifty-minute hour ends. Eight hundred forty ticks, if I'm counting both the clock and the watch.

My phone vibrates in the pocket of my leather jacket, which is draped across the chair to my right. I tried to mix things up a bit today, so I sat on the couch instead. "It's warming up outside. Last week, that blizzard. What'd they call it? Greta? I think it's weird that they name winter storms now. I thought that was just for hurricanes. Anyway, I had to chip, like, an inch of ice off my car in the middle of the night, and it had me thinking."

Dr. Shue nods. "What were you thinking about that night?"

"About the vic, the frozen one. The perp strangled her and tossed her body into a bus shelter. It had frozen solid before anybody bothered to call 9-1-1." At least we got the guy. We indicted him yesterday and celebrated last night. And I didn't drink too much, even though the boss was buying rounds. I was proud of myself. It's the little things.

"You were thinking about the victim while you were chipping ice off of your car?"

"Well, no. I'd just gotten the call on that vic. I'm not sure what I was thinking about."

"What happens if you go back to that moment and try to remember?"

Dr. Shue and I are so good at this little game we play. I was actually contemplating what it would be like to have a normal job that let me sleep regular hours, but I don't say that, because then she'll want to talk about sleep habits or something, and the thought makes my neck tense. "You know, how it might be nice to stay inside when the weather says there's gonna be a foot of drifting snow, gusting winds, and an occasional power outage."

"Do you want to use this time to talk about the weather?" Dr. Shue asks. "Is that effective?"

The shrink and her tough love. Jesus.

"Forgive me for sounding like a psychologist, here, Liz. But I really think you might benefit from using our time together to evaluate what you want and how you want your life to be instead of how you can make yourself feel worse."

My phone gives a short little reminder buzz. The clock and my watch keep ticking, out of sync in a way that feels oddly reassuring. Four minutes to go. "How do I want my life to be?" I ask.

"You tell me." She uncrosses and recrosses her legs, and I entertain myself by listening to the swish of the fabric. "Let's go back and start at the beginning. What made you want to be a cop?"

That's not the beginning, but I'll leave it there. "Since I was a teenager, I just knew. It was a calling." I'm using a sarcastic tone of voice that doesn't match how serious all of this really is, and my guess is that she knows that. She's not stupid, and I'm not stupid enough to think she is.

"Did anything happen in your life to make you think that law enforcement was the only choice for you?"

"You've read my police jacket." There's the tense neck, and we're not even talking about my sleeping habits, but I sidestep her question by chuckling. I can't tell if she buys it or not.

She writes something on her pad with her fancy fountain pen. "Take me through how you got to Special Homicide, then." She's using a gentle tone in spite of—maybe because of—my reticence.

I take a deep breath and let it out slowly through my mouth. "I need to catch the worst of them. Not cases but people. You know, the ones whose motive is power and control. It's not supposed to matter to a cop, but motives... I care about motives." I pause and fiddle with my shoelace.

"Before I got this gig, I was a sex crimes detective, without the homicide part, for just over three years. Before that, patrol for four." I gaze out the window. "I mean, you know all of that. You've read my file."

"Yes, I have read the file."

"I just… I craved the dirt, the grit of the homicide job. It's like I need it."

"What does it do for you?"

"I'm good at solving puzzles. And I guess I thought I could make a difference." I laugh again, but this time it's genuine because I see how naïve I was when I thought I could change the world. "The work I do matters, in some small way. They call me when the violated end up dead." I search her face, wondering if that'll be enough to placate her for the day. "Or when it's some high-profile thing. They like putting cameras on us." *Good for us, right?*

"I hear pride in your voice when you talk about your job. Where does that pride come from, do you think?"

Pride? I'm not sure about pride. But maybe I am proud of what I do. "We're an elite group." I wince and uncross my legs. "That sounds bad. I don't mean it that way. I just mean we're good. They recruited Goran—my partner—and me, what, five years ago now? Something about 'filling a gap' in the department."

She nods.

I give one of those half-assed little chuckles. "They kept citing a 'disturbing rise in these kinds of crimes.' You know, since homicide and sex crimes go so well together. And of course, the whole PR thing. People want to think they're safe at night."

She writes on her pad again. "How do you cope? It must be hard. Your job must be more difficult than most other detectives'." This isn't the first time she's asked this question, though she's asked it in several different ways over the past few weeks.

"Well, I see Josh sometimes. You remember me telling you about him. My best friend for forever."

She nods and pushes her glasses up on her nose. "Any other ways that you give your brain a break?" I catch her eyes flicking to the third timepiece in the room, the digital clock on my left.

"Not really." *I work out compulsively. I hang out with my cat. I read. I*

7

pretty much gave up on having a personal life, or whatever the hours outside of work are called.

"This is something we're going to return to again and again, Liz, so think about adding to your list of ways to practice self-care."

Inwardly, I roll my eyes.

"Nice job today." She gives me a warm smile and sets the notepad on the table next to her chair. "I'll see you next week. Regular time?"

It's quiet when I get outside, save for a lone siren in the distance. Most of the city is deserted after five o'clock, and tonight is no exception. When the suits go home to the suburbs, it becomes a labyrinth of bums, kids going to concerts, and lurkers in dark corners.

I unlock my black VW Passat, which I bought used when I made detective, slide into the leather driver's seat, and crank the key in the ignition. The stereo comes on, and Henry Rollins shouts about pulling out his brain stem over a funk-punk bass hook, comforting me. Okay, Shue, there's something else for the list: music.

The first time I met Dr. Shue, I was coming unglued and doing my damnedest to hide it. Lieutenant Fishner had just taken my gun and my badge because I'd shot and killed a man in an alley. My options, beyond saying screw it to the whole job, were the department shrink, whom I'd heard bad things about, or an outside shrink on a menu of about ten names. So I closed my eyes and dropped my forefinger onto the list. It landed closest to "Grace Shue."

The shooting was justified. It took Internal Affairs only a week to figure that out, despite their long-winded, labyrinthine attempts to do damage control with the public—officer-involved shootings don't play well in the media. The guy would have killed my partner, and I care too much about Tom Goran to let that happen. The last thing any of us ever wants is to shoot somebody. But they train us, and sometimes, training takes over. I came around the corner, saw the gun pointed at my partner, then heard three explosions. I dropped the guy with two rounds to the chest, and I'm not sure how discussing it will change anything. I've never talked about it with anyone but IAU, except for the shrink in her nice slacks and her swanky office by the lake, and she always wants me to go deeper, to figure out how I really feel about it.

I'll be honest. I have nightmares that are worse than the ones I used to have. And maybe I'm in the beginning of an existential crisis. But whatever. I don't have time for that.

I look at my phone and decide to ignore the text message from my brother. Christopher gets needy sometimes, and it's not a good idea to encourage him.

In spite of the bite in the air, I crack the window. The wind off Lake Erie smells of Cleveland, my hometown, the place I swore to protect all those years ago when I was fresh faced and excited and thought I'd be the best cop in the world. It's a fairly typical Rust Belt city, downtrodden but not dead yet, coming back to life in some ways. The public schools aren't great, the homeless rate is pretty high, and there's more violent crime than there should be, but I'll argue with anyone who calls Cleveland "the mistake on the lake."

The perfect city doesn't exist, anyway. Put enough people together in a room, and there's going to be some kind of conflict. The same goes for a concrete jungle.

I hit the gym for a quick workout and get home a little after nine. I clean the cat box and take a shower. Then I pour myself my bourbon ration for the day, grit my teeth, and call my brother back because it's been a while since I talked to him. When he doesn't answer, I briefly consider calling my best friend, Josh, to catch up and make good on what I said to Shue earlier about friends, but I'm tired of talking today.

I grab my red Gibson guitar and plug it into the big amplifier in the corner of my living room. I play a few tentative chords as the amp warms up. Then I'm off, lost, consumed by the coordination of my right hand and my left.

Later, I find one of those police procedurals on TV and watch while scratching Ivan's ears and enjoying the vibration of his purr against my thigh. My favorite character, an incredibly sexy female detective, is about to kick down a door to catch a scumbag. She kicks it three times before it bursts open, then she's in his fleabag apartment with her weapon drawn. If any detective had hair that long, she'd pull it back and keep it that way all the time, not just when she wants to look sexy for the camera.

On police shows, they always get a search warrant in a few minutes. And when they enter a place, they find exactly what they're looking for within even fewer minutes. Then they Mirandize the suspect right away, which we never do. Usually the person we're arresting is so upset that all we do is exchange obscenities until he's in custody. But at least they've gotten one detail correct: she keeps her weapon down and to the right, holding it with both hands, thumbs forward, in a classic two-handed grip. It's always easier to bring it up than down if you have to shoot.

A part of me says screw realism, anyway. People only want a little taste—hints of crime scene photos, blood, and Stryker saws. They don't want to see the real stuff.

I pour myself one last splash of bourbon. "Rations are idiotic," I tell Ivan as I slide down onto the couch.

The phone on the coffee table is silent, leaving me to my solitude instead of back out into the streets of Cleveland with my gun and my badge. I doze off before I can make the move to the bedroom for sleep.

CHAPTER TWO

AWAKEN WITH A THICK FEELING in my throat, as if I've been screaming. My phone is buzzing away on the floor. *Damn it.* Those four hours were the longest stretch of uninterrupted sleep I've had in as many days. I grope around until I find my cell underneath the coffee table. "Boyle," I mumble.

The voice on the other end is gruff and insistent. "Body in the Flats," Lieutenant Fishner says. "It's a kid. Definitely not an accident. This'll be a big one."

After she gives me the location, I clear my throat, trying to process what I've just heard and waiting for the synapses to start firing.

"Boyle, are you listening? Get here now."

"I'll be there in twenty minutes." I drag myself off the couch and stumble into the bathroom. After flipping on the light, I gaze at my face in the mirror. The red in my light-gray eyes makes them look cold. Gray-blue fills in the recesses underneath them. There's a little bit of gray in my dark-auburn hair, too. I recognize myself, yet mirror-me isn't what I expect to see. I guess, maybe especially in these weird moments in the middle of the night, that I expect her to be younger, smiling, still in uniform, and definitely without that frown mark between her eyes.

I brush my teeth and wash my face with cold water. After running my wet hands through my jaw-length mop, I smear some deodorant under my arms. I hope I don't look too terrible.

I toss some clean jeans, a CDP T-shirt, and a dark-gray Cleveland Browns hoodie out of the dresser onto the bed. Its clean sheets have been untouched and pillows unmoved for probably close to a week. I dress quickly and put on my boots. I've been out of uniform for a while, but I still wear tacticals. I've always had a thing for combat boots.

I grab my leather jacket from the back of the couch and pick up my Glock and gold shield on the way out.

As I drive through Cleveland Heights and into Cleveland proper, my mind drifts. After I shot and killed that guy about six weeks ago and started attending the requisite head shrinking, I found out the average life span for sex-crimes detectives. We last three years before a transfer or retirement. Three years before we can't take it anymore and move back to vice or narcotics or, if we've really lost it, property crimes or lakeshore patrol. The worst cases exit with a self-inflicted service-weapon gunshot to the head. There aren't stats for people in squads like mine, but I'm willing to bet they're pretty grim.

"You know," Shue said two weeks ago, "there are other options in your pay grade. You could still solve cases, just… easier ones."

I was sitting in that tan leather chair, staring at a point somewhere along her substantial bookshelf. I thought maybe I should consider moving to Homicide proper. Maybe cut-and-dried—well, not literally, but whatever, relatively unmolested—dead bodies would be easier.

But every single one of us has a hot button, the kind of case that twists the viscera. Mine happens to be tragic families, and I would run into those in any kind of detective work. Narcotics? Tragic families. Vice? Tragic families. Property crimes? Right.

Besides, no one can unsee what they've already seen. There is no magic mind eraser.

The *Plain Dealer* ran an article on me about a year ago. It's weird to be interviewed for the newspaper. Profiled, I guess I mean. I'm not sure if I can still muster the compassion the reporter played up in the article. Maybe I've become one of the cerebral, detached ones. I don't like that thought.

I sometimes wonder if it's the thrill that keeps me going, if I'm addicted to it in some twisted way. I hadn't said that to the paper, and I haven't uttered it in Shue's presence, either. But sometimes I think the opposite.

Sometimes this shit gets to me.

Like tonight.

Another kid.

There's barely any traffic this time of night, so it doesn't take me long to get through downtown, down the hill, and to the Flats. Still, Goran lives closer to the scene, so I know he'll be there before me. I hope he brings coffee. I turn onto Merwin Avenue, right on the east bank of the Cuyahoga River, and wedge the Passat in next to Goran's rusty old Taurus, which he's parked in a lot about half a block away from the gathering of zone cars, patrol officers, paramedics, and gawking civilians. The water laps against a brick retaining wall that runs perpendicular to the narrow alleys between the buildings on my left. To my right stands a row of early-twentieth-century brick buildings that used to house tradesmen, shops, and bars. Now they're mostly dark, save for the bars and struggling nightclubs that haven't shuttered yet and the new upscale-housing construction up the hill.

It's cold even for March. My breath fogs out into the darkness. The smell of fish, booze, and industrial dust hits me as I make my way down the block, to the alcove—a boarded-up doorway, covered by the original awning—where the body lies. Last call is in about five minutes, but even dive bar clocks are always fast, so there's an exodus. Drunk college kids leave the two trendy—the *Plain Dealer* calls them "up-and-coming"—bars across the street and try to get past the police tape to their cars. Uniforms detain them to ask questions. I feel my senses sharpen to a fine point.

The guy could be in any one of these bars, any of these cars, in any abandoned building, any alley. He could be going anywhere in this city on Lake Erie that, in times like this, feels both too big and too small.

Red-and-blue lights flash against Tom Goran's torso as he turns and spots me. "Boyle," he calls. "Over here."

My partner is standing near the alcove across from a wider alley where the bars' dumpsters are. He towers over a green sheet that shrouds a formless object lying against the painted plywood that covers what used to be the door to a club. I make a mental note that the perp didn't leave the victim behind the dumpsters in the alley, because he wanted someone to find the body. I flash my badge at the uniform behind the crime scene tape, sign in on the scene register, then slip under the tape.

We were supposed to be off for three days after the indictment we got yesterday. I guess it doesn't really matter that the next case was supposed to go to somebody else. Sometimes things just don't work out the way we think they will.

Goran holds out a cup of coffee and studies my face when I reach him. "Did you get any sleep?"

"A little. Enough." I take the Styrofoam cup and eye his rumpled clothing. "You? Is there cream in here?"

"I'm okay. I could use about five more cups of coffee. And of course there's cream in there." He winks at me as he pulls his knit watch cap down over his ears so that it covers his graying hair.

His wife, Vera, calls him a "silver fox." He's a pretty good-looking dude. Tom—short for Tomislov—and I have been partners since Lieutenant Fishner recruited us. Goran's a great guy in that Cleveland-Croatian-Catholic-conservative way. There are rumors about him, rumors about me. Being a cop is a lot like being in high school, and we laugh about it all the time, especially since he's not my type at all. When I date—which I don't, at least not recently—I date women. The *Plain Dealer* didn't mention that in the profile, but I guess it's just as well.

He drains his coffee and hands me the empty cup. I pocket the lid, slide my own cup inside his, and drink half of what's left.

"Damn, it's cold tonight," he says as he buttons his peacoat. He's had that coat about twenty years, since he was in the navy. "Where's your poofy coat? No gloves? What, you trying to prove you're Wonder Woman or something?"

"I thought it was almost April. And Goran, I *am* Wonder Woman." I strike a superhero stance, and he chuckles.

Lieutenant Rick Castor, my old boss who is now the head of Homicide, ambles over. "Hey, Boyle," he growls, yet his eyes are warm. "This one's all yours. I'm going back to bed. Call me if you need me." He turns and walks away.

Homicide hands cases off this quickly only if something is really off. The wind blows down from the lake and against our backs. I feel as though I'm finally moving past whatever that couch maybe-dream was. Those are the worst because they mess with my brain. I know I've had them, but I don't recall details. All I know is that I wake up confused and sweating, with my heart pounding, my jaw sore, and a raw feeling in my throat. Maybe it's for the best that I don't remember.

"Yeah, well, get your cape and tights," Goran says. "I got a feeling this is gonna be a doozie."

"What're we looking at?"

When we catch the case instead of our very capable fellow detectives, especially when we're due for days off, it's probably something high profile that the media will sink their fangs into and shake, as murderous dogs do. The brass likes putting Goran and me in front of TV cameras. We're both decent enough on the witness stand, and the fact that our case clearance rate is among the highest in the area certainly doesn't hurt our reputations. Goran's a smart guy. I've seen him convince a waffling jury before. When he thinks it's going to be bad, it's probably going to be really bad.

I hand Goran the coffee cups then pull a latex glove out of my jacket pocket. Sliding it on and squatting down almost in slow motion, I swallow to push down the acid collecting behind my rib cage. I pull the sheet back to get a look at the victim. He couldn't be more than five or six. The bile rises. *Deep breaths. One, two, three.*

Child victims. I always think next time I won't freak out, next time I won't puke. Then the next time comes, and I'm on the floor in a bathroom somewhere, trying to pull it together before anyone hears me.

"Was he covered when they found him?" I ask.

"Yeah." He shines his flashlight onto the sheet so I can see better.

Reddish-blond hair that looks freshly cut almost conceals the sizable dent in the left side of his skull. He's wearing a red Spiderman sweatshirt, blue jeans, black Converse tennis shoes, and no jacket. There's very little blood. I'm grateful his eyes are closed. I notice his left arm looks too short. Maybe a birth defect? I lean forward to try to see more of that side of the body. *Damn it, no.* I feel something hot and greasy uncoil in my chest and press against my sternum.

I look up at Goran to give my eyes a break from the view. "Who found him?"

"Guy over there, talking to the unis." Goran gestures with his notebook toward a college-aged man of about average height. "I'm gonna head over there in a minute and get his statement."

The guy is about sixty pounds overweight and carrying it all in the front. His reddish stubbly mustache and beard were probably grown to cover the double chin, and he's wearing one of those knit hats with a logo on it, leather gloves, and a scarf but no coat. He's crying, complete with streaming snot and tears, while the uni tries to look sympathetic. A second guy, a tall man in a gray suit, stands off to one side with his arms crossed and his brow furrowed.

I point at him. "Who's that dude, the one in the suit? We talk to him yet?"

"Not yet. He's all yours."

I turn back to the corpse. In my experience, most homicide victims know their killers. And when someone takes the time to swaddle the body like this, we might be looking for a relative or a close friend, someone with a shred of remorse, someone who might be easy to track down once he starts feeling bad and is compelled to confess. But there isn't enough regret in the universe, not for this.

I pull the sheet back over the boy. "Let's get the lab out here. Watson on his way?" The deputy medical examiner is usually pretty quick to a scene, even though he has a wife and four kids.

"Yeah."

"Let's take a look around, establish a bigger perimeter." I scan the area, noting the flurry of uniforms holding back curious onlookers. "Scene's secure. You talk to the guy who found the body, then we'll do the grid search. Are unis on the canvas?" I pull myself up out of the squat. "Did you talk to the first responders?"

He nods and searches my face. "You okay?"

I wish he would stop asking me that. "Not really, no." I maintain eye contact. "Any ID yet?" I don't expect one with a kid, since they don't have driver's licenses, but I have to ask.

"No, but I put the word in to Missing Persons."

"Roberts and Dom on their way? Fishner?"

"The guys'll be here any minute. Fishner's meeting us back at the squad. She was here a little bit ago with Castor."

The Flats is pretty much right in the middle of Cleveland, straddling the river between the East Side and its West Side rival. I search the street in front of the alcove, moving in a spiral out from the body, careful not to disturb anything. The crime scene unit will be here soon to take pictures and gather physical evidence. Within the hour, we'll have an entire team of cops and techs working this dead little boy.

It isn't generally regarded as a dangerous part of town, especially now that they're sprucing it up, building townhomes for the bankers and lawyers.

I used to come here in my college days, but it looks a lot different with a badge and a gun instead of a chain wallet and a concert ticket.

There are other parts of Cleveland where I wouldn't take my worst enemy, places that help make us one of the most violent cities in the Midwest. But even in the Flats, there were fourteen rapes and six suspicious deaths last year, so this isn't unfamiliar territory for us. What usually brings CDP to this part of town is drunk college kids misbehaving. Sex Crimes gets calls mostly for groping and date rapes, generally easy-to-solve stuff.

I recall one case in particular from a few months ago, though, one that haunts me. Over on the west bank of the river but still in the Flats, a guy raped a seventeen-year-old girl, a Chinese immigrant, then threw her out a warehouse window. He left no DNA, no fibers, nothing on the body. The only physical evidence was a hair on the ground outside the warehouse, and that could have come from anybody. It was the cleanest rape we'd ever seen. I'll try not to think of how he must have disinfected her body.

He'd pierced her heart with an ice pick before strangling her from behind and tossing her out the window. The ME report stated that she was alive for about an hour before a homeless woman found her in the bushes and called us from one of the last remaining pay phones in the city. Cause of death was a massive cerebral hemorrhage caused by blunt force trauma. Her heart kept beating even with the ice pick stuck in it, and he didn't do the job with the ligature. She'd smacked her head when she'd fallen three stories to the ground.

We never found him. We interviewed a lot of people and followed several leads. There was one suspicious guy, and Goran and I are still sure he did it. The guy lived in the same building as the girl and worked at a chemical plant as a janitor. The girl's friends told us that they ran into him a lot at the bus stop and that he was a creep, always asking the vic out, even though he was way too old for her. He had a record but nothing violent. We could tell something was off, but we couldn't get enough evidence for a search warrant, so he was off the hook.

I look back at the mound under the sheet and vow to find whoever killed this little boy.

CHAPTER THREE

THE MEDIA PARASITES ARE STARTING to gather along the edge of the yellow tape as I turn to head to the alley to look around by the dumpsters. The nightclub two doors down looks different than it did in my late-nineties heyday. It used to be Jack's Down Under, but now it's Jack's Concert Club. I guess Jack wanted to class up the place, but I'm willing to bet it's still a dive, even though they book bigger names these days. Fewer punk bands play at Jack's now, but the floor is probably still sticky, and the place most likely still smells of old fryer grease and sweat.

I spot an ATM across the street from Jack's, just to the left of where I'm standing. *Surveillance footage, maybe.* I turn to head into the alley beside the alcove and hear rustling behind me and spin back around.

I catch movement between two dumpsters across the narrow street, about halfway down another alley but visible from here. "Hey!" I call to the person rolling out of a tattered sleeping bag. "Police. Stop!" He could have had a perfect view of the alley, the alcove, the scene.

He tries to stand and stumbles as I jog over to him. "Mehrrr," he says. "Mfff, hmmm, mehrrr."

"Sir, how long have you been here? And where are you going?" I try to catch Goran's eye, but he's busy with leather-gloved college guy, who has stopped crying and is leaning against the back of a patrol car.

"Hey, laaaaaady." Sleeping-bag guy has dirty, matted hair and a scruffy beard. His clothes are torn, and even from a few feet away, he smells like a combination of a sewage treatment plant and cheap gin. "You got a smoke for me?" He grins.

I smile at him and say a tiny little prayer: *maybe he saw something.* "Answer a couple questions?" I slide my notebook and pen out of my jacket pocket.

He slumps down against the dumpster closest to his sleeping bag. He's too drunk, maybe too cold. Even if he did see something, he probably doesn't remember. It's clear that he's in no condition to murder a little boy, at least not in the way it looks as though the kid was killed, and he wouldn't have access to a clean bedsheet, either. If he did, he'd keep it.

I squat next to him anyway and point at my badge clipped to my lapel. "What's your name?"

"Anthony Dwayne Smith. I live here. Well, over there." He gestures west, across the river.

"Anthony, why are you on this side tonight?"

"That place." He points at a café down the road. "Always throw food out on Thursday nights. 'Cept not tonight, no sirree. I got nothin' tonight 'cept a little pint. Coulda used a fifth." He chuckles and coughs.

I look back and forth between his two glassy eyes. He relaxes a little.

Please, give us something, anything to go on. "Will you come to the station so we can ask you a few more questions?" When he doesn't respond, I ask, "Did you see anything weird tonight, Anthony?"

"Weird?" His eyes move to where the uniforms are working around the green sheet. "Shit."

"There's a body over there, Anthony. You hear anything?"

He shakes his head. "I been asleep."

"And earlier? Earlier in the night? Anything wake you up, anything strange?"

A few seconds tick by. He rubs the back of his hand across his face. Suddenly, his eyes open wider, and he looks more alert. "I mighta seen some dude over there. He was carryin' somethin'. He looked, I dunno, sketchy. And a car... I'm not sure when... there was a car sped away. That way, I think." He gestures to his right, up Center Street, which leads directly to the Shoreway, a pretty major east-west artery.

"What happened to the car?" I move a bit closer and try not to breathe through my nose. "Do you see the guy or the car anywhere right now?" I don't have a visual on either of our two witnesses, and I hope to everything holy that someone interviewed both of them.

19

He looks around then shakes his head. "Nah, he gone. Least I can't see him." He laughs too loudly. "But I mighta—what's the word? Heh heh—hallucinated him in the first place."

Fucking hell. "Do you remember what the vehicle looked like? Was anyone driving it?"

"Of course, lady! How else a car gonna move? It gonna drive itself?" His chuckle sputters into a cough.

I gesture at a uniform to come over here.

The officer, obviously a rookie—I can tell from the way she carries herself, all swagger with nothing behind it yet—approaches. She nods at me. "Detective Boyle, hello."

I squint at her gleaming name badge then tell Anthony, "Officer Colby is going to take you someplace warm." I'm using my witness voice, the soft, soothing one that often gets people—potential witnesses—to talk to me. "She'll make sure you get something to eat, maybe that smoke." I stand up and jot down his name and the location on a new page, wondering what happened to make him homeless.

"Aw, hell no! I didn't do a damn thing!" he yells. "I didn't see nothin', neither, 'cept some stupid dude!" He tries to climb to his feet again.

A lot of the homeless in Cleveland are homeless, at least in part, because they're mentally ill. Anthony is clearly drunk, but I'm not getting a crazy vibe off of him, which makes him a viable enough witness, assuming he doesn't change his story a million times or show up in court completely hammered. If we can get him to sit still long enough, we might get a solid lead out of him. And he'll get a hot meal and a safe place to sleep for a few hours.

"Get up, sir," Colby barks.

I shoot her a look, and she freezes in place. I guess I sometimes look more severe than I intend, but whatever. It gets the job done.

I squat back down and put my hand on his shoulder, softening my features in sympathy to show that she shouldn't have shouted at him that way. "Anthony, we just need your help," I explain, almost in a whisper. "A little boy's body is over there, and if you know—if you saw anything, it might really help us."

"Getcher hand offa me." He brushes my hand off his shoulder. "Fuck you! I ain't gonna help no cops. Fuckin' cops. Pigs. Ha-ha! Oink! I smell bacon! Hell no. No way, José." When I don't respond to his diatribe, he looks over at the green sheet. "A little boy? He dead?"

I use my liberated hand to steady my squat. "Anthony, please. Aren't you hungry?" I wonder what he's seen, beyond whatever went down tonight. My guess is a lot.

"'Course I'm hungry. You got a smoke?" His jaw moves as if he's chewing, and he gestures at me for a cigarette. He's missing a couple of teeth, and the remaining ones don't look as though they'll be staying long. "He dead, or what?"

"Yeah, Anthony, he's dead. You're going to ride with Officer Colby"—I wave my other hand at her—"to the station, and she's going to chat with you for a few minutes. You can eat, maybe take a nap, and I'll see you in a little while, okay?"

"All right, yeah, damn it. Fine. But I want a cheeseburger and fries and a Marlboro, a'ight? Menthol, if you got it. And a Coke."

"Sure, okay." I stand and hold out my hand to help him up.

He grasps it and almost pulls me down on top of him as he rises. He's shaky but not completely crocked, and I'm thinking that some food and a smoke might be exactly what he needs to remember what he saw.

"Keep an eye on him," I tell Colby. "Don't let him leave until I get his statement. If you want to take a preliminary, be my guest. Get him whatever he wants from McDonald's. Afterward, leave him alone to sleep."

"Yes, Detective."

"And Colby? Find him a cigarette, all right? I've got a stash in my top desk drawer if you need 'em." I don't smoke. I call them my witness smokes. They're probably pretty stale by now, but no one's ever complained.

She leads Anthony Dwayne Smith to her zone car, helps him into the backseat, and closes his door.

I hope he doesn't start thinking he's under arrest. Witnesses sometimes clam up and shut down when they're locked in the back of a police car with no way out.

As Colby pulls away, I head back over to talk to Gray Suit, but I don't see him. *Good, patrol is talking to him already.* "Hey," I call to the young patrol officer that I saw near Suit Man earlier. "You see that tall guy in a gray suit? Which zone car has him?"

He walks over to me but doesn't get too close. "Guy in a gray suit?"

"Yeah. Tall guy." I hold one hand about six inches above my head. "He was here five minutes ago. Where'd you guys put him?"

"Uh... I... I don't know," he replies.

"You *don't know*?" I glare at his name badge and feel my face get hot. He shakes his head and looks away.

"You don't know, or you *do* know but you know you fucked up?"

"I think he left. I mean, he mighta left after we talked to him."

"Did you get his license number and address? His phone number?"

He makes brief eye contact and looks away again. "Uh... no."

"You better be kidding me." I feel as if my spine is going to explode out of the back of my neck, and I don't like it at all. I've got to get a grip on this bubbling in my chest before I have a heart attack. "You let him go. You let the guy in the suit go with no info." I shake my head. "What about college boy?"

"Your partner's with him. I'm sorry. We heard—"

I stare him down. "How long have you had this job, Officer Gable? Do you like it?" I'm using my scary-calm voice, even though what I'd like to do is yell and scream, maybe throw a couple of punches. "Who's your partner?"

He gestures toward a shorter, stockier, slightly older guy.

"Call him over here."

"Ramirez!" he shouts, raising a hand when the other man turns around.

Ramirez trudges over as if we have all the time in the world. He takes a wide-legged stance, one of those cop poses, next to his partner.

I look back and forth between them, pen against notebook page, and it isn't lost on me that Gable looks relieved, happy to let Ramirez do the talking. "Tell me what you two have gotten on Gray Suit. Who the hell is he? I assume you at least got his name?"

Ramirez tips his head at Gable, who flips open his notebook. "His name's Brian Little. Says he's an investment banker at Merrill Lynch. Down here to—his word—'decompress' for a while. Claims he had a bad day at work. Says he was at Winky's and heard a commotion in the street, so he came out to see what was happening."

So you talked to him and got that much but couldn't get an address? What the fuck? "Did you tell him not to go anywhere?"

"Of course," Ramirez says. "In fact, I made it pretty fuckin' clear. I told him to stand right there"—he points at a spot next to a fire hydrant—"until either you or your partner could get over here. He knew not to leave."

Guy standing next to a dead body who leaves before detectives can talk to him? Yeah, that's suspicious. I don't ask why no one bothered to follow procedure and put him in a zone car.

"Look," Ramirez says, "there was a loud noise, some kind of scuffle over there." He points across the street at another twenty-years-past-its-prime rock-and-roll club. "We thought it was worth checking out. We took our eyes off him for thirty seconds. There wasn't anything interesting about him, anyway. He said he came outside, saw shit going down, and got curious. He realized this other dude had found a body. That's when we showed up. He didn't see anything, except the other guy freaking out. It seemed routine. We followed procedure."

"Yeah," Gable says, braver sounding with his partner beside him. "We got a photo. We did what we were supposed to do."

You didn't do even a third of what you're supposed to do. I hand him a business card. "Email the photo to that address. Now."

He takes my card and nods vigorously.

"I need to talk to him. So you need to find him. Fucking stat." I spin around to walk away. I turn back and see them still standing there. "By 'fucking stat,' I mean *right now*," I say with a sweep of my arm.

As the two uniforms finally move their asses, I hear Goran's steady footsteps behind me.

"I'm getting photos." He raises a digital camera. "Where's the guy in the suit? What'd you get on him?"

"Uniforms let him go." I flex my jaw and reel off the information the uniforms gave.

He chomps his gum. "At least they got that, right?"

"What about your guy, college boy?"

"Sean Miller. Down here looking for a good time. Lives over on the East Side, spent most of his time over there, too." He tips his head in the direction of Winky's, which used to be a Hooters and still tries to be like Hooters but fails. "Found the kid a little before one thirty, called 9-1-1. He saw the body when he was walking back to his car. He was pretty cooked and more than a little freaked out."

"We'll have to verify that he was in there. Brian Little, too." I look at the restaurant. "Terrible food. Always has been. Remember that Hooters slogan? 'More than a mouthful.'"

He chortles. "Yeah, you aren't kidding about the food. Anyway, I told Miller not to go anywhere. He'll be in tomorrow afternoon to answer some more questions." He shakes his head and smirks. "More than a mouthful."

"Watson's here." I point at the Cuyahoga County Medical Examiner's black SUV.

As we approach, Michael Watson is pulling the sheet back from the little boy. "Happy first day of spring, Detectives," he says in a deep baritone without turning around. "Did you get good angles on all of this?" he asks Monica, his assistant.

She nods after taking two more pictures of the victim. She looks tired but gives us a little smile and wave.

Watson points at the boy's feet. "Get a couple shots of this, down here. We'll need to remember the way it's folded like that."

Monica takes more photos while we watch then puts the sheet into an evidence bag.

Watson slides a thermometer into the child's right side, where his liver is. "We'll be ready to go with the body in ten minutes, so get the guys over here," he tells Monica.

She repeats her boss's order into a small radio.

The thermometer beeps, and Watson hits a button on it to save the reading. "I'd say he's been here for about two hours, maybe three, but dead for longer. From rigor and liver temp and given how cold it is out here, I'd put time of death at about seven thirty, eight o'clock last night." He slides the thermometer out.

The kid was found at one thirty. The body was probably dropped somewhere between midnight and one, given Watson's timeline. And he was killed four or five hours before that.

"Blunt force trauma here." Watson points at the dent in the victim's skull and looks up at me. "You look like you could use some sleep."

"Right, thanks," I reply. "How're you?"

"Not too bad, all things considered." He flips the body over. "The first thing we need to do is figure out the deal with the missing hand. Looks like branch cutters or some similar instrument. See?" He holds up the small wrist.

I grimace but lean forward to get a closer look.

Watson uses his left forefinger and thumb to demonstrate. "It looks like a blade came down on either side in a single motion. Branch cutters, maybe loppers or bolt cutters. Probably a garden tool." Monica edges in and takes a photograph. "He's also got some bruising here"—Watson gestures at the child's rib cage—"that looks pre-mortem. I'll get to the autopsy tomorrow or the next day." After Monica gets her photos, he rolls the body back over.

"Tomorrow, please?"

"I'll do my best." He gives me a look, but I'm too tired to know what it means. "I will say that he wasn't killed here. There isn't enough blood. He's awfully clean."

"Another scene somewhere," I mutter. "Any sign of sexual assault?"

"Not that I can tell, but—like always—the autopsy will tell us for sure." He straightens. He's taller than either one of us and has to be over six five. He has several college basketball trophies in his office, along with a picture of him with a very young LeBron James, Cleveland's golden child, the one who we all hoped would make the Cavs into something and revitalize the city.

I step back and swallow a few times to get the acid out of my throat.

Watson's dark-brown eyes search my face. "You okay?"

"Yeah, just wired," I lie. "Thanks, Doc." I turn to my partner. "Let's work the grid."

Goran and I head back into the alley by the alcove. I hope to find the murder weapon, but we both know that's not going to happen. *Child victim. Mutilated, abused. This won't be easy.*

My phone buzzes with the email from Ramirez. The photo of Brian Little is dark and underexposed but could be usable for an ID.

After we work the scene, we start on the most important part of the job: talking to people. No one stands out among the group of bar owners, drunks, teenagers, and a couple of musician types who have gathered in the street, so we head over to Winky's. I pull the door open and am blasted by the smell of cheap beer, fryer grease, and sadness. No one comes to greet us—the hostess stand is unattended—so we head back to the bar.

One of the Winky's waitresses, Jen Kline, a petite brunette in her early twenties with a bad red dye job, meets us at the bar then takes us to a rickety table in the corner for her interview.

After we show her pictures, she says Sean Miller and Brian Little were both in the restaurant for a couple of hours. "That guy"—she points at my phone when I show her the photo of Little again—"was here before the other guy."

"When did the other one get here?" Goran asks.

"Maybe around eleven? I'm not exactly sure. They sat two seats away from each other at the bar. You know, joked about the basketball game."

I nod. "Did it seem like they knew each other?"

"Maybe? I don't really know. I was the only one working the bar, and from nine to eleven is our busy time."

"Did you notice anything else about either of them, even something that might seem insignificant?" I ask.

"One of them, the weird-looking guy in the suit, took a lot of phone calls." She makes a thinking face. "He looked like he was doing something important. He got up and left a couple of times, too. I figured he was just going to the bathroom or out to smoke."

Goran pretends to be disinterested, but I know he's making a mental recording of the conversation. He's like that.

"About what time was he here?" I ask.

"He came in around nine. I remember because I took a break right after he got here. He left right around midnight. He was a dick. He tipped me two dollars on a twenty-two tab. Then he came back later and stayed and watched the rest of the game and SportsCenter. I don't know. He was here late."

I glance at Goran out of the corner of my eye and catch the almost imperceptible shift in the set of his jaw. "How long was he gone?"

She shrugs. "Like I said, it was busy for once. More than ten minutes. Less than two hours."

So Little was in the bar, left right around the time the body was dumped, then came back. Anthony said he saw some guy drive off in a car, but that could have been anyone. Generally, a killer would want to put as much distance between himself and the vic as possible, but sometimes, for whatever sick reason, they like to stick around. It gives me the creeps just thinking about some guy sitting at the bar, making cracks about the game, when all along his car is outside with a little boy's body in the trunk.

"Does he come in here a lot?"

She shrugs again. "I only remember him from last night. No clue if he's in here a lot."

"What about the other guy, Sean Miller?" Goran asks. He's probably stepping in to let me process—in a nice, calm way—the fact that a likely perp was at the scene and a couple of uniforms let him walk.

Jen nods. "Yeah, he's a regular, friends with one of the bartenders. Cheeseburger, fries, and a basket of hot wings. I don't remember when he got here or when he left last night. Like I said, maybe around eleven? I only noticed the other guy 'cause he was kind of a dick."

I write "soft alibi" in my notebook next to Miller's name.

"Anything else?" Goran asks.

She shakes her head. "I don't get into other people's drama. I'm not even supposed to be here tonight." She rolls her eyes. "I usually work days. I've been subbing for Allie all week."

I'm skeptical. Almost every server I've met loves getting involved with drama. It's part of the restaurant business.

"Who is Allie, and why are you subbing for her?" he asks.

"She works here. I dunno. She called and needed a sub. I could use the money, so here I am."

I make a note of this next to her name in my notebook. "Jen, do you have an ID that I could see? It's routine."

She shakes her head. "Shit, no. I left it at home. But I live over in Tremont." She rattles off an address, and I write it down along with her phone number.

"Can you get us a list of the other servers who were on tonight?" Goran asks.

"Sure, yeah. Just let me go get it." She stands, tosses her hair off her shoulders, then walks down the hallway next to us and disappears through a swinging door.

Goran stifles a yawn then pops a toothpick in his mouth. I attempt a smile but know it looks fake and forced. A couple of minutes later, Jen returns with a piece of paper. I glance at the list before folding the page and sliding it into my notebook.

"Thanks, Jen." I hand her a business card. "Call me if you remember anything else."

Goran and I go outside. No one else saw a thing, at least according to Roberts and Domislaw, two of our guys who were on the canvas with a couple of more senior patrol officers. The owners of the clubs are more worried about how this will affect their businesses than about the fact that a child's body was found on their doorstep.

———— •••• ————

I swing by the gas station for more coffee before heading to the station to interview Anthony. I put my phone on speaker and call my partner. "All right, so if we can get the witness, Anthony, to put Brian Little dropping the body, then we're golden, especially if they get anything off the vic. DNA, hair—"

"Yeah, and Watson'll run prints. We'll find him, Liz."

I pull into the parking lot. "You look into Miller and Little, and I'll start the board." I'm more visual than Goran, and his handwriting is atrocious.

He swings his car into the spot next to mine, and we get out and meet in front of our vehicles.

I tip my head at his Taurus. "You need to get those brakes fixed."

"Yeah, yeah." He takes his coffee from my outstretched hand.

It's nearly dawn, one of my favorite times of day. The city will lurch to life as the sun rises behind Terminal Tower and illuminates the chugga-chug of the smokestacks to our east.

I toss my jacket over the back of my chair and swig a big mouthful of coffee from my paper cup. "Fucking gas-station coffee." I wince. "Battery acid."

"You know it always is. I can make some—"

"Oh, right, like that's not just as bad." We plop down in our chairs and stare at each other for a minute. "How fast do you think Watson'll work this?"

"Tomorrow." He flips open his laptop as I stand. "I'm gonna check Missing Persons now, since I didn't hear back from them." He looks at his notes. "Hey, you know what? That guy, the one who found the kid? Sean Miller. He works at CSU."

Cleveland State, my alma mater. I drag the rolling dry-erase board over to our desks and sketch out what we have so far. "We both know it's more likely the other guy, who's probably on a fucking airplane by now."

"Don't forget Jen Kline's missing ID," he says.

I add that information to the board then open my laptop. After verifying Kline's address with the Bureau of Motor Vehicles, I type my suspect's name into the database. "Hey, there's a Brian Little not far from here." Even though the guy in the picture doesn't look much like Gray Suit from the scene, it's worth a trip. Driver's license photos can be as deceiving as underexposed patrol photos from crime scenes, and this guy is the right height and weight. "It's too early to call Merrill Lynch."

Goran grunts then tosses his empty coffee cup into the trash can.

"Nice shot," I say.

"So you're thinking this Brian Little guy is good for it?"

"He's sure as shit suspicious, don't you think? Leaving the scene like that, leaving Winky's on and off, hanging out next to a dead body?"

"Any other Brian Littles in the database?"

"A couple. None of them are as tall as this guy, though. I mean, he could lie about his weight, but six four is hard to fake." I jot down Brian Little's address in my notebook. "Let's go talk to him when I'm done with Anthony. We gotta be smooth. Becker will never get us a warrant until we know for sure it was branch cutters and until we find the fucking branch cutters and get his DNA off them." I chuckle at the image of the prosecutor pounding on her desk and demanding more evidence. "In fact, he probably has to be holding them."

Goran raises an index finger. "One—and I know you know this, Boyle—we can't assume that this Brian Little guy is our perp, so we can't even *think* about warrants yet. You and your impulsive streak are gonna get us both sent out to Property Crimes." He grins. He knows full well that my impulsive streak is a perfect match for his overly cautious, methodical nature.

I roll my eyes. "We'd get sent back to one of the districts before Property Crimes. And I know you know this, Goran."

He chuckles and holds up two fingers. "And two, I can't figure out why you and Becker can't just get along."

I get to my feet and grab my coffee. "You know why. Because she's an uptight, arrogant asshole, and the way she behaved on the O'Rourke case was way out of line." She yelled at me in front of my entire squad for bagging evidence that was in plain sight but wasn't in the warrant. And the evidence that I got broke the case wide open.

He shakes his head. "You have too much in common."

I scoop the Nerf football off my desk and toss it at him. It bounces off his shoulder. "Too slow," I say. "We need to work on those old-man reflexes."

He makes one hand into a crank and uses it to raise his middle finger at me.

My phone vibrates. I pull it out and check the screen.

Christopher: *I need to talk to you.*

I decide to ignore it. He should have answered his phone last night, when I wasn't working and had time to chat about the weather or his money problems or whatever catastrophe is on his menu today. I shove my phone back into my pocket. Seeing the picture of Ivan on my desk, I make a mental note to buy cat food before he starts the eat-the-plants-and-puke-on-the-bed cycle of feline anger.

I pull on my jacket and grab the pack of cigarettes from my desk drawer so I can take Anthony outside to smoke before I get his statement. I hope the food and sleep have sobered him up enough to give me something. But when I get to the interview room, I glance through the one-way mirror and see only burger wrappers and a Coke can. I push open the door. The room is empty.

I jog down the hall, looking into all of the interview rooms. No Anthony. I yank open the men's room door.

"Hey!" a uniform says, shielding himself behind the urinal.

"Don't flatter yourself. You see a guy in here? Little taller than me, African-American, kind of smelly? Long hair and beard?"

He keeps his crotch covered. "Nope, not in here."

I turn to leave and catch a glimpse of Colby coming out of the file room down the hall. "Hey! Where the hell is my witness?"

The male uniform edges past me and moves a few feet down the hallway. He stands there with his back against the wall.

Colby looks as if I've slapped her, and I kind of want to. "Um, what?" she asks, almost in a whisper. "What do you mean?"

"Come over here. Now." I resist the urge to grab her and shove her into the empty interview room.

She tips her head down and takes a few steps toward me. She stops before she's in reach.

I jab a finger in the direction of the interview room. "Do you see him in there?" My anger is under control but simmering beneath the surface and creeping up into the base of my skull. "He was a witness in a fucking child murder case, Officer Colby. Child murder, maybe rape. Abuse. He's homeless. Are we going to find him now?" I enunciate clearly, wanting her to hear every syllable, every letter of my words.

"I-I'm sorry. I-I don't—"

The blood rushes to my head and face and pounds there. "Why didn't you lock the door?" It's not a question. When she doesn't reply, I add, "Did you get a prelim?" That's not a question, either.

She shakes her head. "I'll go find—"

"Yes, you *will* go find him. Take your friend here"—I stop and squint at his name badge—"Jones. Take your friend Jones and find my witness."

Colby and Jones slink toward the squad room. I lean against the wall and wait for the blood to drain from my cheeks and neck. My heartbeat returns to somewhere in the healthy range as I breathe. They'll find him, I tell myself.

Goran comes around the corner as I'm straightening. "Whoa, Liz, what was that about? You scared the shit out of those rookies!" He chuckles. "They looked like a couple of little kids rushing out of here."

I run my hands through my hair at the temples and squeeze.

"Wonder Woman doesn't lose her cool, Liz." He attempts a smile, but that weird concerned look of his appears again. He punches my shoulder. "There's no time for a meltdown. Watson called and said he thinks he has an ID. Safe-T-Kids."

"What, that fingerprint program?" Safe-T-Kids lets parents fingerprint their children to have the prints entered into local and federal databases. As its name suggests, the goal is to find them if they're abducted. The cynic in me thinks the printing provides a false sense of security—for the program to work, the kid has to be found, and a lot of abducted kids aren't—but it can also be helpful in terrible situations such as this one.

"Yeah. We need to talk to the kid's parents. They live about twenty minutes from here." He gestures at his rumpled clothes. "I figured we might want to get cleaned up first."

"Okay, I'll call them after I shower. Plan to head over to Brian Little's house afterward."

"Take your time. I'm gonna find us some real coffee and something to eat after I change clothes."

My phone buzzes again, undoubtedly another text message from my brother. I don't bother to look. *Some of us have real problems, Christopher.*

CHAPTER FOUR

OUR NEWISH UNMARKED CAR, A black Dodge Charger, is idling in the parking lot. We'd almost had to fight Domislaw and Roberts for it, until Goran pulled rank.

"We've been here longer," he said. "We have special detail." They had no argument for that. In fact, none of the other cops in Homicide did, either. In retrospect, this is strange. Maybe they figure we deserve it since we catch the creepy cases that nobody else even wants to think about.

The sun has been up for about an hour, and it feels as though it might warm up a little bit today. I saunter—some would say strut, and Goran calls it "the Boyle walk"—over to the car and yank the passenger door open. "Hey."

"Feeling better yet, Boyle? That shower help?"

"Yeah, I guess." I climb in and yank the door shut behind me.

"Good." He hands me a cup of coffee and gestures at a bagel on the console.

"Thanks."

Goran pulls out of the parking lot and onto the main street. I munch on the bagel, washing down bites with sips of coffee, and gaze out the window. People are starting to wake up, move around, get going for the day.

"Traffic on Mayfield is going to be a bitch," I say.

Goran nods and makes a right so we're heading east. "The parents at home?"

"Yeah. I'm guessing they know this isn't a good visit." I flick a piece of lint from my pants and gaze over at his profile. He shaved and changed his clothes, so he's looking presentable.

Goran slams on the brakes to avoid rear-ending a garbage truck.

"Jesus," I say. "Keep us in one piece, okay?"

"I did! I stopped!"

I pull out my notebook. "Kevin Whittle. Age five. Been missing since last Saturday. Parents have called their precinct ten-plus times a day since then. Citywide alert went out Monday morning."

He glances at me. "Parents have gotta be going crazy. What's their story? You get anything?"

"They're both professors at Cleveland State. He's in history, she's—Christ, Tom," I say as he almost rams the garbage truck again. "Do you want me to drive?"

He rolls his eyes. "Eat your bagel."

I shake my head. "She's in sociology."

He swerves to avoid a white Mercedes trying to make an illegal right turn. "So a possible connection to Sean Miller."

"I know her. The mom," I tell him after a pause. One of my degrees from CSU is in criminal sociology. "Teresa Whittle. I had a couple of seminars with her." She encouraged me to go to law school, even offered to write a letter of recommendation. That didn't quite happen. I'm more of a learn-on-the-job kind of gal. She, along with a list of other people, was a little disappointed, maybe even disheartened, when I told her I was going to the police academy instead.

"You and your degrees." He pops a piece of Doublemint into his mouth. "Some of us had to go to night school." He's smiling, but he harasses me all the time about having a college education. He's from the good old days when cops didn't need more than an associate's degree or a few years in the military to get hired. Over beers, he's admitted that he's always wanted more, maybe even law school. I've told him to go for it, that life's too short to feel stuck in place. "It's too late now," he said last time we talked about it. "I got a wife and kids."

"What do you think of the missing hand?" he asks. "Creepy."

"Too early to tell. My guess is that the blow to the head is what killed him, though, not exsanguination." I imagine the kind of force that would make a mark like that in a skull. Rage could provoke that. But the missing hand adds a level of detail that we don't usually see in rage killings. It's a more specific MO that I hope isn't the start of some serial thing.

We pull up outside a well-kept house in Forest Hills, out on the far East Side.

Goran parks the car behind a red Toyota Prius. It has a green CSU sticker on it, and I wonder if it's theirs. There are no other cars in the driveway, nor is there one in the open garage. One of those Little Tikes play sets sits in the side yard, and three bikes—two adult-sized, one much smaller—lean in the garage.

I unfasten my seat belt and open the door. "Let me break the news to Teresa, okay? There's no way she did this. I used to know her decently well."

"What, no way she killed her kid and lopped off his hand with some kind of garden tool?"

I ignore him and step out of the car. He rounds the car and walks with me toward the porch.

Before we get there, someone peeks out from behind the curtains on the front window, then the front door opens. "Detectives," a man calls in a nasally voice. "Please come in." He looks as if he gets about as much sleep as I do.

"Hi, Dr. Whittle," I say when we reach him. I show him my badge. "I'm Detective Boyle, and this is Detective Goran. We're here to talk with you about your son."

"Thank God," he replies. "And please, call me Peter." He's about four inches shorter than I am and slight, with bony shoulders, small wire-rim glasses, and a receding hairline. His salt-and-pepper beard is relatively well kept, given that his son has been missing for a week. "We're losing our minds. I'm glad they sent you to talk to us." He gestures for us to come inside, and we follow him into the living room. "Please have a seat. I'll go get my wife." He heads up a carpeted stairway.

An overstuffed hunter-green sofa sits against the front window, and two easy chairs are across from it. In between is a cherrywood coffee table. Tan carpet covers the floor, and the room is decorated with a couple of big potted plants and, on the walls, some British-looking hunting prints with shiny horses, guys in red jackets, and dogs. It's not my taste, but it's tasteful. Next to the front door is an umbrella stand with three umbrellas, two adult-sized ones and one for a kid. Next to that sits a pair of little kid's brown Wellington boots.

Family pictures line the mantel. I walk over to take a look, but I avoid the ones with Kevin's smiling face in them. An older couple in one, based on the resemblance, must be Peter Whittle's parents. The man looks familiar, but I can't quite place him.

Teresa Whittle appears in a doorway that I assume leads to the kitchen. I recognize her immediately—same shoulder-length dirty-blond hair, tortoiseshell glasses, and slacks-and-sweater combo she wore in my senior seminar. She's gained a little weight, probably pregnancy pounds she never lost. Her face looks different, drawn, her large features hollow.

"Hello, Dr. Whittle," I say. When she looks confused, I say, "It's Elizabeth, Elizabeth Boyle."

Recognition flickers across her face, and she rushes toward me, beginning to cry. "Elizabeth! What happened? Please tell me what's happened. Did you find him?"

Peter Whittle comes down the stairs. "I'm not... oh, there you are, Teresa. I was just looking for you."

"Why don't you two have a seat?" With a light touch on her arm, I guide her to one of the chairs, and her husband takes a seat on the couch. Goran perches on the edge of the other chair, but I remain standing.

"Did you find him, Elizabeth?" Teresa asks again as she sits. "Please tell me you—"

"Dr. Whittle, we did find Kevin." I say it as gently as I can.

She's making strong eye contact with me, something she always did, but now I see that concern and pain has replaced the confidence, the cool arrogance of old. Goran has his eye on Peter, who's removed his glasses and is squeezing the bridge of his nose.

"And I'm sorry to have to tell you that—"

"No!" she shrieks. "No. Please tell me he's not gone. Please tell me he's okay. His birthday..." She begins to sob. Her husband stands up and goes to her. He takes her into his arms and starts to cry, too. "We're having a party," she whimpers.

I glance at Goran. He looks about as nauseated as I feel. Notifying families has always been my least favorite part of the job. I'd rather watch an autopsy, dig through rotten garbage, or get grilled on the witness stand by a hostile defense attorney. I know how the Whittles feel, and I know there's nothing I can do or say to take away their pain.

Peter looks up, his eyes red. "How do you know?" he whispers.

"We were able to identify him because of the Safe-T-Kids fingerprints you submitted last year," Goran says in a kind voice. "I'm so sorry."

Teresa falls to the floor, screaming, "No, no, no, no, no! Please, not Kevin, please tell me this isn't happening." She buries her face in the carpet. Her husband just stands there, looking helpless. "I knew we should have never let him stay there," she wails after about five uncomfortable minutes of sobbing.

"Where did he stay?" Goran asks Peter.

"With my parents," the man replies in a monotone voice. "We called the police as soon as we knew he was missing."

"When was that?" Goran asks.

"Saturday. We called on Saturday."

So the kid went missing from the grandparents' house. We'll have to check that out.

I stand up and maneuver around the coffee table. Kneeling, I put my hand on Teresa Whittle's back. "I promise we'll find whoever did this." It's not enough, but there's nothing else to say.

She raises her head. Her face is puffy and red. She twists her body and slaps at my hand. Snot drips from her nose, tears from her eyes. I feel something swelling in my chest, pressing out into my ribs.

"Mr. Whittle," Goran says, "I'm sorry, but we need you to make an identification. We can do it now with a photograph, or we can take you down to the morgue and—"

"*No!*" Teresa bellows.

I embrace her, and she lets it all go, sputtering and moaning into my shoulder. I'm on my knees, my spine pressing into the corner of the coffee table. I'm grateful for the pressure, the physical discomfort, because it keeps me present, in the moment.

"Please, Elizabeth. Why did you let this happen?"

I say nothing. I just squeeze her tighter. Hugging people isn't a daily occurrence in my line of work, or in my life, really, but she obviously needs it.

"Mr. Whittle?" Goran holds the photograph in front of Peter.

The man turns his head, tears flowing down his face and into his beard. "I can't. I can't look at it."

Teresa jumps up and snatches the photograph from Goran's hand. "Oh my God," she whispers. "My little boy." She repeats this several times. It rings in my head.

It's exactly what my mother said once, only my dad had to go to the morgue to identify my little sister's body. There were no caring detectives with a photograph at our house, trying to save us from horrific details. When he got home and told her what happened, my mother said, "Oh my God, my little girl." She repeated it all night, all the next day, for the rest of her life, really, until she found vodka and Vicodin.

My brother and I were listening from the top of the creaky stairs in our old house. I feel transported back to that moment, everything indelibly imprinted on my brain: the sobs of my mother, the smell of something burning in the oven, seeing my father break down and cry, feeling my little brother weeping next to me on the landing and putting my arm around him, bringing him to me, my own eyes disturbingly dry.

I stand and move toward Teresa, but she backs away. Shock is setting in—I can see it on her face—so I reach out and take her hand. "Teresa, sit down," I say in my witness voice. "Please."

She lets me guide her over to sit next to her husband, who has fallen back onto the couch. Both of them are stiff and robotic, as if a switch has been shut off inside them.

Goran looks back and forth between their glassy eyes. "Did anything odd happen in the days before your son's disappearance?" Goran asks. "Anything at all, no matter if it seemed insignificant at the time?"

"No, nothing," Peter replies. "It was all completely normal."

"Can you give us a sense of Kevin's typical routine?" Goran asks.

Teresa stiffens as her face turns red, which used to be a sign of passionate anger back when she was my professor. "We already said all of this. How many times are we going to have to answer the same questions?" Anger isn't uncommon for people who are in shock. Sometimes the stages of grief happen all at once.

"We're sorry for all of the questions, and we know that you already gave a report to Missing Persons. We're just trying to cover all of our bases,"

Goran replies. "Do you mind if Detective Boyle takes a look around while I ask just a few more questions?"

"Fine," Peter says. "The police already searched the house when Kevin went missing, but that's fine."

Teresa looks a bit calmer, so I pull a business card out of my wallet and write two phone numbers on the back. I hold it out to her. "Here's my card. My cell phone number is on the back, along with the number for the Hope Foundation. They help people who have lost a family member." *People who have lost a family member to violent crime.*

She takes it and clenches it in her fist without looking at it.

"You should call them. Talk to someone. I know it doesn't seem real right now, but you're going to need to talk to someone."

"Please just go search or look around or whatever you're going to do," she says. "I have a birthday party to plan."

Pulling on a pair of latex gloves, I head upstairs while Goran continues to question them, no doubt about their alibis, Kevin's routine, and whether they've had any visitors lately.

I start with the bathroom, which is the first door on the right. There's nothing in there of note, other than a bottle of erectile dysfunction pills behind the Children's Tylenol.

Their bedroom is similar in its simplicity. It's furnished in a minimalist style, with nothing lying around. I even look under the bed. Nothing. The closet has clothes and shoes in it. I can't really dig through their drawers while they're downstairs in shock, but I'm not getting the sense that they're hiding anything in here, anyway.

The study has two desks with a laptop computer on each and a truckload of books divided by academic discipline. A wireless modem and some file folders sit on top of one bookshelf. Nothing sinister as far as my eye can see. In the closet is one of those document safes. It's unlocked, so I take a look inside. Deeds for their house and car, passports, about two thousand bucks in cash, and what looks like a key for a safe-deposit box.

Nothing is out of the ordinary. There's no massive porn stash or box of sex toys, no weird keepsakes or collections, no signs of any hobbies. Even the artwork is bland, department store stuff, other than the hunting prints in the living room. If someone searched my apartment, in about five minutes, he or she would find out all kinds of things about me and what I like.

Kevin's room is decorated in a typical little-kid motif. One wall has owl decals on it, and the others are light green and plastered with the boy's artwork. Most of his pictures are labeled or at least recognizable, with the kid and his parents, or the kid and his grandparents, or some combination of the same. A woman with yellow hair, probably a teacher or aunt, appears in a couple of the pictures. Everyone smiles in U's with big dimples at the ends.

His bedspread has cartoon trains on it. Against one wall is a shelf with a menagerie of stuffed animals and an assortment of books. A couple of what look like well-loved animals—a gray dog and a brown camel, their fur matted and worn in sections—lie on the bed.

He has a lot of books. I'd be willing to bet they read to him every night before he went to sleep. If I had a kid, I'd do the same thing. That kind of stuff matters.

In the closet are a variety of board games, coloring books, and some clothes. Stackable bins hold his socks and underwear. Just inside the bedroom door is a white-noise machine like the kind therapists keep outside their doors.

The bed is made, and the window is locked from the inside. I see no signs of foul play. I glance at the dog and the camel, careful not to think too much about my own stuffed dog from when I was a kid and the fact that I couldn't quite love him the same way after my sister died.

On the nightstand, next to a book about a cat who goes hiking and gets lost in the woods but is ultimately found, is one of those old-school magic lamps, the kind where the lampshade rotates and casts light in the shadows on the walls at night.

I go downstairs to rejoin the grim living room scene. Peter and Goran are still seated, but Teresa has moved into another phase of shock that some people experience, one in which she rambles about a variety of things, seemingly all at once. She's over by the mantel, looking at the pictures and mumbling something about knowing better than to let Peter's parents keep Kevin so often. She says, "It's my fault" a couple of times. She tries to tell us all about the birthday party they're planning. There's going to be a magician who can make balloon animals, and she mentions how adorable it is that Kevin loves animals so much. She keeps the verbs in the present tense, as though he's still alive and will be in attendance. They've been discussing the possibility of getting a cat or a dog for his birthday present.

Sometimes people talk just so we won't leave. Once we leave, there's nothing to fill the silence, and they're left with the reality that something unspeakable has happened to their loved one. They're left to sit and stare at each other, to figure out what to do about dinner and funeral arrangements and to wonder how on earth something so horrible could happen to them.

"Thanks for letting me take a look around," I say. "Is there anyone we can call for you? A friend, a neighbor? Maybe some company would be good." I'm going off script again, prompted as much by my own memories as I am by their shock and agony.

"No, no," she says, using a finger to trace the shelf of the mantel. "I'm just going to make something to eat and take a little nap. Kevin will be home soon. We'll be fine."

I glance over at Peter, who is staring out the front window. *You won't be fine. You'll never be fine again.* Goran stands and, catching my eye, gives a little nod.

I move over to the front door. "Please call us if you think of anything. Anything at all. Day or night. Give me a call." I point at my card, which she's left on the mantel.

"Okay," Peter replies, getting to his feet. "Thank you."

"Goodbye, Elizabeth," Teresa says as Goran and I file through the front door.

I let Goran go first so he can't see my face. At the car, I glance back at the house, but the Whittles aren't at the door or windows. I drop into my seat with a sigh.

Goran climbs behind the wheel, starts the engine, and belts up. "All right, so if he was with the grandparents when he went missing, then—hey, are you all right?"

"Not really." I meet his eyes. "No, not really."

"Look, Liz—"

"No, Tom."

"It's not—"

"No, Tom."

He shakes his head and pulls out of the driveway.

"We need to get surveillance footage from every single fucking place down there," I mutter. "Maybe we'll get footage of the body drop. And we have to talk to the grandparents."

The good news, obtained by Goran while I was upstairs, is that both parents have an alibi that's easy to verify. On Thursday night, Peter and Teresa had friends over to talk about how to find Kevin. Goran got the friends' phone number, so I decide to get that out of the way. A woman, Joan, answers when I call. I get her information and ask her a few questions. She confirms the time she and her husband spent with the Whittles on the night in question then goes off on a tearful diatribe about how terrible all of this is.

When I'm finally able to make a polite excuse and hang up, I call my friend Cassie at the Hope Foundation. I give her the Whittles' information and tell her what happened to Kevin.

"Oh, that's horrible," she says. "I'll get someone over there today."

"Thanks, Cassie. Say hi to Greg for me." I hang up as Goran makes a left turn to cut through a much different neighborhood, one left behind in the gentrification boom of a couple of years back. The houses are large and used to be majestic, but most have fallen into disrepair. Some are boarded up, and others have been converted into four, six, or eight apartments each.

We drive the rest of the twenty minutes to Brian Little's house in silence.

CHAPTER FIVE

WE PULL UP IN FRONT of a navy-blue Cape Cod in an area where the factory workers used to live back when the steel mills were going full force, a place where people once let their kids ride bikes in the street, mostly unsupervised, while they waxed their American-made cars in their driveways. It's still solidly middle class, but the demographics have shifted to include more people of color, something a lot of the older residents resent.

We get out of the car and make our way up a narrow sidewalk. I eyeball the landscaping, which used to be nice but has become overgrown. On the porch is a set of chairs and a table, the kind many Clevelanders store in basements or garages during the winter. A layer of fine dust—my dad used to call it "winter dirt"—covers each piece.

Goran knocks on the door while I peer inside a window to the right. What's left of the furniture is covered in sheets and towels. Stacks of boxes and papers sit in the middle of the living room. *Shit, he's in the wind.*

"It looks like nobody's been here for a while. Stuff is all over the place. No lights on."

"Are you sure this is the address?" Goran asks. He points at the mailbox, which has a "vacant" tag affixed to it.

"Yeah. I'm gonna check around back, look to see if the electric meter is running." I turn to head down the porch steps.

"Can I help you?" an elderly woman calls from the end of the gravel driveway next door.

"Ma'am, we're Cleveland police," I say as she totters toward us and up the front walk. She looks as though she could use a cane or a walker.

"Well, I'd like to see some identification, please." She sets her mouth into a haughty little pout. She's got to be close to ninety.

I pull my police ID out of my pocket and hand it to her. She studies it then gives it back and looks at Goran expectantly until he does the same.

"What could the police possibly be doing here? And homicide detectives, at that." She tut-tuts. "This is a very nice neighborhood, you know." She makes herself comfortable on one of the porch chairs. "At least it was before the undesirables moved in." She tips her head at an African-American man vacuuming his car across the street. "My name is Mary Parsalite."

"We're looking for Brian Little." I realize there's an edge to my voice. Racism doesn't sit well with me. But I need the information, so I soften my tone. "Does he live here?"

A pensive expression crosses her face, and she looks back and forth between Goran and me. "No, I'm sorry. Brian passed away last year. It was so sad. He was such a nice man. Brian used to mow my lawn. It's just so terrible what happened to him. Such a nice young man." She adjusts one of her knee-high stockings. Her ankles look swollen.

"Can you tell us what happened to Brian?" Goran asks.

"Oh, he was in a motorcycle accident a few months ago, right before Thanksgiving, I think it was. Back when we had that stretch of warm weather? That was so strange for November, wasn't it?"

Goran nods.

"Brian flew fifty feet into the air when a tanker truck hit him. Died on the spot, right there in the road. No funeral, either. It was so sad. Too bad he didn't have any family that cared. They could have gotten a nice settlement."

"So the house has been vacant all this time?"

"Well, I think Brian had money, what with all the improvements he was always making to the house. And the yard! You should have seen it before. He'd dress up and go to work every day in a nice suit and then come home, change clothes, and get right to work. He used to get me groceries sometimes, too. And he had those motorcycles—dangerous machines, those are. It's so sad that he died like that. I couldn't believe it. At least it was quick, I suppose. Lingering is worse, isn't it? My friend's sister just died of some kind of rare blood cancer. It took her four years. Four years! They did everything they could, but it was one of those cases even the doctors—and they're smart doctors, over there at the clinic—couldn't figure out." She picks at something that's stuck to the table and readjusts herself in her seat.

"Did Brian have any family at all?" I ask.

"No, just some lady friends that would come over from time to time, but I guess that's a young man's prerogative." She shakes her head in a disapproving sort of way then squints at a point off in the distance. "Now that I think of it, he might have had a sister. Yes, he did. But she lives out west somewhere, maybe Colorado or California? One of those *C* states. Bunch of liberal hippies out there, you ask me. That sister of his probably does drugs. That's why she never visited."

I kind of want to shake her, but she's old and obviously doesn't have anyone else to yammer on to. "And no one is living here now?"

"No, I already said that, didn't I? Ha-ha. My memory isn't what it used to be. Now that I think of it, there was maybe a realtor or something here not long ago, but it's been quiet. Not sure what happened to Brian's cat. Maybe Betsy down the street took it in. Lord knows she loves cats. She has to have six, maybe eight or ten by now. I can't even imagine what her place must smell like. Cats, they like to pee on things, and she doesn't let 'em outside." She lowers her voice and tilts her head toward the neighbor, who's winding up the cord to his Shop-Vac. "I wouldn't either, not anymore."

Goran quickly thanks her for her time, probably to keep me from explaining the finer points of being more tolerant. But she rattles on for at least five more minutes about the neighborhood, Brian Little, her late husband—who had been a steelworker—how the world has gone to hell in a handbasket, and why motorcycles should be illegal. I get antsy and shift my weight from foot to foot.

"I can see that you have other work to do," she finally says, "but feel free to stop by anytime if you have any updates."

Updates on what? I'm glad, not for the first time since I've been partnered with him, that Goran is good at seeming patient and kind because I can't deal with this woman right now.

"Well, that was a bust," I say once we're back in the car.

Goran grins. "What, you didn't appreciate her opinions? C'mon, Liz, the sister is probably on drugs because she lives in a *C* state. Give the old gal some credit." He hits the left-turn signal at the stop sign. "Listen, it's noon already. I know you haven't slept enough 'cause I know you, and I'm beat, myself. We need to sleep." He makes the turn.

I grin at him. "Didn't you sleep a couple of nights ago?"

"I wish, but no, I was up almost all night with Hannah, who's sick again."

I shrink away from him and make a face. "What does she have?"

"The flu. The same flu we all had three weeks ago. She's late to the party."

I shudder. "That flu was nothing to fuck with."

"Look, Sean Miller is due into the station at four. We're crap if we're zombies. We can at least catch a couple of hours. You know I'm right." He glances over at me as though he expects a battle, as if I don't need to sleep just like everybody else.

"Yeah, we all know about how well trying to sleep in the middle of the day usually goes," I grumble.

———————— •••• ————————

I park my Passat in the parking lot behind my building, but after getting out, I traipse down the driveway to the front door. I always go through the front because the back stairs feel as if they're about to cave in. The door has been spray painted with some kind of vowelless word. In spite of my exhaustion, I take the stairs two at a time, catching my own eye in the ancient, blackening mirror on the first landing. I avoid the mirrors on the next two.

I move down the hallway to 3D, last door on the right. Almost fifteen years ago, I was thrilled to get the east-facing apartment with three bay windows in the spacious living room. I'd been through my first bad breakup and needed light, and the way the sun hits the gray walls and the light oak woodwork in the morning is perfect. Between that, the hardwood floors, the giant bathroom, and the thick walls that meant I could blast music at all hours, I'd signed the lease on the spot. The couch and a couple of armchairs surround three sides of an oak coffee table and face a smallish flat-screen TV that sits between built-in bookcases that hold my Bose stereo, iPod, and, well, books. Even with all those standard living-room furnishings, there's still plenty of space for my three guitars and very loud amplifier in the far corner next to the bookcase.

I dead bolt the door and draw the chain then drop my gear on the

45

couch next to Ivan the Terrible—or Ivan the Great, depending on what he's up to—who is fast asleep and oblivious to my presence.

"*Privet*, Ivan," I say. It's the only Russian I know.

He opens one yellow eye then yawns before going back to sleep. Not all of us are inveterate insomniacs.

I tidy the kitchen and dump some food into Ivan's bowl. *Shit, I forgot to buy cat food.* I make yet another mental note to do so later. Back in the living room, I flick on the TV. The afternoon news is on, and they're still covering "the tragic story of the shocking murder of a local boy." I mute it and hope they don't release details they shouldn't.

I notice that my answering machine light—I still have a landline because I refuse to give my mother my cell number—is blinking. Caller ID says my brother called yesterday, and Mom called this morning.

I hit the button. The first message is just a dial tone because Christopher isn't one for leaving voicemails. The second starts with static on the line, then my mother says, "Lizbeth, please call me when you get this. Nothing urgent, just a quick question." Her voice sounds clearer, more with-it, than usual.

She's had a problem with booze and pills since my dad died. She ended up having to leave her job as a pharmacy technician, but East Side Pharmacy was good to her. They didn't press charges or call in the DEA, even though they should have. She'd worked there for a long time, and Leo, the pharmacist and owner, wanted her to be able to get disability. They'd been surprised, but I wasn't shocked. I'd seen her just minutes after she found my father hanging next to his heavy bag in the basement. We had just decided to go pick out the Christmas tree, and she went to the basement to get him. We didn't get a tree that year.

Christopher has been in jail before for minor stuff: public intoxication, public indecency for peeing on buildings—he's lucky he's not a registered sex offender for that one—vandalism, and various other kinds of stupidity. He's thirty-two, only three years younger than I am, and his voice still cracks sometimes. That would be endearing to most people, I suppose. Maybe it at least partially explains all the younger girlfriends. A good-sized hunk of a blond man who behaves like a teenaged boy is attractive to some women. I wonder whether he's ever going to grow up, or if he's going to keep living his life as though it's some big, long, stupid party.

I consider calling my mom since I haven't spoken to her in almost a month. I decide against it. I should feel guilty, but I don't. But the fact that I don't feel guilty makes me feel guilty. It's a vicious circle.

I switch on the Bose, but I want something quieter than the Rollins Band from last night. I scroll through the menu until I find Charlie Mingus's "Goodbye Pork Pie Hat." I was a punk rock kid, and I keep the distorted guitar stuff in heavy rotation. But I like a little bit of everything, and I'll listen to anything once.

"You have the life, cat," I tell Ivan. I give his jet-black head a scratch before heading down the hallway.

After another quick shower—I never feel clean if I only shower at work—I try to catch a couple of hours' sleep, but the Sandman doesn't come. He never does, not when I need him. I lie there, squeezing my eyes shut and trying to force my brain to slow down before the neurons short out somewhere in there and the circuit breaks and stops on the memory of what happened to my sister and my dad and my mom and my poor, stupid brother. A lot of the time, I don't notice the pain. It's just part of me. Trying to sleep is another story.

Dr. Shue thinks I should take some vacation time and go somewhere warm and sunny, unplug for a few days. But where would I go? And what would I do there? I can't really see myself on a beach, sipping a daiquiri next to a bunch of newlyweds. I'm more of a beer-and-dark-bar kind of gal. Besides, it only takes me about ten minutes to get one hell of a nasty sunburn. I'm not sure I'd want to go on vacation alone, anyway, even though I probably seem like the type who would.

I will my hand not to reach out and open the drawer to my nightstand. I refuse to take out the picture, still in its frame, of the woman I'm sure I'll never stop loving.

Shue made me identify my tragic flaw: I'm both impulsive and an overthinker. Those things don't match up very well. I don't want to be cynical or nihilistic. The cynical ones end up eating the gun, and really, at the end of the day, some things do have meaning.

CHAPTER SIX

AFTER A FITFUL HOUR OF trying to force sleep, I get up, wash the dishes, and put on a pot of coffee. While the coffee is brewing, I scarf an apple and a granola bar, standing over the sink. Ivan weaves his way between my legs, almost tripping me when I'm putting the dishes away, so I find a can of tuna in the cabinet and open it for him while he meows. He tries to trip me again when I reach down for his bowl, and he purrs loudly as I scrape the tuna into it.

"Damn it, cat, cut it out. I have work to do today and don't have time to go to the ER."

After I get dressed, I go back to the kitchen, where I grab two travel mugs from the cabinet: lots of cream in mine, black for Goran. I know I'll beat him to the station because a kid sick with the flu can't make for an easy escape, and Vera will try to make him eat something.

Back in the squad room, after I set Goran's travel mug on his desk, I call and talk to the HR people at Merrill Lynch and confirm that the Brian Little who worked there died a few months ago. I get on the *Plain Dealer*'s website and search for news of the motorcycle accident, which I find easily, thanks to Mary Parsalite's memory of when he died. I sit at my desk for a minute, forearms on my knees. I stare at my well-worn cop boots then look at my cracked coffee mug and my shabby, scratched-up desk. Even my police-issued laptop has seen better days. *Look at that dent in the side. How the hell did that happen?*

Who the hell strangles a little boy then cuts off his hand? The killer left one hand and the teeth, so it wasn't to conceal the kid's identity. Is the green sheet significant? Why did he move the body? Where's that other crime scene?

I slam my computer shut and pound on my desk until my fist hurts. Goran, who snuck in and sat at his desk without my noticing, takes a sip of coffee and eyes me pointedly.

"I still can't believe they let that guy go," I say.

"Who, not-Brian Little?" He raises his mug. "Thanks for the coffee."

"Yeah. There are only four Brian Littles in the tri-county area. The rest are all in southern Ohio. There's the dead one, two that are too short, and one that's the wrong color. And"—I point at him—"don't steal my mug this time."

"Think there's some kind of identity theft going on?"

I shrug. "At this point, anything could be going on. What I know for sure is that Gray Suit isn't Brian Little, which makes him even more suspicious."

"Okay, well, I'll let you tell Fishner that we're adding ID theft to our repertoire." He does the thing with his lips that means he's kidding but not really.

We gaze at each other for a moment and read each other's thoughts. I'm hoping that Fishner doesn't rip us a new one. She's been concerned about me lately. "Add her to the list," I said when Goran told me that. "And the line forms to the left if you want to have an intervention." I think I might have laughed.

I look up at the clock above Fishner's office door. "Shit, Goran. It's four fifteen. Wasn't Miller supposed to show at four?"

I wait until four thirty before calling the number Sean Miller gave Goran at the scene. One of those automated voices recites the number and asks me to leave a message, and I comply.

"We gotta go tell her. I'm half surprised she hasn't demanded a full briefing yet." I glance over at the lieutenant's office.

Goran follows my gaze and sighs. We both push our chairs back and stand. "Good luck with this one," Goran whispers as we trudge toward her office.

"Same to you, partner." I knock on the door.

Fishner calls out for us to come in, and we step inside. Sometimes—and I hate to say this because I know what it means, and I don't mean it that way—Lieutenant Fishner looks like a rat, like the kind some people keep as pets. She's in shape and kind of pretty in certain light, but other times she looks like a damn rodent.

I give her an extremely abridged rundown. She stands next to her file cabinet and stares at me with those beady eyes. I entertain—okay, distract—myself by imagining her with twitching whiskers.

When I finish talking, she doesn't respond immediately, as though she's waiting for more. Then she says, "Boyle, tell me what *happened*. Beyond whatever that little speech of yours just was."

I fill her in, leaving out the part about my almost-meltdown in the hallway and the incompetence that led to it. I try never to put blame on another cop unless he or she has done something completely egregious.

"Why didn't you get Anthony Smith's statement at the scene? Why have a rookie bring him here?" She moves behind her big desk and sits in her chair, creating distance between us. Her voice is calm. She's good at that.

"I couldn't." I launch into my explanation of the situation with Anthony, his drunken confusion, his need for food and a cigarette, and the fact that I talked to him first because I thought patrol had Gray Suit under control. I don't give the uniforms' names, either—it's cop law not to, so she doesn't ask. I stress how I needed to keep looking for the murder weapon or any other physical evidence. *You know, boss, I wanted to follow procedure and shit.* I don't tell her that we might have lost Sean Miller, too. That would be too much like nailing my own coffin closed.

But hell. Either I should have canvassed the Flats or I should have detained Little or I should have talked to Anthony. Whatever I didn't do is always the thing I should have done. But one or two detectives can't do everything. That's why we have all these other people, other sets of eyes, other moving parts. Anthony would have stayed by that dumpster all night. I should have talked to the other guy first.

"Detectives"—though she threw the *s* on the end of the word, her eyes are on me—"I expect that you will find *both* of these people, question them again, and report back to me by tomorrow afternoon." She tosses her pen onto the desk. She's got to be catching crap from the captain. Dead kid equals antsy brass.

"Yes, Lieutenant. We'll find them," I reply, properly contrite.

She turns to Goran. "You're planning on talking to the guy who found the body, right? I want to sit in on that. When will he be here?"

"He was supposed to be here at four," Goran says to the floor.

After a few beats, Fishner says, "You do realize a little boy was killed, right?"

I flinch. Goran does, too. *One day in, and it's already a clusterfuck.*

He takes a deep breath. "Yes, Lieutenant. We know. We'll find them. Miller'll be here any minute, I'm sure." But he doesn't sound sure at all.

She levels an even stare at us. "I'm authorizing OT for this if you need it. Get it done. But I want you to be very careful with the Whittles. And now that I mention it, let me approve the OT before you take it. In other words, I need to know your every move on this." Her tone makes me feel like a stupid child. "They're important people. I'll tell you when to talk to them. I need to make some phone calls first." She's got to have something to tell her boss. To her credit, she's had my back before, and she's a good cop. She helped to clear me with IAU after I shot that guy, among other things, but she sure knows how to get our attention in this office, and maybe how to motivate us, all without raising her voice.

"What do you mean, 'important people'?" I ask.

"Graham Whittle, the victim's grandfather, was that hedge fund manager. You know the one." Her phone chirps, and after glancing at the screen, she grimaces and presses the ignore button. "Like I said. Wait until I give you the green light to talk to them. I don't want any misunderstandings here."

That's why I'd recognized the guy in that picture on Teresa's mantel. Graham Whittle once bilked a bunch of people out of their pensions before getting out of the capitalism game right before the stock market crashed a few years back. I'm betting he has quite a list of enemies.

"Let me know once you've located your missing witnesses." Her landline phone rings on her desk. "And keep me posted about the forensics," she adds. "I have to take this. Keep me in the loop, detectives. Close the door on your way out, please."

Goran closes the door behind us and pulls his phone out of his pocket. "Watson has an autopsy report for us."

The ME usually moves child victims to the top of the list, to help the families get some closure or whatever, but it's still fast. "Let's go," I mutter. "I'm driving."

"Good thing it's a short drive," he replies. "You scare me."

"Hey, Roberts!" I call across the squad room as I'm pulling on my jacket.

The younger detective sets his spoon and jar of peanut butter, which he consumes way too much of, down on his desk and gives me a little salute.

"See what you can find on this Sean Miller guy, okay? His info is in the system. Try to locate him, and let us know if you do."

He swallows. "Ten-four, Boyle."

Goran and I take the stairs and head out the back way. I hop into the driver's seat before Goran can argue.

"What are you thinking right now?" he asks, buckling his seat belt.

"Gray Suit is my main focus."

He nods. "What do you think the deal is with the grandparents and the LT?"

I make a right onto East Thirteenth. "Who knows? She's gotta be catching shit. Politics. Did you talk to anyone in Missing Persons? Who was on the case down there?"

"Olsen. I talked to him. He's happy to hand it over. It was a complete dead end."

I pull into the morgue parking lot and swing the Charger into the spot closest to the door. Goran and I get out of the car and meet near the front bumper.

He gestures for me to go ahead of him. "It smells like rain."

"Yeah, the forecast called for it later tonight." I yank the glass door open and lead the way down the corridor. "Fishner is gonna be way up our asses on this one. Did you see that face she made back there? Hold on." I stop at the water fountain and grab a quick drink, then we finish the trek to Watson's office. The low lamplight is a welcome break from the fluorescence of the hallway.

"Detectives, come on in." Watson pushes his leather office chair back from his wooden desk. "Come on around here." He points at his two computer monitors. "We'll start with the good news. I see no signs of sexual abuse, chronic or acute."

Merciful caveat. "Time of death?" I ask.

"Hasn't changed. Seven thirty, eight o'clock."

"That pretty much exonerates his parents," I tell Goran. "They were at that dinner thing with their friends."

Watson clicks through photos of Kevin's lifeless body on one monitor, stopping at a close-up of his cleaved skull. On the other screen, he brings up a picture of a garden shovel. "This is my guess with regards to the fractured skull. The edge of the tool came down—definitely down, not from the side—on the left side of the skull, causing this divot and radial fractures." As he speaks, he points at areas on the skull and the garden shovel to illustrate. "But blunt-force trauma isn't what killed him, interestingly enough. My official cause of death is exsanguination due to severed appendage." He clicks through to a picture of Kevin's truncated wrist on one monitor then displays a pair of branch cutters on the other. "These are standard branch cutters, the kind you'd get at any major hardware store, the largest size available. The marks on the wrist bones match the curvature of these blades." He zooms in on the branch cutters.

I'm getting that feeling in my gut again. Goran puts a hand on my elbow, and his touch calms me.

"None of this happened at the first crime scene. There would have been more blood, possibly skull fragments and hair. You're looking for a shovel and branch cutters, and whatever did this." He brings up pictures of the child's rib cage. "He has bruising here, anterior"—he clicks again—"and here, posterior. It looks to me like he was punched and kicked."

I swallow hard. Abused-kid cases are even worse than random, regular kid cases.

"When do you think the abuse occurred?" Goran asks. "Is this something that could have happened at home, over time, or just before death?"

Watson nods. "The missing persons report says he was missing for several days. This bruising occurred during that time span. My guess is just before death. It's all in my full report." He clicks some more.

How the hell am I going to tell Teresa and Peter Whittle about this?

"What's that?" Goran asks, pointing at some small red marks on the screen.

"That's the victim's left shoulder," Watson says, "magnified. Those are needle marks. There are five or six of them. My guess is that someone drugged him with a sedative and that he was unconscious or semiconscious when he was beaten and kicked, given the lack of defensive wounds on his arms and intact hand."

Maybe I'll start there. If he was passed out when the abuse happened or even when he was killed, maybe he didn't suffer. "You're running tox, right? How long on that?"

Watson nods. "A couple of days. I'll call you as soon as I know something. There's one more thing." He frowns. "Even though there's no evidence of sexual assault, I found a pubic hair on the sheet. I'm running preliminary DNA. No match yet. I'll send it over to the lab."

"Anything else?" Goran asks.

Watson sits back in his chair. "Those are the main points. The rest is in the report. If I were you, I'd work on finding where he was murdered. It's definitely homicide."

"Thanks, Doc," I say. "We'll wait to hear from you on the rest."

As I'm on the way back down the overly bright hallway, uneasiness bubbles in my guts. "Why cut off the hand? Was it a mistake?"

Goran shakes his head. "Maybe the perp was planning to send proof of life, for ransom or something."

"Yeah, no tourniquet marks. If it was a mistake, the guy would have tried to stop the bleeding." He shudders and holds the front door open for me.

"It's creepy, Goran. Creepier than most."

"Yep."

"Look, Kevin's grandparents live about fifteen minutes from here. We could swing by and get the lay of the land."

"Boyle, it's too late for that today, and you heard Fishner. She's not messing around right now. Let's just head back, get the paperwork done, and hope we catch a break. We'll try to figure out what's going on with Miller while Fishner plays politician."

"Fucking busywork. We need to talk to them as soon as we can then follow up with the lab about DNA and whether we got anything at the scene."

"I talked to Olsen from Missing Persons. He said they did the regular search of their house, followed protocol. Long story short, they didn't get anything at the scene. But at least Watson got the short and curly, right?" He grins.

"Six days," I mutter. "He was missing six days."

"Yeah, and no Amber Alert, because Missing Persons couldn't confirm whether it was an abduction."

I don't have a response. An Amber Alert could have helped, but not necessarily, and what's done is done. At least we have some evidence, even if all of our witnesses are missing. And I take a little comfort in knowing that the kid might not have felt too much pain. Fear, yes, but maybe not pain.

Back in the squad room, we divvy up the paperwork and start on our reports. I check the news online and am unsurprised to learn that the "gruesome murder of a local boy" is splattered across all of the major local websites. When Jack Domislaw and Mike Roberts approach my desk, I look up.

"We got a line on Miller," Roberts says. "We got lucky in the database search. He's down in Summit County, possible drunk and disorderly early this morning." He flips open his notebook. "Second collar for public intox. Couldn't make bail today, so he's in for the night. We're gonna try to get him in here. We've got to follow up on a few things from last week's case—the LT is on the warpath today—but we thought you should know we aren't asleep at the wheel on this one."

I add the information to my notes. "Where'd he get picked up?"

"Cuyahoga Falls. He claimed he was walking home... to Cleveland. Standard-issue dumbass. That's, what, forty-five miles? It'd take him ten hours to walk that."

"All right. Thanks for the info, guys."

As the pair walk away, Goran says, "We gotta talk to him about Little or whoever-the-hell. They were at Winky's together, or at least at the same time, so maybe Miller knows him."

I nod. "Yeah, at the very least, they've talked, and he could know the guy's real name. And that explains why he didn't show up today. Do we have time to head down to Summit County and grill him now?"

Goran shakes his head. "First thing tomorrow, Liz. Let him sober up and get his act together. If Fishner wants in on this, we need him making sense."

My phone vibrates, and I pick it up. The text message from Colby gives me a little surge of adrenaline: *I've got a line on Anthony Smith. May have found out where he sleeps. Will call if I get info.*

Ten-four, I type. My stomach growls. Shue would ask me if I know how important food is for "normal metabolic and neurological functioning." The only thing I've eaten in the past eighteen hours is that bagel in the car this morning, an apple, and a granola bar. Not nearly enough protein.

As I'm contemplating the assortment of takeout menus from my desk drawer, Goran announces that his wife is going to bring us dinner. Perking up a little, I toss the menus back in and slam the drawer. Vera's meals are hearty Eastern European fare.

"She bringing the girls?" I ask. They're adorable, and I could use a dose of cute right now.

"Nah, they're with my folks. Vera needed a couple of hours off from Hannah and her coughing." His eyes flick to the photograph he keeps on his desk, and there's a twitch of a smile.

Vera is a terrific lady. She'd have to be to live with Goran. If I hadn't spent enough time with them at their house over in Old Brooklyn, I'd have trouble envisioning him with a wife and kids. He's always seemed like more of a loner, the flirt-with-the-bartender-then-go-home-alone type. I'm probably projecting.

She shows up a few minutes later, bearing lamb skewers, potatoes fried with onions, and a heavy walnut roll. We scarf down the food as if we're homeless dogs.

She glances around the squad room. "You coming home soon?" she asks her husband.

He smiles and puts his arm around her. "Eventually," he says. "I'm sorry."

We all do it. We all apologize to people who think they understand but never will and never can.

Her dark eyes flash. She appreciates what Goran and I do, but she also needs him at home from time to time. Raising two little girls can't be easy, even with his parents around to help. She pulls out of his embrace. "Tomislav, please. Your girls need to see you. Hannah has asked for you twelve times since you left this afternoon."

I grab my empty coffee cup and stand. "I'll be right back."

She catches my gaze and holds it, imploring me to make him go home. I haven't seen her in a while, and she looks different. Her hair is shorter, and she's maybe lost a few pounds since the holidays when they had me over to exchange Christmas presents because they felt bad about me being alone.

Everyone close to me knows I screwed up my last relationship, the one that made me feel like a human being for the first time since I was a kid. I screwed it up in ways that embarrass me. I hate the pity, and I despise the fact that there's nothing I can do about it now.

"Thanks for dinner, Vera," I say, patting my stomach.

"My pleasure, Liz." Her Croatian accent is still thick, even though she's lived here for over ten years now. "Always good to see you." She smiles with genuine warmth.

Our interactions haven't always been so great. There were a few weeks right after I was assigned to be Goran's partner when she was jealous. We'd been on nights back then, and I'd heard her yelling at him over the phone about his new "pretty woman cop" partner and didn't he know how much she loved him. One night about two months after we were partnered, he asked me if he could tell her that she didn't have anything to worry about. It was endearing, the way he danced around just asking me if I'm gay. She chilled out after that, and once we hung out a few times and she got to know me better, she loosened up even more.

I return the smile and turn to my partner. "Go home. I got this."

Goran sets his jaw. "Liz, I—"

Vera scowls at him. We're ganging up on him, and all three of us know that he doesn't have a choice. "Come home, Tomislav. It's already getting dark. Your girls miss you. I miss you."

I nod. "As you always like to point out, and I quote, 'Case'll still be here tomorrow, partner.'"

He points at me with the stick of gum he's just unwrapped. "You have to sleep at some point. I'm serious. 'Cause we both know you didn't this afternoon. Then you can finish those reports."

The suggestion of sleep trips a switch in my brain, and I yawn and stretch in a most unladylike way. I feel sleep beckoning. The substantial meal has hastened it. "Yeah, I'll grab a quick nap, but screw the reports. I'm gonna go out and look for Anthony, since he's the only real lead we have right now."

He winks at me. "Don't do anything crazy. Mind your p's and q's."

I give Vera a hug and thank her again for dinner. "I'll see you bright and early, Goran," I call as I head over to my locker to secure my weapon.

We have a room down the hall—I think it used to be a broom closet—with a set of bunk beds for these occasions. We call it the Z-room, or the Z for short. I hit the restroom then the bottom bunk. I'm out before I know it.

CHAPTER SEVEN

T HE RINGING PHONE PULLS ME out from under the heavy weight of dreamless sleep. I pick up the phone—*how the hell did it get all the way over there?*— and Colby's number flashes on the screen. "Boyle."

"I think he's down by Settlers' Landing," Colby says. "Word is he sleeps in the park. I'll be there in twenty minutes."

I know where she means—it's part of the Flats beat. "What, by the dog park? I'm on my way. If you find him, pick him up and bring him here." I hold the phone with my right hand and use my left to rub my sore jaw, which I must have been clenching again.

"Ten-four, Detective."

Maybe she'll make a decent cop after all. I look at my watch—3:22 a.m. Wow, that was more rest than I've gotten in one stretch in a long, long time. I'm sure Ivan is asleep on my bed, with or without me. I'm glad I don't have a dog that needs to be walked in the mornings. Ivan is pretty self-sufficient.

I stand up, shove the phone in my pocket, and go back to the squad room. At my desk, I grab my witness smokes, a portable radio, and my leather jacket.

In the parking lot, I spot Roberts and Domislaw getting out of their car. Dom immediately lights up because Roberts won't let him smoke in the car, so it's probably been a couple of hours since he got his last nicotine fix.

"Hey, Boyle," he drawls between labored breaths. Dom is a big dude, about six three and three hundred pounds. He had trouble passing last year's physical. His doctor told him to lay off the cheeseburgers and quit smoking, but I always see him consuming something, threatening to retire between bites and puffs and grunts.

"Goran go home?" Roberts asks. Mike Roberts's five-foot-six frame looks small next to his partner. But Roberts is in far better shape. He works out like a fiend and has a bodybuilder's muscle-bound shoulders.

I nod. "Yeah, hours ago. He needed to see his kids."

"You done for the day?" Roberts asks. "Gonna go shred it up?" He grins and plays air guitar. They all think it's funny that I'm a musician.

I chuckle and open my car door. "Nah, I'm back on." I wave. "'Night, guys."

I fire up the V8 and let it warm up for a minute. Domislaw drops his cigarette and crushes it with a large shoe before they go inside. I head southeast on Superior and let my brain go blank for a few minutes. *See, Shue? Taking a brain break.*

In the late '90s, CDP raided and closed six clubs for health and fire code violations here on the crummy side of the river. A developer picked up most of the properties pretty cheap. He wants to turn it into a residential area with retail space below fancy luxury apartments. It looks as though he's getting ready to begin demolition. Lining the street are some chained-off areas, construction equipment, and quite a few dumpsters.

The Flats had its heyday, but especially over here on the downtown side, it was relatively short-lived. Three drowning deaths in the river in 2000, combined with an uptick in the homeless population and a brief surge in person-on-person crime, kind of scared people away. This side of the river is nothing like it was when I was a teenager. It used to be all hustle and bustle, sex and drugs and rock and roll, but now it's deserted, save for the strip clubs and the shooting galleries inside the abandoned warehouses.

I ease the car down Lockwood Street, and I'm hit with a spooky feeling. I shouldn't be down here alone, because even Boyle needs backup, and I'm usually not stupid or careless enough to think otherwise. I glide past the old warehouse where the girl had been tossed and coast the car to a stop in front of what used to be my favorite punk club. It's boarded up now, abandoned. Down the road is the park, which the city seems to be trying to class up a bit, but behind me is a stretch of "gentleman's clubs." I'm convinced that phrase is one of the worst euphemisms in the English language.

Not far from here is the Cuyahoga Casket Company, and across the street from that is a tow truck place. It's all old industrial, death, and vice. I'm across the river, about two miles from where we found Kevin Whittle's body, but it's still the Flats. I hope Colby did her homework and knows what she's talking about. I radio her zone car to ask where she is.

"That way soon. ETA six minutes."

I get back in the car and sit tight. I'm not going into the park alone.

In the side mirror, I spot a couple of suits staggering out of the Hustler Club. As they approach the Charger, I wonder if they're heading for the big BMW parked in front of me. They stop when they reach my rear bumper. I put my right hand on my Glock as I open the door with my left. As soon as my boots hit the pavement, I hear laughter.

"Put yer dick away, bro," one of them says.

"Heeey!" The taller one fumbles at his fly, trying to zip his pants. Apparently, he was planning on pissing on my car. "Hoooooo-ie!"

"Nice try, guys," I say, my hand still on my gun.

Pants Zipper elbows his buddy in the side. "Take a look at this one," he slurs. "Wassup?"

"All right, guys, I'm CDP." I open the left side of my leather jacket so they can see the badge clipped to my belt. "Now knock it off. Call a cab, and get out of here."

"My car's right there!" the shorter one says. "We're jus' gonna—"

"You're just gonna take out your phone and call a cab, or I'm just going to have patrol come down here and bust you for DUI."

"Aw, maaaaaaan."

His eyes are bloodshot, and he's having trouble standing. I would be surprised if he could even get the key into the ignition. "Now," I order in a stern tone.

"What a fuckin' *bitch*," the tall one says.

A bitch who doesn't want you to get killed. "Sit down over there"—I gesture with my left hand—"on that bench."

The short one opens his mouth then leans forward. I jump back just in time and manage to avoid the backsplash. He doesn't, and the vomit splatters his pants.

"Real nice, bro. Good *job*," the tall one says then giggles. "Didja puke on her shoes?" He starts laughing so hard that tears roll down his cheeks.

"Sorry, ossifer," the short one says. "Oopsie-daisies."

These guys are real clichés. Ossifer? Oopsie-daisies? Really? "Detective." I can't help myself. I can be so petty.

"Sorry, *Detective*." They both break into another laughing fit.

A patrol car rounds the corner by the park and heads this way. Colby's blond hair is visible against the driver's headrest. I almost chuckle. The old hands always make the rookies drive. They say you get a better feel for the city that way. I wonder who her partner is.

They pull over to where I'm standing, and Marcus Morrison says, "Hey, Boyle."

I smile. "Morrison, how are you?" He's a decent cop. We went through the academy together, and it surprises me that he's still in a radio car, even though he always said he had no desire to be a detective. Just wants to do his twenty-five-and-out, I suppose. I've heard he's gotten into golf and bought a boat. Morrison and I hung out a couple of times, back in the day, and he'd asked me out, like on a date, as recently as a year or so ago. He's a tall, good-looking man, and I was flattered. I turned him down gently, saying I was just coming out of a bad relationship.

He steps out of the car. "What do we got here?" he asks, looking pointedly at the two drunks.

The guys immediately plop onto the bench. Morrison winks at me as Colby sidles up beside him.

"Coupla drunks," I say. "I told them to call a cab instead of trying to drive that Beamer."

He eyes the pair. "You call that cab yet? Don't *make* me put you in this car."

They laugh and point at each other. "Didja call?" one asks. "No, didjoo call?" the other replies.

Morrison shakes his head and turns back to me. "What brings you down to this neck of the woods?"

"Working the kid vic from last night. Looking for a guy who might've seen something." I don't mention his partner's role in the Anthony debacle.

He looks at Colby. "What, that homeless guy you were talking about?"

Out of the corner of my eye, I see a dark figure running into the park. "Over there," I whisper. "Go," I tell her. "Morrison, keep an eye on these guys. Make them call their cab."

Colby must have seen the figure, too, because she takes off before I finish talking. I follow her, leaving Morrison with the drunks.

"Ruuuuuuuuun!" the short one yells after me.

"Shut the hell up!" Morrison bellows.

It's times like this that I'm glad I keep myself in good shape. I wonder how Anthony can run so fast. Assuming Anthony is the person we're chasing, that is. He's the right height and build.

The park is darker than I anticipated. With all of its emphasis on crime reduction these days, I'm surprised the city hasn't installed a few more of the fancy retro lights back in here so that the suits moving into the town houses can walk their purebred dogs after dark. Once we've run for about half a mile, Colby slows to a jog, panting a little.

I pass her with a wave and close in on the man. "Anthony? Hey, Anthony, stop! It's me, Liz!"

Too late, I remember that I never told him my first name. Maybe that's a good thing. Maybe wondering who Liz is will slow him down a little bit. He runs behind some bushes against the picnic shelter next to the river. A soft cough is barely audible over a train horn in the distance.

I slow to a fast walk. "Anthony? Is that you?"

"Who the fuck are you? What do you want?"

I stride over to the bushes and part them. Anthony is sitting against the brick wall of the picnic shelter, gasping for air.

Recognition flickers across his face. "Oh, it's you."

In the beam of the one working light back here, I notice for the first time that he's handsome under all that hair. He has a strong jawline, full lips, a straight nose, and high cheekbones. He seems more with-it today. Maybe he hasn't had his pint yet. "Anthony, I've been looking for you." I search his dark eyes. "Will you come out of the bushes?"

He tries to get up but falls back. "Can't. I'm stuck." He chortles. Maybe he had that pint after all.

I hold out my hand, and he grasps it. His grip is much stronger than I expect. Colby walks up on my right, but I ignore her and focus on Anthony.

When he manages to get to his feet, I lead him into the picnic shelter. "Have a seat, Anthony."

He eases his weight down onto one of the benches. I take a quick look around. Graffiti covers the walls and some of the tables. Empty beer cans litter the floor. On the back wall, a padlocked door leads to a unisex bathroom. Beside that is a water fountain that you couldn't pay me enough to drink out of.

Morrison's voice crackles on her radio. "Ten-four," Colby replies. "Subject located."

"What you mean *suspect located*? I didn't do nothin'!" Anthony jumps up and looks as if he's about to run.

I grab his arm and pull him back down. "Anthony, she said *subject*. It's cop talk. It just means you're someone I want to talk to. Relax." A lot of people respond to force. Some become completely submissive and practically fall all over themselves as soon as they see a badge. But Anthony isn't one of those people, and he's made that clear with his body language, the running, and the flash of anger at Colby.

"Oh." He looks at me. "Can I get another cheeseburger? Or maybe some tacos?"

I maintain eye contact and nod. "Yeah, but you have to promise not to bolt this time."

"A'ight." He flashes me a sheepish grin and shakes his head. "I'm sorry."

We head back to the cars. I let Colby lead, with Anthony between us. I notice a taxi rounding the bend to pick up the drunks.

Once the taxi is back on the road and Anthony is safely in the back of the zone car, I tell Colby and Morrison, "I'll follow you to Taco Bell."

I park in the lot adjacent to the restaurant and watch the patrol car move through the drive-through line. Colby places the order, and she and Morrison talk while they wait for the food. She cracks a smile at one point in response to something Anthony says from the backseat.

As I follow them back onto the street, I wonder what Colby's story is, why she wanted to be a cop. She's probably still on probation. Losing Anthony last night could have cost her the job. I was like her once: fresh out of the academy, shiny name badge, polished boots, belt and holster still stiff and new. Young, strong, I thought I knew a lot more than I did, that textbooks and the firing range had taught me a thing or two, that I was pretty smart. I acted the badass, and it took me screwing up with a material witness in a homicide investigation my third year on the job to learn that I wasn't quite as good as I imagined. Maybe it's best Colby learns that lesson early.

I wanted to be a cop because I always knew that law and justice aren't the same thing, and I hoped that maybe I could bring justice to the law. I've come close a few times—at least I like to think so—with some cases I've closed that silenced the demons for a day or so. But other cases have done the opposite.

Back at the station, Morrison lets Anthony out of the car and tosses me the bag of food. "We've got another call," he says. "Gotta go."

Colby waves as they pull out of the parking lot.

Anthony bounces beside me like a hyperactive four-year-old. "Hey, Liz, can I get another smoke?"

"You want to eat first?" I don't think he's going to try to run, but I'd rather have him in the interview room instead of out here.

"Nah, I'll smoke, eat, then smoke again." He smiles. "If you got more smokes, that is."

I hand him a cigarette and light it for him. He pulls a drag deep into his lungs. The cigarette shakes in his hand.

"You all right?" I ask.

He moves a loose rock around with the toe of one of his worn-out running shoes. "Yeah, just didn't get my pint today. I be a'ight. I just don't wanna be involved in any of this shit. Muthafucka better off if he stay silent, you know? Talkin' to cops is a good way to get fucked up."

"Right, but we're talking about a little boy here."

"I know it. I know. Why you think I'm standin' here?" He takes another puff.

"I could try to get you into a shelter."

"Nah. I'm a'ight."

He finishes his cigarette and carefully puts it out on the side of the trash can before tossing the butt inside. *How did he end up on the street?*

He looks me up and down and grins. "Girl, that jacket look just like Shaft's."

"How do you know it isn't?" I grin. "Come on. Let's go inside."

Once we're in the interview room, I get out my notebook and prompt Anthony to go over his description of "the dude" he saw in the middle of the night, the one who might have been "carryin' somethin'."

"White dude. I dunno. It was dark."

"Was he tall? Short?"

He shrugs.

I slide the photo of not-Brian-Little across the table. "Is this him?"

He squints at it. "That's a shitty photo. I seen that dude, though."

"When was this?"

"You think I got a watch? I don't know. It was dark. I fell asleep. Next thing I know, there's cars and shit, and you comin' at me askin' me about a body." He frowns. "Dude had some kinda bag or somethin'."

I point at the picture. "This guy?"

"I dunno. Coulda been."

"Could you tell if there was anything in the bag?"

"Yeah, looked like it. It was a big bag." He holds his hands about four feet apart.

"What kind of bag? Like a duffel bag? A gym bag?"

"Nah, it looked like one of those... shit, I don't know. Like a laundry bag, maybe."

We looked through the dumpsters at the scene and didn't find a bag. "Anthony, did you see what he did with the bag?"

"Nah."

I lean back in my chair. "Anything else?" I'm not expecting more, but it never hurts to ask.

His forehead gets all creased up. "Yeah, there was a chick out there, too."

I sit up. "A woman?"

He nods. "Yeah. She came out the back of Winky's, but she wasn't dressed like no waitress there."

"Do you remember anything else about her? Height, weight, what she was wearing?"

"She had on a baseball hat. Jeans, maybe. That's what I remember. The waitresses there usually ain't got much on. Dark hair, I think."

"Did you see her around the same time as the dude with the bag?"

He scratches his head. "I think so. Somethin' woke me up. I was awake for a minute. But I was kinda out of it, you know. Hard for me to remember what I seen when."

"And the car? You saw or heard a car drive away?"

"Yeah. Heard it."

"Did you see who got into the car?"

He shakes his head.

"The woman with the baseball cap? The dude with the bag? Either of them?"

He shakes his head again. "Man, I was just tryin' to get some rest. I just heard it drive by. It went by real fast, real loud. That's the only reason I remember."

"You didn't see it drive away?"

"I saw just the back of it. It was black. A regular black car."

"Sedan? Hatchback? Four-door or two?"

He shakes his head. "Just a regular car. Not a hatchback. I think it was a four-door." He yawns. "Hey, I'm getting real tired. Mind if I take a little nap? I might remember more if I wasn't so damn tired."

Knowing I'm not going to get any more from him right now, I get to my feet. "That's fine. Sure." I head for the door.

"Would you shut the light out?" he asks as he uses his arms to make a pillow for his head.

I flip the light switch and step out of the room. In the hallway, I gently turn the lock on the door, hoping he won't hear it and freak out at being locked in. After a few beats of silence from inside the room, I go back to the squad room and add the information from Anthony's statement to the crime board.

I text Goran: *Found Anthony Smith. Gray Suit is all yours.* Then I settle in, thinking that I'll catch up on some paperwork before I doze off. I start a to-do list in my notebook:

Talk to Sean Miller about Gray Suit.

Talk to grandparents.

I decide I need some coffee if I'm going to stay awake, so I get up and trudge down the hall to the break room.

CHAPTER EIGHT

AWAKE IN A POOL OF my own drool. Once my brain starts to work, I say a little thank-you that no one saw me sleeping at my desk. At first, I wonder why no one else is here. *Right, it's Saturday.* I look at my watch. *Roberts and Dom worked all night. Fishner should be here any minute now.* I hear movement down the hall—probably the rest of Homicide, working their not-kid cases—and decide against calling Goran, figuring he needs his beauty sleep and he'll be here by nine.

I grab my mug and walk down the hall for a fill-up. I'm pouring the coffee when I remember that Anthony is asleep in my interview room. I take a couple of gulps of coffee before going to wake him.

I open the interview room door and flip the light on. "Hey, Anthony."

He raises his head. "Damn, it sure makes a difference to sleep where it's warm."

"You want a cup of coffee?" I ask.

"Nah, but maybe some water." He stretches his shoulders.

"You got it." When I turn to leave, I almost run into Lieutenant Fishner. She's at least six inches shorter than I am, which means that I'm looking down at her. I sometimes feel this strange urge to bend my knees when I have to stand next to her.

"Detective," she says, "a moment?"

I follow her into the observation room to the left. *Shit, I was supposed to call her when I found him.*

"Who is that?" she asks. "A suspect?"

"The wit. Anthony Smith."

She looks relieved. "Did you talk to him?"

"Yeah, last night. The notes are on the board." I give her the rundown.

"Okay, good." She gives me a tight nod. "How long has he been here?"

I watch Anthony through the mirror that separates the interview room from the observation room. He's fidgeting. He probably needs a cigarette, and he definitely needs a drink. "I located him last night, thanks to a tip from patrol."

She crosses her arms but doesn't say anything about the fact that I didn't call her right away. "We need to clean up the rest of this mess. I just talked to the grandparents. They're expecting you this afternoon." She takes in a deep breath. "And I said that I'd like for you to keep me in the loop, but you talked to him without me. Why is that?"

"I'm sorry. I completely forgot."

"Boyle, I expect information. A slow drip of it."

"Yes, Lieutenant. I just want to run down to Summit County and talk to Sean Miller before I go to the grandparents' house. I'll be back by one o'clock. Let me get the wit some water, then—"

"Where's your partner?" she asks, glancing at her watch.

"His kid is sick. She has that flu that's going around. I'm sure he'll be here by nine, though."

After a light knock on the door, First Assistant Prosecuting Attorney Julia Becker enters the room. She's dressed down. I don't remember ever seeing her in jeans, even designer ones. She stops next to Fishner and gestures at the two-way mirror. "What's going on here?" she asks. Her voice is deep for a woman, almost husky, and she always enunciates perfectly.

I fill her in, in less detail than what I gave to Fishner.

"This man's statement will hardly stand up in court."

"We can make it work," I mutter, suppressing the urge to roll my eyes.

"I think we're done here," Fishner says.

I walk back out into the hallway and push open the door to the interview room. "All right, Anthony, let's go."

Looking relieved, he grabs his grimy coat off the back of the chair. We stop at the vending machine for a bottle of water then head back to the Flats.

He points at a covered bus stop ahead. "You can drop me off there."

After pulling over, I write my cell phone number on the back of a business card and hand it to him, along with the rest of my witness smokes, the lighter, and ten dollars. "Get yourself some breakfast."

"Thanks, Shaft," he says, shoving my gifts into his shirt pocket.

I know he's going to drink the money, but I don't care. "Look, I need you to stick around this area."

"Where'm I gonna go?" he asks with a little laugh.

"Hey, Anthony, thanks," I call to him as he shuffles away. He throws up a hand and waves as I drive off.

I call Goran, and he answers by yawning.

"That's a nice greeting."

"Sorry. Hannah was up all night again, still coughing. I think she's on the mend, but damned if she's sleeping."

"Tell her Aunt Liz says to get better soon. Listen, I need to get cat food and run home before Ivan destroys my apartment."

He laughs. "Beware the angry cat. I'll be in in about an hour, and I'm starting on the first floor, looking at surveillance. I'm hoping for a hit on Suit Guy. I'll keep you posted."

I'm emotionally exhausted, and I feel it pulling down on my shoulders as I guide the Charger onto Lorain Avenue. I'm so tired that it feels as if sheep are counting me. I think about an old appointment with Dr. Shue.

"Are you still having nightmares?" she asked.

"No, I'm fine. No more nightmares." Nightmares only happen to people who sleep for more than four hours at a time on a regular basis.

"The drinking?"

"I've cut back," I replied. Yeah, I know the statistics. So I ration myself now, for the most part. I didn't always, and I don't always. But it's under control.

I sighed and looked her in the eye when she kept going with the questions. I was going crazy, but not from the shooting, or the loneliness or guilt or whatever she thought was wrong with me. I was losing it because I had to sit at a desk and do paperwork all day, and I had too much time to practice the time-honored art of self-evaluation, the very thing that most cops try to avoid. It gets us into trouble, especially when we don't much care for what we see. Things definitely got better when I was released for duty.

As I'm turning in to the parking lot to switch vehicles, Fishner calls my cell. I answer quickly, trying to get back on her good side. "Detective Boyle."

"Front desk says the victim's grandparents are on their way up to talk to us. I need you here."

"Right now?" I ask, imagining my poor, hungry cat probably shredding my couch as revenge for being left alone all night.

"They're in the building. On their way upstairs. Now."

I put my phone in my pocket, park, and enter the building. They came here instead of waiting for me to drive out to Larchmere later this afternoon. Either there's something in particular they need to tell us, or they're hiding something that they don't want us to see at their house.

When I barrel out of the elevator, I see an elderly couple sitting on the bench in the hallway. "Are you Mr. and Mrs. Whittle?" I ask.

The man stands up. "Yes. I'm Graham, and this is Elaine. We're here to see Detectives Boyle and Goran." He's about seventy with white hair, glasses, and small hazel eyes. His thin face and narrow shoulders make him look like an older version of Peter Whittle. It's kind of hard to imagine him as *the* Graham Whittle, the financial guy who *allegedly* stole from all those people and somehow escaped federal prison. His head shot on the news made him look bigger.

"I'm Detective Boyle. Detective Goran is my partner. Can I get you something to drink? Coffee, water?"

"No. Thank you."

Elaine is weeping quietly. She holds an embroidered handkerchief over the bottom half of her face. A big tear drops out of one eye and lands on her tan leather purse. She rubs at it with an arthritic thumb.

"Ma'am?" I kneel next to her. "Are you okay?" *What a stupid question.*

"No," she whimpers. "We should have called. We should have called."

I put my hand on her shoulder and give it a light squeeze. Her bones feel too light, like a sparrow's. "Are you sure I can't get you anything?"

"No," Graham Whittle replies. "No, we're fine." He doesn't look at either of us, doesn't acknowledge his wife's tears.

"Well, Detective Goran isn't here right now, but we don't want to make you wait. Lieutenant Fishner and I just have a few questions," I say.

"A lieutenant?" Graham starts to smile but then catches himself. "Okay."

I lead the Whittles through the squad room to Fishner's office. She's sitting at the table for four to the right of the pair of leather visitors' chairs. The tangle of file folders that usually graces the table is stacked on the floor in front of the filing cabinet behind her desk. She stands and shakes their hands, offering her condolences for their loss.

"Please, have a seat." Fishner wears a kind expression that softens her features, making her appear younger than the late forties I'm sure she is. "Detective Boyle and I are going to ask you a few questions, okay? Can we get you anything? Something to drink? Coffee? Water?" *Just a few questions.* We can't come out and say that we're going to interrogate someone—people don't like that at all.

"No, we're fine," Graham says as he settles into a chair.

"Detective?" Fishner says. She usually plays observer in situations like this, probably because she thinks faster than she speaks.

"Can I take your coats?" I ask.

"We should have called," Elaine says as she struggles to remove her jacket without standing.

I go over and help her out of it. "Sir?"

"I'm fine with it here." He wrenches his arms out of his suede coat then drapes it over the back of his chair. He shoots his wife a hard look.

I hang Elaine's coat on Fishner's rack then sit in the remaining chair. They don't look rich. Their jackets are more than a couple of years old, and neither of them is flaunting anything name brand. His shirt isn't starched, and his watch is plain. I don't see any jewelry, other than their tasteful wedding bands. It's possible they're hiding millions in offshore bank accounts, I suppose. But they certainly don't live up to the hype.

"We should have called the police," Elaine tells the table. "We should have called right away once he disappeared. We never should have waited. This is horrible, just horrible." She starts to cry again.

Graham flexes his jaw and crosses his arms in front of his chest. "We were afraid to call." He directs his comments to Fishner rather than me. "We were hoping we'd find him, that he'd just wandered off. And then we thought… well, we thought if someone had taken him, they'd be after money. We thought we'd get a note or a phone call, you know, for ransom. We thought Kevin would be safer if we didn't involve the police."

"Let's back up just a little bit," Fishner says. "Can you tell us, step by step, what happened? What made you want to come in today instead of waiting for the detectives to come to your home?"

"We had to get this out," Elaine says in a voice thick with tears. "We lost you a day. An extra day the police could have been looking for Kevin…"

"Take us through what happened," Fishner says.

Graham clears his throat. "Peter asked us to look after Kevin on weekdays, while they were at work."

"He'd just gotten a promotion," Elaine adds, "to interim department chair."

"That promotion meant that he had to work regular hours in addition to his weird professor hours," Graham adds.

"When did the babysitting start?" I ask.

"End of August, year before last," Graham replies. "It was mostly because of Teresa and that stupid book. She was on a deadline."

"And she was teaching three classes," Elaine quickly throws in.

Graham sets his jaw. "She never seemed to have time for anything but her manuscript and grading papers. So we agreed to help, but then the hours got longer and longer, sometimes stretching into several days and nights at a time." He coughs.

"And Graham has a bad heart, so it was hard on us," Elaine adds.

"Is this a medical condition?" I ask. *It could be a euphemism for maybe stealing all that money and getting away with it.*

"Angina and a bad mitral valve," he replies. "I've been putting off the surgery—it's open-heart surgery, nothing to mess with—until Kevin starts school."

"How many days a week did you usually watch Kevin, especially in these past couple of months?" I ask.

"Five," he says. "Weekdays."

"How often did he typically stay overnight?"

"Two, maybe three nights a week."

"And this went on for how long?"

Elaine opens her mouth to speak, but her husband interrupts her. "I told you," he says. "About a year and a half." He shifts in his chair.

She doesn't look at any of us. "We should have called," she whispers.

He scowls. "Damn it, Elaine, just stop it."

"Okay," I say in my soothing witness voice. "Okay. Take us through what happened leading up to that, okay?"

Graham gives his wife another harsh glare, but she ignores it. "Everything was going along just fine until last Friday around noon," she says. "I was at the grocery store when Graham had an angina attack while he and Kevin were playing hide-and-seek outside."

Graham nods.

"Hide-and-seek in March?" I ask, trying to get them to confirm that this occurred last Friday, which was one of those weird Midwestern March days that tricks us into thinking spring has arrived.

Graham nods. "Yes. It was almost fifty, and we'd been cooped up indoors for weeks, so we went out. Kevin was excited about it. I had an attack and went inside—very briefly, I might add—to get my medicine. When I came back, Kevin was… gone."

There's something in Elaine's face that bothers me. She averts her eyes whenever I try to look at her. At one point, she even covers them with her hand. I'm certain she didn't kill her grandson. She wouldn't have the physical strength. But that doesn't mean she's completely innocent.

I switch tactics. "Why didn't you tell Peter and Teresa right away, when Kevin went missing?" They lied to Kevin's parents for an entire day, which is maybe what sickens me most.

They look at each other.

"We agreed that it would be best," Graham replies. He clears his throat. "We said Kevin wanted to spend the night."

"And they didn't want to talk to him, say good night, that sort of thing?"

"I said he was in the bath," Elaine whispers.

"Whose idea was it to keep it from his parents?" I ask.

"We thought for sure it was about money. Everyone always thinks we have money," Graham says, and I swear he looks ashamed. "But we don't. Not really. We live beyond our means."

"I see." *Since you tried to pay back what you stole*, I don't say. I also don't bring up the fact that I'll be going through their bank records.

"I didn't take that money," he declares. "I know this isn't about me, but I need for you to know that." He jabs at his sternum with a thumb. "I took the fall to save my company."

"Graham, please," his wife says. She turns to me. "Please. I'm so sorry. We should have called. We should have told Peter and Teresa. We should have…" She looks away.

His nostrils flare. "It must have been about money. I think something went wrong. We were sure we'd get a ransom note or something. We have an unlisted number. Maybe they lost their nerve. But it must have been about money. Who'd want to hurt Kevin?"

Elaine sputters into sobs.

That oily feeling stirs my guts again, and I hand her some tissues. "I saw a lot of Kevin's artwork at Peter and Teresa's house. Some of the pictures have a woman with yellow hair in them. Do you know who that is?"

They glance at each other, then Elaine looks away. "Our neighbor is a blonde," Graham Whittle says.

"How well do you know this neighbor?" I ask.

"Decently well. She gets our mail for us when she's out of town, and sometimes she lets Kevin play with her dog."

"Would Kevin have drawn pictures of her?"

"Yes," Graham replies. "He said that woman in the drawings was her."

Elaine stares at the table.

"We need to ask if anyone can verify your whereabouts on Thursday night," I say. When they look stricken, I tell them that it's just a formality, completely routine.

He makes a fist. "We were at home, trying to figure out where the hell Kevin was. All of this is ridiculous. Now, are we free to go?" He stands up from the table. "I don't like being accused of things I didn't do."

I get up and meet his gaze. "Sir, I understand. We're not accusing you of anything. We just have a few more questions. Everything we ask is to help find Kevin's killer. Please sit back down."

He deflates a little and returns to his seat. His wife never left her chair.

"Is there anyone who can verify your whereabouts on Thursday night?" I ask again.

"Probably either of our neighbors," he replies. "The car was out front. I didn't pull it into the garage until late."

"You only have one car?"

He nods.

I take down the neighbors' names and phone numbers on Fishner's legal pad. "Do you have a security system or anything that you might have set?" I ask. "Something that could verify that neither of you left that night?"

Elaine turns to him. "Did you set it?" she asks.

He shakes his head. "I don't remember."

I write down the security system information on the pad so I can check with the company later. "Do you know anyone named Brian Little or Sean Miller?"

He frowns. "No. Why? Are they suspects?"

"Just persons of interest. How about you, Mrs. Whittle?"

She shakes her head. "No."

"Have you received any threats? To you, your property, that kind of thing?"

They both look at me, at each other, then back at me. Graham clears his throat. "After I was accused of doing those terrible things—things I never did—I've received quite a few threats." He flexes his jaw and looks out the window.

His wife puts a hand on his arm. "Tell them, Graham. You have to tell them." When he doesn't respond, she says, "About three months ago, a former associate of Graham's contacted me," she says. "Louis Randolph."

"Randolph didn't have anything to do with this," he mutters.

I write his name on the pad. *Okay, good. Something to go on.*

Elaine glances at her husband. "He's never gotten over what happened. He's convinced that Graham stole his money."

"He's always been an asshole," the man mumbles.

"Graham!"

"I'm sorry, but he has." He looks at me. "He worked for me for a long time. I caught him following me about a year ago, so I guess he knew that we were caring for my grandson." *Worked for me. My son. My wife. My grandson. Such ownership.*

"Is there anything else you can tell us, Mrs. Whittle, about the manner in which Mr. Randolph contacted you?" Fishner asks. "Are you sure it was him?"

"It was him. I'd recognize his voice anywhere," she says. "He called me at home. He said he would get his money back or something terrible would happen. He told me to look over my shoulder everywhere I went. He said that hurting me would be the best way to get back at my husband." She sighs and slumps a little in her chair. "It was about a hundred thousand dollars. Right, Graham?" She turns to me. "Do you think he did this?"

"What does Randolph look like?" I ask.

"He's stupid looking," Graham replies. "Never has clothes that fit. I

always told him that going to a tailor was a good idea. Did he listen? No."
He huffs. "I didn't take his money. He lost that hundred thousand investing
badly. He's not very bright, that Randolph."

I pull the picture of Brian Little up on my phone and show it to them.
"Have you ever seen this man before?"

"No, he doesn't look familiar," Graham says after a brief hesitation, and
Elaine shakes her head.

I scroll to Sean Miller's photo. "How about him?" I ask.

They lean forward and squint at the screen. "No," Graham replies as his
wife shakes her head.

"Is there anything else we should know?" I ask.

"No, not that we can think of right now," he replies.

"Please don't take this the wrong way," Fishner says in her nice voice,
"but I have to ask that you not leave Cleveland until we get all of this
sorted out. Someone will be by to take a look at your house and property,
too, okay?"

"Someone was already there," Graham says. "Olsen. He was already
there."

"Since then, Mr. Whittle, this has turned from a missing persons case
into a homicide," I reply.

He looks shocked, and Elaine gasps, but they both nod.

"Okay," I say, pulling a business card out of my wallet. I scrawl my
cell phone number on the back. "Here's my card, with my direct line on
the back. Call me if you think of anything—*anything*." I hand the card to
Elaine, and she slides it into her purse, nodding.

"Thanks for coming in today," Fishner says, standing. "Detective Boyle
will show you out."

After they leave, a quick internet search takes me to the website for
Louis Randolph's new company. On the directory page are pictures of staff,
but next to his name is a gray box that contains the words "Photo Coming
Soon." I take a detour through various online social networks. No photos
there, either.

I fill in the crime board with the information gleaned from the interview
then stand back, leaning against my desk, to take it in. I'm a visual person,
and it's time to assess what we have, look for patterns.

Who: Kevin Whittle, unknown suspect

What: Kidnapped, murdered, mutilated

Where: Kidnapped from grandparents' home, body discovered in Flats

When: Time of death - Approximately 7:30 to 8:00 p.m. Thursday

Persons of interest: Brian Little, Sean Miller, Louis Randolph

I study the photographs from the scene and my sketches of the alcove, the alley, and the position of the body. "Roberts," I call across the squad room. "When did you get here?"

"Not long ago. This case is rubbing me the wrong way. I couldn't sleep, so I came back."

"Yeah, I understand. Hey, look into this guy, Louis Randolph. We need his address, financials, anything you can get. And check out this security company and these neighbors. Try to verify what Graham Whittle told me." I fill him in and grab my coat. "I'm on my way to Akron to get Sean Miller"—I tip my head at Fishner's office—"in case she forgets and wonders where I am."

"You got it," he replies.

CHAPTER NINE

O N MY WAY TO SUMMIT County, Josh calls, but I let it go to voicemail. Seeing my best friend's name gets my mind wandering. He was popular, but I was *that* kid in high school, the weird one with the blue Mohawk. I kept to myself most of the time, but I led my team to the state soccer championship and played guitar in a band. I pretended nothing could touch me, even while I was taking care of my younger brother when he had the stomach flu, helping him with his homework, and making crap dinners out of a box or can because Mom was too shitfaced to care. I was the kid who made it work in spite of it all. Maybe *to* spite it all. Music, soccer, and solitude: those were my solace. All that was after my mom moved us to Willoughby, away from the home we'd grown up in and known our whole lives. Josh and I were neighbors until then. We've known each other since we were born two months apart. Well, since we became sentient, anyway.

Josh was there when my sister went missing, and he was there the day the cops came to tell us they'd found a body that might be hers.

We'd been having a lip-synch contest on his front porch when the patrol car pulled up in front of my house. At first, I expected my sister to hop out and go running up to our front door, but instead, two cops got out. Plainclothes detectives, I know now, with badges clipped to their lapels. The looks on their faces said she wasn't with them. Josh—still "J.J." then—saw them at the same time I did, and some instinct compelled him to shut off the boom box and take my hand. We were sitting there, holding hands, when I heard my mother wail through the open windows of our living room. We didn't say anything when my dad came outside, got in the car, and followed those cops to the morgue.

I didn't become a cop for some kind of atonement, though. It was kind of because my little sister was raped and murdered and then my dad killed himself over it. But it also wasn't. I struggle to keep it from defining me. I shove it in the back of my mind with the reptile functions. Tragic family cases flip that switch, and I don't like it. It makes me feel erratic and unpredictable.

"You need some fucking therapy," Josh said when I told him the department had mandated me to see someone after shooting that perp. "You have for years."

He'd said something else before that, too, one time when he was pissed off at me for blowing off his partner's birthday party. "You'd better start telling me what the hell is going on with you. You need to start caring as much about living people as you do about murder victims." I'd heard that kind of thing before, just not from him.

I shake my head and flip on the radio. Scanning through the stations, I look for something upbeat. Nothing sounds good, so I shut it off and hit the off-ramp to go into downtown Akron. At the jail, I park in a visitors' spot and stride into the reception area.

The deputy at the front desk narrows her eyes at my badge. "Police ID."

I slide my ID out of its case and hand it to her. She takes it over to the photocopier without a word, then she returns. She holds it out to me. "Is this a custody transfer, or did someone post bail?"

"Custody transfer," I reply.

She taps on her keyboard. "It looks like bail just came through."

"Well, he's still coming with me. Care to tell me who posted that bail?"

"A bondsman out of Cuyahoga Falls. That's all the information I have right now." She slides me a clipboard. "Here, you need to fill this out."

I sign the paperwork that says Summit County is releasing Sean Miller into my custody. She tells me it will be a few minutes, so I go over to a chair in the corner and call Goran. "Hey," I tell his voicemail, "get someone to find out who posted Sean Miller's bail."

I thumb through an ancient copy of *People* then flip to the back, but someone has already filled in the crossword. I toss it back on the table and gaze at the more-ancient TV in the upper corner of the room, which is playing that courtroom reality show with the feisty judge and redheaded bailiff. After an hour, I get up and remind the deputy that I'm still waiting.

"He should be out in twenty minutes," she replies. She sounds like a robot, but I don't tell her that.

Thirty minutes later, Sean, hands cuffed behind him, is escorted through a large metal door. When he reaches me, he asks, "Am I still under arrest?" He looks exactly as I remember from the crime scene, down to the clothes.

"We'll talk about that later," I reply.

The deputy uncuffs him and gives me a little salute.

"Don't get any ideas, Sean," I say. "You're coming with me."

"My friend was supposed to come pick me up. Who are you?"

"Yeah, well, change of plans."

The deputy hands Miller a plastic bag with his personal effects and asks him to sign for them. He scrawls his name on the form and takes the bag without verifying its contents.

"Who are you?" he repeats on the way to the car. "You're obviously a cop, but what the hell?"

"I'm your ride. Detective Boyle, Cleveland Special Homicide."

"Shit, is this about that kid?" He blinks and looks around.

I grab his elbow and lead him to the car. "Yeah, it's about the kid." I open the back door. "Get in. Don't hit your head."

Once he's in the car, I slide behind the wheel then angle the rearview mirror so I can watch him through the safety cage. "Remind me what happened down there the other night."

He avoids my eyes in the mirror. "I already told you."

"No, you told my partner. Now you're gonna tell me." I pull out onto the road.

He repeats the same story he gave to Goran at the scene, which matches what Anthony told me. The whole time, though, he seems nervous. He keeps glancing at me in the rearview mirror but looks away when I try to make eye contact.

"Why'd you come down here?" I ask. "Seems weird to me. You know, just after you find a little kid's body, you leave the city... When we've arranged to see you downtown later that afternoon. Blowing off a meeting with detectives isn't a good move, Sean. We need to talk to you about what happened."

"I have family in the Falls. I freaked out. I needed to get out of Cleveland."

I let silence envelop us for the six minutes it takes to get out of town and onto the interstate. The sun has come out and is bright enough that I don my sunglasses. "Tell me about the guy you were talking to the night you found the little boy."

He gnaws on a thumbnail and stares at the seat next to him. "What guy? I don't know that guy."

"Which guy don't you know?"

"Whatever guy you're talking about. I don't know him."

"That doesn't make any sense."

"I just don't know any guys, okay?"

"The guy who sat near you at Winky's, Sean. The guy who was standing next to you after you found the body. That guy. I hear that you were friendly with him, that you talked about the basketball game that night."

"I don't know who that guy is. I mean, I've seen him around, like at Winky's. But I'm not friends with him or anything. You should ask them about him, not me."

"How long were you at Winky's that night?"

"I don't remember. I just went there to eat dinner and watch the game."

"You don't remember what time you got there?"

He shrugs and picks at something stuck to the front of his shirt. "I don't know, maybe around nine. I really don't remember."

"You go there a lot? You know someone who works there, right?"

"I know a few people who work there."

"Your girlfriend, maybe?" *Woman in a baseball cap?*

He shakes his head. "I don't have a girlfriend right now."

"Did you see anything suspicious when you were in there that night?"

He glares at me. "Look, I told you. I didn't see or hear anything. I hang out there sometimes. I know some of the bartenders. That's *it*. Okay?"

He's not under arrest anymore, and I can't legally hold him. He gazes out the window, shifting his eyes to the mirror every couple of minutes. At one point, he squeezes the bridge of his nose, then when he catches me watching him, he stops.

I pull up in front of his house on the East Side. "You know, Sean, your alibi for that night is pretty soft, and it makes me wonder what you're hiding. Do you know a guy by the name of Brian Little?"

He shakes his head.

I turn around, and he looks as though I've slapped him. "Tall guy, weird, shiny suit?"

"I *said* I don't know any guys."

I point at a white Chevy pickup in the driveway. "Is that your truck?" He nods.

"How'd you get all the way to the Falls without your truck?"

"I got a ride. Friend picked me up." He reaches for the door handle.

"A friend with what color car? Who's the friend?"

"Uh… blue. A blue one. And it's a Jeep, not a car." He blinks fast three times. "And it's just a guy I know from work."

No black sedan. Anthony was certain he saw a black sedan. "What's the guy's name?"

"Listen, I told you I don't know anything." He jiggles the door handle and scowls. "Let me out. You're harassing me, and I didn't do anything."

"What's your friend's name?"

"Jim. I don't know his last name. We aren't that close. I needed a ride, and he gave it to me."

I thought you didn't know any guys. I get out and open his door. "Sean, don't leave Cleveland again until I give you the green light. I mean it. You don't want us thinking you're involved with this. So if you think of anything you might want to tell me, something to add to the statement you gave at the scene, here's my card."

"Sure, okay." He takes the card. "But I don't know anything else."

I stay long enough to watch him amble up the front walk. He doesn't look back at me before closing the front door behind him.

I swing by the pet store on Mayfield, but they're out of Ivan's grain-free, super-duper-nutrition-for-indoor-cats brand. I hate feeding him other crap, but he's hungry, I need to get back to work, and something is better than nothing. The kid at the register can't be more than sixteen.

"Hi there, ma'am. Will this be all?" His name tag is one of those hastily made jobbies, created with a cheap label maker.

"Actually, hold on." I grab a bottle of orange juice from the cooler and a catnip mouse from a bin on the counter. "This, too."

He catches a glimpse of my gold shield. "You a police officer?"

I smile. Something about him makes me want to take him home and give him a bowl of soup. "Indeed I am." I hand him thirty bucks.

"My dad was a cop," he says. *Was* a cop. Dead or retired? Anyone's guess. He gives me my change. "You need a bag?"

"No, thanks." I can't figure out how to convey how endearing I find him, so I just continue to smile. "Thanks, Sammy. Have a good one."

"You too, Officer." He grins. "Careful out there."

As I'm pulling into my building's parking lot, my phone beeps with a text from Goran: *Fishner wants to know where you are.*

Feeding the cat. Back soon.

Once fed and after a dramatic trip through the dining room with his catnip mouse, Ivan returns to his perpetual position on the couch. *Lazy ass.* I flip on a couple of lamps in the living room, just in case it's another late night.

Roberts calls while I'm on the way to the station. "Alarm wasn't set, but the Whittles' neighbors are able to put their car in front of their house on the night Kevin was killed. One said Graham Whittle pulled it into the garage at about ten. She remembers because she was outside with her dog, and when she went back in, the ten o'clock news had just started."

I thank him then hang up and call Goran.

"Where have you been? How long does it take to feed that cat of yours?"

"Talking to Sean Miller then feeding Ivan, in that order."

"You get anything on Miller? I got your voicemail. Miller's sister posted his bail. She lives in Cuyahoga Falls."

"Something isn't right, but I had nothing to hold him on. His story hasn't changed, and he swears he doesn't know Gray Suit or anyone named Brian Little. Any news on your end?"

"Well, Louis Randolph has been out of town, in San Francisco for a real estate conference since last Wednesday. His secretary confirmed that he called her from a four-one-five area code on Thursday evening. It's not all bad, though."

"Do tell."

"Surveillance camera from the ATM down near the scene cross-checked with a club who actually gave us video," Goran says. "Time stamp around midnight, Brian Little comes out of the Emerald Club, carrying a large canvas bag. So now we just have to find out who he really is."

The Emerald Club is across the street from where Sean Miller found the body, up the road a bit, on the corner. It's another "gentleman's club," only the owners don't throw the euphemism around very much. They're trashy, and they know it. Actually, the last time I was there, it seemed as though they embrace it.

"Since when does the Emerald have cameras that work?" I ask. I worked a couple of sex crimes cases stemming from there a few years back. Videos could have been useful.

"Since those unsolved rapes. They got sick of having vice around all the time, I guess, so they fixed 'em."

"Or they're doing something else and want to monitor who comes in and out." I hear him tapping on a keyboard and Fishner's voice in the background.

"Uh-huh. It looks like maybe he works there. He has that look about him, if you know what I mean." He chomps his gum. "We're working on getting footage from a couple other places, too. There's another ATM down the road. If we can get him dropping the body... Hold on." His voice sounds farther away as he talks to someone else. "Boyle talked to him this afternoon, boss." Someone says something in the background, and he responds, "Yeah, she says she'll have the report to you by tomorrow morning."

"ASAP," Fishner replies. "It's already six thirty. What's taking her so long?"

I don't ask how they got information from a club that's notorious for being uncooperative with the police. They're probably trying to conceal more sinister activities and figure that throwing us a little something will keep us from digging too deep.

"You heard that, right?" Goran asks me. "She wants that report, stat."

"You sure it's him?" I ask.

"It's definitely him."

"Good," I say. "Fucking-great-good. I'll meet you in the Flats. It's best if a woman goes in to talk to the dancers—you know, camaraderie—so why don't you guys wait for me there?"

"You got it. See you there."

CHAPTER TEN

AFTER A QUICK STOP FOR some sandwiches and about a gallon of coffee, I drive to the Flats. The area looks much different without the swirling red-and-blue lights and flurry of uniforms. It's quiet for a Saturday evening. I notice a few teenagers heading into Jack's Concert Club, but I don't recognize the band names on the billboard. The kids look too young to be out in this part of town without their parents, but I probably did too, once.

I go all the way to the end of Riverbed Street. Crime scene tape blows in the breeze that comes down off the lake. No wind could break that stuff. Someone yanked on it until it snapped. As I pass the alcove, my gaze flicks to the dumpsters and Anthony's spot, then to the café down the road that didn't throw food out that night. I maneuver the car around and stop for a minute before heading back the other way.

Same Flats. The city can try to class it up, but it's still the same grungy mess it's always been. I roll down the windows and let the breeze blow through. The smell hits me less hard today than it did on the night Kevin Whittle died, but it's still there, still Cleveland. I roll up the passenger window and try not to think about depressing stuff.

Easing down the street, I look for Goran and Roberts. I know they'll be parked near, but not directly across from, the Emerald Club. I can see its sign, a green sort of vaguely gemstone-shaped neon thing, but no junky old Taurus. My phone vibrates in my pocket, and I answer without checking the caller ID.

"What'd you think, you were gonna sneak up on us?" Goran asks. "I hope you brought food."

"Where are you?"

"Corner of Superior and Elm," he says.

I hang up and make a right turn. Roberts has wedged the car in a space with the front bumper almost touching the back of a good-sized windowless van and the rear bumper close to a rusted-out Honda. I pull up parallel to them.

Goran looks disheveled. It's becoming a thing with him. Maybe he wants to be that detective, the sloppy guy in the trench coat. I toss the bag of subs through the open window, and it lands in Roberts's lap. I hand him the coffee and two cups.

"We can cover the alley"—Goran gestures with his toothpick—"and the front entrance. You gonna go talk to the dancers like you said?"

"Yeah. If Little happens to be in there, he might see me and run, so be on the lookout. C'mon. We'll use the Charger."

He nods and joins me in the car. I end up parking pretty close to the alleyway that runs behind the Emerald. As I get out, I notice a midsized black Lexus sedan parked illegally behind the club's back door. "Check that plate," I say through the open window.

When I open the heavy front door, the stench hits me like a fist. The club smells like stale beer and sweat and urinal cakes.

"You got a dude with you?" the bouncer, a very large man with a bad goatee and a ponytail and big silver jewelry, asks. "No bitches without dudes."

I badge him. "I'm not here to give you a hard time. I'm looking for someone, and it's not you."

He squints at my ID. "Yeah, whatever. Wait here."

When he walks away, I saunter over to the bar, where an attractive African-American woman is wiping out a glass.

"I didn't see and don't know shit," she says before I can even speak. Her eyes gleam in the low light. She can't be more than twenty-two.

"Okay." I take a seat at the bar.

The two customers a few stools over glance at me then move to a table in front of the stage. Bouncer Bob reappears from down a narrow hallway to the left of the stage, which comes out about twenty feet into the center of the room, complete with a pole and two strippers on said pole. I scan the crowd. Just a bunch of sad sacks waving dollar bills at women who are probably trying to put themselves through college. They all look way too young. The women, I mean. The men look way too old.

"I told you to wait over there," the bouncer says, pointing at the door.

"I don't listen very well," I reply. "And I said before that I'm not here to give you a hard time. So why don't you go back over there and sit down?"

He tries to puff out his chest. "Johnny won't like this," he growls.

"Fine with me."

He calls me a bitch under his breath as he turns and goes back to his post. There, he plops down on his stool and glares at me.

Out of the corner of my eye, I see a smile tug at the bartender's face. "What's your name?" I ask her.

"I said I didn't see and don't know shit." She has a scar under one eye, the kind you get when somebody wearing a big ring punches you in the face. She's tried to conceal it with makeup, and I vaguely wonder what else the makeup is hiding.

"Okay, then this'll be easy," I reply in a soft voice. I'm not trying to be a hard-ass with her. The bouncer wouldn't have told me anything, even if he saw someone kill the kid and then drop the body. But this woman, she might. "Who's Johnny?" I ask.

"Manager." She picks up a glass. "You want something to drink or what?"

"I'm fine. Thanks. Were you here on Thursday night?"

She nods and wipes the glass with a white cloth. "You should get something to drink," she says without moving her lips. "It'll look less weird that way."

"Club soda. How about Johnny? Was he here?"

"He's always here." She fills a highball glass with ice and club soda. After jamming a lime slice onto the rim, she passes me the drink. "Pretend it's booze."

I take a sip. "What does Johnny look like?" He wasn't in charge the last time I was here.

"Short and fat. Hairy. Wears a lot of gold bling. Nasty as hell," she says. "Hold on. I gotta help those guys over there."

I follow her gaze to three men who are right in front of the stage. One of them is waving a twenty and asking a tall blonde for a lap dance. The bartender grabs a round tray, puts three Bud Lights and three shots of Wild Turkey on it, and goes over to serve them.

I bring the picture of Brian Little up on my phone and slide it across the bar so that it's waiting when she returns. She looks nervous, her eyes darting all around. Bouncer Bob isn't staring anymore.

"Just nod if you've seen him before," I whisper.

Her head bobs once.

"Do you know his name?" I ask.

She shakes her head, but I'm pretty sure she's lying.

"Can you take a break? I'll meet you wherever."

She shakes her head then searches my eyes. Something has softened in hers, some sort of acknowledgment that maybe I'm not so bad, maybe I want to keep her safe. "I don't get a break," she says. "Only the dancers get breaks. I'm the new girl." She forces a laugh and glances at the pole, where a different woman is upside down and backward.

"Why are you afraid?" I ask.

"Is that a real question?"

"Are you afraid of the man in the picture?"

"Yeah, him and all these other nasty-ass motherfuckers." She forces a grin. She makes strong eye contact then whispers, "Ricky Harris."

I keep my expression flat. "He work here?"

She shakes her head. "Not exactly."

"What's your name?" I ask.

She starts wiping down the spot next to me. "You can call me Cleopatra."

"Thursday night, was he here?"

She nods, the movement almost imperceptible to anyone not sitting right next to her. I'm impressed.

"But he wasn't here all night?"

She shakes her head slightly.

"Is he here now?" I ask.

After a slight hesitation, she shrugs.

I slide a business card under my cocktail napkin. "If you think of anything I might want to know," I say as I stand. I toss a five-dollar bill on the bar.

"Okay, yeah." As I start to turn away, she adds, "When he's not here, he hangs out across the way."

"Winky's?"

She nods.

I try to hide my surprise. Jen Kline didn't say he was a regular, but then I remember that it wasn't her usual shift. On my way out the door, I tell the bouncer to have a wonderful evening. I go back to the car and give Goran the download.

"He might be in there now," I say, tipping my head at the Emerald. "The bartender wasn't sure. I'm going to Winky's for a minute. I'll be right back."

He nods. "Hell yeah. We'll cover this shithole."

Winky's isn't very busy, either. A few youngish guys sit in a booth across from the bar, which is in the center of the space. A group of what looks like out-of-town businessmen is rooted in a corner booth, and a couple of stragglers perch at the bar.

I take a seat at the bar, across from a man who looks as if his dog just died. His head is in his hands, and a half-empty pitcher of pissy-looking beer sits to his right. He has a white line on his finger where a wedding ring once might have been, and I briefly wonder what his story is as I scan the space for Ricky Harris.

After about five minutes, the bartender comes over. She looks me up and down a couple of times as she asks me if I'd like to see a menu. I guess women in here alone are kind of an anomaly, but at least we're allowed in here without a guy. She's in her midtwenties with longish dark hair—dyed, based on her skin tone—pulled into a sloppy bun. Her little tank top allows her to show off a three-quarter sleeve of tattoos on her left arm.

"No menu," I reply. "Just a coffee, please."

She grins. "You probably don't want the coffee. I think it's been on since this morning. How about a beer? Or a bloody Mary? I make a great margarita, too. Just ask those guys over there." She gestures with her eyes to the booth of young guys.

"Water, thanks."

When she sets the water down in front of me, I catch a Day-of-the-Dead skull on her forearm.

"Straw?" She reaches for a glass that contains individually wrapped ones but maintains eye contact.

"No, thanks," I reply. When she doesn't walk away, I figure that I might as well ask my questions. "Slow night?"

"Yeah, everybody got scared away after they found that little boy." She looks down at the bar with a sad expression. "Did you hear about that? It's terrible. I can't believe that happens."

"Yeah, it's awful," I reply. "How long have you worked here?"

Her eyebrows rise. "Why?"

"Detective Boyle, CDP." I lean back far enough to reveal the shield on my belt. "Is Jen Kline here?"

"No, she usually works lunch." She starts wiping down the bar with a white towel that's seen better days. "I don't know. I've been here about a year now, I guess. Are you investigating what happened to him?"

I take a sip of water and nod.

"It's terrible," she repeats. "I can't believe someone would do something like that. I can't even imagine what would make someone do that."

It happens all the time, more times than you want to know. "Were you working that night?"

"Who, me? No, I had the night off."

"Do you know most of the other servers?" I try to picture the schedule Jen had given us. There were no full names, just first and last initials.

"I know a few, I guess."

"I was talking to Jen last time I was here."

"Yeah, Jen's nice. She just had a baby about six months ago. I'm pretty sure she's gonna quit. The little boy getting murdered really fucked with her."

"Did Jen tell you anything about what she saw that night?" It wouldn't help in court, but it's good to get a read on what they tell each other.

Her brow furrows. She's wearing a lot of mascara. "Not really. Just that everything got crazy that night, once the little boy was found." She looks around but doesn't continue.

I take another drink of my water. "Did she tell you anything else?"

"Nope." She shakes her head. "Look, I really need to get back to work." She gestures at the guys in the booth, who are all pointing at their empty margarita pitcher.

"Do you know a tall guy, dresses kind of flashy? Comes in here a couple times a week to hang out? Have you seen a guy like that today?"

Something shifts behind her eyes, but I can't get a solid read on it. She's good at the poker face.

"There are a lot of guys like that in the world. I don't really get involved with the customers."

"Does the name Ricky Harris mean anything?" I ask.

Her eyes widen, but then she says, "No, I don't think so." She yanks a tequila bottle off the shelf on the wall. "Is that all? I really need to get back to work."

"Thank you for your time." I toss a dollar on the bar, along with my business card. "Will you give me a call if you think of anything else?"

"Sure. Thanks." She turns to walk away, leaving the card and the dollar on the bar.

"What's your name again?" I ask as I stand up.

"It's Elizabeth. Have a good night," she calls over her shoulder with a smile and a little wave.

At least it'll be easy to remember her name.

When I get back to the car, I open the driver's-side door. "Move. I'm driving tonight. You scare me."

Goran grunts and climbs out. While he walks around, I plop down behind the wheel and readjust the mirrors. I edge the car back about a block, not directly in front of the club but so that the front entrance is visible.

"What'd we get on that Lexus?" I ask once he's settled in the passenger seat.

"It's registered to Johnny Lamont. He runs the Emerald. Roberts is having Dom check into it."

Neither one of us discusses how difficult it is to do surveillance down here, in this network of alleys and side streets. The Emerald is even more problematic because it's on the corner, with intersecting alleys behind it. We'd need a whole lot more police to cover every possible escape route down here.

Goran and I chat about his kids and other stuff while we wait. Stakeouts can be pretty boring, so I consider it a bonus that I actually enjoy talking to my partner.

About three hours later, just before midnight, Roberts calls my cell. "White van approaching from the east." After a pause, he adds, "Van is stopping behind the Emerald." Another pause. "Suspect matching the description just exited van. He's carrying a black bag."

"Ten-four," I reply. "You cover the back, and we'll move closer to the entrance before we go inside to talk to him."

"Wait—he's going back to the van. Looking at his phone. Maybe he forgot something. Let's block him in. You take the east end of the alley, and I'll cover this side."

I drive around to the back of the building and park across the mouth of the alley. The man looks in our direction then whips his head around and sees Roberts's car. He drops the bag and breaks into a run, heading toward us. Roberts throws open his door.

"Shit, Tom," I say. "That's him. Let's go."

Goran jumps out of the car. The man is faster than he looks, and he cuts to the right down a narrow alley perpendicular to the one we're on before Goran or Roberts can get to him. I slam the Charger into reverse, spin around, and cut through the parking lot behind a self-storage place. The guy sprints out between two buildings. I pick up speed and hope I don't run my partner over as I fishtail back out onto the main road. Swinging around, I cut the man off. A few seconds later, Goran tackles him into the side of the car.

"Fuck you!" the guy screams as Goran pushes his face down on the hood. "I didn't do anything! What the fuck?"

Goran pulls the suspect upright. "Why run, then?" He flips the guy around and cuffs him in one motion. "Try running now, asshole." He spits his gum onto the ground.

I unclip my seat belt. None of the coffee spilled. I should have been a stunt driver. Roberts appears from the alley, and I see that he's holding the guy's bag.

I hop out of the car. I step between Goran and the guy. This is definitely our guy, with that big nose and weird hairline. He's wearing clothes that are both too big and too small, probably because he's tall and doesn't have a tailor. "Hi, Brian. Or should I call you Ricky?" I ask, holding my partner back with an outstretched hand. It's a fake gesture meant to scare the guy. Goran doesn't hit people.

Surprise crosses his face, then he mumbles, "I didn't do anything."

"Yeah, we heard that."

"Fuck you," Ricky replies.

"No, thanks," I reply as I start to frisk him. "Oh, what's this?" I ask, pulling a .22 out of his waistband. "Is this legal? Probably not. It looks like you're under arrest." I find a buck knife in his sock. "Hmmm... this looks a little bigger than legal, too." I flip it open. Legal is a four-inch blade, but this is six, easy.

"Fuck you," Ricky repeats. "You planted those on me."

"Nice vocabulary." I yank his wallet out of his back pocket then spin him around and into the side of the car. "Question is, what's in the bag? Are we arresting you for weapons or something else? Detective Roberts is going to open it and see." I gesture at Roberts, who slides on a pair of latex gloves.

"I didn't do anything. Fuck you."

"Hey, I already turned you down. Didn't anyone teach you that when a girl says no, she means no? Consent matters, Ricky."

"Bag's empty," Roberts says, but "empty" doesn't mean the bag didn't once contain Kevin Whittle.

"Search the van," Goran responds, taking the empty bag. Roberts nods and trots back down the alley.

The first license in the guy's wallet belongs to Richard Harris. A second one in a concealed slot has the name Brian Little. They both say he's six foot six, two hundred ten pounds with a date of birth of August 2, the day after mine. Richard Harris's address is in Ohio City. The wallet also holds three hundred dollars and several credit cards with different names on them, including a Chase Visa for Brian Little.

"Put him in the car," I tell Goran. "We have enough."

"Fuck you," Ricky repeats.

"You should shut the fuck up, since you're already under arrest," I reply as Goran pops open the rear door. He puts the suspect in the car none too gently, but he does do the hand-on-the-head thing to avoid marking the guy up.

Ricky finally decides to keep his mouth shut after I read him his rights, and he doesn't say a word on the way back to the station. That's a relief, since the broken-record act was getting old. After locking him in the interview room, Goran and I give each other a high five in spite of ourselves. We go to the kitchen. Someone's made a fresh pot of coffee, so I pour us a couple of cups.

"How long are we going to let him sit there?" Goran asks.

"At least another fifteen minutes. What an asshole."

He grins. "Think he's our guy?"

"Are you kidding? I mean, why run like that? Van, bag, Emerald Club connection, Winky's connection. The list goes on. Did you talk to the LT?" I dump the rest of the container of cream into my mug.

"Yeah, I sent her a text while you were in the bathroom. We're good. She sounded like she was out on the town or something."

Leaning back against the counter, I laugh at the image of Fishner out on the town, maybe at the club. "Think she's having a good time? Partying down somewhere?"

He chuckles. "She said to go ahead and talk to him without her."

"Really? Even with her big 'babysit Boyle' initiative?"

He ignores my question. "I think Harris is good for it," Goran says. "Everything you just said, plus the surveillance video. Maybe Roberts will get something in the van, the kid's DNA or something."

I toss back the rest of my coffee. "Let's go talk to him. Let's make him nice and uncomfortable."

We go to the observation room and watch him for about five minutes. Right when he starts to jiggle his left leg under the table, I give Goran the signal, and we go out into the hall.

Goran slams open the door to the interview room. "What were you doing down there with that bag?"

"I didn't do shit," Ricky says.

I sit down across from him. "We'll find out about the bag in a bit. Even better, what were you doing down there on Thursday night?"

"Thursday night? I don't know. Did something happen on Thursday night?"

"You know what happened, Ricky. You were there. Question is, why'd you disappear when we got there? Doesn't that seem strange? I mean, if it were me? I would have stuck around to answer questions, you know, clear my good name. Unless I did something real bad."

"Bitch, I work down there. I went outside to smoke. I talked to those cops. What do you want from me? I didn't do shit."

"People who didn't do shit don't usually run, twice, from the police, asshole," Goran growls.

Ricky stands as if he's going to leave, but Goran shoves him back down into the chair.

Ricky hunches over. "You can't do that, man. This is harassment. I told you I didn't do anything. Am I under arrest?"

"Yeah, we told you that already," Goran replies. "Remember back there in the car when my partner read you your rights? You know you're under arrest. So you want to come clean on the murder or just talk about those weapons and that credit card?"

"Where do you work?" I ask.

He sneers. "I'm self-employed."

"Yeah, what do you do?"

"None of your business. And I want a lawyer before I listen to any more of your stupid questions."

I lean forward. "You know, Ricky, it can feel good to tell the truth. Get it off your chest," I say in a mock-empathetic tone.

His leg bounces faster under the table. "I didn't kill anyone, and that gun, you fucking planted it on me. This is bullshit. I'm not saying anything else until my lawyer gets here."

"Just tell me why you killed him, Ricky," I say.

He blinks fast a few times but doesn't say anything.

"He was a little boy, Ricky. I'm trying to figure out why you'd do that to him. You don't really seem to me like you have the balls to kill anyone." I'm reaching here, but I've got to shake him up a bit. We don't have any hard evidence. If he did kill Kevin, our only chance is to break him down until he slips.

"I'm no fucking pervert, and I didn't do shit to no kid. Lawyer."

"Okay, then tell me about the Emerald Club."

He eyes my ID and laughs. "Boyle. I know a guy with that same name."

"Let's go call your lawyer, asshole," Goran says.

After he makes the call, we put him back in the interview room, hands cuffed behind him, to let him stew. Without any physical evidence, there's no way in hell we can book him for the murder.

Goran and I doze at our desks for the couple of hours it takes his sleazy lawyer to get here. Goran sees him before I do and rolls his eyes. "Marty McPherson," he mutters.

"I wonder if he's wearing a suit that fits today."

"Nope."

McPherson comes over to our desks, wearing his trademark annoying grin. We exchange fake pleasantries for about two minutes, then I get up and start down the hall. I let the defense attorney into the interrogation room, where Ricky makes a big show of demanding that I uncuff him.

"Detective, it's unconscionable for you to keep this man handcuffed like this," McPherson says, faking his best concerned look.

"As a favor to you, Marty." I remove the cuff from Ricky's right wrist and fasten it to the metal loop built into the table. I stare at the attorney to see if he'll argue. When he doesn't say anything, I wave and go back to my desk.

After an hour or so, just before six a.m., McPherson emerges from the hallway. "Mr. Harris is ready to answer some questions."

Goran and I go back in to continue the questioning. Ricky admits that the gun is illegal but then claims it's not his. We can keep him on that, but bail will be negligible, and now that he knows we're on to him, he'll probably run.

Sitting in a chair with one arm shackled to a table is no fun, I guess. Ricky starts running his mouth, ignoring McPherson's frequent interruptions to remind him to stick to the facts. More than once, Ricky includes suggestions that we go fuck ourselves. Goran and I exchange glances. *Whatever.* This guy is in jail for at least twenty-four hours, so we can take our time with him.

"Where were you on Thursday night?" I ask again.

He narrows his eyes. "From seven on, I was at the club, hosting a party."

"How late did your party run?"

He shrugs.

"What'd you do after the party?"

McPherson holds up a finger. "You don't have to answer that."

"I have nothing to hide. I stopped in at Winky's for some food."

"What time did you get there?"

"Ten? I don't know. I don't keep a logbook."

"So you were at the Emerald until ten o'clock?"

Time of death was estimated between seven and eight. It's close. I wonder if we have those security tapes from earlier that evening, because I'd like to see if he really was there at seven, and what time he left. That kid was being held somewhere for six and a half days, and it doesn't sound as though Ricky had time to leave and do the deed. But if the kid was there that night, tied up in the back of his car or bound and gagged in some back room in the Emerald, killing him would have taken only minutes. My stomach churns. I wonder why Ricky would dump the body so close to where he hangs out. It would make more sense to dump it in the river, but maybe he was pressed for time.

"Do you know a guy by the name of Sean Miller?" I ask.

McPherson rolls his eyes. "What does this have to do with why Mr. Harris is here? You arrested him for an illegal firearm, correct? He already answered those questions. I'd like to speak with the prosecutor."

"This is a homicide investigation," Goran says, turning to Ricky. "Do you know Sean Miller?"

"Fuck if I know. Get me some water."

"You know this isn't just going to go away," Goran says. He turns to me. "I'll be right back."

Harris leans back in his chair, his leg still jiggling. "I have an alibi. I told you I was at the club. Thirty people can put me there."

I slide a legal pad across the table then stand. "Give me a list of names. Then you're going to tell me all about how you killed that little boy and left him in that alley. We'll get evidence from the van. It's best for you to cooperate."

"Detective, unless you are going to arrest my client for this homicide, we both know that he doesn't have to provide that information."

"Yes, he does," I growl.

Ricky laughs. "Oh, aren't you cute when you're angry?"

I want to punch him in the face. "Names. Start writing. Now."

"What do you think, Marty?" Ricky asks his attorney. "Think I should give her the names?"

McPherson juts out his chin and stares at me. Finally, he says, "If you have an alibi, Ricky, you should go ahead and offer proof."

Ricky picks up the pen. "Fuck it. I'm sick of this. Here are your stupid names." He scrawls eight names on the pad then pushes it my way. "You took my phone. Find their numbers yourself."

"That's not thirty. Tell me what happened, Ricky."

He fakes a yawn and looks around. "When?"

I clench my jaw and make a fist.

"What, you're gonna hit me? Violate my rights in a whole new way? I mean, I hear about police violence all the time, but this is ballsy. Are you getting all of this, McPherson?"

The attorney folds his arms across his chest and tries to look menacing. I kick the chair back into the wall and take a step toward Ricky.

Becker opens the door. "Detective Boyle? A moment, please?"

The burning feeling is back in my neck. *What the fuck is she doing here? Fishner probably called her, which means that Fishner is out there, too.*

"Oh, good," McPherson says. "I'd like to talk to her about how poorly you've treated my client."

"Who's that hottie, *Detective Boyle*?" Ricky asks.

I resist the urge to throw him up against the wall and turn to leave instead.

"Bye," he calls to my back. He leans in and says something inaudible to McPherson.

I go into the observation room, where Fishner and Becker are waiting. Becker stares at me, her mouth slightly open. She's worried that I'm going to lose my temper. I'm not. It's under control.

"Boyle," Fishner says, "you need to calm down. Now."

"I need to check his alibi and talk to Roberts about the van."

"Go get some air. We'll check it." Fishner checks her watch. "We only have nine hours before we have to cut him loose, Liz, and I want you at the burial. Then you need to go home and sleep. You're way too punchy. Look at yourself. You're making a fist. You just threatened that man in front of his attorney. I mean it."

"What do you mean, cut him loose? That alibi is *bullshit*. And we can hold him for—"

She leans toward me. "I said *go*." Her voice is low, and her mouth is too near my ear for comfort. "We'll take care of Harris. He looks good for this. I'll spend some time with him and see if he'll break. Go to the burial. You need to be there. Please don't make me do paperwork." By "do paperwork," she means put me on the desk and off the case. She might actually do it this time, since I'm not giving her much confidence in my ability to maintain my cool.

I take a deep breath and nod.

She straightens. "The burial is at noon." She stares at me without blinking. "It's eight thirty now. Go get some air, get cleaned up, and go. I mean it. We'll take care of the rest of this."

I don't respond.

"Your other option is some more time off. Maybe you came back too soon, Boyle."

I level my blank cop-face at her. "Yes, Lieutenant. I'll go to the burial." I had no idea that much time had passed, and it kind of freaks me out a little bit. I blink hard and scrub my face with a hand.

As I'm stepping out of the room, Goran shows up carrying a cup of coffee and a bottle of water. He gives me a questioning look. I nod and keep moving.

Before I get to my desk, I hear Becker say that they need to book Ricky on the weapons and ID theft or cut him loose. "We don't have any evidence *at all* to charge him with murder," she adds.

CHAPTER ELEVEN

TAKE THE STAIRS AND HEAD for the back way. I slam the metal door open hard, but the sound it makes isn't satisfying enough, so I slam it again. It bounces back at me, and I kick it closed.

The sun is deceptive. It's one of those days that looks like spring but feels more like winter. It can't be more than forty-five degrees, but I lean for a few minutes on the concrete ledge across from the station. After a few deep breaths, I push off the ledge and go to the Charger.

I wouldn't have hit Ricky Harris. They misread me back there. I was just being bad cop, just playing a role. At least, I think that's what I was doing. Maybe I did come back too soon. Maybe I'm getting too emotionally involved, and it's clouding my judgment. There's never been a time, at least in my professional life, when I've been overly subjective about a case. Getting too emotionally involved is murky territory. It's dangerous.

Kevin.

Kevin Whittle, aged five. Didn't talk much but drew lots of pictures.

They were going to have a party. His birthday is today.

Nothing like burying your kid on his birthday. Jesus, those poor people.

He liked toy trains and animals. His parents read to him every night. He had a caring grandmother who doted on him.

There are only a few motives for murder: revenge, money, hate, some sort of personal vendetta, or to keep a secret. Maybe Kevin saw somebody do something that somebody didn't want anyone to know about. With a child victim, the list of possible motives is even shorter than with adults. It's unlikely that a quiet little boy provoked all-out rage. So it looks like money, secret, or personal vendetta. But since he was held for six days before he was killed, someone was waiting for something.

Riverside Cemetery is way over on the West Side, and the drive gives me too much time to think about Ricky Harris and Kevin Whittle and what it all means, about how small the coffin will be. For some reason, they decided not to have a service at a funeral home, just the graveside thing, so this is it... goodbye to Kevin.

I arrive about ten minutes late because of traffic on 480. I don't want to interrupt the service, and I'm only here to watch for suspicious people, lurkers, outbursts, and that sort of thing, so I pull off the narrow cemetery road on the right, away from the gathering.

The grouping of people standing around the open grave is small, just Teresa, Peter, Graham and Elaine, a few middle-aged couples, a handful of elderly people, and a couple of little kids who obviously have no clue why they're there. My eyes are drawn to the small white casket, and I can't look away from the thing. He's in there, the little boy. Today is his birthday. *Deep breaths.*

I can smell the imminent rain, and I curse myself for not bringing an umbrella. Sitting in the car and observing from afar won't get the job done. I climb out, shut the car door as quietly as possible, and stand among a small grouping of trees. I spot only one news station van over by the road. I guess the murder of Kevin Whittle is already old news. Movement to my left catches my eye, but when I turn to look, all I see is a groundskeeper on a golf cart.

A woman is officiating the service. She isn't dressed in religious garb, so I guess this is more a closure thing than a God thing. At some point, Peter Whittle says a few words, and everyone cries.

After they lower the casket into the ground, Teresa loses her mind, way beyond typical graveside grief. She turns to Graham Whittle, raises her fists, and starts screaming at him. "You fucking asshole! This is all your fault!" Her face turns purple, then she punches him in the jaw.

Graham steps back, hands in front of him as if to ward her off.

Peter jumps between them. "Teresa, please—"

She shoves him away. "*I will not!* You know exactly what I'm talking about!"

The official-looking woman puts her hand on Teresa's shoulder and whispers something to the distraught mother. Teresa allows the woman to take her by the arm and lead her back to the grave. The woman says something I can't hear and gestures at the hole in the ground. Teresa collapses, sobbing beside her son's grave.

I wonder if she just needs someone to blame. I glance over at Graham Whittle. He has his face in his hands as he turns to walk away.

As the rest of the group begins to disperse, I take one more look around to see their reactions to Teresa's fit. No one appears to be acting oddly, and I don't see anyone who obviously doesn't belong. I walk back to my car and get in. I feel the tears pushing hard on the backs of my eyes, but I ignore them.

Do not think about your dead sister.

Don't think about her or your dad.

That shit is over and done with and has been for twenty-five years.

Just as I start the car, my cell phone rings. The caller ID shows my brother's name. I'm feeling so guilty, thinking about all those years ago, that I can't stop myself from answering. I'm dreading what problem it's going to be this time, but to my surprise, Christopher sounds pretty good. He starts telling me about this new girl he's seeing. He met her at the tattoo parlor, and she loves David Lynch movies as much as he does.

Christopher has a hard time keeping a girlfriend. I guess we have that in common. He wants to be reliable. I know he does, because I'm similar. But the problem is that he routinely forgets important details, like that he's arranged to meet a woman somewhere for dinner. Then he feels terrible, tries to apologize, and professes his undying affection. He's sincere, but they don't buy it. I can't imagine why they would.

For me, it's easier to be alone, even though it really isn't. If I were with someone, I wouldn't be myself anymore. I would be someone else. And I don't know how that someone else would behave.

"She's cool as hell," my brother says. "She's had kind of a fucked-up life. Her mom used to beat the crap out of her for being left-handed. Can you believe that? I mean, who does that? So her aunt got her into foster care or something. But she still went to college and stuff. I showed her that newspaper article about you. She was really interested and wants to meet you. Mom, too. And seriously, Liz, *Eraserhead* is, like, her second-favorite movie. We're gonna go to that thing they're putting on, the big Lynch festival, this weekend. I can't wait."

I don't say anything about how my brother is a complete weirdo for loving creepy David Lynch movies. The whole woman-in-the-radiator thing gives me the shivers. It's like watching a nightmare unfold on a movie screen.

I worry about Christopher going for damaged women, like those who had fucked-up childhoods, just because he's damaged, too. But I guess for people like us that's how it goes, and this new woman sounds pretty okay. If there's hope for Christopher, I guess maybe there's some for me.

"What were you texting about the other day?" I ask. "You seemed kind of anxious. You sent a lot of messages."

He goes quiet.

"Christopher?"

"Sorry, Liz. I was just... well, I was kind of fucked up, I guess."

Dammit, I was hoping he really was clean now.

"I think someone spiked my drink or something. Honestly, Liz. It was all pretty... well, I just freaked out, I guess. But it's fine now," he says. "Don't worry about me."

"Christopher, I'm not back on 'til later. Want to get lunch? I'll be home in a bit, and we can catch up." I have until four o'clock, I figure. And the way Fishner looked at me, even that might be too soon.

———— •••• ————

Rain clouds continue to darken the sky to the west as I pull into the parking lot behind my apartment building. It's Sunday, which means Kevin Whittle has been dead for three days, and if Ricky Harris's alibi checks, we've made no progress whatsoever.

I pull open the front door and stop at my mailbox, which I haven't checked in three days. It's stuffed with a couple of bills, the new *Rolling Stone*, and one of those packets filled with useless coupons. The last item is a thick envelope postmarked in Cincinnati that looks as though it might hold a wedding invitation. I squint at the handwriting then shove it inside the magazine. I'm not real big on weddings.

Upstairs, I toss the mail onto the table then take care of the litter box and feed Ivan while he meows and figure-eights around my legs. After starting a pot of coffee, I grab the dust mop and run it across the hardwood.

"Geez, Ivan," I yell, "you're molting."

He's sitting in the bay window now, making weird clicking sounds at a crow outside. It would be nice if spring arrived on time this year. I laugh at myself. Not a chance. This is Cleveland. It can snow in June.

I try to take a nap, but of course, it doesn't happen. With a sigh, I get up to answer the doorbell. "Hey."

My brother smiles and steps inside. "How's cop world?"

I can't tell him stuff about blood and perverts and dead kids with missing hands. He's way too sensitive for what I see every day. "Ah, you know. Same old, same old."

"So tell me, detective-sister." He's on one knee, scratching the base of Ivan's tail but looking up at me as I walk to the kitchen. Ivan likes Christopher more than anyone else. It used to bother me. "Do any of those, you know, those drinks you can drink? Do those work? I'm applying for this city job. And it's not that great. Okay, I'd be a garbage man"—he laughs—"but it pays, like, twenty-four bucks an hour..." His voice trails off when I reappear from the kitchen.

I'm not hiding my irritation very well. I remember the last time I had to get him out of jail, when he was busted with heroin. He claims he never shot it, that he just smoked it. I choose to believe him because it's easier that way, even though the detective in me wants to push up his shirtsleeves and look for tracks. He winces and stands up, leaving Ivan, then flops onto the couch. He puts his big work boots on my coffee table.

Damn it, Christopher, Christ only knows where those boots have been. "Let's go get something to eat," I say. "And no, that stuff doesn't work. It just messes up your kidneys. Drink a shitload of water, take B vitamins before the test to make your piss yellow, and tell them you took a lot of ibuprofen in the last six hours. Put it off as long as you can, a month or more if you can swing it."

He grins. "Smart detective-sister."

He's the smart one, probably smarter than I am, but he sure doesn't act like it. You'd never know it by talking to him, either, unless you got him started on quantum physics or organic chemistry. How he knows about such things I will never understand. He's a genius living the life of a loser.

"Where do you want to eat?" I ask.

"Guido's?"

I nod. Guido's is a Cleveland Heights staple, untouched by the gentrification that's raised the facades and the rents in the rest of the neighborhood. It's a quick trip there, just through a couple of parking lots from the back of my building.

Christopher asks me what kind of pizza I want, and I tell him to decide. I take a table by the window and wait, but even when he brings the slice and sits down, I can't concentrate on the food or the conversation. I keep wondering if they're still interviewing Ricky and if they've gotten anything else out of him. I can't get my phone out fast enough when it rings. I gesture at my brother to keep eating and mouth that I'll be right back as I get up. Once I'm outside, I answer, "Boyle."

"All right, bad news," Goran says. "Harris's alibi checked out. Becker said she couldn't get an arrest warrant, so Fishner cut him loose. We're keeping a tail on him, though."

"Shit." The tension wraps itself around my neck and throat. I look up at the green-and-white awning overhead. It's finally begun to rain, and a cold breeze gusts across the lake and into my face. A truck goes by, and the diesel fumes assault my nose. "You're kidding."

"I'm not kidding." He goes on about how Becker wasn't happy that we didn't have more evidence to book him before we brought him in, especially since McPherson is talking about harassment.

"What about the weapons? The ID theft?"

"Nah, she said those were a waste of time and we need to get him on charges that matter. I was kind of still hoping Watson would come back with something on that hair, but he called just after you left. He's got nothing."

He keeps talking, and I fiddle with a hinge on Guido's front door while I listen with half an ear. A teenaged couple wants to get inside, and the boy gestures at me, asking with his eyes for me to move.

I try to return his smile as I slide to the side. "What about the bag and the van? And why did he leave Winky's and come back?"

"The bag is in the lab, and the van is in impound, but he's getting it out today. He says it's a laundry bag that he had because he'd taken some of the club's linens to the Laundromat. He says if he left Winky's, it was just to go outside and smoke."

"Uh-huh," I mutter. "Why leave the crime scene? And why do the club's laundry if he's 'self-employed'?"

"He said he went out for a cigarette and saw Miller shouting outside, so he went over to see what was up. Then when the cops showed up, he gave them the stolen ID by accident, then he freaked. I mean, he's some kind of fraudster, no doubt. But the ID thing, I think it was a genuine mistake. He didn't mean to hand it over. I guess he figured if we ran a check on it, we'd pull him in, so he beat it."

I grunt in reply. It sucks that the story actually makes sense.

"Becker said we can't get a warrant, and honestly, she's right. Property Crimes is watching him. They'll get him one of these days for something. But we got nothin' on him. What else can we do?" He stops talking, and I hear him chomping his gum. "Are you all right? Why are you breathing like that? What's going on?" He chuckles. "Oh, wait, are you *busy*?"

In spite of the dread settling in the pit of my stomach, I bark a laugh. "No, you perv. You think I'd answer the phone?" I'm grateful for this moment of humor, for the tiny hint of a genuine smile that threatens to creep across my face. When was the last time I was *busy*, anyway? Hell, it's been a year, almost to the day, since Cora and I ended it. Her birthday is coming up. Maybe I should send a card. *No, stop it with the distractions.* "I'm thinking," I say. "Look, I'll be back in a couple hours. I want to—"

"Boss lady said to tell you not to come back today. Take the rest of the day. Sleep. I'm gonna try to catch a couple hours, myself. I'll call you later if anything happens."

"Yeah, but—"

"Boyle, Fishner is at the end of her rope with you, and we're at a standstill. Roberts is gonna try to get more footage from those dumps in the Flats, but aside from that, we're out of leads."

I mutter a goodbye and slide the phone back into my pocket. I watch some cars go past. Sunday-afternoon shoppers enter and exit the little boutiques along Coventry Road. There's a mom with her two kids on their way into the pet store. She looks about my age, but I can see from here that she has a big diamond, probably set in platinum, on her left hand. Her kids are well dressed and well behaved. The older boy holds the door for his mom and brother. They're all smiling, and it kind of makes me want to puke.

Christopher comes barreling out of the door, holding a foil-wrapped slice of pizza. "Hey, I thought you were never coming back."

He looks so much like our father that I almost want to cry or scream or something. My dad, a straightlaced former Marine, would never do the stupid things that Christopher does. Dad was an amateur boxer in the service and kept in shape with the heavy bag and speed bag he hung in our basement. When I was eight or nine, I showed an interest, so he taught me how to fight. It must have been amusing for him to watch his lanky, awkward daughter make two fists and bash that bag with her bare hands. The gloves had been too big back then. I only did it to be close to him. In a way, I might still spend all of that time at the gym to be close to him.

"Sorry," I tell my brother. "Work call."

Christopher holds the pizza out to me.

"You can have it," I say.

"Aw, c'mon, sis. You only had, like, two bites. Aren't you hungry?"

"Nah, I'm good."

Back at my apartment, we make small talk about his new girlfriend and possible job, both of us avoiding the topic of our mom. After he's gone, I actually fall asleep for a few hours. I dream about Cora, my ex, having a birthday party. We're smiling and laughing, and it's as though no time has passed, as if we never ended it, as if I wasn't completely terrified of someone knowing me so well.

But then it turns into some sort of psychedelic autopsy. Watson hands me my liver and tells me to weigh it, and the sting of regret as I lie on the cold steel table is worse than the pain when he saws through my sternum. My heart is the size of a basketball, and it weighs too much. He makes a big deal about it before free-throwing it into a jar of formaldehyde.

———— •••• ————

When I awaken, it's dark outside. The phone is buzzing, so I grab it off the coffee table on my way to the kitchen for my bourbon ration.

"Hey, girl!" Josh chirps. "What're you doing? You should come down here!" There's a lot of noise in the background. He's probably at Bounce, and even though it's early, he's likely surrounded by several sexy young things hot on the prowl, even on a Sunday.

"Hey, Josh." I pour just a tad more than my allotted amount into the glass.

"Girl, I'm so serious, it's a great night to be out, to be alive! It might be early, but it's fabulous!"

"I can't, Joshie. I'm on a case." I walk back down the hallway.

"Rough one?"

"You could say that." *If you only knew.*

"If I only knew what?"

"Did I say that out loud?"

"Are you all right?"

"Yeah, I think so. Kid case. No real suspects. Went to the funeral. It was fucked." I plop down next to my gun belt on the bed and run my fingers along the stitches in the black leather.

"I'm coming over."

"No, no. Really. I gotta get back to work."

He sighs. "Call me when you can. I'm on days all week, so just let me know." He puts up with too much shit from me. We both know it.

"Thanks. See you soon."

I set my glass and phone on the dresser and go into my closet. Kneeling in front of the safe in the back corner, I punch in the combination. I eject the magazine from my Glock before shoving the weapon, holster, and heavy leather cuff case inside.

I change into my oxblood Doc Marten eight-eyes. The cat opens one eye and stares at me as I drain my glass. I slide the sleeve of my leather jacket out from under him, put it on, and slip my shield into the left inside pocket, not that I'll need it, but better safe than sorry.

I go to an old metal-club-turned-hipster-hangout that I haven't been to in years. After ordering a double bourbon and a beer, I try to make myself invisible in a far corner.

First on my list for tomorrow is the grandparents' house, yard, and garage. If that's where Kevin disappeared, even if someone has been there already, I've got to go look.

I order another round and put my notebook away.

CHAPTER TWELVE

MONDAY MORNING, WHEN I GET back to my gym locker after working the lingering booze out of my system, I have three missed calls from Jo Micalec, our senior lab tech. That strikes me as weird, because it's only seven thirty. I call her back right away.

"Hey, Liz. I'm really sorry to bother you so early. But you need to know this, and you need to hear it from me."

"What? You get something on the bag? The van?" I shove my sweaty gym clothes into my locker. She's used to my brusque phone voice, so I'm not worried that she'll take it personally.

"Nothing on the bag yet. It's about this hair. The one Watson got off the sheet."

The hair. *Please let it be a match for Ricky.* "Okay. What about it?"

"It's a match to you."

I sit down on the bench in front of my locker. "What?"

"It's a match to you, Liz."

I blink a couple of times. "That's impossible. Why would you even think that?"

"Well, after Watson didn't get any hits, I ran it through the state employee system, thinking we might get a match from one of the universities or from a city employee. But the mitochondrial DNA matches yours. So it's not *your* hair, but it is someone related to you on your mother's side. Is your mom still alive? Do you have any siblings? Anyone on that side of your family nearby so we can get swabs from them?"

Christopher. Shit, what did you do? He might be a hapless, bumbling pain in the ass, but he's not violent. He's always been the gentlest person in my life, way nicer than I am. He's the soft one, the caring nurturer. The humid air of the locker room starts to suffocate me.

"Liz?"

My breathing has become too shallow, but my lungs don't cooperate when I will them to inhale deeper. "Yeah, I'm here." Something bubbles in my chest, pressing down into my stomach like a vise, something like rage or regret or maybe fear. "Okay," I say, and I don't like the quavering in my voice. I get up and walk back to the shower area, hoping no one else is in there. "Can you sit on this for a couple of hours?"

She takes a few seconds to respond. "Sure, Liz, but you know I have to give it to Fishner. I can try to stall, but—"

"Thanks, Jo. I'll call you back. Bye." I hang up the phone and shove it back into my pocket. Leaning against the sink, I try to take deep breaths. My vision goes white around the edges. I stumble back over to the bench and bend forward to put my head between my legs.

There's no way Christopher did anything to that kid. He couldn't have. It has to be a mistake. I'm lucky to make it to the toilet before I vomit.

Once I'm cleaned up and calmer, I send Goran a text that says I'm running late and to cover for me with Fishner. I walk out to my car.

Maybe someone Christopher knew, or even a stranger, picked up one of his hairs by accident and left it on that sheet. He works in a restaurant. He has contact with hundreds of people on a weekly basis. But it's a pubic hair. I wonder if someone planted it there, trying to frame him. Even as sweet as my brother is, he's pissed off a few people along the way.

I grab a bottle of water off the passenger seat and swallow gulp after gulp. I think about sending Christopher to Boston, where we have a semi-estranged aunt and uncle. No, I'm a terrible liar when it comes to my brother. I would lose my job, and they'd find him, anyway. I can't ask Jo to cover it up. She'll have to tell Fishner. Maybe I should tell him to go talk to Fishner. I'd be off the case, and I'm committed to finding Kevin's killer. I owe it to Teresa. I owe it to Kevin.

But one way or another, I'll have to tell Fishner, and there's no way she's going to let me stay on this now. I squeeze the bridge of my nose. *Damn it, Christopher.*

I'm going to have to get Christopher in for a DNA swab then come up with a reason why we're running a cotton swab through his mouth. I'll have to explain to Fishner that some inexplicable crazy thing is going on, that it can't possibly be what it looks like.

First, I have to talk to him. I drive over to his place and pull up in front of his apartment building and sit for a couple of minutes, wondering if he'll notice the red in my eyes.

I ring the doorbell then immediately knock hard three times. When he opens the door, I can tell he just crawled out of bed.

"What're you doing here?" he asks, rubbing his eyes.

"Do you have a few minutes?"

He yawns. "I haven't even had a cup of coffee yet." He doesn't move out of the doorway.

"Christopher, can I please come in?"

"Why do you look like that? Is Mom okay?"

"Yeah, Mom's fine. I just need to ask you a question." I step forward. It takes him a moment to get the hint and move out of the way. During those seconds, I have to restrain myself from shoving him to the side.

"Well, come on in, I guess. I'm gonna put on a pot of coffee. Sit down."

Instead, I follow him into the kitchen.

He goes straight for the sink and fills the pot with water. "Liz, you look really upset. What's going on? Why are you being so weird? You're not acting like yourself at all." He dumps the water into the coffee maker, fills the basket with coffee, then turns on the machine.

I want to tell him that I'm being unlike myself because I'm starting to not like myself very much, and I think I'd rather be like someone else, someone normal, someone kind and soft, someone who likes to take vacations and spend time with family and friends instead of digging through piles of bloody clothes and watching autopsies. But if I were someone else, I wouldn't know him, and this wouldn't be happening. "Did you do something that I need to know about?"

He cracks a grin. "Sis, I've done a lot of things, but you don't want to know about any of them." He chuckles as if he's replaying something humorous in his head.

"Christopher, I'm not trying to be funny. I'm serious."

He turns and pulls two mugs out of the cabinet. "No, I don't think so."

111

He opens the refrigerator and retrieves the half-and-half. "Lots of cream, no sugar, right?"

"Sure, yeah."

He pours the cups and hands me one. Leaning against the counter, he takes a sip. "So, seriously, why are you here so early in the morning?"

I see no way to deliver this gently, and I'm running out of patience, anyway. I just blurt it out. "Christopher, your DNA was found on a murder victim. Did you kill someone?"

He laughs. "Jesus, Liz, don't fuck with me. All this for a joke? That's like the time you—"

"I'm serious. *This* is serious. You need to tell me, honestly, what you've been doing for the past several days."

"Of course I didn't kill anyone. And no, I don't need to tell you anything." He pushes past me and goes into the living room.

"I need to figure out how to protect you here, and I can't do that if you won't talk to me."

He slams his coffee onto the table hard enough that some of it shoots up out of the cup and onto the wood. He crosses his arms in front of his chest. "I don't need you to protect me." His eyes are fierce, but I can tell he's terrified. "Do you understand?" he asks in a low, measured voice. "I don't need you to protect me. I'm a *grown man*."

"Now is not the time for your masculine bullshit."

He turns and faces his front window. The rain has stopped, and the sun is shining, glistening off the damp surfaces as if it's spring. Minutes tick by.

I lean against the wall and cross my arms. "Have you done something?"

"No. I mean, nothing that would get me into trouble. Drugs." He blinks hard. "Nothing detectives would care about. Tell me what's going on. Please."

I can't tell him anything. That would compromise the investigation and probably make me the target of another IAU probe.

I'm soft as a kitten with kids, victims, a lot of witnesses, and grieving families, but there's a fine line here. "I can't really give you details, and you don't want to know them, anyway. Christopher, please, I need to question you officially. You have to come with me."

He points at me. "No, *you please*. I'm not going anywhere."

Sucked into his childish display, I jab a finger back at him. "Don't you fucking point your finger at me."

He steps over and gets in my face. Towering over me, he points at me again. His fair skin is flushed, and the vein in his forehead pulses with his heartbeat. I have that same vein, so seeing my brother angry is like looking at my own reflection in some kind of distorted fun house mirror.

The conversation stops and starts like this over the course of an hour. We move from anger to sadness to dejection to denial and back through all of them again, with some other uncomfortable silent emotions mixed in. Shortly after I make him tell me about his sex life and he breaks down, he's on the floor with his back against the couch, crying, embarrassed.

But one of his pubic hairs was on that sheet. I can't stop. "I have to know," I say as calmly as I can. "I have to try to help you." I avoid the word "protect."

I hold him on the couch while he cries in frustration and fear. I don't cry, and it feels as if we're little again. It strikes me that I would give anything, I would throw it all away, if it meant that I could defend him from this investigation, from the unpleasant details of my job that he's becoming involved in for reasons that I'm certain are not his fault. If I could shield him from me.

"You have to let me take you to the station. We need to go now. We can get you a lawyer."

He wipes his eyes. "A *lawyer*? Are you serious?"

I nod. "Yes, you need a lawyer."

"Man, I am so fucked," he mutters.

"I have to go to the bathroom. Please don't go anywhere. Just stay right here, on this couch, and when I'm done, we'll take care of this."

He nods.

I go into the bathroom and sit on the floor with my back against the tile wall. I press my face into a towel that smells like his aftershave and draw my knees to my chest. Then I fall into silent, rhythmic sobs. The pain reminds me that I'm alive. After I pull it together, I make a quick call to Jessie Hedges, one of the only good criminal defense attorneys in the area that our squad hasn't alienated. I briefly explain what's going on.

"Did he do it? What's his story?"

Anger surges through me. I want to scream and rant at this woman for even asking such a thing. Then I realize that I'm going to have to get used to people asking it. Some won't even bother asking. They'll just assume he did it. And if I want this woman's help, I can't go off the deep end. "He's an idiot. He's done drugs, probably other minor stuff. But there's no way he killed a kid." *There's no way in hell he cut off Kevin Whittle's hand. That takes a special kind of monster.*

"I can meet him in an hour," she replies. "My retainer is twenty-five hundred."

"I don't have my checkbook on me, but I'm good for it."

We agree to meet at the station, then I hang up. I was in the bathroom for only ten minutes, but when I walk out, he's gone. *Fuck.* I yank my cell phone out of my pocket and call him.

"Hey, it's Chris," his voicemail says. "Leave a message."

I drive to the restaurant where he works. I know he won't be there. They don't open until eleven. But I'm not sure what else to do.

The sun blinds me, so I pull my sunglasses out of the console and slide them over my eyes. I crank up the stereo. P.J. Harvey is singing "Rid of Me," the title track on one of the best albums of '93. She yells and screams in a deep alto, trying on different characters, becoming someone else on every track. This is the only one of her albums where she sounds like this. She's raw, frenetic, almost unhinged, which totally matches my mood.

As I figured, Christopher's not at the restaurant, so I point the Passat northeast and hit I-90. I'm going to have to talk to her, because I know he's there. He goes to her when he can't talk to me. Somehow, in the twenty minutes it takes me to get to Euclid, where my mother lives, I start to feel more human and get some perspective.

There's bound to be evidence that will prove my brother's innocence. Fishner will have to believe me. I've never given her reason not to. I'll do whatever is necessary: work the case as if my life depends on it, be a character witness, go to bat for him. He's cleaned up his act, at least for the most part, so he'll have to give a statement and a swab, and we should be able to clear him. That doesn't stop me from feeling as if I'm going to explode.

I pull into the parking lot of Mom's apartment building and maneuver around several chuckholes in the asphalt before swinging into a spot about a hundred feet from the front door. I should have called first. I never know what I'm walking into with her. But I'm here now, so I might as well just deal. I consider leaving my gun in the lockbox in the trunk but decide against it. This neighborhood sucks, and the last thing I need is a stolen service weapon. I pull my leather jacket tighter around me to cover it, then I unclip my badge from my belt and slide it into my pocket.

The complex is a dump. She moved here about ten years ago when she lost her job. Her disability checks wouldn't cover the place in Willoughby. The glass front door is covered in handprints and snot prints and I don't want to know what else. Hoping the intercom works, I press the button marked 211 - Margaret Boyle.

"Who is it?" Her voice crackles through the speaker. She sounds different than I remember.

"Mom, it's me."

The door buzzes, and I yank the handle. Walking through the big lobby area, I think this place used to be a hotel, long ago converted into low-income, state-supported housing. It's a far cry from our former middle-class existence. I can't believe she lives here. I don't want her living here.

Both elevators have Out of Order signs taped over the doors. My mouth falls open. This is an eight-story building. Those poor people on the top floor must be in very good shape.

The stairway is gritty, with the paint peeling off the floor and unrepaired holes in the walls, like something out of a cop movie, when they're chasing some degenerate up or down, in the dark, with guns drawn. It smells like piss, something a movie can't really convey. A broken toaster is smashed in one corner of the first landing.

I push open the metal door to the second floor. Her apartment is first on the right. I knock sharply a couple of times.

"Lizbeth, is that you?" Mom calls from behind the door.

"Yeah, Mom, it's me."

She pulls the door open. She looks better than I expect. Her color is good, and she's dressed in a pair of green corduroys and lighter-green sweater. I try not to let the relief show on my face. I can't remember the last time I saw her in anything but her ratty old bathrobe, and it's still pretty early in the day. I suppress the urge to push her out of the way so I can find my brother.

She hugs me and sighs when her elbow brushes against my gun as she steps back. She's almost as tall as I am. "I've missed you." She smiles. "I need to ask you about my brakes." She winks at me.

I sit down on the sofa—always a "sofa" for her, never a "couch"—and scan the room. It's clean and put together, looking much better than it did the last time I was here. I don't see any vodka or pill bottles, which is a major improvement. I allow myself a sliver, just a tiny glimmer, of hope, even though I know how dangerous that is. "How are you, Mom?"

She meets my gaze with light-gray eyes the same color as mine. "I'm better. I'm going to meetings." Her graying auburn hair is pushed behind her ears. It's longer than before, down to her shoulders, but still wavy. "Two weeks."

I hear a symphony coming from the stereo in another room. I nod, even though I know better than to get too happy about it. We've been down this road before. "That's great. Dvorak, huh?" I allow a flicker of a smile to cross my face.

She seems pleased. "Yes, it is."

An image flashes into my mind of her teaching me about classical music when I was about five. We were sitting at our kitchen table, listening to snippets of various symphonies. My favorite was Beethoven's Seventh. She used to play piano and tried to get me to take lessons. That kind of lost importance at some point. Another sudden, vivid memory hits me hard. I see her practicing Chopin, with a cigarette dangling out of her mouth and a half-empty bottle of vodka on top of the piano, while I got ready to take Christopher to his sixth-grade parent-teacher meeting.

Enough nostalgia or whatever that feeling is. I decide a change of subject is in order. What I really want to do is grab her and shake her until she tells me where my brother is, but I know that will only make things worse. "You look like you've lost weight."

She smiles. "Just a little. Water weight." She pats her stomach with both hands.

"Mom, I've been trying to get in touch with Christopher. He's not at home. I just wondered... have you seen him?"

"Oh, you know Christopher. He's so busy these days."

"Yeah." I don't believe her, but confrontation is the wrong way to go with Mom.

"You want something to drink? Water, coffee?"

"Sure. Coffee, yeah." There's a little edge to my voice that I know I have to soften if I want her to help me. I can't believe this is happening. I wonder what the latest is at the station and if they've got new leads. Well, anything besides the one Jo Micalec dumped on me at seven this morning.

We sit on the sofa and make small talk for a while, and I avoid snapping at her again. She drinks a couple of cups of coffee complete with fresh cream, which I interpret as another good sign. When she's off the wagon, she doesn't keep perishables in the house.

I don't take off my jacket. Even though she felt it, I don't want her to see my gun and know that I'm actually here on kind of a police matter. Her eyes are clear. She talks with her hands as she always does, as I do. She prattles on about her brake problem, the meetings, and how she's doing really, wonderfully well. She even invites me to dinner next weekend, adding how nice it would be with just the three of us.

I surreptitiously glance at the clock on the side table while she talks. She doesn't seem to notice. Kevin Whittle has been dead for four and a half days now. My phone vibrates at 9:04. *Shit, we need to get to the station before they come after Christopher.* The muscles in my shoulders turn into rocks.

I hold up my index finger. "Just a second, Mom. I'll be right back." Pulling my phone out of my pocket, I move into the kitchen. Checking the screen, I see Fishner's name. *Damn it, Tom. I asked you to cover for me.* "Boyle."

"Boyle, are you planning to come to work today, or did you decide you need more time off?"

I'm staring at my mom's refrigerator, at the pictures on the freezer door. There we are at Christmas last year. I was wearing black, as usual. My hair was longer then, almost to my shoulders. Christopher was wearing his new Browns jersey. Mom looks sloshed. There's me at about six, playing in a sandbox with Josh. Next to that is a gangly Christopher at my high school graduation, standing with my mom and me. I have blue hair and a lot of eye makeup. Below that is a small photo of Jupiter, a black-and-white dog we had when I was a kid.

Up high, another photo shows Dad wearing boxing gloves and a white undershirt. It must be a picture from the service. I trace around the sides of the photograph with my index finger. "Yeah, Lieutenant. I'm dealing with a family thing right now, but I'll be there soon. Sorry. I'll explain when I get there."

"You need to get back here for the briefing then go talk to the rest of the Winky's people before you go speak to the grandparents again."

"Yes, Lieutenant." I put the phone back in my pocket before returning to the living room.

As soon as my butt hits the couch cushion, Mom says, "Hey, maybe you should come to my church. It's in Midtown. That's where my AA meetings are, too. I went to one this morning." She reaches for her cup. "Oh, I'm out. I'll go put on a fresh pot."

While she's in the kitchen, I take a look around. The bedroom is clean. The gray carpet looks freshly vacuumed, and the bed is made. The blinds are open, letting in a ray of sunshine. A mystery novel by a popular author is on the nightstand next to a clock radio that's set to the correct time. All these I take as promising signs. I don't have time to search the closet, but a quick glance doesn't reveal anything suspicious. There's nothing under the bed except a pair of slippers and her fat orange tabby cat, Bubbles.

I walk over to the bathroom door, but the knob won't turn. I knock, gently enough that she won't hear it from down the hall. "Christopher, open the fucking door."

He doesn't reply.

"Mom, I need to pee," I call out. "Why's the bathroom locked?"

She appears in the hallway with a worried look on her face. "I, ah, I accidentally locked it. The maintenance man is on his way to open it for me." She's lying. I know because she has a tell. She always looks down and to the left when she's lying.

"Mom, I need to talk to you, and I need for you to be okay about it."

Her eyes search mine, worry creasing her brow. "What about?" I catch her glancing in the direction of the bathroom door.

I lose my nerve. "I really need to know where Christopher is. He's helping me with something for work."

"He was going to go to breakfast with me before my meeting. I'll get him." She walks past me to the bathroom door.

I hope this isn't going to make her relapse. *Please, dear God, I don't even know if you exist—in fact, I'm pretty sure you don't, but if you do, please.* He'll try to stay calm in front of her. He knows I wouldn't tell her details. We both try to act casual, normal, around Mom.

"Christopher," she says through the door, "come out. Lizbeth needs to talk to you. She says you're helping her."

"Okay, just a sec," he replies. I hear a quaver in his voice.

"Promise me you'll take care of him," she whispers.

A long time ago, I made the same promise to my dad. "I will."

She squeezes my arm as he emerges, red faced and red eyed. I pretend that I don't think it's at all strange that he was hiding in the bathroom or that it took her pleading through the cheap door to get him out.

She doesn't like that he can't go to breakfast with her now, since he has to help me with this case. That's what we tell her, at least, even repeating it a couple of times. She's upset, but we all manage to hold it together and avoid a big scene. I offer to give her a ride to meet her friend at St. Martha's, since her brakes are bad. It's on the way, anyway. She agrees.

Mom is scary smart. She used to do logic problems for fun and could have had any academic career in the universe, but she was content to work at the pharmacy and tend to us like a good old-fashioned Irish Catholic. She senses that something is going on. I'm sure of it. But she won't say anything. He's not in jail, and she's not getting some phone call in the middle of the night to say he's in trouble. So she can go to mass and her meetings and read her novel and do her damn puzzles and remain unaware of all the craziness, at least for now. I hope I'm not going to have to tell her that he's been arrested for murdering a five-year-old.

A part of me wants to tell her to fend for herself, that I'm dealing with something much bigger than giving her a ride to church, but then I think better of it. I force a smile and hurry her into the car. She spends the entire ride talking nonstop about how great it is that all three of us are in the same place for once, and I almost tell her to shut up but clench my jaw instead.

"Are you all right, Lizbeth?"

"Yup, I'm just peachy." I make a fist. She would lie to the police to protect Christopher, and then they'd both be in jail. It's almost funny, and I stifle a laugh, knowing that I'm having some kind of weird, inappropriate response to the situation.

When we arrive at the church, I get out of the car and help her to make sure she doesn't leave her purse or something. "Do you need me to pick you up, Mom?"

"No, I can get a ride home from Angie. Thank you for the ride." She reaches out and squeezes my hand then gives me a wan smile. I pull her into a hug, and she stiffens, probably in surprise, but then relaxes into it.

Christopher gets out of the backseat and hugs her. "Bye, Mom."

"Bye, Christopher. I'll see you tomorrow, right?"

He nods. "Sure, Mom."

"When are you two coming over? We should go to dinner next week. Wouldn't that be nice?"

I try to smile, but I know it's distorted. "I'll call you."

"But we could just—"

"Okay, fine. Dinner next Wednesday. See you then."

Mom squeezes my shoulder then heads up the steps to join another woman. She turns and waves with a smile before they both disappear inside. Christopher continues to stand beside the car, the passenger door hanging open.

"Get in the car," I tell him. He looks as though he might run away, so I gently take his arm. "Christopher, please get in the car. We need to get this over with. We need to get you to the station before they come after you. It's better. Get in the car."

CHAPTER THIRTEEN

WHEN WE GET TO THE station, Jessie Hedges is sitting by the elevator. I introduce her to Christopher then lead them directly to the interrogation room. I ignore all the stares as we pass through the squad room.

"Christopher, I need you to wait here for a few minutes while I talk to my boss. Talk to your lawyer. Be honest with her."

"Can I have something to drink?"

"In a bit. Just wait here."

The second I walk back into the squad room, Fishner is on me like a mongoose on a cobra. "Who is that? I thought you had a family thing! Instead you bring in another suspect? Who already has Jessie Hedges working for him?"

Sitting at his desk, Goran raises his eyebrows at me.

I remove my jacket and carefully hang it on the back of my chair. "That's the family thing."

Fishner points at her door. "My office. Now."

Goran makes the "you're in trouble" face at me before turning back to his paperwork. I stride into Fishner's office.

"Close the door," she says as she moves behind her desk. Once I sit down, she says, "Tell me what's going on."

I try to explain everything in a nice, calm tone. "He's my brother. Jo called me and said that the hair turned up a hit to my mitochondrial DNA. I talked to him, and I'm sure he didn't do it. He's an idiot, but he's not a murderer. We got Hedges, and here we are."

She hasn't blinked in ninety seconds. She leans forward and pinches the bridge of her nose. "I can't believe Jo didn't call me right away. That *you* didn't call me." She shakes her head. "This is a shit show."

I just stare at her. She's pretty much nailed it. I start counting the second hand ticking on my big silver watch.

"All right, here's what we're going to do," she says right after I get to a hundred eighty-two. "We have to talk to him as if we think he did it, Boyle. It's the only physical evidence we have right now. Sure, he's your brother, but we're the police."

"I know."

"If the media gets wind of it, will you be all right?"

No, I won't. I shrug. "I guess."

She picks up her cell phone. "I'm calling Becker. She should be here for this. We'll try to keep it quiet and hope that, one, you're right that he didn't do it, and two, that we can find evidence to prove that."

I drum my fingers on the chair arm. "Is she going to keep her mouth shut?"

"Of course she will." She stares at me. "Boyle, I am really concerned about you, about all of this. You know that you can't be involved in this." She points at me. "Go finish your paperwork. Get Goran in here. He and I will handle the interview. You have to step back. You know that."

Part of me wants to argue, but another part is relieved that Fishner and Goran will take over and shoulder some of this burden. "Okay."

"That's an order," she says as if I argued with her. "Desk. Catch up on your paperwork. Until I tell you otherwise." She makes a typing gesture.

I get up and go back to the squad room. After sending Goran to her office, I plop down behind my desk and fake doing paperwork until they emerge to go down the hall. Once they're in the interrogation room, I slip into the observation room.

Julia Becker steps in a minute later. "Are you supposed to be in here?" she asks.

We both look through the mirror. Goran is sitting across the table from Christopher, while Fishner leans in the corner, in her typical Fishner way. Christopher's got his head in his hands, and Jessie Hedges, sitting next to him, leans over and whispers something to him.

"No, but he's my brother." *I promised I'd take care of him.*

Goran asks Christopher a couple of softball questions, which my brother answers in a soft voice.

"This, Detective"—Becker gestures with her bottled water at the three people in the interview room—"does not look good." She stares at me. What is she looking for in my face?

What the hell am I supposed to say? Of course it doesn't look good. It looks like a steaming pile of smelly shit.

"You're here because we found physical evidence linking you to the murder of Kevin Whittle," Goran says to Christopher, who looks as though he might cry.

Hedges folds her hands on the table. "Do you have a question?"

Becker turns the volume down on the audio monitor and turns to me. "Did he do it?" She seems semi-concerned. Her eyebrows are raised in a way I haven't seen more than a handful of times. "If he did it," she says, "we need to charge him now, today. The media isn't going to let this go. We have to tell the press—"

"No." Simple. "There is no way in hell he'd cut off a kid's hand. Just no way."

"Then explain the DNA." She taps on a file folder in front of her. "If this susp—man was not your brother, what would you think?"

I think about that for a few seconds. "I would think that we need more evidence. A murder weapon, a motive. And I'd grill the hell out of him until you let me search his apartment." I'm lying, and I know it. I would think that he was the killer, and I'd nail his ass to the wall until he confessed. I'd play bad cop to Goran's good cop. I'd scare the crap out of someone like Christopher. "If we found anything there, I'd arrest him for murder." I don't mention that I already looked through his apartment and didn't find any green sheets, branch cutters, garden shovels, or evidence of blood.

"We can't risk our careers for this."

"Julia, if you knew my brother, you'd get it."

She turns the volume back up on the audio feed.

"I didn't kill anyone. I swear to God," Christopher says, tears in his eyes.

"How do you think your DNA got onto the sheet at the crime scene?" Goran asks.

"Look," Christopher says. "I know what this looks like, okay? But I swear I didn't do anything. I would never do anything like this. Ask Liz.

She'll tell you." He swipes at his tears. "The only thing I can think is that one of my, um, hairs got onto the sheet when I was, um, well…" He rubs his hands on his pants legs. "There are a couple of possibilities, I guess," he mumbles.

I wonder what's coming. Jessie Hedges leans over and whispers something to him.

Christopher nods. "See, a friend of mine—okay, not a friend. A guy I know talked me into doing something I didn't want to do."

"Go on," Fishner says.

He winces and looks down at the table. "Okay, I know the kid, that poor dead kid, was wrapped in a green sheet. I saw that on the news." The goons on Channel 3 released the detail about the sheet, but at least they didn't say anything about the missing hand. "Green sheets. Shit." He cradles his head in his hands.

"Mr. Boyle?" Fishner says. *Mr. Boyle. Really.*

"Call me Chris. Please." He takes in a deep breath. "Look, okay. There's this guy, Ricky—"

"Ricky Harris?" Goran asks.

My throat tightens. Christopher nods and looks back and forth between them.

"Chris, just tell us what you know," Goran says. "We'll do our best to help you. If it's not related to this case, we'll let it go. Okay?" This is something Goran would say to get anyone to talk. I hope he means it this time.

"Does Ricky know I'm here?"

"Why would he?" Goran asks.

Christopher narrows his eyes. "Is my sister watching?"

"No, she's working on something else," Fishner replies.

He nods. "Okay. Well, Ricky hangs out a lot at the Emerald, you know. And I've done him a couple of favors, and he said he wanted to repay me."

"What kind of favors?" Fishner asks.

Becker shifts behind me, and I force myself to breathe.

"You don't have to answer that," Hedges says.

Christopher shakes his head. "It's okay. I might as well be honest. It was just a couple of deliveries. I told him I was done, though. I'm not doing that anymore."

"Drugs?" Fishner asks.

"I don't know. He never said, and I didn't ask. He'd shoot me a text, and I'd swing by, grab whatever he gave me, and take it to wherever he said it had to go. I think it was just weed, but I don't know. I borrowed a really nice car a couple of times, and a van, too."

You poor, sad, stupid fuck.

"And what did he usually give you in exchange for doing these deliveries?"

"Oxycontin. Well, Percocet, usually." Christopher takes a sip of his drink. "Anyway, he texted me to meet him at the Emerald Thursday night. He said he had something for me. I figured it was to... um... pay me for my last delivery. Ricky was supposed to come outside and give me the stuff like usual, but instead he told me to come inside. He said he was working the door, and he'd get me in free 'cause there was a party, some guy's birthday or something."

Damn it. Christopher was in the Flats on Thursday night. Kevin's body was found early on Friday morning. That puts my brother way too close to the scene.

"Go on," Goran says.

"I didn't want to go in. I hate places like that, but I needed the pills." He lowers his head and talks to the table. "See, I kind of hate my life sometimes, and a little oxy is one way to get through the day."

His words are like an uppercut to my solar plexus. *This* was why my brother kept calling and texting me, and I ignored him just when he needed me most. If I'd called him back that day, we might not even be sitting here.

"What time did you get there?" Goran asks.

"It was about six o'clock. I went in, and Ricky gave me a drink then offered me a lap dance from a stripper. I turned that down. I have a girlfriend, and I don't really get into that kind of thing, anyway. But Ricky said I had to stay for the party, that he had a surprise for me. I was thinking maybe the surprise was some blow or something, you know, that kind of thing. So I went to the bar and sat down. Some woman brought me a beer, said it was from Ricky."

"Who?" Goran asks. "Do you remember her name?"

"Yeah, 'cause it was funny. Her name was Cleopatra. I'm guessing that's not her real name." Christopher lets out a nervous laugh. "I drank the beer while I texted with my girlfriend. I really just wanted to get my stuff and leave, but I needed to wait for Ricky."

"Was Ricky Harris with you that whole time?"

I know what Goran's asking. Kevin Whittle's time of death was between seven and eight that night. If Ricky Harris was with Christopher that whole time, that will cement Harris's alibi and maybe give Christopher one.

Christopher nods. "Yeah. I mean, not sitting next to me or anything, but he was in the same room the whole time."

"How long were you at the bar?"

"Well, I ended up drinking two beers, so I guess about an hour."

"And what happened then?"

"I went to the bathroom because I didn't feel well. That's where it gets fuzzy. I can't really remember. I think somebody put something in one of the beers." He stares at the wall for a second. "I remember trying to get back down the hallway from the bathroom and feeling really sick. I decided I was just going to leave. I thought maybe I was getting the flu or something. I fell down, and I think I hit my head. Someone, maybe Ricky, told somebody to put me 'in there.' I didn't know where 'in there' was. I tried to ask, but I think that's when I passed out."

Yes! An alibi. If Christopher was out cold in the Emerald Club, he couldn't have been dropping a body off in an alley. All we have to do is verify that he was there when he says he was. Becker could calculate some kind of preemptive strike in case the defense uses the DNA as reasonable doubt. She could put me on the stand and ask the right questions.

"What happened next?" Goran asks.

"I woke up in some closet, like where they keep the tablecloths and napkins and stuff. I checked my phone, and it was Friday. I had a horrible headache. It was weird—that's never happened to me before."

"What time was it?"

"I dunno. All I remember is seeing the day of the week. I was still pretty confused and having a little trouble seeing, so I couldn't make out the smaller numbers for the time. I got up and headed for the front door. On my way out, I saw Ricky sitting at the bar with Johnny."

"Who is Johnny?"

"I'd only seen him once before. Ricky just said the guy's name was Johnny. He never told me his last name, and I never talked to the guy. He's older and kinda skeevy." He shakes his head. "They asked me what the fuck happened then laughed. I just kept walking and got out of there."

"And this was Thursday night and into Friday morning, is that right?" Fishner asks.

He nods. "There's something else," he says. "They use green sheets at the Emerald, back in their private rooms. But other places use 'em, too. See, Ricky uses the laundry bags for the deliveries. Sometimes that's what I deliver, you know, in the van."

"So the... clients, they just take the stuff out of the laundry bag?"

Christopher gives a little half-hearted chuckle. "No, they take the whole bag. I don't even get out of the van. They just take the bag out of the side door."

"So these sheets get around." Fishner frowns. "Chris, do you remember the addresses you've delivered to? Any regulars?"

"Well, there's this one dude on the East Side. He's Ricky's best customer. He has a lot of parties. He invited me to the last one."

"You know his name?"

"Um... Sean... um... Miles, Monroe, Miller, something like that. Nice enough guy, I guess. I've hung out with him a few times."

I back away from the glass and bump into Julia Becker.

Fishner asks my brother what Miller looks like, and Christopher describes him perfectly.

"That should be enough for a warrant," Julia Becker says. She starts to say something else, but I'm already halfway out the door.

CHAPTER FOURTEEN

BEATING EVERYONE TO SEAN MILLER's house isn't exactly "doing paperwork," but if this lead breaks open the case, Fishner won't be too upset. Then again, it might give her serious ideas about chaining me to the desk. That's a risk I'll have to take, though, because there's no way she'll let me go get him, not with my brother involved in this.

I pluck my jacket from the back of my chair. "I'm gonna go grab a bite to eat," I tell Roberts. He just nods without looking up from his screen.

In the car, all I can think about is Christopher. *Someone—Sean Miller?—murdered a little kid then cut off his fucking hand. That's brutal. Christopher may even be connected to the person who did it. Could Christopher have killed that boy? No. There's no way. I mean, anyone could be pushed into violence with the right motivation. But not many people could be pushed into murdering a kid, and even fewer into cutting off the child's hand. My brother is not one of those people.*

As I'm turning onto Chester, Fishner calls. I don't answer, and she doesn't leave a message.

It takes me about half an hour to get to Sean Miller's house, one of those nondescript one-story jobbies that's mixed in with bigger houses in a modest neighborhood. I roll past it slowly but keep going up the block in case he's home and paranoid. At the stop sign, I turn the Charger around and park across the street, about a hundred feet from his front sidewalk. The white paint is peeling, and the front flower beds have become weed patches. Everything is dead, still waiting for spring. The white Chevy pickup that was there before is parked in front of his garage. The boarded-up house on the left looks abandoned. Fishner calls again, and I ignore it again, but she still doesn't leave a message.

I have to wait for the warrant. But I'll already be here, so I might as well help with the search. As long as I don't answer my phone when Fishner calls, I won't have to lie to her. I'm not being completely disobedient.

I don't know how quickly Becker can get a warrant for Miller's place. It depends on the judge and could take anywhere from a couple of hours to all day. Fishner most likely has Goran finishing up with Christopher and doing the warrant paperwork. Our signed affidavit will state that we have evidence that might lead to other evidence, and Becker will take it before a judge and ask for the warrant. She'll need to convince the judge that we have enough for the warrant. Judges are serious about that pesky Constitution and its irksome Fourth Amendment.

After about forty-five minutes, I start to get antsy, so I take a risk and get out of the car. It's stupid, but I don't care because my brother's ass is on the line here. I stroll toward the house, pretending to be out for a walk. The blinds are drawn on the front windows, so I climb the four rickety wooden steps and take a look around the small porch. Budweiser and Coors Light cans litter a square of tattered AstroTurf. An old lawn chair sits in the corner, behind a piece of broken plywood and some wet cardboard boxes. I spot the board for that yard game, Cornhole. A couple of cans of paint sit to my right.

A dog starts barking inside the house. It sounds big and mean. I back down the steps and sidestep into the neighbor's yard. I move down their gravel driveway to get a look at the back of Sean's house. From their backyard, I should be able to see most of his. This is another risk. If someone is home, they could come outside and ask me what I'm doing. I concoct a story: an elderly woman saw my unmarked car and flagged me down up the street. She lost her dog. And because I'm here to protect and serve, I'm helping her look. It's a Jack Russell named Salsa. Lies are always more believable with details.

I slip beside the house and head to the far back corner of the neighbor's yard. All the blinds are drawn on Miller's windows on this side, too, and the window on the side garage door is covered with newspaper. The back door of the house looks as though it hasn't been opened in a long time, given that ivy is growing up and across it. An old wooden privacy fence runs across three backyards, including Miller's. There's really nothing more I can think to do that won't get me in more trouble. With a sigh, I walk back to the car to wait for the warrant.

At one o'clock, Fishner calls and leaves a message telling me to call her when I'm done eating lunch because she has a lot for me to do. I don't obey, and an hour and a half later, I catch sight of a big man lumbering up the block, carrying what looks to be a case of beer.

Miller meanders up the front steps, fumbles with the lock, then goes inside.

My phone beeps once with a text message from Goran: *Where are you? I'm on my way to Miller's with the warrant. Boss is sending backup. Get back to work before she blows a gasket.*

Adrenaline hits me, and I bark out a laugh. I'm getting giddy because we're so close to getting him. He's in there with his stupid case of beer, with all of his blinds drawn and no clue that he's a sitting duck.

I don't take my eyes off Miller's house until an unmarked Taurus from the motor pool turns onto the street. I ease the Charger back up the block and park it right in front of Miller's house.

Goran climbs out of the Taurus. He shakes his head when he spots me getting out of my car. "What, your phone is dead all of a sudden?" He knows what I'm doing. He knows me.

I cross my arms. "Is Christopher all right?"

"Boyle, you can't be here. You've lost your mind. Fishner is gonna—"

"Is Christopher all right?"

"He's fine. We'll cut him loose later today, assuming we can verify his alibi. At least, that's my guess." Goran tilts his head toward the Charger and wedges a toothpick between two bottom teeth. "Way to take the car and risk your shield."

I shrug. "Until she tells me I'm off the case, I'm on the case."

"Don't handle evidence or talk to Miller, or we'll both be up shit creek. Okay? At least give me that much."

I roll my eyes. "Sure thing, boss."

"Liz, I mean it. Please."

I nod because I know he's right.

A patrol car rounds the corner and pulls up behind the Taurus. Two uniforms get out and join us by the Charger. The taller, older one introduces himself as Crouse, then he waves at his partner and says, "Dietz."

"How do you want to run this?" Crouse asks. "Do we know if the guy is at home?"

"He's here," I reply.

Goran gives me the please-don't-screw-this-up look.

I treat his look pretty much the way I treated Fishner's calls. "I've been surveilling the property since eleven twenty. The suspect arrived here, on foot and carrying a case of beer, at approximately two fifteen. He went into the house and hasn't come back out. I took a look around, and the back door appears to be sealed or otherwise unusable. All of the blinds are drawn."

"The warrant allows us to search this property," Goran says, "including the house, garage, and vehicle, for evidence of stolen property and drugs. We're also looking for a large laundry bag, a pair of branch cutters, a garden shovel, and any evidence of violence." He points at Dietz. "Go around back and secure that door."

"Ten-four," Dietz says. He jogs over to the house and rounds the corner.

The three of us traverse the crumbling walkway to the porch and go up the steps. The dog is going bonkers. Goran knocks on the door, and for some reason, the dog stops barking, but Miller doesn't answer.

Goran pounds harder. "Sean Miller, this is the Cleveland Department of Police. We have a search warrant for your property. Open up."

Miller opens the door a couple of inches. "What do you want?" He seems blurry, somehow, as if he's somewhere else. The dog growls behind him.

Goran badges him. "Remember me? I'm Detective Goran, and this is Detective Boyle. We have a search warrant. You need to let us in. Let's do this the easy way, okay?"

"What do you want?" He points at me. "I just talked to you."

Goran responds before I can say anything. "We have some more questions, and we need to take a look around. Again, Mr. Miller, my suggestion is that we do this the easy way."

Miller looks as if he's toying with the idea of slamming the door in my partner's face. I try to see inside, but the dog provides an incentive not to move too quickly or too much.

Goran switches to his good-cop voice. "Mr. Miller, you've been helpful to our investigation so far. Why don't you let us in so we can figure out what really happened with that kid? We just have a couple more questions. You want to keep helping us."

Good cop works. Miller opens the door, restraining the dog by a purple collar. "You won't find what you're looking for in here," he says. His eyes are swollen and red, and he looks as though he hasn't shaved in a couple of weeks. His red mustache hangs over his upper lip, while the lower one is cracked and chapped. He's wearing the same clothes he had on Thursday night when he found Kevin Whittle, and they don't appear to have been washed in the interim. A smell that's a combination of laundry that sat in the washer too long and straight-up body odor wafts over to my nose.

The dog looks like a shepherd mix, probably half pit bull based on the size of the head and jaws. I refuse to judge a dog by its breed or its owner, and I hope this one makes me continue to feel good about that.

Goran serves the warrant and explains what it covers. "You're going to sit with Officer Crouse while we conduct our search."

"Sure, yeah, okay. C'mon, Peaches." He turns to lead the way inside, pulling the dog with him. Crouse radios his partner and tells him to come inside, following Miller.

The house is small with a simple layout, so it shouldn't take long to search. A long hallway leads from the front door to the back of the house, so I walk the length to get the setup. On one side are doors to the living room, bathroom, and bedroom, and the dining room and kitchen are on the other. At the rear of the kitchen is the back door, which is blocked with a table holding a dirty microwave and a box of trash bags. I wave at Dietz and motion for him to go around and come inside.

I move back down the hallway and join Goran, Crouse, and Miller. The living room looks like a frat party gone bad. Beer cans and bottles litter the coffee table and floor. Even though it's only March, fruit flies have taken over, enchanted by the smell of vinegar. Dietz walks through the front door, and the dog lets out a deep bark.

"Control the dog, please," Crouse says in a stern voice.

Miller tells Peaches to "lie down," and she goes directly into a wire crate in the corner. He latches the door, and she curls up on a couple of old towels.

Crouse shoves some garbage aside and plants his ass on the coffee table, which is probably safest. It's hard for bugs to live in a wooden table, but there's always the possibility that it's sticky. "Hey, come over here," he tells Miller. "Let's chat for a minute."

Miller goes over and sits down on the stained gray-blue couch across from Crouse. Dietz moves and stands in a classic cop stance in the doorway leading to the living room.

Goran and I head into the dining room, which is equally trashed. There's no table, just an ancient sideboard and three cheap secondhand chairs that don't match. One is overturned on top of an old TV. A nasty stench rises from a couple of trash bags in the corner, and flies buzz around them.

My boots stick to the floor as I walk, and I try not to think about maggots. "This is fucking disgusting," I mutter.

"Hey, you wanted to be here." He winks and tosses me a pair of latex gloves.

"So now I'm allowed to touch things?"

"No, but you should wear the gloves, anyway. Like you said, this is disgusting." He shoves a trash bag out of the way and looks underneath it.

"Goran, is Christopher all right? Is someone taking him home?"

"Well, he's not very happy, with you or with any of what's going on, and he's freaked out. Wouldn't you be if your DNA was found on a murder victim?"

I pretend not to notice a pair of dirty boxers on top of another trash bag. "Yeah, I would. I need to call him."

"Liz, let him chill out a little bit first, okay? Roberts is working on his alibis. He claims he was at work when the kid was abducted, and that'll be easy to verify." He opens the door to a sideboard that's seen much better days. "There's just garbage in here. Let's keep looking. Living room next."

I know they can't let him go until they know what his movements looked like on the day Kevin was abducted, during the time he was held, and the entire night of the murder, but I'm aching to protect my little brother. "I don't like it. You know he didn't do it, and Fishner should let him go."

Goran stops in the hallway and turns to me. "If the alibis check, he's gonna be okay." He taps my shoulder. "Okay?"

"Are they calling our mother? Is she one of these alibis?" I don't want to deal with her. I don't want her to drink and eat pills, either.

"Yeah, but it's gonna be okay."

I nod, but I still don't like it. I grit my teeth and follow him down the hallway.

Dietz steps to the side and lets us back into the living room, where Miller and Crouse are chatting. Goran goes over and rummages through a fake-wood entertainment center. The dog growls at us from her crate. I don't want to interrupt, so I do-si-do past her and stand against the mantel, which is covered with beer cans and broken bottles.

Miller's eyes—his whole head, really—follow me, but too slowly. His pupils are big, so it's not heroin. He's not acting sped, so it's not coke, crack, or meth. It could be acid, maybe Molly, or ecstasy. "I had an epic party a couple weeks ago," he says. He gnaws on his lower lip until it bleeds. "Over a hundred peeps." My brother was one of those peeps. "Huge," he says, gesturing around to convey how crowded it must have been. I struggle to imagine over a hundred people crammed into here. "I guess I haven't cleaned up yet." He guffaws.

Crouse nods. "Dude, that sounds awesome. Hey, why were you in the Falls?"

"I was pretty upset when I found that kid down in the Flats," Miller replies, rubbing his forehead with the back of his hand, "so I decided to get the hell out of here. I went to see some family."

Goran catches my eye and tilts his head at the hallway. We slide past the dog then Dietz and walk down the hallway. I wish I had one of those white biohazard suits. I'm sure there are mice or cockroaches, maybe both.

The bedroom seems cleaner than the rest of the house, so we start there. A mattress and box spring with no frame are jammed into one corner. Goran pulls them away from the wall and finds only a crushed beer can and an overturned ashtray. Next, he rakes through a closetful of dirty laundry. He finds a collection of porno mags in the particleboard dresser, but it's just regular stuff, nothing illegal. In the corner opposite the makeshift bed, Goran finds a bong and a decent-sized bag of marijuana.

I summon Dietz in to bag it. "Dump the water first," I tell him, and he smirks.

The bathroom is next. I've seen a lot of disgusting things in the twelve years I've been a cop, but there's something about other people's dirty, sticky bathrooms that still frays my viscera. I hold my breath and follow my partner through the door. A half inch of slime and white crust covers nearly every surface.

Goran yanks open the medicine cabinet and picks up a prescription bottle of Vicodin from the top shelf. "Is everyone eating pills?" The label, dated about a year ago, has the name Marnie Phillips printed on it. I wonder who Marnie is and what she needed it for. I write her name in my notebook.

We hit the kitchen next, which is less foul than I feared. Goran shoves some dirty dishes out of the way and looks in the sink. Nothing of note. Next, he checks the freezer: a half-empty box of ham-and-cheese Hot Pockets, an almost-empty plastic bottle of cheap vodka, and three empty ice trays. The refrigerator holds a case of Coors Light, an old pizza box, and a crusty bottle of ketchup.

We move the microwave and its table out of the way to get to the door, which opens to the backyard. "This better not be poison ivy," Goran mutters as we struggle through the vine.

A narrow sidewalk leads to the garage. Three metal trash cans stand in what used to be a flower bed to the right of the structure.

Goran tries the side door of the garage first. A glance through a sizeable crack in the wood tells me that there's no vehicle in there. But I do see blood. Someone tried to clean it up but did a bad job. It's smeared around the cracked concrete floor. Some dirt, which looks like potting soil, and dried leaves are scattered around, as if he'd thought to hide the stain.

"Goran, look at this. Blood." I push on the door. I want to open the big garage door, but that could disturb other evidence.

He shines his pocket flashlight beam into the space. "Holy shit." He gives the door a swift kick right at the lock, and it springs open. The smell of bleach wafts out, but bleach can't get rid of blood evidence.

He stays in the doorway and pulls out his radio. "I'm calling for Crime Scene and more backup."

"Don't tell Fishner I'm here."

He juts his chin out at me then starts talking to dispatch, asking for two more patrol units and the mobile crime scene lab. Then he pulls out his phone.

I hold out my hand. "Since I'm not allowed to touch anything, how about I take the pictures?"

He hesitates but passes me the phone. "Okay, but I took them."

"Of course you did." I take pictures of everything. Some old bikes lean in one corner, covered in cobwebs. A snow shovel is propped against the far wall. There are more garbage bags, and one has maggots crawling along the bottom. "Hell, can't you put out your damn trash? I mean, they'll even come and pick it up from the curb once a week."

Goran chuckles. "Does this guy seem like the kind of guy who puts his trash on the curb? He'd rather keep it in his dining room."

A few garden tools hang from nails on the right wall. I don't see any branch cutters, but there's a shovel like the one Watson thinks the perp used to crack Kevin's skull. An aluminum ladder dangles from a peg, and a rusty red lawnmower that looks as though it's leaking oil or gasoline or both sits in another corner, near some more old paint cans and a dried-out paintbrush. I spot what looks like blood spatter on that wall, so I snap a few more pictures.

I wave a hand around the garage. "Well, everything, other than the garbage, looks clean. It doesn't jibe with the rest of the house or the condition of the yard. So it's a good guess why that bleach smell is so strong."

Goran nods. "Up there," he says, pointing.

I follow his finger and see a small loft. A tent bag, some folding chairs, and a Coleman stove block my view of the rear of the platform. I take some more pictures then move the ladder to lean it against the edge of the loft. "You want me to go up?" I ask, knowing Goran hates ladders.

"Yeah, but don't touch anything," he replies.

"Make sure I don't fall backward off this thing."

He doesn't laugh, but he does come over and hold the ladder. I climb up and start snapping more pictures. There are a couple of garbage bags and a lot more camping equipment. Up close, I can tell that the stuff hasn't been used for a while. There are a couple of coolers, some fishing rods, and a tackle box. A layer of black dust covers almost everything. The tent is half hanging out of the bag, which clearly doesn't belong with the tent.

I feel a little surge of adrenaline. "Holy shit. That's a laundry bag like the one Anthony described, and it looks a lot like the one we took off Ricky Harris." I take several pictures of the tent in the bag before I push the tent out of the way.

"Hey," Goran says. "I told you not to touch anything."

"I just moved the tent a little. I've got pics." My phone vibrates in my jacket pocket, and I pause to pull it out and look at it. It's Fishner. I hit the ignore button and take three more photos of the bag before I unzip it. "It's jewelry. Some Rolex knockoffs, that kind of thing."

"Anything else?"

I see a tool bag. "Yeah." I unzip it. "Whoa. Two bricks of what looks like coke and at least two pounds of weed." After getting a few more pictures, I hastily descend the ladder. "We need more evidence bags. A lot of them. And get someone looking through those trash cans for evidence of bleach, maybe a bucket. Also, we need to bag that shovel." I point at the one hanging on the wall.

He grins. "What, are you in charge now?"

"Goran, don't fuck around. This is it. This is where Kevin Whittle was murdered. Come on." I push past him, back out into the yard.

The stuff we found will be enough to put Miller back in the box and grill him until he tells us what he did to Kevin Whittle. We have seventy-two hours from the time we take him in. Remembering the dog, I call dispatch and request that they send Animal Control.

Goran chomps his gum. "You just blew your cover. Now Fishner's gonna know you were here instead of on some four-hour lunch. All I ask is that you tell her I told you not to touch anything or talk to Miller. Oh, and you were never out of my sight. Now give me back my phone."

I pass him his phone, and he starts flipping through the pictures. A patrol car parks out front, and two more uniforms get out.

"Hey, back here!" I call.

When they reach us, Goran orders, "Tape off the backyard, and don't let anyone near this garage until Crime Scene gets here."

Goran and I go back to the living room, where Miller and Crouse are still talking. Crouse has his head cocked to one side. His notebook is out, and I can see from the doorway that he's filled at least a page.

Goran walks over to stand beside the couch. "Mr. Miller, we need to discuss what we found in your garage."

Miller's mouth falls open, and for a second, I wonder if he even understood what my partner said. Not that I care. What I really want to do is throw him on the floor and cuff him. Dietz shifts from foot to foot. The dog moves around, and I notice she's too big for her crate.

Miller jumps to his feet. "Hey, wait. I didn't say you could look out there."

"Actually, you didn't have to," Goran says. "Remember that search warrant?"

Miller suddenly turns and tries to leap over the back of the couch. I'm between him and the door, but it doesn't matter. Goran tackles him from behind, and they end up on the floor in front of me. The dog lurches into the kennel door, growling, her hackles raised. As my partner yanks Miller's hands behind his back to cuff him, Peaches lunges again. The crate door flies open. Peaches heads straight for Goran. Crouse, still sitting on the coffee table, thrusts out his leg and gives her a swift kick in the ribs. She staggers to the side with a small yelp, but she doesn't appear hurt. Dietz quickly draws his weapon and points it at her. Crouse stands and mirrors his partner.

"No!" I yell. "Miller, control your dog, or this officer is going to shoot her!"

"Peaches!" Miller shrieks, his voice about an octave higher than it was before. "Peaches, go lie down!"

Amazingly, Peaches lowers her head and slinks back into the kennel. Dietz nudges the door shut with his boot then fiddles with the latch, keeping a wary eye on the dog. For good measure, he slides the coffee table over in front of the door, for all the good that will do.

I'd heard just last week about a patrol officer shooting a guy's dog in the process of an arrest somewhere in Texas. The dog was only doing its job, trying to protect its owner. This dog is obedient as hell. She ignored her instinct to rip out our throats in order to please him. I feel this weird surge of gratitude toward Miller for not setting the dog on us. I would have hated to see her killed.

Goran finishes cuffing Miller then pulls him to his feet. "You wanna resist arrest? We can add that to the list."

"What am I under arrest for?" Miller asks in a whiny voice.

"For felony possession of narcotics and stolen property." It's a strategy move. We're hoping he'll crack and confess to Kevin Whittle's murder, but right now we just need to get him into custody. "Get him out of here," Goran tells Crouse and Dietz. "Read him his rights and take him downtown."

"I told you I didn't do anything!" Miller screams. His face is red, and he looks as though he might cry. "I didn't do anything!"

As the uniforms are pulling away to take Miller downtown, Crime Scene pulls into the driveway and parks behind the Charger.

Goran meets them at the door. "Out back in the garage. Bag everything. Type the blood as soon as you can."

My phone buzzes in my pocket. I pull it out and answer without thinking.

"Long lunch, Boyle?"

I know there's no point in lying, so I just ask, "Did you cut my brother loose?"

"Not yet. Let's see what happens with this new evidence." She sighs. "Boyle, I told you to do paperwork. This is way out of line." She's got the teeth-clenched voice, the one that means I'm probably in some seriously deep water. "We'll talk about this later. Animal Control is on its way. You and Goran get back here as soon as you're done there, and come to my office first."

Goran and I watch the crime techs go over the area, but they don't find anything more than we did. We leave a couple of hours later, while they're still dusting for prints. On the way back to the station, I wonder what will happen to Peaches.

CHAPTER FIFTEEN

"**H**E'S OBVIOUSLY UNDER THE INFLUENCE," Becker is saying as Goran and I walk into Fishner's office. "I can't take him to arraignment like this, even for narcotics possession, not given what's happening with Chris Boyle and the fact that Liz was at that scene. I have to play this very safe." She glances over at me and blinks.

"We'll just sit on him, then," I say. "We've got seventy-two hours. It'll clear his system by morning. We have plenty of time to crack him."

Fishner levels her gaze at me. "Counselor, give us a minute, please." She doesn't look at Becker or Goran because she's focused on me. She stands up and crosses her arms as the prosecutor leaves the office, shutting the door behind her.

"His lawyer is on the way," Fishner says.

We stare at each other for a few seconds. "Lieutenant, look—"

"No."

"I just—"

"You. Just."

I look away and run my hand through my hair. When I look back, I cringe before I can stop myself. She's been mad before but never like this. I'm a little scared that I've crossed the line and may have truly screwed up this time. I try to catch Goran's eye, but he's focused on a point somewhere on Fishner's desk.

She takes three long, even breaths. "Detective Boyle, let me ask you a question." Her voice sounds weird and tight, even though she's speaking in low tones. "What, exactly, was unclear about my orders to stay on the desk and catch up on paperwork?"

I don't say anything. I look at the floor.

"And you." She jabs a finger at Goran. "You allowed this to happen? Was there something unclear in my orders? Detective Goran, this surprises me, coming from you. I'm disappointed."

"I apologize, Lieutenant," he says.

She gives him a tight nod. "Go write your search report. Wait for me before you talk to Miller."

I turn to follow him.

"Not you, Boyle. Sit down."

Goran slinks through the door and closes it gently behind him.

"Sit down," she repeats, and I do as I'm told. "Answer me." She uncrosses her arms and recrosses them in the other direction. "In case you forgot the question, or maybe you weren't listening in the first place, I'll ask it again. What, exactly, was unclear about my orders to stay on the desk?"

I glance at the windowed wall. The blinds aren't closed all the way. The guys are trying not to watch, but I know they're out there gossiping, every one of them relieved they aren't in here with me. Not that I'd be any different.

"Lieutenant, I—"

"Look at me."

I raise my eyes to hers.

"Go home, Detective."

"But what about Miller? He—"

"No. Go home." Her nostrils flare.

In her mind, I should have waited. But I shouldn't have. I did the right thing. We have him now, and that's what matters. The drugs will wear off, and we'll nail him. Then I can tell Teresa and Peter Whittle that we caught their son's killer. It won't mean much to them, but it's something. It might not help their grief, but it could be justice.

"This is such a blatant disregard for authority that I'm not even sure what to do with you."

She's relaxing a little bit now. I can tell because her voice sounds closer to normal. I don't want her to get scary again, so I keep my mouth shut.

141

"An attorney could say that you tainted—or planted—evidence because your brother is involved." After a pause, she adds, "You know that, right?"

I nod.

"Look, I know you hate it when anyone worries about you, but maybe if I put it to you this way, you'll listen. First, killing that guy, which, okay, that was a good shoot. But then you turned to shit for weeks. Liz, officer-involved shootings are nothing to laugh at. You've been on edge ever since. Don't think I haven't heard about you bawling out the rookies. Don't think I haven't noticed how close to the wire you look these days. Even on the best day of the best week, Special Homicide burns people out." She leans a hip against her desk. "You need to step back. What happened today with your brother could jeopardize this whole case, your closure rate, your squad. You know that."

I lean forward, my hands on my knees. I have nothing to say that's going to help the situation. It's not going to jeopardize the case or my closure rate or the squad. She's exaggerating. I squeeze my knees until my knuckles turn white.

Fishner's gaze flicks to my hands. "The biggest problem with all of this? You're turning into some kind of raging, rogue detective. You know that shit doesn't fly with me, Liz. You *know* it doesn't. You're good, but you're not that good. No one is irreplaceable." She uncrosses her arms and places her hands flat on her desk. "This bullshit with your brother is... I don't even know the word. It's unbelievable. You were about to smack Ricky Harris around in there yesterday, too, in front of his lawyer."

I don't tell her that I wasn't going to touch him. At this point, arguing could set her off even more.

"You *defied my direct order* by going to the Miller property. And now? Now we have an inebriated suspect and the possibility that none of what you found will be admissible. Now you have to go home, which means no sleep for the rest of your squad. You need to step back, and I will do paperwork to make that happen if need be. But I hope you're smart enough to keep this out of your jacket. We'd both hate to see you back in one of the districts or in Property Crimes. Like I said, some of us care about rules."

I just stare at her.

"Goodbye, Liz," she says.

"Yes, Lieutenant," I reply around the lump in my throat. Suppressing the urge to run, I walk out of the office.

In the squad room, the guys are pretending to be working really hard on paperwork. Goran glances up as I walk to my desk for my jacket and keys. I make a face at him, and he wiggles his eyebrows. I give him a tight nod.

"Hey, nice job, Boyle," Domislaw grunts from his desk.

I fake a smile for him and nod.

"Liz," Julia Becker calls.

I look over and see her standing in front of the vending machine. She grabs her Diet Coke from the slot and starts strutting my way, one foot in front of the other as if she's on a runway. I am so over all of this, and I'm sure it shows.

"Relax," she says when she's about three feet away from me.

I catch a whiff of her good perfume. She smiles. I wonder if she knows that we call her a shark and an ice maiden. I don't say anything. I just look at her.

"I think I know why you did what you did." She pauses as if waiting for a response, but I keep zipped. "It might not be by the book, exactly, but we all suspect the lab is going to tell us that the evidence you found is damning for Sean Miller. Damning enough to book him, in all likelihood." She's smiling with her eyes but not her lips. "It looks like a decent case to me."

Why does she enunciate like that? Seriously, don't most people speak differently than they write? Lawyers. Sheesh. I'm drained, coming down hard off the adrenaline, feeling hollow pressure in my head and a weird sort of tingling in my hands. "All right, I'm gonna head home," I say.

"I'll see you tomorrow." She puts her hand on my arm. "Take care of yourself. I'm going to go watch an interrogation now."

After Becker leaves, Goran stands up and tells me to follow him. We go into the stairwell, where one of the fluorescent lights blinks and buzzes above us. I feel light-headed and strange. I haven't eaten anything since… I can't remember.

He leans back against the wall and raises his eyebrows. The flickering light casts harsh shadows on his face.

I fiddle with the clasp on my watch. "What?"

"Where do I even start?"

I sigh and roll my eyes.

He shakes his head. "Why didn't you tell me what was going on with Chris? As soon as it happened, as soon as Jo called you?"

"I don't know." I shrug. "I wanted to keep you out of it. I figured the fewer people involved, the better for Christopher. I knew she wasn't going to let me interview him, and I wanted it to be you who did. If you'd known, then…"

He takes a breath, his blue eyes back on mine, unwavering. "The better for Chris or for you?" He's staring me down. He's not going to let it go.

"For all of us," I lie.

He pops a piece of gum into his mouth. "Liz, come on."

"What?"

"Talk to me."

Goran is the only one on the squad who knows anything about me. Well, I'm guessing Fishner knows some things, since she has access to my personnel file. I'm sure there's stuff in my jacket about my dead dad and sister, but she's never said anything, and I'd just as soon keep it that way. But Goran… I told him all about it one night, drunk and emotional, after we'd collared a guy who'd done bad shit to a girl who'd been about the same age as my sister when a guy did bad shit to her. I can only hope he knows me well enough to give me a break on this.

I glance at the ceiling then look back at him. "What do you want to know, Tom?"

He smiles at me the same way he might look at one of his kids. This time, maybe for the first time since I've known him, it doesn't piss me off. It comforts me.

"Are you going off the deep end? 'Cause if you are, I need to know. I'm your partner." He grins. "Sometimes your friend."

"What do you mean? I'm not going off the deep end. In fact, as you well know, we just arrested Sean Miller, and now you're going to grill the shit out of him. I'm fine."

He stares at me and chews his gum.

"I'm not going off the fucking deep end, Tom."

"You still talking to that shrink?"

For a second, I imagine Shue in her office, gazing through her glasses and into my eyes, probing. "Yeah, I have a couple more appointments," I mumble.

I know Goran would never talk to a shrink unless it was mandatory, and until about two days ago, I felt the same way. But I don't want to become a statistic.

"You need to talk to *somebody*, and it's obviously not gonna be me." He looks hurt for a second, then he's all cop again.

I reach for his arm and close my fingers around his elbow. "I'm sorry."

He chomps his gum and squeezes my shoulder hard. The whole thing—and I'm not exactly a petite woman—fits into the palm of his big hand. "When you want to talk, say the word." He smiles and releases me. "I mean it."

I give him a half smile.

"Good job showing up today," he says as he opens the door to the stairwell. "I knew you would. That guy is such an asshole." He slips back into the hall.

I take the stairs down to the first floor. In my car, I grab a stale protein bar from my glove box and scarf it on the way to the gym for the second time today. I can't believe the call about my brother was just this morning. I feel as if days have passed since then.

At the gym, I go straight for the heavy bag. Punching things feels good. It helps me get the tension out of my shoulders. I don't like being in trouble, but at least we got Sean Miller into custody. Christopher can probably get immunity for testifying against Miller, and maybe against Ricky Harris. Miller and Harris can both go to prison.

I take a quick shower after my workout. As I'm getting dressed, I'm startled by an instinct to call Cora, my ex, and tell her about what's going on. I shake it off, grab my stuff, and head home. I stop at a convenience store on the way and buy a six-pack of dark beer.

At home, Ivan is glad to see me. Before I even crack a beer, I feed him, fill his water bowl, and scoop the litter box. I look at my six-pack and consider how much more effective that bottle of bourbon on top of my refrigerator would be, but I decide against it. Prying off the cap on my first bottle, I congratulate myself for showing such restraint.

A couple of hours later, as I'm draining my fourth beer, my phone buzzes. "Boyle."

"Hey," Goran says. "Chris's alibis check out. He was at the Emerald

Club during the time of the murder, and he was at work the day Kevin was abducted."

"What about the rest of the time? It needs to be tight."

"He was with his girlfriend a couple of nights, worked several double shifts, had dinner with your mom, all like he said. He's pretty much in the clear."

"Thank God. Thanks for letting me know. Anything on Miller?"

Goran says, "Miller claims he found the vic's body in his garage and panicked, so he cleaned up then did a dump job."

I take a few seconds to let that sink in. "Wait a minute. He copped to dumping the body?" I feel my shoulders and neck relax. "Okay. Fuck yeah, Tom. Good. We can close this shit out."

"Yeah, but he swears up and down that was it. He has no idea what happened. And he lawyered up."

"Who's his lawyer?"

"Rodriguez. So far, he's not saying anything about Miller being intoxicated or about you being there, uh, against everyone's better judgment. Good work, Boyle, even if it's just dumb luck and even if you're a pain in the ass."

Rodriguez is a Legal Aid lawyer who's been around for a while. He's a nice enough guy but a terrible defense attorney. So there is a silver lining. Everything will stay in the record with that guy at the defense table. I'm sure Becker is elated. "Okay, it could definitely be worse."

"Anyway, Miller's story is that a few people had access to his house, and he's been out of town a couple of times in the past few weeks. I guess he's well known for his *epic* house parties, which bring all kinds of lowlifes to his place. So he claims that the killer could have been anyone."

"It doesn't look good, though. I mean, he did dump a kid's body in the Flats, and he admitted it." I pad down the hallway to the kitchen, where I toss my bottle into the recycle bin and open another beer.

"Yeah. Miller said he gave copies of his house and garage keys to his sister. She feeds the dog when he's out of town. But he says he doesn't lock the garage much, anyway."

"Uh-huh. Likely story." I take a sip.

"He says he doesn't think it was locked when he went to Pittsburgh on his trip last week. Anyone could have gotten in."

I walk back down the hallway and plop down on the couch. "Why not call the police? I mean, if I found a dead body in my garage, I'd call the police. Unless I'd put it there, of course. But hey, maybe that's just me."

"Yeah, I probably would, too," he replies.

I grab my notebook from the coffee table and flip it open. "So how long is Miller saying he was out of town? Kevin was abducted on Friday, and his body was found on Thursday. So if Miller's telling the truth, could someone have been holding Kevin in the garage that whole time? It's pretty soundproof in there, relatively isolated."

The sound of paper rustling comes over the line, probably Goran checking his notes. "He claims he was gone Monday through Thursday."

"Does he have tickets or reservations or something to prove his alibi?"

"He drove, so no plane tickets. We can check gas stations if he didn't save any receipts and can remember where he stopped. He came home Thursday around nine a.m. He says the garage door was stuck so he parked in the driveway. He went into the garage later that evening to check out the door, and that's when he found the body. He says he put the kid's body in the laundry bag then stuck it in the trunk of his car. He was going to drive up to the lake, but he changed his mind. He said he couldn't stomach the idea of the kid never being found, never getting a decent burial. So he drove down to the Flats, but it was busy down there, still early. He went to Winky's and got drunk. When it got to that dead time, he got the bag out of the car, laid the kid out near the dumpsters, where it was kind of screened from the bar, and started to raise hell. He said he was so upset it all came pretty naturally."

I remember the man I saw that day. Miller had been a snotty, sniveling wreck. "Yeah, I can see that. When did he clean up the garage? Before or after dropping the body?"

"After moving the body into the car but before dropping it in the Flats. He also admits that he bought drugs from Ricky Harris, so there's that. He basically corroborates what Chris said about all of that."

"Anything on the neighborhood canvass?" I ask.

"'Course not. No one saw or heard a thing."

"Any line on Miller's parents? Maybe we could talk to them."

"No parents. He and his sister were brought up in foster care, or so he claims. The sister is the owner of the black sedan your wit saw. Miller's

Chevy's been broken down for a while, so he borrowed her car that week. He drove it to Pittsburgh, came back, then used it to take Kevin's body down to the Flats. He'd just taken it back to her on Friday morning when he got picked up for drunk and disorderly."

"Oh, that's convenient, isn't it? He just happened to be driving a borrowed car the night he needed to get rid of a dead body."

"Yeah, he's full of shit," Goran replies.

"And he lied to me about some friend of his giving him a ride to his sister's. I wonder if he had her car cleaned before returning it. Did you get the sister's address?"

"Yep. She's clean, no record."

"Any other relatives? Any connections to anyone else?"

"Not as far as I can tell."

"But what the hell? Who would take Kevin to Miller's house—to his garage— just to kill him? It makes no sense. There was blood all over the place, Tom. It wasn't just someone dumping a body. They took him there, and they killed him there. And it just happens to be the couple of days Miller was away?"

"He says a lot of people knew he was going away. He was going up to see a buddy in Pittsburgh—one of his 'connections.' Apparently, he was bragging about it at the party, how he was going to come back with some grade-A goods. He says upwards of a hundred people could have known he'd be out of town those days."

"All right, so what's Fishner's plan? We keeping Miller on the drugs?"

"Yeah, we're keeping him on the murder, too. We're gonna go at him hard again first thing in the morning, just on the drugs and stolen property stuff for starters." A pinging sound comes over the line, and I know he just spit his gum into a trash can. "You can take care of all your hunches tomorrow, partner," he says. "Right now, I'm just happy we have Miller. I mean, you risked your shield to get him."

"Yeah. Call me tomorrow and give me an update, okay?"

"You coming in tomorrow?"

"Yeah, but I'm guessing I'll be at a desk for a while."

We say our goodbyes and hang up. I go to the kitchen for my last beer. Miller's not copping to the murder. I thought for sure he would. And although I would love to think he's just holding out on us, I can't make myself believe it. Something is off. Things aren't lining up in my brain the way they should. But I know better than to say this out loud.

There's one thing that's going to make me sleep easier tonight, though: my brother is going to be okay. I decide it's time to give him a call, but he doesn't answer.

"Hey, it's me," I say to his voicemail. "I'm sorry about everything. It's gonna be okay. Call me." After a beat, I add, "I love you, little brother."

I wonder where he is. Maybe he's at Mom's. I can't remember the last time she's been sober for this long, and I hope it lasts. I have to admit that it would be nice to have her back after all these years. I also know that hope is a dangerous thing.

Back in the early '90s, my dad was under investigation for my little sister's rape and murder. That was back in the days before Cleveland did much with DNA. Even though other states were starting to catch on by then—I think Florida put a guy away using DNA evidence in '87 or something—Ohio was a little slow. Blood typing, which is much less detailed, said it could have been Dad. That shitty little shred of evidence looked good enough to those cold cops. Dad was never arrested because his alibi checked out, but they didn't let up. They harassed him for two years. He never complained about it, though. He wasn't a complainer.

They never found out who did it. They never even had any good leads. I've looked at the files again and again, but I couldn't find anything solid, either. Usually those kinds of assholes, once they get a taste, do it over and over until we get them, but I couldn't even find any other linked crimes. Maybe the guy moved out of town. Maybe he died. Maybe he's in prison for something else. I'll never know.

Anyway, after my dad died, Mom got really into pills. It started with a couple of Vicodins here and there, then she moved on to oxycodone. I suspect methadone was added to that list later. She would spend entire weeks blissed out in her bedroom while I took care of Christopher and did my best to keep the house. After about four years, she stopped paying the mortgage altogether, so we lost the house and had to move. I did the same thing at our Willoughby apartment. That went on until I was eighteen and moved out. By then, Christopher could take care of himself, or so I told myself.

The death of a child often tears families apart. I don't know which one of Kevin Whittle's family members will come undone, but when it happens, it won't be pretty.

Showers at the gym never really make me feel clean enough, so I head to the bathroom for a long, hot shower. Something happens in there: I start to cry. And then I *let* myself cry. I put both hands on the tile wall, the water beating down on my body, and I weep for several minutes.

Finally, all cried out, I get out and throw on some sweats. While I'm ordering takeout, Ivan creeps along the edge of the area rug then curls up next to me on the couch.

CHAPTER SIXTEEN

WAKE UP EARLY, BUT I lie still, contemplating my dream. In it, I was in a cemetery that looked like a huge, old library, one of those with a sliding ladder and big leather-bound books, but it was outside. Dark-red bricks lined the sides of where I stood and the wall opposite the books, but they were made out of grass and formed a patchwork tapestry. A woman stood a few feet in front of me. I've heard that when we dream, we never see a face we've never seen before, so I'm trying to place her. She explained that each of the grass bricks represented an experience that a person had worked through, that the experience could become a brick only if the person had dealt with it. She walked over to a bunch of what looked like old vaudeville steamer trunks in the far corner and tugged one over to me.

We put a bunch of stuff in it: a diary filled with pages scribbled in my handwriting, a ragged doll, some bits of fabric, some old books, a couple of vinyl records, and a lock of dark hair tied with a red ribbon. We scooped up some dirt and sprinkled it all over the contents before closing the lid. Then she pointed up at the wall of books-slash-bricks and told me to put the trunk away. In that surreal way of dreams, I was able to get the trunk up the ladder and into a space that perfectly fit it. The wall sealed around the trunk, as if it had been waiting for that day. All the books turned into other trunks, then they all became grass bricks. After I climbed down, the ladder disappeared, and the woman was gone.

I was all alone in this huge space with the weird grass bricks. I sat on the ground and wondered where my trunk had gone, but I was okay with it disappearing like that. Then I wake up.

I sit up and look around my bedroom. It feels good to wake up in my bed again. On my way to the kitchen for coffee, my phone beeps, reminding me that I have an appointment with Shue this morning. My first instinct is to cancel, but then I remember Goran's face yesterday, how dejected he looked when I didn't tell him what was happening with my brother. If we add defying my boss's explicit orders and flashing back to my screwed-up adolescence and coming unglued in the shower to the list, it's probably good that I'm seeing her today. Maybe this crap could actually help me. *At least give it a try,* I tell myself. *Maybe it's not all bad. Maybe you can fix it.*

After I've eaten a bowl of cereal and gotten dressed, I shoot Goran a text telling him that I'll be late. I don't tell him what the appointment is. *Ten-four,* he replies as I'm starting the car.

After I fill Shue in on what's going on with work, I tell her about the dream. She's thrilled that I remember it and that it wasn't a nightmare. She asks what I think the dream means.

I think about that for a minute. "On the way here, I listened to a CD Josh made for me."

"Josh is your best friend, right?"

"Yeah. And there were two songs on it that made sense."

"Had you heard them before?"

"One of them, yeah. The other one, no. Anyway, there's this line in the one I hadn't heard before. It's by a singer named Gillian Welch. Do you know her?"

She nods. "Yes, I like her very much." She knows I usually listen to heavy, angry stuff, so she's probably happy to discover that I have a heart.

I like a lot of music. Someone I cared about once told me that I have a musical brain. I might have been devoutly punk rock in my misguided youth, but I like anything that sounds good and has some semblance of emotional honesty to it. "Okay, so it's the line in 'Look at Miss Ohio' about wanting to do right, maybe sometime later. Not now. And the whole song, you know, it's slower and draggier than what I usually listen to, but it's about this Miss Ohio character who just does whatever she wants. Even though her mom wants all this shit for her, she gets in a convertible and drives away." I run my hands through my hair. "You know the song."

She smiles as if I've uncovered some big secret about something. "What's the other song?"

"It's called 'Bottle Up and Explode.' I never liked it before. I thought it was some sappy sad-sack emo crap, but now I think I understand it."

"What do you think it means now?"

I shrug, about to blow her off and invent a meaning. But then I think about how screwed up the Christopher business is and how screwed up I am, and reconsider. "It's about not hiding feelings anymore."

She just stares at me.

"What?" I ask.

"You tell me."

I gesture at her notebook. "You haven't written on your pad in over two minutes."

"Good observation."

"I've been thinking about Cora a lot again." I almost tell her about the psychedelic autopsy dream and the impulse to make that phone call last night, but I decide against it. I want this to work, but I can't make myself spill my guts about everything.

She nods. "Did you ever stop thinking about her?"

I shake my head. "Not really."

"Liz, we both know that circumstances in your life—not just your childhood but your entire career and many of your adult experiences—have made you wary of people, unwilling to trust even those with good intentions."

I blink at her. *The road to hell is paved with good intentions, right?*

"Wondering—and this applies to most people—if a potential friend or lover wants to harm you or how she *could* harm you will, at least subconsciously, mean that you will not allow her to get close to you. Forgive me for saying this because I think I can predict your reaction, but I have something I want you to think about."

"What?"

"'The universe will reward you for taking risks on its behalf.'" She goes all Zen with her eyes half closed and wearing a little half smile.

"Who says shit like that?" I chuckle.

She grins. "Well, it's from a personal-development expert with New Age tendencies."

"Yeah, I'm not surprised. Seriously. I can't imagine ever saying anything like that." My impulse is to tell her to go to hell with her taking-risks crap, but then I remember the deal I made with myself this morning.

"Pooh-pooh it if you want, but you need friends, Liz. You're right when you say that."

"I will pooh-pooh it." I stare at a spot on my jeans, wondering what it is. "I want to be a nice person. Normal." I pick at the spot with a fingernail. It looks like red wine. Maybe blood. "I'm kind of afraid I'm losing it," I say with some finality as I look up from the stain.

"What does that mean?"

"I'm not controlling myself very well. I'm still doing things I shouldn't be doing. I'm on the desk again because I went a little nuts yesterday. And the night we caught this case, I went off on a rookie, scared the shit out of her. My partner thinks I'm losing it."

"Why does it bother you that you scared the other officer?"

I blurt, "Because that rookie is a lot like I once was." I stop in surprise. I didn't even realize that was the reason for my irritation until I said it out loud. "At least I think she is."

"Is this significant, do you think?"

"Back then, I didn't have anybody to stop me from fucking up. So with her, I was just trying, you know, to get my message through. It seemed like maybe it worked."

She writes something on her pad. "Do you think you could have gotten your message through without intimidating her?"

"No, not if she's a lot like I once was."

"What I'm hearing is that you're conflicted. Your outward behavior doesn't seem to align with your feelings. Is that accurate?"

"I don't even know what the hell that means." When she just stares at me, I sigh. "Okay, fine. My outward behavior doesn't align with my feelings. Except it does. I think I do a lot of these things to try to help people I care about, or people who remind me of me, but then I come unhinged." I fiddle with my watch clasp then catch her watching me and stop. "When I come unhinged, I say and do things I regret, which partially explains why Cora and I broke up." I chuckle, trying to lighten the mood. "And even sitting here and saying this shit right now, I'm pretty sure I'll regret it later."

She gives me a soft smile. "Why will you regret it later?"

"Because it goes against everything I believe. This woo-woo shit"—I wave my hands around—"it's not my thing."

"What is your thing, then?"

"Well, I have a list of things I'm not going to do anymore. Does that count?"

She frowns, but almost immediately, she makes her expression neutral again. "What will that help you accomplish?"

"It'll help me get my shit straight. If I have a list of things I'm not doing, then I won't do them."

She gets up and goes to her desk. "I want to remind you again that this is a process." She rummages through a drawer and pulls out a notebook with a black-and-white marbled cover like the ones I used in school. "I'd rather see you make a list of things you *are* going to do instead of ones you're *not*." She hands me the notebook before sitting back in her chair.

I just stare at her, holding the notebook as if it's covered in blood.

"That will transfer strength to you," she says, "rather than just offering the outward appearance of toughness." She searches my face. "Think of it as being like the other to-do lists you like to make."

A light comes on in my head. I get it. After all this time, I think I get it. I tuck the notebook between my leg and the arm of the chair.

"This takes time," she says. "All of these things take time. Let's work on trying to see gray areas instead of black and white ones."

I laugh, but it's forced. "At least you aren't asking me to make a collage again." She wanted me to do that once, and I have to draw the line somewhere. I pull the notebook out and look at it. "The cover is black and white." I grin. "I don't see any gray areas."

She chuckles. "Just try it," she says. "You can write your list of 'don'ts' in here if you want. But think about turning them into positive statements. They'll have more meaning that way." She glances at the clock. "See you next week?"

"Yeah," I say.

I hustle out of there. Jogging down the stairs, I check my voicemail. I'm surprised to find a message from Elaine Whittle. She must have retrieved my business card from her purse and remembered something I might want to know, as the detective of record on the case. All she says is that she wants to talk to me. Her voice is sad and weak and bedraggled.

I know what Fishner would say: "Stay on the desk. Tell them someone else will be by to talk. Send Goran." But the woman called *me*. I slip back out to my car and send Fishner a text telling her that I'll be back in two hours. I say a little prayer that this won't get me shipped back to one of the districts.

It doesn't take long to get to their house. When I pull up in their driveway, I see a blond woman in the neighboring yard. She has a dog, a boxer mix, on a long leash. I figure she's the blonde in Kevin's picture, so I get out and trot over to talk to her.

"Hi there. I'm Detective Elizabeth Boyle, CDP." I hold out my badge.

"Oh, hi," she replies. "Um... I'm not sure what to say. I've never talked to a detective before. Is this about Kevin?"

I nod.

She waves at her dog. "This is Rufus. I'm Caroline. I'm happy to help in any way that I can."

I pet Rufus, who drools and gives me a friendly enough canine gaze. "Last Thursday night, do you remember anything about your neighbors' activities?"

She purses her lips. "Yeah, actually, because I was going on a late-ish run with Rufus. Graham was outside checking the mailbox."

"What time was this?"

"Probably a little before eight." She makes a hand motion in front of the dog's face. "Sit, Rufus."

"Okay, thanks. Do you remember any strange vehicles in the vicinity? That day or any other time?"

She knits her eyebrows and scratches Rufus behind the ears. "Not really. I mean, I don't really pay attention, you know?"

I pull out a business card. "If you think of anything, will you give me a call?"

She grins. She's the type to smile at anything and make it look effortless. "Sure, of course."

"Thanks for your time, Caroline."

"If I think of anything, I'll call you," she says, turning away. She calls for Rufus to follow her, and he seems thrilled to get to move again.

I go back to the Whittles' house and ring the doorbell. Their house is

156

nice. It's not a huge suburban mansion, which I expected, but a remodeled city property.

When Graham opens the door, he looks haggard and unshaven. "Detective Boyle," he says with no hesitation, "come in." Either he has a terrific memory, or he was expecting me.

I step into the foyer. Elaine comes from another room and stands behind Graham. She looks at her husband then back at me and shakes her head.

I take the hint and focus on Graham. I pull Sean Miller's photo up on my phone and hold it out for him to see. "Do you recognize this man?"

He squints at it for several seconds then shakes his head. "No. I've never seen him before."

"Okay. Does Kevin have a room here?"

He nods.

"You mind if I take a look?"

"No. That's fine. It's upstairs, the first door on the left. I'll show you."

I was hoping that he would stay downstairs and Elaine would come up and talk to me, but that's not how it's working out. Graham stands outside the door while I look around Kevin's bedroom. It looks a lot like the one at his parents' house. Crime Scene was just here yesterday, so I don't expect to find anything, and it turns out I'm not wrong with that expectation. The window is shut and locked. I see no signs of any kind of foul play, at least other than the fingerprint powder all over everything, but I do take note of the absence of stuffed animals on the bed. A couple are on a shelf in the corner but none on the bed. More little-kid drawings hang on the wall, and I'm surprised by how many include the neighbor with yellow hair. I didn't get the impression they were that close.

My cell rings, and Goran's name appears on the screen. I move to the far corner of the room and try to keep my voice quiet so Graham can't hear. "Boyle."

"We booked Miller on the drugs and stolen property," Goran says. "He sang like a canary about the Emerald Club. Fishner sent me back to the Emerald, and it's a huge waste of my time, but whatever. Lamont—the manager—couldn't tell me dick about the possible connections between Miller and that place. Good news for your Ricky, though. One of the dancers alibied him for time of the abduction, too. Says he was there that whole afternoon."

So it looks as though Harris is well clear. Miller dropped the body and insists he did it alone. Christopher was with Harris for the time of the actual murder. The afternoon Kevin disappeared, Ricky was in the club and has an alibi, Christopher was at work, and Miller claims he was out of town. "Uh-huh," I whisper.

"Lamont offered more videotape," Goran says.

"Call you back?" I ask.

"Sure. Okay." He hangs up.

When I emerge from Kevin's room, Graham says, "Forgive me, Detective Boyle, but I have to go take my medicine. I'm sorry. Is that okay?" He certainly seems more contrite today than he did in Fishner's office.

"Sure, of course," I reply. "Do you mind if I take a look in the backyard?"

"No, that's no problem at all. Go ahead downstairs." He gestures at the staircase then goes the opposite way down the hall.

Elaine waits until he turns in to another room then asks, "Would you like a cup of coffee? I can make some coffee." She nervously looks over her shoulder.

I know she wants to talk, but I also know this is my one chance to get a look around their house. Even though Crime Scene was here yesterday, sometimes it helps to get an idea of what an abductor saw. "Sure, that would be fine. I'm just going to look around in the backyard, then I'll come inside."

I leave her reaching for the coffee filters and head out the kitchen door. I move in a spiral out from the deck to the far reaches of the property then back again. As I'm about to step onto the deck stairs, I spot the edge of something white peeking out from under the wood. I bend over to take a closer look.

It's a business card. But the odd thing is that I recognize the name. It belongs to my old partner, Dwayne Arya. I rode in a patrol car with him for a couple of years, at the beginning of my career, playing Colby to his Morrison. Arya isn't even CDP anymore. He moved to California and became a private investigator after his parents died and he got a big inheritance. As far as I know, he hasn't been in Cleveland since then, so it's not as if he or anyone else would need to pass out his card in this neighborhood.

I take two photos with my phone then use my pen to flip over the card. A number is written on the back. It looks familiar, and I think it may be his old cell phone number. Underneath the number, in block print, are the words "Nothing beautiful without struggle." I try to imagine him writing such a thing. Not likely. His writing was never that neat, anyway.

I'm losing track of time again, so I try to think this through. Crime Scene was here yesterday, the day the Christopher shit happened. Sunday. It rained part of last night, but the card isn't wet. So someone was here between the time it stopped raining last night and right now, and that someone was carrying Arya's card.

I take several more photographs and pull an evidence bag from my inside jacket pocket. Using my pen, I slide the card into the bag and seal it. I look at the number on the bag again. Curiosity overwhelms me. I call the number. A young-sounding woman answers on the second ring.

"May I speak to Dwayne Arya, please?"

"I'm sorry. You have the wrong number."

"How long have you had this number?" I ask.

"Uh... who is this?"

"My name is Liz. I'm looking for someone. It's important. How long have you had this number?" I hate repeating myself, but whatever.

"I've had it for, like, four years."

"Thanks." I hang up and call Goran. "What time was Crime Scene done at the grandparents' house?"

"Just a sec." I hear him clicking on his computer. "Report says five p.m."

"Sean Miller was with us at five and in the box with you by the time the rain started."

"Um... yeah. Where are you?" he asks. I can almost hear the wheels spinning in his head. "And what are you talking about?"

"I'm in the Whittles' yard. Before you say anything, Elaine called me. I'm going to tell Fishner, so settle down."

"Holy hell, Liz! Do you *want* to get suspended?"

"No, and I won't. This is important. Thanks and bye." I hang up.

Elaine comes outside as I'm approaching the steps. I smile at her and start up the stairs. Graham must still be upstairs, and I wonder if he's okay.

"Mind if I take you up on that cup of coffee?"

She nods. "Of course," she says, almost in a whisper.

We sit at the kitchen island, and she pours two cups of coffee. She slides one over in front of me, and I thank her.

I show her the card. "Do you recognize this?"

She peers at it then shrugs. "One of your team must have dropped it yesterday, right?"

"Do you have motion lights or anything outside?"

She shakes her head. "They all come on automatically when it gets dark."

"Did you see anyone outside late last night, maybe even earlier this morning?"

"No. Do you think someone was out there?"

"I'm not sure yet. Do you use your alarm system regularly?"

She nods. "Yes. We use it every night."

"Make sure you set it, okay?" I run my hand through my hair and stare at her.

She nods again then takes a deep breath that sounds rattly and vaguely unhealthy. "Graham is upstairs," she whispers. "There's something we didn't tell you. That I need to tell you. That's why I called today. I can't keep it inside anymore."

I take out my notebook. "What do you want to tell me?"

"Someone else was involved. With Kevin." She looks back and forth as though she's worried that Graham might come downstairs any minute now.

"What do you mean? Who was involved?" I ask, masking my irritation that she's only now telling me this.

"Kevin was outside playing with Graham in the backyard. He had an angina attack—it's much worse than he lets on—and he went inside to get his medicine."

"Then what happened?"

"When he got back, Kevin was gone. He called me—I was at the grocery store—he called me and was more upset than I think I've ever heard him. When I got home... I've never seen him like that," she whispers. "I had no idea what to do. We should have called the police. But we called Allie. We thought she could help."

"Who is Allie?" *Who the hell calls someone named Allie instead of the police?*

"I can't believe this is happening," Elaine whispers.

"I know," I murmur. "I'm so very sorry." Sometimes, I'm just good-cop, but right now I'm really sorry. They're as stupid as my brother, and I can't help wondering how things might be different if they *had* called the police right away.

She swipes at her tears with a napkin. "Everything we've done has been wrong. Everything."

I nod. "It's okay." I carefully cover her arthritic hand with my own. "You didn't know. You did your best."

"Thank you for being kind." She sniffs and rubs her free hand across her face. "We hired Allie when Peter and Teresa asked us to keep Kevin more often. We told you the truth about everything else. All we left out was Allie. I don't want her to get in trouble. She's such a nice girl. She's like a daughter to us in some ways. She's trying to get her life together. I just feel so terrible for not telling you sooner, for not telling Peter and Teresa."

I look up from my notebook and see Graham Whittle in the doorway, looking stricken.

He steps into the room. "Elaine, why are you telling her all of this?"

Elaine jumps a little then juts out her chin. "Because they need to know the truth so they can find who killed Kevin." She turns back to me. "I wonder if introducing Kevin to so many outsiders made him more likely to go off with a stranger." She shakes her head.

"Sir," I say, "it's okay. I just need to know everything." I use a soothing tone, hoping he doesn't get as petulant as he was in Fishner's office the other day. "Just have a seat and tell me everything."

He blinks then sits down next to his wife. She reaches over and takes his hand.

I nod at her. "Mr. Whittle, the more you can tell me, the likelier it is that we can find who did this."

"We hired her about a year ago," he says. He seems even smaller now. "It got to be too much." He puts his hand on his chest. "My heart." He shakes his head.

"Teresa asked us who she was," Elaine says, "a couple of months after Kevin started drawing her picture."

And you lied to her. I really want to ask why, but I know this will go better if I just let them talk.

Graham's shoulders droop. "I didn't want my son to think we couldn't handle the boy. That's why we didn't tell him. Or you. We didn't want them to know. All of this is my fault." He sags even lower in his chair. "I told

Elaine not to say anything because it's my fault. We couldn't care for Kevin properly because of my heart."

"Medical problems happen," I reply. I don't really know what else to say.

He turns to Elaine. "I'm sorry I told you not to say anything. Maybe we could have figured this out days ago." He covers his heart again with his hand, and I hope he's not going to die right here and now. "We should have gone to the police sooner."

Elaine takes his hand from his chest and holds it in both of hers. She starts to cry again, and he puts his arms around her.

When she pulls herself together after a couple of minutes, I ask, "How many days a week did she watch Kevin?" *And why in the world would you think your nanny could help, instead of the police?*

"Three," Graham says.

"And just to clarify, this went on for how long?"

"A little over a year."

"Friday, the day Kevin was kidnapped, was that one of her regular days? Was she here?"

"No. We called her after we couldn't find him. We thought maybe she could help." He won't make eye contact with me, and the way he glances around the room makes me think he's still not telling me something. "She's a nice girl. She took Kevin's disappearing hard."

"When was the last time you heard from her?" I ask.

"She stayed over the night he went missing," Elaine says. "She was supposed to go to her other job, but she was determined to find Kevin. She went out and looked all through the neighborhood." She focuses on a point past my shoulder, as if she's trying to find the words, then her bleary eyes meet mine. "She was sure she'd find him. She was worried, like we were, that he'd get hurt."

Holy hell. Okay, so you hire a nanny without telling the kid's parents. Then he goes missing, and instead of calling the police or telling anyone anything… I try not to sigh or make a face.

"Allie would never do anything to hurt Kevin," Graham says. "She's a class act."

Allie. The name is familiar. I focus on that for a minute. *Allie who didn't make it to her other job that night.* A switch flips somewhere in my mind. *Jen Kline. Winky's.* She was covering for someone named Allie.

"What's Allie's last name?" I ask.

"Cox," he replies. "Allie Cox."

"What's her other job?" I ask.

"She's a server somewhere in the Flats," Graham replies.

That's it. That's her. "A.C." was on the schedule. My heartbeat speeds up, but I breathe through it. *Allie Cox as Miller's accomplice.* It's possible. "Can you give me her address and phone number?"

Elaine nods and pulls a piece of paper from her pocket. She obviously knew I would ask for that information once she spilled about the nanny. The address is in Cleveland Heights and not far from my house.

I sit with them for a few more minutes and ask more questions about Allie, such as her age, height, weight, and any relevant details. "Thank you for coming clean with me," I say, standing. "Please call me if you think of anything else I might need to know."

"We will," Graham replies. "Bye."

I jog to my car. When I get behind the wheel, I call Goran. He doesn't answer, so I leave him a voicemail. "Ask Miller if he knows someone named Allie Cox. Figure out if there's a connection."

I leave the neighborhood and pull into a gas station, where I briefly debate paying Allie Cox a visit. I think better of it, though, when I imagine the kind of trouble I would be in if I did. Sitting in the parking lot, I use my phone to search online for Allie Cox. I finally locate a Facebook account that seems to fit. The profile picture is of a young woman in front of a field of wildflowers. She's looking off to the side, so all I can tell is that she has long blondish hair. I look through her friends list and find Jen Kline's name. Allie's page shows lots of pictures. She and the other Winky's bartender, Elizabeth, are in some from a party.

I go back to Allie's friends list. There's an older woman with the same last name, and I'm guessing it's her mom. When I go to the woman's page, I see lots of RIP and condolences posts. If it is Allie's mom, she died a few months ago.

I try to call Goran again, but he still doesn't answer. I hope he's not angry with me for practically hanging up on him earlier.

I call Roberts. "Get me info on Allie Cox," I say. "I have to run over to the lab."

"What? I'm halfway back to—"

"Roberts, I'm serious. Database search. Please and thank you and bye."

"Bye."

I point the Passat east on Woodland and hit the gas.

Of course Elaine and Graham Whittle didn't want to tell their son that they outsourced Kevin's care. But there could be more to it than that, some reason why they sat on the information so long.

My phone buzzes in my pocket as I'm leaving the lab, where I handed Arya's card off to Jo Micalec.

"I looked her up," Roberts says. "No criminal record. The only hit I got was the BMV. Blonde, brown eyes, five two, one ten. I just texted you her picture."

"What else did you get on her?"

"Not a lot. She got a degree from CSU in early childhood education and has a teaching license but no job. No traffic tickets. Nada. Totally clean."

I unlock the car and climb inside. "She been here her whole life?"

"From the looks of it, yeah. Born in Cleveland. Went to Shaker Heights for high school. Parents divorced when she was eleven. Mom died late last year, breast cancer. Dad's still alive, still lives in Shaker."

"Any connection to Miller other than the restaurant?"

"Nope, at least not on paper."

"Vehicle?"

"Oh seven Focus, black."

"Could be the car Anthony saw," I mutter. Miller could have lied about using his sister's car, covering for his accomplice. "Thanks, Roberts. Get Cleveland Heights to sit on her. I don't want her disappearing. I'll try to get over there today." I'll have to ask Fishner first.

"Ten-four."

When I get back to the squad room, Fishner is in her office. Becker is with her, which means I'll only have to go through this once. As I approach the door, Fishner waves for me to enter.

I fill them in, trying to convey the urgency of the situation with Allie Cox. "I'm sorry that I went to the grandparents' house without asking, but they needed to talk. She called me, and I thought it was—"

Fishner points at me. "I want you on Cox. I want you to bond with her." She nods as if confirming something in her mind. "If we get her to finger Miller, we can wrap this up. It's time. This has gone on too long. We need to close this."

I try to keep my mouth from falling open. Just hours ago, she was putting me on desk duty, but now I get access to a prime suspect or witness or both. "Okay. I'll get on that now." I turn to leave before she can change her mind.

"Boyle."

I freeze. *Damn!* "Yes?"

"*We* are going to talk to Allie Cox." She stands. "You drive."

I narrowly manage to avoid rolling my eyes or saying anything about not needing a babysitter. "Just give me two minutes."

"I'll meet you at the elevator."

CHAPTER SEVENTEEN

SOMETHING OCCURS TO ME AS I walk to my desk. Anthony mentioned that he saw a woman in a baseball cap coming out the back door of Winky's the night Kevin was killed. Allie was supposed to be out sick that night, but she could have still been there. She would have access to the back entrance, stockroom, and staff areas. Kevin could have been held in one of those places before someone killed him in Miller's garage.

I glance over at Goran's desk and see his cell phone sitting next to his lamp. I go over and pick it up. The screen shows several missed calls, all from me. Good. He's not ignoring me because he's mad that I practically hung up on him earlier. "Roberts," I whisper, "where's Goran?"

"In the box with Miller." He shoves half a bagel into his mouth and chews.

"Again?"

He nods.

Fishner wants to keep an eye on me, even with her prime suspect in interrogation. She must be confident that Miller is our perp. "Boss lady and I are going to talk to Cox. Tell Goran, okay?"

"Ten-four," he says around a mouthful of bagel.

Fishner and I spend an awkward fifty seconds in the elevator—I counted—and an even more awkward fifteen minutes in the car. It's as if neither of us know how to behave when she's out in the field, which doesn't happen much anymore. I slide the car into a parking space in front of Allie Cox's apartment building.

"You're talking to her," Fishner says.

"Okay." *Then why are you here? I'd rather have Goran here. I don't know how you work.*

I walk up to the building and hold open the front door for Fishner. The elevator ride to the second floor is mercifully quick. I say a little prayer that she'll keep quiet. She must have been a decent detective at one point to get where she is, but I feel as though this is my case. I knock on the door to Apartment 2B.

Allie opens the door. "Yes?"

"We're here with Cleveland Police," I say.

I catch a glimpse of another woman inside before she pulls the door closed. Allie is wearing jeans and a CSU fleece jacket. She's one of those who doesn't need to make any effort to look good: flawless skin, healthy hair, the kind of bone structure that pisses some people off because they're jealous. "Is this about Kevin?" she asks.

"Yes. We just have a few questions. I'm Detective Boyle. This is Lieutenant Fishner."

"Do you have some ID or something?" She doesn't make eye contact with either of us. We show her our IDs, but she looks disinterested and faint, almost to the point of passing out.

"Allie, are you okay?" I ask.

"Yeah, I'm fine." For a moment I wonder how true that is. She still hasn't looked at me, and it's disconcerting. We stand in silence for a few beats. "Do you want to talk out here, or can we come inside?"

When she finally meets my eyes, there's something hollow about her expression. It's the kind of sad that goes beyond situational grief. Her sadness doesn't ameliorate my suspicion, though. "Out here is better," she says.

I decide to start by playing good cop. "Thanks for talking to us, Allie. We appreciate any help you can give us."

She sighs. "I can't believe this is happening. The one good thing in my life. Gone. Fuck. I knew I should have called the police. But Graham said they probably just wanted money and not to."

"I'm sorry for your loss."

"One after the other," she whispers, looking at the floor.

Fishner leans against the wall behind me but doesn't say anything.

"Do you mean your mom?" I ask.

167

She looks a little surprised. Most people do, once they realize that we know more about them than they might like. "Yeah, my mom. And Kevin. And the job. And my so-called friends. And my dad."

"What about your dad?" I ask. "Isn't he still alive?"

"Yeah, technically."

I wait for her to tell me more, but she doesn't. "Allie, I know this is hard. But I need to ask you some questions. They might feel intrusive, and I apologize in advance if they do."

She nods.

"Where were you on Thursday night?"

"The night Kevin was killed?" She blinks hard and looks away. The light above us flickers as if it's about to go out, but then it stays on. "I was here, at home."

"Yes. Is there anyone who can verify your whereabouts?"

"No. I was home alone. I took a couple Xanax, you know, tried to put everything out of my mind."

I wonder what she means by "everything." "So you weren't down in the Flats, by Winky's?"

"No, I called off." She narrows her eyes. "You know what? I ordered food. It got here at, like, a quarter to eight. I fell asleep, and the guy was pounding on the door, so my neighbor called to wake me up." She lets out a little chuckle. "I'm not supposed to take Xanax and drink like that, but whatever. Anyway, the delivery guy and my neighbor, they both saw me that night. I probably have the receipt."

"What restaurant?"

"Malibu Jack's."

I make a note. "Do you remember the driver's name?"

"No. I mean, I don't think he even told me."

"What's your neighbor's name?"

"It's Ellen Preakness." She pulls out her phone, taps the screen a couple of times, then holds it out for me. "She lives downstairs, Apartment 1C. She's probably home right now. She works nights."

I copy the woman's name and phone number into my notebook. "Why didn't you come forward right away, after we found Kevin's body? You heard about it, right?"

She doesn't reply.

"Why didn't you come to the police when he went missing?"

"Of course I heard about it. They called me when they couldn't find him. I went and stayed the night, thinking he would come back. Maybe he was just playing around or something. He's a good hider. Was a good hider."

"Who called you?"

"Elaine called me."

"Where were you last Friday afternoon, the day Kevin was kidnapped?"

"I was about to go to my other job, the one at Winky's. I work Friday nights."

"Why have you been calling off from that job all week? Have you been sick?"

"Because I'm fucking *distraught*." She blinks back tears. "Wouldn't you be? If someone you loved was fucking dead?"

I ignore her question. I don't have time to worry about her feelings, and for all I know, she's faking the grief. "Where were you between five last night and eight this morning?" I'm digging because of the business card. I didn't tell Fishner about that yet, and I hope she doesn't question why I'm asking.

Allie makes a face. "Here, sleeping. I've been sleeping a lot."

"Do you have any enemies?"

"Not really."

Fishner moves a little farther away from us. I'm glad she's working to fade into the background. Allie will talk more if she feels we're alone together.

I lean back against the wall and relax my hands at my sides, trying to convey that this is just a relaxed little chat. "How long have you known the Whittles?" I'm not getting a sense that she did it. I also don't think she's a good enough liar to throw me off. I've been wrong before, but what I'm beginning to think is that she's living in some kind of abject internal misery that she doesn't talk about.

"I've been working for them for a little over a year. They pay me pretty well. And I really love Kevin." She squeezes her eyes closed for a second. "*Loved* Kevin."

"How much do they pay?" I ask.

"Five hundred a week. For three days. Cash."

I make a note. "How would you describe your relationship with Elaine and Graham?"

I'm pretty sure she flinches when I say Graham. She starts prattling nervously about Elaine. She overuses adjectives like "nice" and "wonderful" and "nurturing" and says Elaine is like a mother to her.

"And Graham? Do you get along with him?"

She lowers her gaze. A tear trickles down her cheek.

"Allie? Do you have a problem with Graham? It's okay to talk to me."

Fishner takes another step to the side, farther out of Allie's line of sight but still in mine.

Allie sniffs. "He wanted me to do stuff with him," she says, wiping tears with the back of her hand.

Fishner flinches, and I have to work to control my expression.

"Did you?" I ask.

A dark look crosses her features. "No, I didn't. And every fucking day I wondered if he'd fire me for it." Her face is reddening, and her hands clench into fists. "Whatever." She shakes her head. "It doesn't matter."

"What did he want you to do?"

She blushes. "He said that since I worked at Winky's, I was probably used to…" She looks down at her hands and interlaces her fingers. "He wanted me to blow him. But I wouldn't. I'm done with that. I'm trying to get my shit together." She raises her head and juts out her chin. "Good thing he didn't force himself on me, though. I would have fucked him up. All he did was talk a big game. He thinks he's God's gift. That's it."

The second part of my gut feeling comes back with a surge: motive. "Did Kevin ever hear or see any of these advances?"

She meets my eyes and sets her jaw. Her tense face provides a contrast to my intentionally relaxed one. "Of course not. Graham only made comments when we were alone. Kevin never heard anything."

Realizing I'm not going to get anything more with the head-on approach, I switch subjects. "Take me through the whole day that Kevin disappeared."

"Elaine called me in a total panic that Friday afternoon. She asked me if I'd come by and picked up Kevin without telling them. I used to take him on little day trips sometimes, and Elaine seemed like she hoped we'd gone on one. But of course, we hadn't. I would never do that without telling them."

"What time did she call you?"

"I was getting ready to go to work at my full-time job, the one at Winky's." She says this with downcast eyes and the hint of a blush, as if I might judge her for working there in the way that Graham Whittle did. "So it was about three o'clock. My shift starts—started—at four."

"What did you do after you got off the phone?"

"I freaked the fuck out is what I did. I really love—loved—that kid. I pulled on a sweatshirt, called off work, and drove to the Whittles'. We looked everywhere. I ran through that whole yard, back into the park, everywhere, but we didn't find anything. It's like he just… disappeared. It was like he was never even there, even though Graham said they were playing outside."

"Did you look out back, past the fence?"

"Of course. Do you think we're stupid?"

"Under the porch?" I notice Fishner crossing her arms and staring at me, but I keep my eyes on Allie.

Allie looks at me as if I'm insane. "Yes, we checked everywhere."

"Did you see anything under there, any sign that Kevin might have been there?"

She blinks at me. "No."

"Can you think of anyone who might want to harm Kevin? Or you? Or the Whittles?"

"Not off the top of my head, no."

"Have you let anyone borrow your car recently?"

"No," she says. "Who would want to borrow my car?"

"A friend, maybe?"

She shakes her head. "Never."

"Okay. I'm sorry, but I have to ask this. Did you kill Kevin Whittle?"

"Are you serious?" She slides down the wall and starts to cry.

I don't say anything. I just stand there, looking down at her.

"No. I would never. I would never. No." She weeps silently.

Fishner pulls two tissues out of her bag and hands them to me, and I hand them to Allie. I let ninety seconds tick by. "Allie, what can you tell me about Sean Miller?"

She raises her head. "Who?"

I pull his picture up on my phone and show it to her. "Sean Miller. Do you know him?"

She gets up off the floor. "Yeah. I know him, but I didn't remember his name. He's a regular at the restaurant. Always orders a ton of food and eats it all. He asked me out once." She searches my face. "Wait a minute." She jabs a finger at my phone. "Do you think he did it?"

I try to look sympathetic and supportive. "Allie, are you on medication right now?"

She nods. "Yeah. Xanax. Just one, though."

"Whose decision was it not to call the police when Kevin disappeared?"

She starts to cry again. "Graham told me not to. I couldn't even go to the funeral. I couldn't face him. I knew I should have called. Fuck, I should have called. And I didn't because I was too chickenshit." She leans against the wall and cradles her head in her hands.

I nod and wait a couple of minutes for her to pull herself together again. The second hand on my watch ticks away. "Is there anything else that I should know?"

She looks at the wall, at the floor, then back at me. "No."

"You sure?"

She hesitates. "Yeah, I'm sure."

I stare at her for a few beats, but she doesn't say anything else. "What are you going to do now?"

"Hell if I know," she replies. "I'm probably fired from the restaurant. I've been a mess. I'm a mess. I guess I'll be a sub or something."

"You mean like a substitute teacher?"

She nods.

"You seem pretty put together to me. You're going through a hard time."

She turns her eyes to meet mine but looks straight through me. "Yeah, I always have seemed that way. I've always seemed that way."

I hand her a business card with my cell phone number and the number for Victims' Assistance on the back.

Fishner comes over and stands beside me. "Allie, we have to ask you not to leave the city. We may have more questions later. Call us if you think of anything, okay? And talk to a grief counselor at Victims' Assistance. They can help you."

She gives us a wan smile. "Thank you."

When Allie turns to open her door, I glance inside. Elizabeth, the bartender from Winky's, is sitting on the couch.

We go downstairs and knock on Ellen Preakness's door to check Allie's alibi. The only response is yapping from a small dog. I slide a card under the door with a note asking her to give me a call.

Fishner and I don't say much on the way to the station. I wonder what she was like as a detective. *Did she talk to her partner, or did they just work in silence like this? Who was her partner? What's her story?* We part ways at the station, Fishner to her office and me to my desk.

I call the restaurant and verify Allie's story about getting the food delivery the night Kevin died. My stomach grumbles, and I realize it's lunchtime. I go out and grab a sandwich from my favorite food truck in Public Square. I eat sitting on a bench and watching the people walk by.

My phone rings as I'm taking the last bite. "Boyle."

"Hi, Detective Boyle? This is Ellen Preakness. I found your card under my door."

"Yes, ma'am. Thank you for calling. We're hoping you can verify that Allie Cox, your upstairs neighbor, was home last Thursday night."

"Hmmm… Oh! Yes, that was the night I had to pound on her door when the deliveryman came. He was from Malibu Jack's. If you haven't eaten there, you should try it."

"And did she answer her door?"

"Yes, she did. She looked tired. She must have fallen asleep, the poor thing."

"Okay, great. Thanks for your time."

The dog yaps in the background. "Is Allie in trouble? That poor girl, I tell you."

"No, she's not in trouble. You've been a big help. Thank you again."

I return to the squad room and find Goran back at his desk. "What's happening?" I ask.

"Same old. I'm just—"

"Did you get anything else on Cox?" Fishner says from behind me. "Any connection to Miller?"

I turn around to face her. "Not as far as I can tell, beyond crossing paths at the restaurant. The neighbor verifies that Cox was at home at the time of the murder. I called Malibu Jack's, too. The guy that was on delivery that night wasn't there, but the woman I talked to verified that someone ordered food delivered to Allie's address. The delivery guy will be back later. I'll just swing by and talk to him."

She nods. "I'm still thinking Miller is our guy."

"Yeah," Goran says. "He's sticking to his line about finding the body, but I figure he's good for it, too. He was in town when Kevin disappeared, and he has no alibi for that afternoon. He was away for a couple of days visiting that *friend* in Pittsburgh, which Miller's druggie ex-roommate in Pittsburgh corroborates, but he could have left the kid in the garage overnight."

Fishner nods. "Cement walls, vacant house next door. Kid was probably drugged, too."

As much as I'd like it to be that simple, I can't buy it. If Miller was involved, he was working with someone. But my gut says it wasn't Allie. And if Miller's telling the truth, I have to wonder who would take a kid to Miller's house to kill him. "Wait. There is one weird thing. I found Dwayne Arya's business card under the Whittles' porch this morning."

"Who is Dwayne Arya?" Fishner asks.

I explain who he is then pull out my phone and show her the picture I took of the card. "I dropped the card off at the lab earlier."

She frowns. "Well, someone from the investigative team must have dropped it."

"I don't think so. It wasn't wet, so it was left there after the rain last night. And who would even be carrying it around, anyway? Arya's been gone for years."

She shakes her head. "Boyle, we need to concentrate on the facts at hand. I just got a report on the blood, and the blood type in Miller's garage matches the vic. On the shovel, too. You two are building a case against Sean Miller. I have a couple of floaters from Homicide coming in later to help you. We need to get this tied up and closed. We'll have a briefing at four thirty."

"Okay," I reply.

"Ten-four, boss," Goran adds.

When Fishner goes into her office, I ask Goran, "What's up with her today?"

"You tell me. Isn't she your new partner?" He grins.

I roll my eyes. "She's babysitting me."

"It's probably for the best, Boyle. She'll keep you out of trouble."

"Whatever."

A couple of hours later, the two floaters Fishner requested arrive for the briefing. Goran is out getting us some real coffee, so I point them toward the break room, where they can get some stale coffee and day-old doughnuts. One of them, Malik Sims, has always been a little resentful of Goran and me because he requested Special Homicide and was passed over. He's a decent detective, though, so I try not to hold it against him. The other one, John Wittenour, has been around the block more times than I can count. I think he was on Goran's softball team a few years back.

Wittenour makes a beeline for the doughnuts. "You want one?" he asks Sims.

"Nah, man, you know I don't eat crap like that." Sims follows me to the briefing room. "He's gonna end up with diabetes one of these days."

Wittenour returns, cramming a doughnut into his mouth. "Hey, Boyle, how's it going?" he asks.

"Not terrible. How are you?" I smile without looking away from the case board. I tend to get possessive of my cases. It's not an especially endearing trait of mine. To put it in Shue's positive terms, maybe I should be more willing to let others help with investigations.

"You know," he replies. "Same as I ever was."

"Right." I have to behave myself today, so I decide to engage a bit more. "I see they brought in the big guns for this one."

That earns a chuckle from the guys.

Wittenour finishes his doughnut. "Man, that was one stale-ass doughnut. So the Whittle murder, huh? Yeah. We've been hearing about that one." He licks his fingers then wipes them on his pants.

I do my best not to make a face. Goran shows up with the coffee, and Roberts and Domislaw trudge in behind him. Rather than letting five hulking dudes make me feel claustrophobic, I stand up and lean against the windowsill. The guys start talking about the virtues of the new indoor driving range. I roll my eyes. I'd rather talk about the shooting range or something like that.

Fishner emerges from her office. "All right, let's go over these details." Her whole spiel takes about forty-five minutes, then the new guys have questions. She and Goran and I take turns answering them. She doles out assignments to the guys then points at me. "I'm still with you. You drive. We'll go back to that bar to get more on Allie Cox."

I nod. "Also, I think we should check with Anthony Dwayne Smith and show him her picture."

"Good. Let's go."

Goran smirks at me. I give him my "at least I'm not on the desk" shrug and head for the elevator.

This time, Fishner makes small talk while I drive. We discuss the crime board and the new guys. Well, "discuss" might be overstating it. She talks, and I make the right noises at appropriate times and focus on not driving too fast.

While we're idling at a stoplight not far from the Flats, I spot a Starbucks. "Do you want coffee?" I ask.

"You and Goran both drink too much coffee." She looks at her phone.

I take that to mean she doesn't want any coffee. I guess that means I don't want any coffee, either. I console myself with the fact that I probably won't get in trouble if my boss is my partner today. I can continue to practice behaving like a model detective and an upstanding citizen.

Winky's is even more depressing than I remember. Marco, the manager, is tending bar. The same sad guy with the pitcher of beer sits in the same sad spot. I take a stool a few down from that guy. When Marco comes over, I introduce Fishner, who remains standing behind me, then ask for a glass of water.

Marco brings the water, and I'm relieved to see that the glass is clean. He looks as if he belongs in a bad reality TV show but seems like a nice enough guy. "Yeah, what happened to that kid is terrible." He shakes his head. "Just terrible."

"What can you tell me about that night?" I ask. "Thursday night. Anything you remember?"

"Typical Thursday. Basketball was on, so we were actually kind of busy. Well, not *busy*, but steady. You know."

I nod and sip my water.

"We're closing soon," he says. "For good. We're all gonna have to find different jobs."

"Yeah, I'm sorry to hear that. Not many jobs out there these days." Idle chatter is not something I want to be engaging in right now, but I want him to relax. "How long have you worked here?"

"About four years. My wife got transferred here for her job, and I had restaurant experience, so there you go. It's not the best place in the world, but it pays the bills." He crosses his arms in front of his chest.

"What can you tell me about Allie Cox?"

He leans back against the counter below the liquor shelves. "Allie? She's great. Everyone likes Allie."

"Was she here last Friday?"

He shakes his head. "No, she called off. Said she had a family emergency. She was supposed to work four to midnight, her regular shift."

"She had another job, right? As a nanny?"

"Yeah. Man, she loved that kid, too. Like he was her own. She brought him in here a couple times when she picked up her paycheck."

"Did you notice anything unusual about how they interacted?"

"Nah." He shrugged. "He seemed like a normal kid, and she's a nice gal."

"Has Allie ever behaved oddly, that you've noticed?"

He makes a thinking face. "Well, she's been calling off all week. Something about her—wait a minute. Tell me it wasn't that kid. The one that got killed, it wasn't him, was it? Shit, that would…"

I take a sip of my water to avoid responding.

"That would really suck for her," he finishes.

I nod and try to look sympathetic. "Does she hang out with a guy named Sean Miller, one of your regulars?"

"I don't think so. But then, I don't really pay attention to her, like, personal stuff."

I show him the mug shot of Miller on my phone. "Do you recognize this man?"

He squints at the screen. "Yeah, I've seen him in here. Never seen him with Allie, though."

"Is there anything else you can tell me about Allie? Anything at all?"

He chuckles. "Yeah. I've only seen her get mad one time, which is pretty rare in this business. They're always mad about something. Allie was different. It was fucking scary. She's usually so calm." He rubs the back of his neck and frowns. "Sarah, one of my other servers, did something to piss her off. They're friends. They used to be roommates, but they still hang out together. Anyway, Allie got pissed off and bounced a beer mug off that wall over there"—he gestures at a divot in the wall above the TV—"like she was

177

a baseball pitcher." He laughs. "It was pretty crazy. It flew back and almost hit me in the face. Surprised it didn't break."

"Did she stay mad long?"

"Nah. It was like a flash, you know, a temper thing. Then it was gone, and we all got back to opening for the day."

"When was this?" Fishner asks.

He raises his shoulders. "Maybe two weeks or so ago."

"Any idea what pissed her off?" she asks. Temper flares are interesting things, especially in the context of a murder investigation.

"No clue. Probably some guy or something." He chuckles.

"Have you heard from Allie in the past few days?" I ask.

"Nah, she's off the schedule for a while. Said she needed some time. Jen picked up most of her shifts, and I hired a new girl."

We talk about Jen Kline for a while. Marco has nothing of interest to tell me.

I slide him a card and ask him to call if he thinks of anything. He nods then steps away. Fishner and I head outside.

"All right, so Cox has a temper," I say as we settle into the car.

Fishner nods. "Keep an eye on her."

I point the car north and hit the gas. "She's sort of out of our jurisdiction." Cleveland Heights tends to get touchy when we invade their territory.

She gazes at me. "I don't mean to start a territory war. I mean *keep an eye* on her." She slides her phone into her pocket and studies my face for a beat too long before looking away.

I drive across the river to Anthony's spot. He's by his dumpster outside the warehouse, and he smiles and waves when I pull over to the curb. When he tries to get up, he's shaky on his feet.

"Hey, Shaft," he calls as I get out of the car. "I can't really walk. Heh heh. What you up to?"

I push the car door closed. "Hi, Anthony. You just sit. I'll come over there." Fishner stays in the car while I trot over to him.

"You got a smoke for me?"

"I'm sorry, I don't." He looks dejected, and I make a mental note to get more witness smokes. "This will only take a second." I pull up the picture of Allie Cox on my phone. "Will you look at this and tell me if you recognize her?" Bending over, I hold it close to his face.

"Heh heh. Okay." He squints at the screen. "I got kinda drunk. I found ten bucks earlier." He shakes his head. "Nah, she don't look familiar to me," he slurs. "I'm sorry."

"Remember that woman you told me about? The one coming out the back of Winky's, wearing a baseball cap?"

He scrunches up his face then nods.

"Think this looks like her?"

"It's possible. Maybe."

That's not going to cut it, especially since she has an alibi. "Anthony, about how tall was she?"

"Baseball cap? I don't know." He peers up at me. "'Bout your height, maybe a little shorter."

According to Allie Cox's driver's license, she's only five two. I pat his shoulder and tell him to take care, and I mean it.

He waves. "Bye, Shaft. Stay safe out there."

Back in the car, I fill Fishner in, not that I have much to tell her. Our next stop is Malibu Jack's. The delivery driver, Ben, is there this time, and he remembers a "sort of out-of-it" young woman who matches Allie's description answering the door. When I show him the photo, he confirms it was Allie.

When Fishner and I get back to the squad room, Goran is at his desk. Fishner goes into her office and closes the door. I plop down in my chair, feeling a bad mood coming on.

"What'd you get?" Goran asks.

"Not a fucking thing."

"Are you having fun with Fishner?"

"Fuck you."

My phone buzzes with a text message from Christopher. *I'm fine*, it says. *Thanks for trying to save my ass.*

I love you. Call me when you can, especially if we're actually having dinner with Mom next week, I reply.

"They'll charge Miller," Goran says.

I shake my head. "It doesn't add up."

"What murder has ever made sense?"

I shift my eyes to him and slow-blink a couple of times. "I'm going home. I'll see you in the morning."

"Bye, Boyle. Behave."

"Nice alliteration, Goran." I switch off my lamp and wave at him on my way out.

Driven mostly by curiosity, I creep past Allie's apartment building on my drive home. Lights are on, and her car is still there. She crosses in front of a window, and I drive away.

CHAPTER EIGHTEEN

I WAKE UP AT 4:23 ON Wednesday morning. I'm not one of those people who can just go back to sleep, so I sit up for a minute, hugging my legs and contemplating a pleasant surprise. I slept in my bed for six hours in a row.

I get dressed then head into the kitchen to feed a meowing Ivan. After he eats, I take a few minutes to pet him while he purrs. I'm sure he's been feeling neglected, but I tell him I'll make it up to him once this case is over. "You're still molting," I tell him as I sweep the collection of cat hair into the trash can.

Even after a trip to the gym, I'm the first in at work. One of the night shift detectives saunters into the break room as I'm making coffee. "Hey, Boyle." He looks spent.

I smile at him. "What's up, Martinez?" I fill the filter with Folgers, glad it's not that battery acid crap in the white can again.

"Caught one tonight. Prostitute dead over off Lorain." The red-light district. Vice has been under a lot of pressure to clean up that area, but whatever they're doing isn't working.

I fill the coffeepot with water and switch on the machine. I hope this dead hooker isn't the start of some serial thing. "Any leads?"

He pinches the bridge of his nose. "Not yet. Her teenage daughter found her." He sighs. "I'm going home. Have a good one."

"Nighty night," I reply as he ambles away.

The coffeepot starts to gurgle, so I grab my black skull-and-crossbones mug out of the dish drainer and root through the refrigerator for the cream.

Coffee in hand, I go to my desk and set the mug down before sitting in the chair.

I prop my feet up on the corner of the desk and stare at the crime board. I hate that I can feel this case slowing down. They're going to have to charge Miller with the murder or release him, and he and his lawyer are sticking to their guns on the he-just-found-the-body line. My own gut feelings aside, I still don't think we have enough to put him away. If Miller didn't kill Kevin, and Harris couldn't have killed Kevin, and Allie has an alibi, and Christopher obviously didn't kill anyone, it comes down to the fact that at seven thirty on Thursday night, someone was in Sean Miller's garage, and that person killed Kevin Whittle.

My mind circles back to motive. If whoever kidnapped Kevin did it for money, I need to take a look into the Whittles' finances. I open my laptop.

The first thing I notice is that the grandparents made weekly five-hundred-dollar cash withdrawals. That confirms Allie Cox's statement. Beyond that, they only have about two thousand in checking, a little over twenty grand in savings, and a money market account that looks as though it's generating enough interest to keep paying their bills for ten or so years. A credit check confirms that they started the process of getting a second mortgage, probably to cover the ransom that no one ever demanded, and this jibes with my general sense that they're stupid but not guilty. So if the killer wanted a huge ransom, he was barking up the wrong tree.

Goran wanders in and greets me, but all I can manage in response is a grunt.

"So it's that kind of day, huh?" He tosses our Nerf football at me.

I bat it away. "Bad mood."

"Oh, the Boyle bad mood. Beware." He sits down at his desk.

"Yeah, you're really on a roll. Keep it going, Goran."

He opens his laptop and starts typing. I get more and more irritated with every minute that passes. *Too much sitting and not enough moving.*

"Chill out, Boyle," Goran says, standing. "I have to go run copies of these pictures, but I'll be back."

"Knock yourself out." I feel my neck and shoulders getting tense, so I do a couple of neck rolls. I start fiddling with my computer, trying to look busy. My phone rings, and I snatch it up. "Boyle."

"Hey, Boyle," Domislaw says. "I got more wit statements from the Emerald."

"And?"

"One of the dancers, Cinnamon, had a fight with her boyfriend that night. She got left with a punch in the face and no ride home. But here's the kicker—she was friendly with Jen Kline, your gal from Winky's, and went to borrow money for a cab. Cinnamon was the gal in the baseball cap. She tossed it on to cover the beginning of the shiner her guy gave her, and she borrowed the jacket from Jen."

"So much for that lead, then," I mumble. "Thanks, Dom."

"You got it," he replies.

A few minutes later, Fishner comes over and plants her bony ass on the edge of Goran's desk. "Sean Miller tried to off himself in his cell early this morning. He's at Metro. Coma. I sent Goran and Roberts to check in on him and talk to the doctors."

"Shit. What the hell?" I almost feel a twinge of sadness. Whether from guilt or from fear of being convicted as a murderer, that man tried to end his own life.

"It confirms that he's good for it."

"Not necessarily. I don't mean to be a pain in the ass, but what if he was just scared?"

She levels an even gaze at me. "Boyle, we had this conversation yesterday." She goes back into her office.

Uh-huh. It's all so easy, isn't it? I go back to my busy work.

After our noon briefing, Fishner leaves for a meeting. I glance at my watch and am genuinely surprised by how quickly the hours have ticked by today, given that this whole stupid day has been a whole lot of sitting and not much moving—pacing around doesn't count. I send Christopher another text message telling him to call me. He's been keeping me at a distance, responding to my texts but not calling me. I'm not surprised.

About forty-five minutes later, I'm pacing back and forth in front of my desk when Julia Becker asks me if Fishner is around.

"No," I reply, crossing my arms in front of my chest.

"I'm heading over to the Black Cat for lunch. Do you want to go?"

I hide my surprise by glancing at my watch. "Sure, but I don't have a lot of time. Just let me get my stuff." I throw on my jacket then grab my gun from my locker.

"Do you need to be armed to eat a sandwich?"

"Yeah."

In the elevator, Julia says, "We're all feeling pressure here. We're going to have to charge Miller today or tomorrow, whether he's awake or not."

I don't respond until we're crossing the lobby. "It wasn't Miller, Julia. I mean, I get where you're going, but—"

She holds up a finger. "Occam's razor."

"Right, whatever." I laugh. I get that the simplest explanation is usually the right one, but the "usually" is what we have to take into consideration here. We can't let an innocent—at least mostly innocent—man go away for capital murder, and the more I think about it, the less convinced I am that Miller did it. There's just so little evidence and no motive.

The wind whips down from the lake and blows Becker's hair across her face. She pushes it behind her ears and hunches her shoulders. It's warmer today but still cool, and she's wearing only a lightweight trench coat over her skirt suit.

I get a text from Goran: *I'm still sitting at MetroHealth waiting for Miller to wake up.*

Yeah, Fishner told me, I reply.

At the counter at the Black Cat Café, a lunchtime favorite among law-and-order types since it's right around the block from the Justice Center, I order a coffee and a turkey club. Julia gets a tuna salad wrap with extra pickles and a Diet Coke. The kid at the counter gives us two plastic number tents, which we take to a table in the back by the bathrooms. It's the only table available, so we take it even though it's the worst one in the joint.

"I know you're stuck on motive," she says. She removes her inadequate coat.

I glance down and think that she's unbuttoned her blouse one button too far. *There's no way she's flirting with me.* "Of course I'm stuck on motive." I hear a little edge to my tone, so I concentrate on being civil.

"Think beyond motive. Follow the evidence. Get me something I can use for an indictment." Becker waves at someone. I turn to look and recognize the guy as a pretty powerful defense attorney and a huge asshole.

"You're friends with him?" I ask nonchalantly. It's hard for me to ignore her cleavage, but I do my best.

She arches one eyebrow. "Always keep your worst enemies closest to you," she whispers.

"Is that what we're doing here?"

The kid brings over the red plastic baskets that contain our sandwiches. "Thanks," I tell him.

She doesn't look away. "No, Liz, I'm pretty sure that's not what we're doing here."

I'm confused, but I don't say as much, especially given that confusion feels better than irritation, at least at this point. Becker sucks Diet Coke through her straw as I plow into my club. I wonder whether the blouse is just a wardrobe malfunction or if Julia Becker is actually flirting with me. She used to hate me—at least it seemed that way—and the keep-your-enemies-close stuff kind of makes sense. Maybe that's what's going on.

"What's happening with the rest of the case?" she asks.

"The most interesting thing I can think of is that I found an old partner's business card in the grandparents' yard, under the porch." I pull out my phone to look at the picture of the card. "It had a weird message on the back, and I keep thinking it means something. 'Nothing beautiful without struggle.'"

She swallows her bite of sandwich. "That's kind of true, though, isn't it?"

"That's not very lawyerlike."

She chuckles. "So, what do you do when you're not working?"

I use the fact that my mouth is full to take some time to consider her question. *She's just being nice. Answer the question.* I swallow. "I'm always at work."

"You can't possibly *always* be at work. Do you *live* at the Justice Center?" Her eyes twinkle.

I struggle to keep my face neutral. "No, I live in Cleveland Heights." *She has no reason to know anything about me, so this is probably just a normal conversation.* "You?"

"Shaker."

"I figured as much. Either that or University Heights. Big, old, nice, expensive houses."

She laughs. "Such assumptions!"

"It fits."

She knits her eyebrows and searches my face. "First of all, my house is not big, nor was it especially expensive. And if we're assuming things, Cleveland Heights fits for you, too. I can see it. Artsy movie theater, good food, rock-and-roll clubs."

"It was better twenty years ago, back when it was still grungy as shit. Now it's all brick sidewalks and fancy streetlights. If I wasn't *always at work*, I might think of moving." *Now I'm flirting. This is getting weird.*

We make more small talk while we finish our food. Afterward, we walk back to work together and say our goodbyes in the lobby.

My slightly elevated mood erodes quickly once I get back to my desk because few things irritate me more than boredom. I set down yet another cup of coffee on my desk. *Maybe I do drink too much java.* I've been typing my report about the search of Miller's house and answering the phone for the better part of two hours, watching the shifting sunlight mark the relentless passage of time outside. It's too quiet in here. I know Goran is still at MetroHealth with Miller, but I have no idea where everyone else is.

The landline on my desk rings, and I grab the handset. "Special Homicide. This is Detective Boyle."

"Detective, this is Alexis Edwards from the *Plain Dealer*. Can you corroborate a tip that you've identified someone other than Sean Miller as a potential suspect in the child murder?"

"What the hell are you talking about?" I slam the phone down.

It rings again a few minutes later. I resist the urge to answer it with a stream of obscenities. "Special Homicide, Detective Boyle."

"Elizabeth?" a woman asks.

Her voice is so soft that I press the phone against my ear in an attempt to hear her better. "Yes. Can I help you?"

She starts to cry.

"Ma'am, are you calling to report a crime?" If so, I'm supposed to tell her to hang up and call 9-1-1.

"It-It's m-me. T-Teresa."

"Dr. Whittle, are you okay?"

"For God's sake, Elizabeth," she snaps. "Call me Teresa."

This indignant woman is the person I used to know, so I relax a little. "Teresa, are you okay?"

"Not really."

"Is there anything I can do?"

"Find the asshole who killed my little boy."

"We're working on it." I'm met with silence on the other end, but I can hear her breathing, and I'm glad she's not crying anymore. With what I hope is a confident tone, I add, "We've got a couple of leads." It's not exactly true, but it'll have to suffice.

"Yeah, I saw that on the fucking news."

"What? You saw what on the news?"

"On the news, it said the man you arrested might not have done it and that now he's in a coma, anyway. Why didn't you tell me?" She sniffs, and I fear more tears are on the way.

"Teresa, please believe me. If I had known that any of this was gonna be on the news, I would have. I'm so sorry." I can't figure out who would have told the media anything, especially since the brass wants us to build a case against Miller.

"Why in the *hell* are you sitting there at the fucking police station instead of *finding who killed my little boy*?"

Good. She's angry. I can deal with that. I also know that sometimes rage helps with grief.

"Teresa, we're all working this case as hard as we can. Half the cops in the city are on it."

"Why the hell aren't *you* on it? You promised that *you* were going to catch him! Why the fuck aren't *you* out there?"

"Look, we're all doing our best. I'm sorry I can't tell you more." I want to promise her that I'll find her son's killer, but I can't make promises I don't know I can keep. I do know I'll do my best, but that's not much comfort to a grieving mother.

"Please. Please just use your fucking brain." She hangs up the phone, leaving me with a weird greasy, twisty feeling in my gut.

I slam the receiver into the base of the phone until I start to worry that it might break. I would just as soon not have to explain that to Fishner. I go to the bathroom, lock myself in the far stall, and lean against the cold tile wall. I think I might puke, but instead, I feel that pressure building behind my eyes, in my neck, and at the top of my chest. I let loose and allow the tears to come.

After my little cry, I feel better. I splash cold water over my face a few times then dry off with paper towels.

When I get back to my desk, I have a text message from an unknown number: *The heaviest penalty for declining to rule is to be ruled by someone inferior to yourself.*

What the hell? I text back: *Wrong number, this is Elizabeth Boyle's phone.* The person doesn't reply. I shrug it off. On the scale of weirdness, I've seen worse.

The wallpaper on my phone is an old picture of Josh and me. I feel bad, remembering how I blew him off last time. I've been blowing everyone off for too long now. Shue is right. I need to start making some changes and get my act together.

I call Josh and ask him to have dinner with me tonight.

———————•••••———————

Just after seven o'clock, Goran and I are dotting the i's and crossing the t's in the last of our reports. Dead ends meet the setting sun, and through the window, I watch a parking lot light turn on and off in an erratic rhythm.

Goran takes a call, and when he hangs up, he says, "Miller is still in a coma, but the doctors say the signs are pretty good. They're hopeful he'll wake up without brain damage."

"Waking up without brain damage is kind of my goal every day." Joking aside, I'm worried. If Miller doesn't wake up, we may never find out who killed Kevin. I tell Goran about my weird text message. "Check it out," I say, showing him my phone. "There's some kind of Nostradamus texting me."

He reads the text. "That's creepy. A penalty for declining to rule? Did someone offer to make you queen or something?"

"Yeah, and I turned it down." I realize he's not joining in my humor. "Hey, come with Josh and me to dinner."

He slumps in his chair. "I can't. Sorry."

"What's your deal, Goran? Why the grumpy face?"

"Vera is royally pissed at me. Today's our anniversary. I was supposed to be home an hour ago." He leans back in his chair and stretches his arms over his head.

"Go home. I'll finish the reports."

"Really? Did you just volunteer to do paperwork?"

"Yeah, and you better leave before I change my mind. Get Vera some flowers on the way home. And take her out to dinner this weekend."

"Thanks, Liz," he replies, and his smile is genuine. "Try to keep your shit together, okay?" He stands and squeezes my shoulder. "Stay out of the deep end."

He grabs his stuff and heads for the elevator. I hear him have a conversation with Becker in the hallway, but I can't make out what they're saying.

Several minutes later, Becker comes over and sets her briefcase down on his desk. "Goran just told me you got a creepy text message."

"It's nothing. Wrong number." *But two makes a pattern, and the business card was creepy, too.*

She takes off her coat. With a combination of relief and mild disappointment, I notice that her blouse is buttoned properly again.

She gestures at Goran's desk. "You mind if I sit here and send a couple of emails?"

"I guess. I mean, if you really want to." I turn back to my computer. *What the hell is this? Does Fishner have Becker involved in the babysit-Boyle service? Twice in one day is odd, even for Julia.*

I make quick work of the reports. After I print and sign them, I take them to Fishner, who tries to give me a hard time about the fact that she told Goran to do them.

"It's his wedding anniversary," I say. "And it's not like we have any traction, anyway."

She nods. Miller's suicide attempt has everyone depressed. "Go home, Boyle. Good night. Close the door on your way out."

When I walk out, Julia is still at Goran's desk. She looks up at me and smiles.

"Do you have dinner plans? Do you want to come to dinner with my friend and me?" It's out of my mouth before I know it, but the universe might reward me for taking risks on its behalf.

"My big plan was to make a salad at home. Nothing exciting whatsoever. Where are you and your friend thinking?" She looks happy, and I vaguely wonder when I last looked happy.

"We haven't picked a place yet. Any ideas?"

"Gomez. It's a great Mexican place in the Heights."

I smile. "Yeah, I live, like, next door, so that sounds great. I could use a margarita or six."

"It's decided then. I'd be happy to go."

I call Josh, but he doesn't answer. He's probably finishing his rounds at the hospital. I leave a voicemail, telling him to meet us at Gomez at eight thirty.

When I hang up, Julia says, "Since you live close by, I imagine we'll drive separately?"

I nod. "Yeah, that's a good plan."

We pack up our belongings and take the stairs down together. Watching her, I wonder if it's hard to do all these flights of stairs in those heels. We part in the lobby, and I go out to my car.

Just as I get behind the wheel, Josh sends me a text, asking who "us" is.

I type: *Julia Becker. Assistant Prosecutor.*

You want me to evaluate her for you?

I stare down at my phone and tap out a reply: *What does that mean?*

You know exactly what that means. It's been almost a year.

No way. I work with her. I'm not even sure I like her. Plus, I think she's straight. I shake my head. I'm about as far from relationship material as a person can get.

We'll see. I'm going to scope her for you, anyway, he replies.

I toss the phone on the passenger seat and start the car. While I'm sitting at a red light, my phone rings. "Boyle here."

"Hi, Detective Boyle. This is Allie Cox. I found the receipt. And, um… there are a couple other things I want to tell you. Can we meet tomorrow morning? I, uh, I think you might be able to help me."

I hear music in the background. "Is this about Kevin? I can be there in ten minutes. There's no need to wait till morning."

"I'm not at home."

"I'll meet you wherever you are. I can be anywhere in the city in less than twenty minutes. If you have info for me, let's talk now." The light turns green, and I press on the accelerator.

"No, that's okay. Never mind," she says.

Shit, I'm pushing too hard. "Allie, if you want to talk, let's talk," I reply in my witness voice. I brake hard behind an old blue Corsica.

"I can't talk now. In the morning. I have to go. Can you meet me at my apartment in the morning?"

"Yes, that's fine. How are you doing?" I ask as I pass the Corsica on the right.

"I'm okay. I mean, I'll be okay. Thanks for asking. Look, I have to go. I'll see you in the morning. Bye, Detective Boyle."

The line goes dead. "What the actual fuck?" I toss my phone on the passenger seat. When Henry Rollins comes on, ranting and raving about how badly cops behave, I turn up the stereo volume. I can't help agreeing with him. I sing along as I pull into my apartment building's parking lot. I'm going to walk to the restaurant, since it's only two blocks away.

I get out, lock the door, and move onto the sidewalk. Taking some deep breaths, I try to get my head out from under the investigation. Things have slowed to the point that the next catch may go to Goran and me, and I don't like it. The Christopher business was like a knife in my side, and I know I have a lot of work to do with him and my mom if I want to be able to say that I have any family at all. The fresh air helps. It's one of those nights that's almost warm, and I vaguely think about opening a window when I get home. I sleep better when the room is cold.

When I enter the restaurant, Julia waves from the bar. I go over and drape my jacket on the back of the barstool next to her.

The bartender steps up immediately. "What'll you have?"

"Margarita on the rocks, no salt."

"Nice choice," Julia says, raising her glass, which is the same drink.

The chef comes out of the back and walks over to us. "Hi, Julia."

Well, no wonder she recommended this place. Apparently, she's a regular.

"Hey, David." Julia waves at me. "This is my friend Liz."

Even though my badge is in my pocket and I've locked my gun in the trunk of my car, he says, "Evening, Detective."

Julia smiles into her margarita. Joe sits down and chats with us for a while. It becomes clear that they know each other far better than as just chef and customer. I ask how they know each other.

Joe responds, "We went to high school together. And then I went to culinary while she got lost in the ivy." They laugh.

I feel a little out of my league. I'm kind of rough around the edges, and sitting here with a polished, Ivy League-educated prosecutor on one side and a classically trained chef on the other feels strange. The margarita helps. I drink it quickly then order another.

Josh breezes in. Add a gifted pediatric oncologist to the mix. "Hey, ladies!" he coos. "What's happening? What are we drinking?"

Who are these people, and why are they hanging out with me? They introduce themselves and slide into comfortable conversation while I take a sip of my margarita. An hour later, our table is ready. We order dinner, and I almost feel like a normal person, out to dinner with friends.

When Josh gets up to go to the bathroom, Julia asks me to show her the business card again. I pass my phone to her. After that, she wants to see the weird text, so I pull that up.

She frowns. "These both sound vaguely reminiscent of Plato's *Republic*. I mean, I'm not certain, but maybe it's worth checking, if you're worried about it. Have you read it?"

I remember Plato. I think he might have been on to something with the whole allegory-of-the-cave thing and the forms in the shadows. "Yeah, about twelve years ago, which is about a hundred in cop years."

She chuckles, and it occurs to me again that I'm having a nice time. I appreciate the sound of her laugh and wonder if, on some level, I *am* attracted to her. I push that away pretty fast, but given the wall we've hit with the case, it feels like some kind of breakthrough. *Maybe Josh is right. Maybe I invited her out not just to melt the historic ice but for some other reason. But I don't think so. The truth is I don't think I'll be over Cora for a very long time.*

I take my phone back. "You're right, though. The weird language and the tone are similar on both. But if they *are* linked..." The thought gives me shivers. If that's the case, it's as if I was—or someone was—meant to find the card. As if it wasn't dropped but planted. I think I'm letting my imagination run away with me. This case is about Kevin Whittle, not about me.

Josh returns to the table. I give Julia a look to let her know to drop the subject.

A few minutes later, Julia looks at her watch. "I have to get going. I have an early meeting tomorrow."

"Are you okay to drive?" I ask.

"I'm fine," she says, pulling on her jacket. "I only had two. And I ate food and drank quite a bit of water. It's you two I worry about."

"We're good," Josh says. "I'll get an Uber, and Liz lives right over there." He points in the direction of my building.

Julia picks up her purse. "Thanks for the invitation. This has been lovely."

"Let's do it again sometime," Josh says while I grin like an idiot.

Julia smiles and waves and breezes out of the restaurant, checking her phone as she walks.

"Let's have another drink," Josh says.

I nod and signal the waiter. We order another round. I sip my margarita while trying to ignore Josh's pointed stare.

"Quit bullshitting me," he says, pushing his glasses up his nose.

"You've been saying that for twenty-five years."

"And yet you keep bullshitting me. You need to move on, Liz. It's been a year. A *year*."

"I don't know what that means." But I do. I'm still hung up on the woman who knew me too well, well enough that it terrified me right out of the relationship. I regret it, and my inveterate inability to have a normal relationship, every day.

"The lawyer is interested in you." He wiggles his eyebrows at me.

"I'm not interested." *But what if I am?* I shake my head.

"You need to move on, Liz. If you're not going to move on, then fix it with Cora, because she's perfect."

"She's not perfect. No one is." *And I can't fix it, anyway. What's done is done.*

He accepts my recalcitrance after a few argumentative minutes and moves on to tell me about his life, his partner, and his job. We talk about him until my own minor personal perils evaporate. When it's time to go, he orders an Uber ride. We wait outside for it. The car pulls up, and we hug.

"Take care of yourself, Liz. And let's do this again soon." He squeezes my hand and turns to walk away.

"Bye, Josh. Love you."

During my walk home, it occurs to me that I didn't know what love was, once. And I might not have known it even as I experienced it. But I know it now. That matters. And it's too late. That matters, too. *What does that mean, Dr. Shue?*

She always writes in ballpoint pen. Cora, not Shue. We had a conversation about it once. I use decent rollerballs, always black. But Cora is a fan of what she calls the "throwaway pen." It's the kind of pen you get as a perk for filling out a loan application or the kind you steal from the bank.

She explained it to me once. "If you use a throwaway pen, you don't miss it if it disappears, and you can just replace it with whatever pen comes next."

I asked her if the ink color mattered.

"Yes, you can just switch because, at the end of the day, it doesn't matter. Your report gets done. You get a high-five from your partner and maybe your boss, and then you go home to the love of your life. So screw it. Who cares about your ink color? There's more to life than continuity."

I told her that it really does matter. I like continuity and consistency and patterns.

She asked me to move in with her, and I threw it all into the fire. After the best months of my life, I balled it up and tossed it in, watched it ignite as if I didn't care, as if it were some shitty old newspaper. I got too immersed in work. I drank too much. I pretended to be someone else, an apathetic, uncaring asshole. And I guess I gave a convincing performance. I thought life would be easier that way, but it hasn't been. It's not.

When I get home, I chug some water to offset the tequila and the regret, then I yank *The Republic* off my bookshelf. I go over to the dining room window. Something moves in the bushes below, and I get an eerie feeling. I tell myself to stop being so jumpy. After an hour of Plato, I turn off the lights and go to bed.

CHAPTER NINETEEN

THE NEXT MORNING, I GO straight to Allie Cox's apartment. As I pull into a parking space, I spot Allie's downstairs neighbor, Ellen Preakness, standing outside. She's wringing her hands and looking around wildly.

I climb out and jog over to her. "Ma'am? Are you okay?"

She puts a hand over her mouth. "Oh my God."

"I'm Detective Boyle." I show her my badge. "We spoke on the phone. Can you tell me what's wrong?"

"U-Upstairs. A-Allie." She points up at the building behind her. "I-I c-called 9-1-1."

"Okay. You wait here." I run up the two flights of stairs.

I have to sidestep a pool of pinkish water to knock on Allie's door. No one answers. The stream seeping out from under the door is probable cause. Holding my service weapon in my right hand and standing beside the wall, I try the knob and whisper a thank-you when it turns easily. I follow the water to the bathroom. The door is open, so I stay to one side of it. I've already guessed what I'm going to find, but I can't be too careful when walking into the unknown.

Weapon raised, I step into the bathroom. The area is tiny with nowhere for anyone to hide. Allie is in the bathtub, and the faucet is still running. I shove my gun back into its holster. I feel for a pulse even though I can tell from the whitish film on her glassy eyes that I won't find one.

I pull on a pair of latex gloves and take some pictures with my phone before shutting off the water. A few minutes in, the paramedics and two

Cleveland Heights patrol officers show up. The paramedics push past, but the cops recognize me as police, so we talk for a minute.

"You're not really in our jurisdiction," the female patrol officer says.

"I know. I had a meeting scheduled with her. Then this happened. Call a homicide detective—she's dead."

"Okay, but we're going to need you to step into the hall. It's just protocol. No offense."

I give her a little salute. "Call the medical examiner," I say before I head out into the hallway.

I pace for a minute, deciding whether to leave, because I know who will probably be showing up soon. But Allie is part of my case. Heights officers are well known for being bored enough to ticket you for going five over the speed limit. They don't work a lot of "real" cases, mostly just burglaries and the occasional assault. But right now, I'm less worried about turf wars, hurt feelings, and whatever that fizzy feeling is in my chest than I am about what happened to Allie and what she wanted to tell me. I can't just go. I break out my phone and start taking pictures of the door and jamb.

"You can't be here." The voice is a familiar soft alto.

I turn around to face her. "Hi, Cora." I feel a surge of something that I ignore. "The door was unlocked. She was involved in a case I'm working. She called me last night. When I got here, the neighbor—"

"I'm serious, Liz." Her dark eyebrows come together in a way that makes a serious frown mark between them. She points down the hallway. "Get out of here." The intensity in her eyes could burn a hole through a phone book.

She steps around me and goes into Allie's living room. I follow her, staying too close, and she ends up in the corner between the couch and a bookshelf. I glance at the pictures lined up in front of the books: a photo of Allie with Jen Kline, one of her with the tattooed bartender from Winky's, one of Allie and her mother. I stifle a gasp when I spot a photo of Allie and Kevin.

"I found her," I say. "The neighbor was outside when I got here. I had an appointment to talk to Cox, the deceased, this morning. When I got here, well…" I gesture around with my hand. "I need to know more. I need to know what happened to her."

She flexes her jaw. "I said I never wanted to see you again. This is—*you are*—way out of line."

I notice a silver strand in her dark hair that wasn't there before. I nod and take a breath. I've been way out of line before, and I know what that means, coming from her. I take another, slower breath. "It's important. It's a kid case, Cora."

She knows my thing with tragic families. She knows more about me than I care to admit. I don't remind her that I can find out everything I need to know from Watson. Our medical examiner and the crime lab serve the entire county, not just Cleveland proper. I maintain eye contact. I don't like being a bully, if that's what I'm doing, but I refuse to back down.

She shakes her head. "Don't touch anything. Not a single thing. This is my scene, and you're lucky as shit that I'm not holding you on suspicion of this. I'm calling the ME, and you are not to leave my sight."

Am I really that predictable? It takes a lot of willpower not to roll my eyes, but I know that gesture would get me kicked out of here in a jiffy. "I understand."

While she makes the phone call, I take the time to study the living room. Allie decorated it tastefully with French-language prints and lots of photographs. She has quite a few books and records. A copy of *Rolling Stone* sits on the coffee table, next to the TV remote and her phone. I pull a new glove out of my jacket and slide it on. But as I reach for the phone, Cora takes two steps my way as if she means business. I shove my hands in my pockets.

I don't see any signs of a struggle, nothing to make me think this was anything but a suicide. *But why would she commit suicide when she had an appointment to talk to me this morning?*

Cora hangs up and puts her phone away. She jabs a finger at the door. "Go wait in the hallway."

Biting back a sarcastic remark, I do as she says. Cora isn't playing a game. She's being a consummate professional and protecting her scene from me, which is exactly what I'd expect of her. I'm lucky she's telling me anything at all, instead of demanding that I leave the premises.

Out in the hallway, I text Goran: *Allie Cox is dead in Cleveland Heights, and you'll never believe who I just ran into. What's happening? You at work yet?*

My phone rings. "I'm driving," Goran says. "On my way to work. What's this about Allie Cox?"

"Dead. Looks like a suicide."

"Man, they're dropping like flies."

"You're telling me. Watson's people are on the way." I glance at the door, which Cora shut behind me. "Cora's here."

"Where?"

"Here. Allie's apartment is in the Heights."

"Whoa. What do you want me to tell Fishner?"

"Don't tell her anything. I'll handle it. Make something up and text me the story. I'm gonna try to sneak back in there and take a better look at the body."

After we hang up, I slip back into the apartment.

"Looks like a severed femoral artery," Cora tells a uniform in the bathroom.

A severed femoral artery will take a person out pretty quickly. I try to become one with the wallpaper while Cora and her guys take a look around. She catches my eye once and scowls, but for a moment, I think I see something other than anger behind her eyes.

Once Watson's crew gets the body out of the tub, I give Cora a questioning look. She frowns but nods. I step over and scan the body before they zip her into a body bag. On her left shoulder is a small puncture mark that I didn't notice earlier. I snap a close-up to add to the ones I took before I was thrown out.

"Find anything?" I ask as I step back from the gurney.

Cora fishes something out of the bathtub. "Box cutter." She squeezes the bridge of her nose between her thumb and forefinger. "I have no idea why I'm cooperating with you, of all people in this fucking universe, but I'll tell you that we found what looks like a suicide note in the bedroom. It was under a bed pillow. But we don't even know if she wrote it. We'll have to run a handwriting comparison."

"Just let me see it." When she hesitates, I add, "Listen, I'm not trying to steal your case or fuck with you. I was invited here by the victim, remember?"

The female uniform tries to push past me to talk to Cora. "Detective, the neighbor is a mess."

"Yeah, I would be too if bloody water was seeping through my ceiling when I woke up in the morning," Cora mutters. "Get her to the hospital. Tell her someone will be by in a little while."

The uniform trots away.

"The suicide note?" I say to remind her, even though I know she hasn't forgotten my request.

She gives me a long, hard stare. "I'll send you a copy of the note once we get it processed."

"And get Watson to look at that left shoulder. Something isn't right. My gut says homicide."

She scans my face. *What is she looking for?* I wonder if she can see the regret under my cop veneer. "I'm going to need a statement from you," she says.

"You still have my number?" I ask.

"Against my better judgment."

"Thanks, Cora."

Without responding, she turns away and goes back to work. I stare at her for a minute before I leave the apartment.

On my way to the station, I make a few calls and learn that Miller didn't make any phone calls from the jail, other than one to his lawyer, who refuses to give me any information. Miller had no visitors, in jail or at the hospital, so it's unlikely that he's responsible for Allie's death, even from a distance. I'm certain that whoever killed Allie killed Kevin. The question is what Allie knew. If I'd driven to her house last night instead of going out to dinner, I might have the answer to Kevin Whittle's murder, and Allie might not be in a body bag right now.

Once I get to the squad room, I ask Goran if Miller's family has been notified.

"I think the hospital called his sister, one Marnie Phillips of Cuyahoga Falls. Are you going to tell me what this morning has been all about?"

"I told you. Allie Cox is dead, and Cora Bosch is the primary on the case. I don't believe it was a suicide, and my gut feeling is that whoever killed her also killed Kevin Whittle."

He leans back in his chair and squints up at me. "Are you all right?"

"Not really. I mean, I was supposed to talk to her this morning, and instead, I found her dead in a bathtub."

"What about the Bosch thing?" He knows most of the long, shitty story. But he also knows I don't like to talk about it, so he doesn't bring it up much.

"I think she'll give me limited info. Who knows with her?" I decide to change the subject. "Right, so Sean Miller doesn't have parents, because he and his sister were long-term foster kids." I walk over to the crime board. "The sister with the black sedan. The sister with keys to Sean's garage. Marnie Phillips."

He flips open his notebook. "That was the name on the Vicodin bottle in Miller's medicine cabinet. Think it could be a prescription drugs racket?"

"Maybe she's not as clean as the system thinks she is." I shuffle a stack of papers on my desk and pull out the preliminary report on Marnie Phillips. "Nada. Totally clean, at least on paper."

"Maybe she was the brains behind the operation?"

"Could be. And there's something else nagging at me. The keys to the garage. Miller said it was left unlocked most of the time, so nobody would have *needed* keys to get in. But this wasn't a crime of opportunity. We agree that this was a planned crime, right?"

He nods.

"It's leaving too much to chance, that the garage would be left unlocked. I'm gonna dig deeper on Marnie."

He stands and stretches his shoulders. "You want coffee?"

"Of course." I flip open my computer.

I dig up some information on Sean Miller's sister. Marnie Phillips, née Miller, married Craig Phillips, aged twenty-seven, four years ago. Marnie Phillips is twenty-four. Her driver's license picture shows a pleasant-enough-looking woman, with shoulder-length dark-brown hair and brown eyes. She's five eight and weighs one seventy. She's a third-grade teacher at Lincoln Elementary, so she's been fingerprinted. Other than a traffic ticket six years ago for making an illegal left turn, she has no record.

I bring up their address on the satellite map. Their house is like every other house in Cuyahoga Falls: a modest gray Colonial with white shutters, some shrubs in the front, and a driveway leading to a two-car garage. An American flag hangs from the porch. A lot of people call the city "Caucasian Falls," because it's the most lily-white section of the Akron-Canton area. Summit County's middle-class white people like to live there so they can brag about low crime rates, good schools, and high property taxes.

Craig Phillips works for the city as a school bus repairman. He had a misdemeanor charge for reckless driving a few years ago and again last year. I read that as DUI, pled down. He got his license back about six months ago. There was a misdemeanor petty theft last year when he stole some candy bars from a gas station, a seven-year-old drug charge, and some older juvenile offenses, but those records are sealed.

When Goran gets back with our coffee, I give him an update on what I've learned so far. He agrees that we need to pay Marnie Phillips a visit. I grab my laptop, and we head to Fishner's office.

Standing just inside the door, I say, "We need to go talk to Miller's sister in the Falls." I hold my breath, waiting for her response. I don't know if she's going to put me back on paperwork, send me home, or insist on riding with me. None of those would be good.

She narrows her eyes at me. "Do you have anything on this sister?"

"Not a lot." Relieved, I sit in one of her visitors' chairs, open my computer, and give her an update on what I've found. "Marnie Phillips seems nice and normal: too nice and normal. Her husband has been in some small stuff but nothing violent."

Fishner knits her eyebrows and nods slowly. "Okay, go talk to them. Keep me posted."

"Ten-four," I reply, standing.

Goran and I gather our gear then go down to the car. On the way there, he keeps telling me to slow down. "You're going to get us killed, and then we'll never know who our perp is. They're probably at work, anyway."

"It's spring break. I'm hoping that means she's home. And I'm only going ninety-two." I guide the Charger onto the off-ramp and slow down.

"Make a left on Second Street," Goran says, looking at his phone.

We pull up in front of their house about five minutes later. No one answers the door, so we take a quick tour around the yard and garage. Everything is locked, including a shed that's secured with a padlock.

"Can I help you?" an old man calls from the front porch next door.

I wave and flash him a big, warm smile. "Hi, I'm Detective Elizabeth Boyle. My partner and I are just here to ask a couple of questions."

He frowns and crosses his arms over his chest. "You're not Cuyahoga Falls. I know our police."

I nod and walk over to him. "That's true. We're here from Cleveland. This is totally routine. Do you know where they are? Or when they'll be back?"

"Nope." He eyes me with suspicion. "You got some ID?"

"Of course, sure." I show him my badge and police ID. "Like I said, this is routine."

He squints at my shield before handing it back to me. "Yeah, they should be home tonight, maybe tomorrow. I don't know where they went, but they asked me to keep an eye on the place."

"You usually watch their house for them?"

"No. They said something about some freak they know trying to get in. I dunno. They always have scumbags over there."

I hand him one of my cards. "Here's my information. Would you mind giving me a call when they get back?"

"Yeah, soon as I see them."

Goran steps in. "Do us a favor and don't let them know we were here, okay?"

The man nods. "Are they in trouble?"

"No, we just have a few questions," my partner replies, and the man nods.

I thank the man, and Goran and I get back in the car.

"So where we going next?" Goran asks.

"The Flats."

He raises an eyebrow at me. "Why there?"

"I want to talk to Anthony again," I say. "I have a picture of Marnie Phillips now."

"What the hell, Boyle." He shakes his head.

"Shit, we're out of gas." I cut across traffic and pull into a gas station.

Goran unfastens his seat belt and starts to open the door. "You want anything?"

"Bottle of water. Thanks." I step out of the car and slide my card into the slot on the gas pump. Just as I'm starting to pump the gas, my phone rings with an unknown number calling. I glance at the sign that tells me not to use my cell phone, that I might go up in flames as a result. "Boyle."

A disembodied woman's voice, one of those that sounds like the computer that answers the phone at credit card companies, says, "Either we shall find what it is we are seeking, or at least we shall free ourselves from the persuasion that we know what we do not know." Then the line goes dead.

"Hello?" I say. When I get no response, I jam my phone back into my pocket. "What the fuck." I yank my notebook out and write down the message as Goran is returning with a Diet Coke and my water.

"Why the face?" he asks across the car. He slides my water across the roof.

"Thanks. Phone call."

"Ha-ha. Who, Fishner?" He opens his door. "I just talked to her. Maybe she called you because she knows you won't listen to me."

I roll my eyes. "Prank call." But it wasn't. At least, it's unlikely that I would get two weird calls in as many days.

"Another one, huh?"

I shoot him a look. He shrugs and gets in the car. I finish topping off the tank. I need to find out who is sending me these messages. And why. After hanging up the nozzle, I twist the gas cap until it clicks three times, then I climb behind the wheel.

He waves his phone at me. "Fishner wants me to check on Miller. And she wants you back at your desk. She said you need to fill her in on why you were first on the Cox scene and talk to her about, quote, 'strategies for cooperating with Cleveland Heights.'" He clears his throat. "Drop me at MetroHealth."

CHAPTER TWENTY

E ARLY THE NEXT DAY, FRIDAY morning, I get a call from the Phillips'
neighbor. I call Goran and tell him we need to head back to the
couple's house.

"I'll meet you at the station in half an hour," he replies.

Goran decides that he's going to drive today, so I gaze out the window
on the way to Cuyahoga Falls. "You're driving like an old man," I mutter
at some point.

"Safety first."

We pull up in front of the Phillips' house and get out of the car. The
neighbor catches us on the street, looking wide-eyed and excited. "There
was a big screaming fight last night, and Craig drove off. He hasn't been
back yet."

Good, we can talk to Marnie alone. "Did you hear what the fight
was about?"

He shakes his head. "No. And it's not a rare thing. They're at it all the
time. Last night was loud, though." There's laughter from across the way,
where three kids are playing in a neighbor's front yard.

"Thanks for your cooperation, sir. We really appreciate it," Goran
replies as I start to walk toward the Phillips' front door. Goran joins me as
the neighbor goes back into his house.

We knock on the door, and Marnie opens it.

"We're here from the Cleveland Department of Police," Goran explains.
"I'm Detective Goran, and this is Detective Boyle." We show her our badges.

She sighs. "What do you want?"

"We just have a few questions."

"Questions about what?"

"Can we come in?" Goran asks. "It shouldn't take long. Just a couple of questions."

"I guess." She eyes me then turns back to Goran. "Can I get you a cup of coffee?" Her eyes are red, and those dark circles under them are pretty severe, given that she's only twenty-four.

"Sure," Goran replies.

She gestures for us to come inside.

"Is your husband home?" I ask.

"No." She leads us to the small kitchen, where she opens a cabinet and removes three mugs. "Cream or sugar?" She keeps addressing Goran, while avoiding looking at me.

"Cream and sugar would be great, thanks," Goran replies.

"Any idea where Craig might be?" I try to catch her eye, but it doesn't work.

She turns to face the coffeepot. "It's spring break, so the buses aren't running. He's a repairman. That's why I'm not at work today, too. I'm a teacher. I figured this was about something he'll probably say he didn't do." She sighs. "He's probably hanging out with his scummy friends down at Billiards Town. It's in North Akron. Want me to call him?"

The clock on the microwave says it's 8:32, which I confirm against my watch. "It's a little early for pool, don't you think?"

She doesn't respond. She seems nervous and maybe angry. I can see the tension in her neck and shoulders, and I recognize it. I'm starting to think she knows exactly where her husband is but doesn't want to tell us that it's somewhere other than Billiards Town.

"Ms. Phillips, we stopped by yesterday, too, but no one was home. Where'd you go?" I ask in my witness voice. "Just getting out of town for a few days?"

She turns and faces me but still doesn't meet my eyes. "Yeah, we went down to Columbus to see a friend. She just had a baby."

"And you got back late last night?" I ask.

She nods.

"Did you go anywhere else last night?"

205

She stares at the floor for a beat before turning to pour the coffee. "No, I was at home." She sets the mugs down on the kitchen table.

It hits me that she looks vaguely familiar, but I can't place her. "Did anything happen when you got home?"

"Craig acted like a prick, and I went off on him. Just another Thursday night." She sits down and takes a sip of her coffee.

"What can you tell us about Sean Miller?" Goran asks.

She sets down her mug and talks to the table. "He's my brother. He tried to kill himself. I got a phone call." She has a look of practiced stoicism, but I can tell she's trying not to cry.

"So you were here all last night, once you got home?"

She lets out a breath. "I just *told* you I was here."

So she has no real alibi for Allie Cox. "Where were you *last* Thursday night, into Friday morning?"

She looks as though she's trying to remember. "Here on Thursday. I probably went to bed early. I don't remember. Friday, I came home from work and waited for Craig so we could go to Columbus. He was out late, though, so we didn't leave until Saturday morning."

And her alibi for Kevin Whittle is shaky. "Out where?"

"I don't know. With his friends. Guy time or something. Look, what is this about? What did he do now?"

"Tell me about Sean's garage," I say as I sit in the chair next to her.

"I don't know anything about Sean's garage. Seriously. What do you think Craig did?"

"You have keys to the garage."

"I have those keys because I've fed his dog a couple of times when he's out of town. But I don't get involved in Sean's life anymore, because... because I thought that staying out of his business and trying to keep him and Craig separated would stop *this* from happening."

"What's *this*? What do you think is happening?"

She squeezes her eyes shut. "*This*. Fucking cops in my house, asking questions."

"What kinds of things is Sean involved with that upset you?" I ask. "I have a little brother, too, Marnie. I know how it can be. Does he hang out with bad people? I get it. So does mine. He makes even the simplest thing into a huge pain in the ass, too. And the thing is, he's not as stupid as he looks. I always have a hard time with that."

She finally looks at me. "Sean hangs out with fucking lowlifes. He makes a living slinging shit food at CSU and dealing drugs. All he does is party. I tried to help him, I really did." She looks down at the table again.

"Does Sean come over a lot?" I ask.

She shakes her head. "Not anymore. I told them they had to stop partying here."

"Who is *they*?"

"Sean and Craig," she replies. "I already said I was trying to keep them separated. They're bad news together."

"What kind of partying?" Goran asks. "Like drug parties?"

"I said that I didn't get involved with that, and I don't know. I don't know what kind of parties. I'm a fucking *teacher*. Do you think I want to end up in *prison*?"

"Is your husband really at Billiards Town now?" Goran asks. "We could catch up with him there, if that's more convenient."

"No. I don't know where he is."

"Would you mind if I use your restroom?" I ask.

She waves toward the doorway. "It's down the hall."

The bathroom is tiny and squeaky clean, and seemingly normal, even if they do have one of those fuzzy toilet lid covers. There's another half-empty bottle of Vicodin in the medicine cabinet with Marnie Phillips's name on it. I flush the toilet for cover then go back out in the hallway and check the bookshelf. On the top shelf is a picture of Marnie at about thirteen, with her arm slung around a redheaded little boy. They're standing outside a house that looks vaguely familiar, but the address isn't visible. The middle shelves contain mostly fiction and some memoirs, along with a couple of pictures from the Phillips' wedding. The bottom shelf holds a row of used college books. Some philosophy books, including *The Complete Plato*, are right in the middle, next to something about assessment in elementary education. I bend down and squint at the Plato, trying to see if the dust layer on top matches the other books, and wondering if Marnie is the one leaving messages for me. I suppose it could be Craig.

As I return to the kitchen, Goran's running names by her.

"Allie Cox?" he asks.

"Never heard that name."

"Elaine Whittle?"

She shakes her head.

"Kevin Whittle?"

"Nope. I swear that I have no idea about anything, other than my brother being in intensive care and that my husband is out doing whatever it is that he does."

Goran nods and stands. "Thanks for your time."

I pass her one of my cards. "Marnie, do us a favor and don't go anywhere, okay? No more trips to Columbus until we can talk to you again. You don't want this to look bad for you."

She looks directly at me. "Okay, Detective Boyle."

When we get back to the car, Goran gets on the phone with Fishner and tells her that we're going to look for Craig. While he's talking, I notice something stuck under the windshield wiper. I get a little wigged out when I see that it's a business card. I lean out the door and reach around the edge of the windshield to snatch it. It's one of my business cards from when I was on patrol: Officer Elizabeth Boyle, Badge #1761. I remember thinking it was pretty great to have business cards.

"What is that?" Goran asks as he slides his phone into his pocket.

"I wish I knew." My stomach drops. *What is that feeling?* It's dread. I have something to do with this. The feeling snakes up like a thin line from the bottom of me. It works its way to the top of my head, and when it gets there, I finally turn the card over.

Written in the same block lettering that was on the back of Arya's card is another message: "It is important that the tales which the young first hear should be models of virtuous thought."

I raise my head and scan the street for suspicious people. I don't see anyone. Even the kids are gone. I pass him the card. "I guess Marnie Phillips isn't the one leaving messages for me."

"Wow. Liz, this isn't good. We were only in there for half an hour." He looks around in the same way I did. "I'll go ask the neighbor if he saw anything." He gets out and goes to the neighbor's door.

While he's gone, I let my head fall back and close my eyes. I really don't need this crap right now.

The driver's side door opens, and Goran slides back behind the wheel.

"Nobody saw a thing." He studies my face. "Are you all right? You look weird and pale."

"I'm fine," I mutter. "Let's go."

A prickly feeling needles me all the way back to Cleveland. *Who is sending me these messages? And why? If someone has information on the Whittle case, why be so cryptic about it? And if the notes aren't supposed to help me but just supposed to taunt me... Is Kevin and Allie's killer behind them?*

CHAPTER TWENTY-ONE

WHEN WE GET BACK TO the station, I tell Goran I need to leave for a few minutes. "I forgot to feed the cat this morning," I offer as my lame excuse.

I can tell he doesn't buy it, but he doesn't press me on it, either. We exit the car, and I go around to get into the driver's seat.

He leans into the open window. "What do you want me to tell Fishner?"

"I don't care. I'm just gonna run home, feed him, and then I'll be back." I make my best blank cop face at him.

He sighs. "Okay, Liz. Whatever you say."

"Thanks. Bye." I put the car into drive and pull away.

A bell is ringing in my head. Marnie seems so familiar, but I can't figure out a connection to the case beyond the possibility that I crossed paths with her at some point while I was on patrol. *But when?* I run through a list of possibilities, given her age and the fact that she's lived in the Falls for almost ten years now. She would likely have been a juvenile, and those cases aren't usually easy to forget.

I text Becker: *I need juvie records on Sean Miller, Marnie Miller, and Craig Phillips ASAP.* She has access that I don't.

Once home, I dead bolt the front door then go into my bedroom. In the closet, next to my gun safe, I have six large plastic totes that contain all my duty notebooks from day one as a rookie to, roughly, last week. Not even Shue knows about them. Everyone would think it was crazy to keep notebooks like this. Actually, I kind of thought it was, too. Until now.

I mash my dress blues against the closet wall then shove a duffel bag and an old pair of boots off the top of the totes before sliding them out into the middle of the floor. The patrol notebooks are on the bottom. Apparently, I take a lot of notes. *See, Shue? I told you.*

I close my eyes and try to place the memory, which is starting to flicker in my brain. I was working the 513 out in the fifth district, driving a radio car with Dwayne Arya in the passenger seat. The location and partner put it early in my career.

The call came while we were getting a cup of coffee at a Dunkin' Donuts on the corner of Shaw and East 113th, our usual coffee spot. I'd been pissed that they were out of heavy cream for my coffee, as usual.

It was dark. I was on midnights, so it was definitely my first or second year on the job. The dispatcher advised... something. Two units needed for a nine-one-one at a house, located at... *Shit, Boyle, keep remembering.*

I can see the house in my head, almost out in East Cleveland. It was a big brick house with a huge front porch and a gravel driveway. Some kids' toys littered the front lawn, which was blanketed with snow. Christmas lights decorated the border of the porch.

Snow and Christmas lights. Arlington and Paxton.

It was about three houses from the corner. Yeah, I remember. Arya made me drive so he could eat his stupid bear claw, or that was his excuse. The old hands always make the rookies drive.

I think the notes I need are in the second box. I pop the cover off and run my fingers down the rows of old notebooks. They smell like old paper and ink. I've always liked that smell.

All the notebooks have a date range printed on the front of them. I've always been obsessive about keeping good notes and keeping evidence clean, that sort of thing. I like to think that it makes up for my sometimes erratic behavior. I locate the eight notebooks from November and December of that year and flip through the first five or so without finding what I'm looking for. I'd forgotten about a lot of this.

"The shit you see on patrol," I whisper.

I locate it about halfway through the last notebook. The date is December 18. I shudder. My dad hanged himself on that date. What I wrote in the notebook matches my memory.

We'd gotten the call at about three in the morning, and we were first on the scene.

A girl, maybe thirteen years old, met us in the front yard. She was followed by a younger boy, both of them wearing only thin pajamas. They ran up to me, the girl crying and shrieking in a way that made her seem much younger. Smudges on her pajamas looked as though they could be blood, and when the boy got closer, I could see that there was blood on his hands and pants. *Are you okay?* I asked them. *Did someone hurt you?* They nodded. I asked their names, but they gave no reply. I asked where their foster parents were. He was silent, and she wailed that she didn't know.

I asked them what was wrong, what happened, and who called 9-1-1. The girl clung to me without responding. I helped her into the back of the zone car and told her to sit tight then lifted the boy in to join her. I remember checking them to make sure they weren't bleeding before locking them in the car.

Hand on his gun, Arya walked toward the house, bellowing an order. I followed him with a flashlight. The radio chattered. The dispatcher said it was a foster home. All the lights were out inside the house. There was only darkness.

I hit the radio and told whoever would listen that we needed Child and Family Services there right away and that we'd stay on-scene until a social worker arrived. We went up the porch steps and entered the house through the front door, calling out that we were police. No answer.

Another girl, a little older than the first, appeared in the hallway by the staircase. She seemed calm. I remember that calm. She directed us to the kitchen. Her voice was like an adult's but in a child's timbre. And her eyes… a shiver went down my spine when I looked into those deep-brown eyes that had seen too much. She was covered in blood, much more blood than the other two, but she didn't seem upset. At first we thought she was hurt, but we checked her out, and she had no injuries. She led us into the kitchen with a weird smile on her face.

In the middle of the kitchen floor was a dead white cat. Its left front paw was severed. Next to it was a ceramic mixing bowl filled with blood. A pair of red-handled hand pruners lay beside the bowl. Blood was splattered on the floor and the white refrigerator.

I don't remember what I said. Probably something to the effect of "Oh, holy shit." We cleared the rest of the house, and I remember wondering why no adults were home in the middle of the night. There's a note in my notebook that there were no signs of forced entry.

Standing in my bedroom, I shake off the memory. I call for Ivan. He comes trotting in and jumps on top of one of the totes.

I don't remember much about those three kids, but I do recall the younger girl telling me about her little brother Sean not talking much ever since the summer before, when something bad had happened in the woods. She wouldn't explain further. She said—and I have this written in the notebook—"If I tell, I'll get hurt, too." *Marnie Miller, aged thirteen,* my notebook says.

I remember thinking that somebody had messed with those kids pretty badly. I also remember giving each of them my card and telling them to call me if they needed anything. I don't remember waiting for the social worker—but someone must have come, or we wouldn't have left—or following up. We got another call, and Arya talked me into leaving.

I have one more note from that night: *What happened? Biological parent showing up to terrorize them? A former resident?* Now I'm sure I was wrong.

I send Becker another text: *I need a list of everyone who stayed in the foster home at the corner of Arlington and Paxton.* I add a date range at the end.

"Wow," I say to my cat. I slide the old notebook into my inside pocket, in front of the current one.

I clean up the mess I made with my search and turn on a couple of lamps in case it gets dark before I get home. I dump some food into Ivan's bowl and give him another scratch. He meows once then walks away.

When I get back to the station, Goran is working at his desk. I stop beside him and wait for him to look up.

"Anything on Miller's condition?" I ask.

"Nothing yet. You look crazy. Are you all right?"

"No, not really. I need to tell you something, but let's do it in Fishner's office so I don't have to go over it twice."

"Okay, let's go." He shuts off his monitor and follows me into the LT's office.

Fishner is on the phone, but she takes one look at my face and tells the person she'll call them back. When she hangs up, she waves at the guest chairs. "What's up, Boyle?"

Goran and I sit down. I fill them in on my hunch and what I found in my old notebook.

Fishner taps a pen on her desk. "If the business cards aren't separate from the killing—maybe killings, plural—there's going to be a real problem." She leans back against the wall as if she's planning to sit there and talk to me all day.

"Yeah, I know." I don't ask her what kind of real problem she has in mind. It's probably something about defense attorneys and how I've compromised the entire investigation just by existing.

"Dot your i's and cross your t's, both of you. I was just on the phone with the captain. We need to get this tied up and, in an ideal world, solve all of this at once."

It's not an ideal world. "Yes, Lieutenant."

"What's your plan?"

"I'm going to look into their juvenile records—what little I can get— and try to find a connection. I'm thinking Craig Phillips is good for this, but I'm still trying to find a pattern."

She nods. "Close the door on your way out."

Becker is waiting when we emerge from Fishner's office. She crooks a finger at me. Goran tells her hello then goes to his desk.

Becker leads me down the hallway. She's holding three file folders under her arm. Two are thick, and one is normal size. "Don't ask me how I got any of this. I'm serious. Don't ask. And don't tell anyone, either. Make it seem like you got all this on your own." She pushes open the door to the Z-room, the room we use for naps on long shifts. "Are you all right?" she asks.

I raise an eyebrow. "Not really." I don't like piles of bodies. Nor do I like finding business cards all over the place or receiving prank phone calls. And I don't like the jurisdiction in which Allie's case is or the fact that I have no evidence on Craig Phillips beyond my gut. *Yet.* I don't have evidence *yet*.

Becker nods and bites her bottom lip.

"Shouldn't we look at this at, I don't know, a table or a desk?" I ask as the door closes behind me.

"No camera can see that I'm showing this to you." Her face is grave, her eyes downcast.

"Wait a minute. Are you breaking the *rules*?" My mouth twitches into a grin in spite of my own gloom. I've never seen Julia Becker break the rules before.

"I'm breaking a *law*, Liz." She hands me the folders, which are heavier than they look. "Don't let these leave your sight for even one minute." She points at me. "I mean it. You're not supposed to have this kind of information. But I know you need it."

"I got it. Thanks."

She pulls the door open. "None of it will be admissible. Speaking of which," she says as she glances at her watch, "I'm due in court. Get those back to me as soon as you're done with them. Lock the door. Not a word to anyone, not even Goran."

When the door closes behind her, I turn the lock. I take a seat on the bottom bunk and open the first folder, the Child and Family Services case file on Craig Phillips.

His social worker's name was Amanda Tanner. She'd been on his case since he entered the system back when he was removed from his single father after a kindergarten teacher got suspicious about some odd behavior and called CFS.

According to her notes, his father was an alcoholic who started beating Craig soon after the mother ran off to Colorado with another man. The abuse escalated to sexual abuse of the kind that no one wants to imagine. The only way they were able to get any information was to have him draw pictures. The first ones are about what I would expect from a child who had gone through what Craig experienced: monsters, penises, a naked man, that kind of thing. The notes mention that he was a good artist, even at six. Eventually, the father confessed and was sent to prison. He was shanked in the shower two years later for stealing another con's peanut butter.

There are photocopies of some of the pictures Craig drew over the years after he entered the system, all dated by hand in Amanda Tanner's handwriting. As he got older, they became disturbing in a different way. Right around the time his dad was killed, he started doing detailed anatomical drawings of the insides of both people and animals. He sketched the person or animal from the outside—as time went on, they got to be good sketches, too, because this guy is quite an artist—and then peeled back the layers, so to speak.

Just after his thirteenth birthday, Craig was accused of felony assault for beating the crap out of an eight-year-old neighbor boy, allegedly because the boy made a joke about Craig's biological mother. The victim's name is redacted in the file, so it will be difficult to follow up on that. As far as I can tell, though, he was never at the foster home at Arlington and Paxton. It looks as if he lived on the West Side for most of his life.

Amanda Tanner and I worked together on another abhorrent case a few years back, right after I started in Special Homicide. She retired last year after ten years of working a caseload that was four times what it should have been. And I think *my* job is hard. *The shit people do to each other boggles my mind.*

I get up to stretch. After grabbing the rickety old wooden chair from the corner, I pull it over to the bunk so I can use the bed as a desk.

The next file is Marnie Miller's. She entered the system after her parents were killed in a car accident when she was four and Sean was two. Their grandparents lived in California and wouldn't take them, so they were placed in a group home until a foster family could be found.

According to the file, the foster family at Arlington and Paxton wanted to adopt Marnie. There's no mention of Sean in those notes.

Someone knocks on the door and jiggles the doorknob, but I ignore it. The last file, Sean Miller's, is the slimmest. It contains a lot of information that mirrors Marnie's but with less detail. For some asinine reason, he'd ended up with a different caseworker, one who wasn't very descriptive.

I check the list Becker included on a sheet of paper between the files. Two boys and five girls are listed. I write their names down in my notebook so I can look them up later. Three of the girls stand out as being the right age as the girl I saw in the house that night: Elizabeth Conrad, Sarah Taylor, and Jenny Perkins.

I flip back through my notes—I've taken eight pages of them—looking for a pattern, some kind of connection.

There's a loud knock on the door. "Boyle!" Fishner bellows. "Wake up and get out here. Now. I need you in my office. Now."

I unlock the door and pull it open. "I'm not sleeping." *Why the hell would I be sleeping?*

She gives me the side-eye and glances at the bunks. "I'm not even going to ask what you've been doing in there for so long."

"I've—"

But she lets the door close in my face.

I gather the files and shoot Becker a text message: *I have to tell Goran and Fishner about the juvie records.*

She replies almost immediately: *None of it is admissible. And you didn't get it from me.*

I know. Thanks for this.

Back in the squad room, I lock the files in my desk. When I enter Fishner's office, I see Goran is already there. "What happened?" I ask.

Fishner tosses me a pair of latex gloves. "Put these on. You need to see this before I send it to the lab."

I notice that Goran and Fishner are both wearing gloves and that the table is covered with a paper evidence bag.

She points at the chair closest to Goran. "We're not going to ignore this, especially given the business cards."

I sit and scooch the chair up to the table. I try to catch Goran's eye, but he's giving all his attention to Fishner.

Fishner pulls her chair over next to mine. "This came today."

She uses a gloved hand to pull a folded piece of paper out of what looks like a handmade manila envelope and a copy of the feature that the *Plain Dealer* ran on me this past summer, the big interview Fishner made me give because CDP was trying to make us look like caring nurturers. There I am, in the photograph, standing in front of my desk with my hands on my hips, looking very cop-like. She passes everything to me, and I hold it gently.

Even through the gloves, I can feel the texture of the heavy white paper, the kind that illustrators and printmakers use. I unfold it over the table and lay it flat. Written across the top is "Haiku for Hero Cop" in black ink. I lay the article next to it.

I start with the envelope. It's postmarked Cleveland. I sniff it and catch a whiff of sandalwood. I wear sandalwood. It looks as though he's tried to copy my handwriting, too. He got some of it correct but missed the fact that when I write, all my *N*s are capitalized. It's never occurred to me that my handwriting might be hard to forge.

I pick up the paper. At the bottom of the page, he's mimicked my full signature. And he's gotten it pretty close. I wonder where he got it—maybe from an old police report, since those things are pretty easy to track down. I start reading the poems.

For Elizabeth,
Genius clever roguish cop
Blind and in the dark.

All the pictures show
Your fucked-up family line,
Your cold silver eyes.

You will never see
Forms moving in gray shadows
Shift into the light.

Hero in Cleveland:
Depraved and indifferent
Gun, badge, radio.

I flip the paper over. More poems.

Ropes hang from ceiling:
Noose on auntie, Boyle,
And a kindred soul.

Everything goes black—
All but this, struggle over.
Can't breathe, can't see, done.

Darkness covers us:
Ontological chaos.
Screaming black abyss.

Good night, sad women.
I might not see you again.
Eternal sleep waits.

"Who the hell is the aunt?" I whisper.

"Do you have any nieces or nephews?" Fishner asks.

"Not that I know of."

"We need to get a handwriting sample of Cox's," Fishner says. "She could have sent this before she killed herself. Work with Heights. Have they sent you a copy of the suicide note yet?"

"What, you think *Allie* sent me this shit? No way. Craig—"

"Finish those reports and then go home," she says. "And for God's sake, be careful. I'll get Heights to sit on your place."

Goran and I leave the office. I head over to my desk to grab my stuff.

"Like she said, be careful," Goran says. "Don't put your gun in the safe anymore." He flicks a wadded-up piece of paper at me and tries to smile. "You can stay with us if you want."

I feel my eyebrows come together, so I will them to separate. "Thanks, but I'll be okay."

"You sure? This is some creepy stuff, and—"

"I'll be okay. Thanks, though."

I sit down and pick up the phone. I call Cora three times before she finally answers.

"What do you want, Liz?"

I put on my most saccharine voice. "Hi, Cora. May I please have a copy of the suicide note? Right now? It might relate to the case we're working. The kid case."

She's silent long enough that I wonder whether she's hung up on me. Then, she gives a dramatic sigh. "Whatever, okay. I'll have a digital copy to you within the hour. But you owe me a drink."

"Thanks, Cora."

"Don't get any ideas about stealing my investigation. Or about anything else."

"Okay. Thanks again." I don't remind her that she never wants to see me again. And I don't tell her that I'd love to buy her a drink.

On the way home, my phone plays the happy chirp I assigned to Cora's text messages, way back when. I make a mental note to change her alert sound. Sitting at a red light, I pull up the text. There's no message, just the attachment that I assume is Allie's suicide note, which can wait until I get home.

Back in my apartment, I put on Nirvana's *In Utero* and make a peanut butter and jelly sandwich. I scarf down the food then bring out my phone.

I'm sorry to whoever finds this.

Please forgive me. I cannot go on knowing.

I can't stand living with Kevin's death.

Never should have gotten so angry.

Never meant to hurt him.

I don't know what else to say.

In the end, it didn't matter if I lived or died.

Detective Boyle, I appreciate you reaching out to me.

"Get in the habit of seeing in the dark."

Allie

The handwriting doesn't look like the stalker's, or whatever we're calling him. I forward the attachment to Fishner and Goran.

The note is bizarre. It's nothing like any suicide note I've ever read. And the "seeing in the dark" line reminds me of those creepy haiku. I'm certain that whoever's stalking me also killed Allie and tried to make it look like suicide. I pour myself my bourbon ration for the day.

Looking for a distraction, I turn on the TV. As soon as I plop down on the couch, Ivan jumps into my lap. I doze off at some point to the sound of his purring.

I wake up at the sound of a loud commercial, advertising some kind of special pillow. I glance at the clock: 2:14. Before I turn off the lights, I make sure the front door is bolted. In the dark, I look outside and spot the Heights unmarked car in the parking lot next to the Passat. My gun goes on the nightstand.

CHAPTER TWENTY-TWO

T HE NEXT MORNING, FISHNER SENDS us after Craig Phillips. Goran and I lead Roberts and Domislaw to Cuyahoga Falls. The nosy-but-helpful neighbor is on his porch when the four of us pull up in front of the Phillips' house. I catch his eye, and he nods before going inside.

"Roberts, Domislaw, one of you take the side door and one take the back door."

They nod, and I wait ninety seconds for them to get in place before I pound on the door with the heel of my hand. Goran stands beside me.

Marnie Phillips opens the door. "Shit, you again? What now?"

"Is your husband at home?" Goran asks.

"No, he said he had to run some errands."

"When is he going to be home?"

"I have no idea."

"We have a few more questions. Can we come in?" I ask.

She rolls her eyes. "Do I really have a choice?" She holds the door open.

I lead her into the living room. I'm not playing good cop today, not when we have Craig right in our crosshairs. "Have a seat, Marnie."

She takes a seat on the couch, so I perch on the coffee table in front of her. I'm going to go at her as if I think she's guilty. If she gives her husband up, this will wrap up nice and tight.

"Marnie, I need you to give us permission to take a look around. It'll look much better for you if you cooperate today. Yesterday was bullshit, and we don't have time for more bullshit right now."

Goran clears his throat from his position in the doorway to the kitchen. I ignore him and stay focused on Marnie.

"What the hell is going on?" she asks. "Didn't I answer your questions already?"

"You tell me what's going on, Marnie. Now, can we take a look around, or should I call the prosecutor and get a warrant? I'll say it again: it's better for you if we don't *need* that warrant." We can't get a warrant, because we'd need Cuyahoga Falls' cooperation, and they're not real well known for cooperating. But she wouldn't know that.

She drops her head. Her longish brown hair hangs in front of her eyes. In some ways, she looks like the stereotypical female con.

I don't want her to think too much. "Look at me," I say.

When she does, I nod. She was the little girl in the bloody pajamas that I tried to help in that police zone car all those years ago.

I lean forward and put my elbows on my knees. My face is less than two feet from hers. She leans back, but there's nowhere to go.

It's time to find out if she knows that her husband is stalking me. "The business cards. The weird note in the mail. The text messages. What do you know about those?"

She shakes her head. "I honestly have no idea what you're talking about." Her hands tremble when she pushes her hair out of her face. "I promise you. What business cards?"

"Is your husband a writer? Tell me what he likes to write about."

She chews on her bottom lip until it starts to bleed. "What are you talking about? Craig is a mechanic, not a writer." She starts to cry.

"Listen, Marnie, I'm not stupid. And neither are you. So it doesn't make much sense to me that you surround yourself with idiots who couldn't put two sentences together, much less quote some dead philosopher all over the place. And that, in my mind, means that *you* are fucking with me, which I don't like very much. That philosophy book on your shelf, when was the last time you looked at it?"

"What philosophy book?"

"*The Republic*. It's next to *Designing Effective Assessment*."

"Uh, it's from my college philosophy class. I like to keep my books," she says.

"When was the last time you looked at it?"

She screws up her eyebrows. "Probably when I was in college?"

"I can take that book into evidence now and arrest you." I pull a search

222

consent form out of my inside pocket and lay it and my pen in front of her. "Or you can sign this form right now. You choose."

She stares at the form for several seconds then covers her face with her hands. "Holy fuck. Fine." She picks up the pen and signs the form. "Look around. You won't find anything."

"Green light," I tell Goran as I slide the form back into my pocket. "Get Roberts and Domislaw."

He nods and moves out of the doorway.

"Where is Craig?" I ask again.

"I don't know."

"Does he hang out in Cleveland a lot?"

"I don't know. Maybe?"

"Does he ever tell you where he's going?"

"Not really, no."

Goran reappears in the doorway. "What's behind the dead bolted door?"

"The basement," she replies in a whisper.

"Why is there a dead bolt on your basement door?"

"I don't know."

The frustration is making my neck hot. "Where are the keys? Or should we kick the door in?" Goran asks.

"He keeps the key with him," she mutters.

Goran turns away and says something to Roberts and Domislaw in the kitchen.

"It opens in, so I'll kick it," Roberts says loud enough for us to hear.

Goran comes back and stands in the doorway again.

"Are they really going to kick the door in?" Marnie asks. "Craig won't be happy."

"What happens when Craig is unhappy?" I ask.

"He acts like a fucking asshole," she mumbles.

"Does he hurt you?"

"Not usually."

Three loud cracks come from the kitchen then a slamming noise. "Got it," Roberts calls.

"Why is your basement door dead bolted?" I ask. "Did Craig have the kid down there for a while before he killed him in Sean's garage?"

She turns white. "Detective, I swear to everything. God, Allah, Satan,

Zeus, whatever. Everything." She swallows hard. "I think I'm going to throw up." She starts to stand, but I push her back down.

"Breathe," I tell her. "Goran, will you get her some water, please?"

He leaves for a minute then comes back with a glass of water. I take it and hand it to Marnie.

"Drink it," I tell her.

As she's sipping the water and trying to hold it together, someone stomps up the basement stairs. I assume it's Roberts and not Domislaw, based on how quickly the footsteps move.

"Boyle, Goran, you need to see what's down there," Roberts says from the doorway to the kitchen. "Now."

"Get in here to sit with her, then," I reply, not looking away from Marnie's terrified eyes.

"What's down there?" she asks.

Roberts comes over and stands next to me. "Go," he tells me.

I push myself off the coffee table. "Keep breathing, Marnie," I say on my way into the kitchen.

I jog down the steep basement stairs then pause to let my eyes adjust to the dim light. It's a pretty clean area. Some boxes labeled "Xmas decorations" sit on a wooden pallet in the far left corner. On the wall to the right are an old couch, a coffee table, and a deflated air mattress. Across from that are a dartboard and a mini refrigerator. I walk over and take a peek inside the fridge: a few cans of Coors Light, a dried-up slice of pizza on a paper plate, and a cellophane-wrapped chunk of what looks like summer sausage. To the left, behind the washer and dryer, is a door that looks as though it could lead outside, if not for that board screwed across it. I remember seeing a bulkhead outside. A makeshift wall separates me from where Domislaw and Goran are standing. I go around it to see what has their attention.

Behind the barrier, the furnace and hot water heater frame the door to an old fruit cellar. Domislaw and Goran stand in the doorway, illuminated from behind by a lightbulb hanging from the ceiling by a cord.

"Not exactly up to code, is it?" I chuckle.

Neither man laughs as they move out of the way.

"Liz, you should see this," Goran says.

As I step forward, I notice the splintered wood on the doorframe. They must have broken it to gain access.

In the middle of the room, an empty fifth of cheap vodka and an ashtray filled with butts sit on the floor next to a wooden stool, the only furniture in the space. The gray cinder-block wall to the left is plastered with images of me. The pictures progress in order, in four rows, beginning with my academy picture in the upper left and ending in the bottom right with a photograph of me kneeling next to Anthony the night we found Kevin Whittle. Some of them are available online, and I recognize several that were cut out of the print version of the *Plain Dealer*. But a couple, including one of me outside Guido's the day I had lunch with Christopher, are candid shots that I've never seen.

The opposite wall is the same style but with photographs of Teresa Whittle that roughly correspond to the timeline depicted on my wall. Kevin is in a few of them. The last eight photos in the series, set off in their own row, are of Kevin with Allie Cox.

"Holy shit. Did you photograph this?" I ask.

Goran nods and waves the camera at me. I look from wall to wall, left to right, trying to match the pictures. Above the top row on my side is a photograph of me at about eight, reaching up to hold my dad's hand. On Teresa's side is a picture of a very young Teresa with another young woman holding a baby. In the middle of the bottom row on my side is a photograph of me with Christopher outside my mom's apartment building. On Teresa's side is a photograph of her with Kevin at the park.

"What the fuck is this?" I point at the overflowing ashtray. "Bag those cigarette butts. DNA." I back out of the room, shaking my head. "This is nuts." Goran puts a hand on my shoulder, but I shake him off. "I'm fine. Let's keep looking around. Get photos of all of this."

I check behind the furnace, and I find a pillow and a green sheet. "Bag this," I tell Dom. "Photograph it first." I turn to Goran. "Green sheet. This is it."

He nods.

"Holy shit, this is it," I repeat.

Behind the water heater is a curtained doorway. "What kind of little shop of horrors is this?" I whisper. I pull back the cloth to reveal a badly installed makeshift bathroom. I search the small area, and behind the toilet, I find something wrapped in a trash bag.

"Dom, in here," I call. "Photograph this," I say, gesturing at the bag.

He takes several shots from different angles, then I gently pull it out from behind the toilet. I open the trash bag and remove a large pair of branch cutters.

"Murder weapon. Holy shit. Photos." I set the branch cutters on the toilet lid so Domislaw can get some more pictures.

Something was under the bag. I bend down to get a closer look. A kid's glove. "Here, too, Dom," I say, pointing.

"There's a lot of physical evidence here," Goran says.

"Good job, Captain Obvious," I snap, but then I feel bad. "I'm sorry. That wall of weirdness freaks me out."

He nods. "Yeah, it's pretty freaky."

"We need to get Crime Scene here right away. Will you call? Ask Jo to come personally. She's the best."

I move back into the larger room so I can breathe. *This is it. We've got him.* I pull out my phone and call Fishner. "Marnie Phillips. Craig Phillips. We got consent to search. There's evidence. Dead bolted basement. Possible murder weapon, a kid's glove, and a weird shrine-like thing with Teresa Whittle and me. It's nuts."

"You're talking too fast, Boyle. Slow down. Start over."

I force myself to slow down and tell her again about finding the murder weapon and the creepy stalking walls.

"Well, we obviously need to run forensics on the branch cutters, but I'll call Teresa now. Good work, Boyle." She tells me to bring Marnie in to the station so we can interview her and, maybe, book her as an accessory.

"I'm going back upstairs," I call to the guys. "Bag everything. Every fucking thing. We've got him."

I jog back upstairs and go into the living room, where Marnie is sitting on the couch, tears rolling down her face. "Marnie? Why are you crying?"

She hunches forward and stares at the coffee table.

I look at Roberts. He just shrugs.

I go over and stand on the other side of the coffee table. "Tell me the deal with the basement." I try to use my witness voice, but the adrenaline interferes.

She doesn't raise her head. "You're talking about the locked room, right? I'm not allowed in there. I'm not really even allowed downstairs."

"You're not allowed in your own basement? You *live* here. What do you mean?"

She stops crying. "It's Craig's area. I don't go in there."

"It's Craig's *area*? What does that mean?"

She doesn't respond.

"You've never once been curious? You never sneak down there when he's not home?"

She shakes her head. "He keeps the key with him. He needs his space. I get it."

"Marnie, quit fucking with me." I stand and lean forward with my hands on the coffee table. "I'm serious. This is getting really irritating."

"I swear to God, I'm not fucking with you! Why would I fuck with you? Why would I?" Her voice has a hysterical edge.

"Maybe because of that night at the foster home," I reply, sitting back down. "Look at me."

She raises her eyes to my face.

I don't know what will get through to her, but I need a reaction of some kind. "Do you keep in touch with Elizabeth and Jennifer and Sarah?"

She shudders and looks back down at the table.

I give her a second, but she remains silent. Someone pulls into the driveway. "Roberts, I'm guessing that's Jo and her team. Can you please take them downstairs if it is?"

He nods and leaves. I move over to sit in the recliner. I try to look relaxed as I lean back and cross my legs.

"It sounds crazy," Marnie whispers, "but I always knew I'd see you again." Something in her eyes tells me that she's going numb. "My life is shitty and pathetic."

I feel an expression on my face, one I'm unfamiliar with, before I make it blank cop-mug again. "Marnie, look. Just tell us about the basement, okay? Have you seen what's down there?"

She shakes her head. "I told you I'm not allowed in there. Craig calls it his 'man cave.' I mean, he dead bolts the fucking cellar and has another lock on that stupid room. God knows what he has in there. He's such an asshole. He keeps saying he's going to redo the basement, put in a better washer and dryer, make a TV room so we can move that giant thing out of here." She gestures at the television. "Of course, he never does any of it. It's all talk. He's such a prick."

"So Craig kept you out of the basement." *Why the hell does she stay married to an asshole who's all talk?*

227

She nods. "I swear to God that I did not do anything. Now or ever before." She meets my eyes. "I've always had good memories of you. You were nice to me. You tried to protect me the night the cat died, way back when."

I force a smile. I kind of feel bad about being so cold right now, but I need to separate myself from the guilt I have about that night ten years ago. It's a moot point. Besides, I'm a different Liz. She's a different Marnie. "We're going to take you up to Cleveland, Marnie, and have a longer conversation there. But tell me again, and I want the truth this time, was Craig with you in Columbus?"

She shakes her head. "No, I went alone," she whispers then starts to cry again.

"And two nights ago. Did Craig come home?"

"Yeah, but then he left again at, like, two thirty."

That window is more than enough time for Craig to have driven to Cleveland and killed Allie Cox. "You have two cars, right? Which one did you take to Columbus?"

"I took the Camry to Columbus. Sean was borrowing the Focus while his truck was broken down."

"How long did Sean have the Focus?"

She shrugs. "I don't know. About ten days, maybe? He brought it back last Friday morning. Just dropped it off, you know."

"And last Thursday night? Were you really in all night?"

"I was. Craig was out. He just said he had something he had to do."

So he could have killed Kevin Whittle. "Why did you lie before, when you said that he was with you?"

She sighs. "I don't know."

"Do you know a man by the name of Ricky Harris?"

She thinks for several seconds. "Craig has a friend named Ricky, but I don't know his last name. He's been here a few times. He knows Sean, too. He's a bad influence. I think he manages one of those strip clubs up there. Craig hangs out there a lot. I'm sorry I didn't tell you that before." She shakes her head. "Look, I know that Craig isn't a good guy, okay? But neither one of us killed anybody."

She looks as though she's telling the truth, but maybe she just doesn't know her husband very well. Believing something and having it be true are different things.

"They always hang out in the basement," she says. "Smoking pot, drinking, acting like assholes."

"Who are 'they'?"

"Sean and Craig. And Sarah's been around more the past few weeks, since she got evicted. She crashed down there for a couple weeks. Her boyfriend's been around, too. Nice guy. Not like the dirtbags she usually dates."

"Who's Sarah? The Sarah from the foster home?" Someone sleeping in the basement explains the air mattress.

She nods. "Sean's and my foster sister. Sean and I are biological siblings. Sarah was the third one in the house. We grew up with her."

The third kid. The older girl. The one who came down the hallway that night with those big, calm eyes.

"It's a kind of bond," she says. "We went through all that shit together. Sean and I had each other, but she had no one. No father, her mom in jail, no other family except for the aunt who put Sarah's mom away then turned her back on Sarah, let her go into that fucked-up system. We've all suffered. The three of us—hell, all four of us—have been through things you wouldn't imagine."

Goran steps into the doorway. "Guess who just came home. We've got him outside."

"Is Jo Micalec here?"

He nods and then disappears.

I get up and walk over to Marnie. "Marnie Phillips, I'm arresting you on the suspicion of homicide." I Mirandize her, even though every instinct in me says she had nothing to do with this. I take her arm and pull her to her feet then handcuff her.

I call for Roberts. When he comes in from the kitchen, I tell him to stay with Marnie. I move quickly through the house and out the front door, where Dom has Craig cuffed in the driveway.

"Fuck you," Craig says when I approach. "Who the fuck are you? What is this about?"

"C'mon, Craig. You know exactly what this is about," I say. I turn to Domislaw. "Read him his rights and impound the car."

"This is bullshit!" Craig yells. "Fuck you, you fucking bitch!"

CHAPTER TWENTY-THREE

WHEN WE GET BACK TO the station, Craig is already ensconced in the interview room.

Fishner strides over, looking proud of us but trying to downplay it because we don't know enough yet. "Goran, you take the first shot at Craig. I don't want him distracted by Boyle." She hands me a file folder. "Domislaw's photos. You weren't kidding when you said that was nuts." I take the folder and tuck it under my arm.

Fishner and I go to the observation room. She turns up the volume on the speakers as we take our seats. Craig is sitting with his elbows on the table and his head in his hands. He has engine grease under his fingernails and wears a dirty Carhartt jacket and stained pants. His work boots are huge. They must be a size thirteen or more. I wonder if any of those dark stains are Kevin Whittle's blood. Allie Cox's blood. He looks up when Goran enters the room.

Goran flips a chair around and sits on it backward. "What do you have to say for yourself?"

Craig's leg jiggles under the table. He throws his greasy hair off his forehead. "Look, if this is about the stolen property, I'll tell you everything. Just promise me I won't do any time."

"We don't give two shits about stolen property," Goran says. "How 'bout that kid you killed? Why don't you take me through what happened?"

Craig blinks hard a couple of times. "Wait a minute. I'm under arrest for *murder*?"

"Capital murder. And we like you for another murder, too. And stalking."

"I want a lawyer. This is bullshit. I—"

I'm through the door before Fishner can stop me. I slide into the interview room and close the door behind me. "Tell me about that room in your basement."

"I didn't mean to call you a bitch," he says, hanging his head. "I'm sorry."

Contrition. That's what I like to see. "The locked room, Craig."

"What room?"

Goran pounds his fist on the table, making our suspect jump a little. "The fucking room, with the stupid lock, that you wallpapered with pictures of Detective Boyle and those other people. The room where you kept that kid. Start there."

Craig shakes his head. "I don't know what you're talking about. I haven't even been in there in months. I was working on the bathroom."

"Oh, yeah?" Goran says. "Fixing the toilet, huh?"

He nods. "Yeah, it wouldn't work. I just got a new kit for it, and—"

"Stop lying, asshole," Goran growls. "You're going away for a real, real long time. You might as well just tell us everything right now."

I take a step closer to the table and slap the file folder down. "Yeah, you're gonna end up with some shitty public defender, and then what? You weren't planning on that when you kidnapped a *five-year-old* from his grandparents' house, were you?"

"Wait a minute," Craig says, holding up his hands. "Listen. I really, truly did not kill anyone. You think I killed a *kid*? Jesus."

Goran and I just stare at him.

"Fuck!" He expels a harsh breath and leans forward. "Fuck," he repeats in a softer voice.

"Why did you kill Allie Cox?" I ask. "And why plant all those business cards? Were you *trying* to get me to come after you?"

"Shit, what?" He puts on an incredulous expression. "Look, I didn't do anything like that. I swear."

"Why are we here then, Craig?" I'm smooth, confident. "Seems to me that we're here because of *something*. Let's start with Allie Cox. How do you know her?"

"I don't know her," he says.

"Did you kill Kevin Whittle?" I ask.

"Who the fuck is that?"

Innocent people often do one of several things. They either behave like Allie Cox did, disbelieving that we're asking whatever question we just posed, or they get angry, like Graham Whittle. Or they freak out, like Marnie. They fall all over themselves trying to prove that they didn't do whatever it is we're asking about. Craig isn't doing any of these things.

"How about Sean Miller? Was he involved?" I ask.

"Fuck if I know what Sean does."

"How long have you known him?"

"A while."

"How long is that?"

"Since Marnie and I got together. Six, seven years, maybe a little more."

"When they were kids?"

He squints at me. "No. I met her when she was in high school."

"So you didn't know them when you were sixteen, seventeen?"

He shakes his head, confusion tugging at his brow. "No, I lived on the West Side then. Marnie and I met at a party when she was in high school, after I moved down to the Falls. I just said that."

"Ever go to Sean's?" I ask. "You have keys to his house, right?"

"Yeah, I've been there. For some parties. Once to feed his dog."

"You have money problems?" I ask.

"Everyone needs money."

"How much money do you need, Craig?"

He tries to stare me down and fails. "Anything would work," he mumbles.

"Here's what I think. You hatched a little plan. You decided to abduct the boy when you thought his grandparents had money. You knew about Graham Whittle, you heard the speculation about how he stole a bunch of money, and you believed it. You thought you were on to something when you found out about the grandson: perfect kidnapping victim. You knew where he'd be. Maybe you got it from Allie. But something went wrong before you could get the money, so you killed him. Allie knew something, and you were afraid she'd tell us. So you killed her, too. Why don't you tell me what she knew, how you met, that kind of thing? We can make this a hell of a lot easier for you if you tell the truth now."

"What the hell are you talking about?"

I open the folder and take my time flipping through the photographs. I pull out the one of the branch cutters in Craig's basement and slide it his way. "Explain that, then." I move that one to the side to reveal the picture of the weird stalker room. "Or how about that?"

He looks stunned. "I have no idea what any of that is. Shit, is that my basement? That's my basement. Oh, shit."

"Listen, asshole," Goran says. "We figured it out. Just wait till we get prints off all that creepy shit in your basement, including the murder weapon."

"But he wanted us to figure it out, Goran," I say. "Either that, or he's one dumb shit."

"No," Craig squeaks. He clears his throat. "I swear, I swear, I *swear*. I didn't do any of that."

"Why kill Allie?" I ask in a softer voice. "What did she know? It just makes no sense to me. Help me make sense of it."

He frowns. "Wait a minute. Do you mean *Sarah's* friend Allie? The blonde?"

I keep my expression blank. *Sarah's friend Allie.*

"I only met her once," he says. "I swear to God I didn't kill anyone."

"Sarah," I say. "Marnie and Sean's foster sister. The one who stayed in your basement. What's her last name?"

"Taylor." He looks confused. "Sarah Taylor. Allie's her friend. They both live up here. They work together."

My heart beats faster. "Where do they work together, Craig?"

"At Winky's. In the Flats." Something happens in his face, like a light coming on behind his eyes. He points at the photo of his basement. "She must have done this. Crazy little bitch. Her or that new boyfriend of hers. I haven't even been in that room in weeks. She got thrown out of her apartment last month—spent all her money on those stupid tattoos—and I gave her the key when she needed a place to crash."

I start to lean forward but catch myself. "Where is she now?"

He shrugs. "At work? She hasn't been around this past week. She's been staying with her boyfriend."

"His name?"

"Chris," Craig says, wild-eyed now. "You think *he* killed a kid?"

"Chris what?"

"I don't know! I don't even know the guy. Big blond fucker, puppy-dog eyes. He knows Sean, I think. Runs some deliveries his way. You think he did this?"

I'm in a nightmare. Hoping against hope, I pull out my phone and scroll through my photos. "Is this him?" I ask, thrusting the screen in front of his face.

Craig squints at the picture of Christopher and my mom. "That's him. That's the guy. Now get me a lawyer. I mean it this time."

CHAPTER TWENTY-FOUR

AT MY DESK, I PULL out my phone. My hands shake as I scroll to Christopher's number. After a few rings, my call goes to voicemail. I hang up and dial again. Voicemail. Christopher's the needy one. He always answers.

That night at the foster home plays in my head like an old home movie, flickering in and out of focus, before the frame melts on the screen. Something hits me, and I call over to Domislaw. "Teresa Whittle," I say. "What was her maiden name?"

Dom runs the search. "Taylor. Teresa Taylor."

My stomach turns. "Siblings?"

"One sister." He taps on his keyboard. "Karen Taylor. She has a record. She did time. Had one kid, a daughter, Sarah. Never married."

Teresa Whittle is Sarah's aunt, the aunt who turned her mother in to CFS, the aunt from the creepy poems. It all snaps together, and I hate, on so many levels, that it makes sense. *It's Sarah Taylor. Christopher's girlfriend, Sarah. It's her.*

My partner comes back to his desk. "Goran, my brother's not answering."

He pulls his coat off the back of his chair. "Let's go. I'll drive."

I don't bother arguing. But when we get to the car, I get in the driver's seat. Goran eyes me for a second then climbs into the passenger side.

My brother's apartment is fifteen minutes away. *Is Sarah there? Is she there with him now?* We can't afford to spook her. If she knows we're closing in, she could kill him or take him hostage.

When we get to Christopher's apartment building, I slam the gearshift into park and wrench the keys from the ignition. I'm at the front steps before Goran is even out of the car. My senses are sharpened to a fine point. Everything looks normal enough on the outside, but Christopher's Cutlass isn't here. I start to get a sinking feeling in my gut. I yank open the door and run up the stairs. On the second floor, loud music—Slayer, to be precise—blasts out into the hallway.

"He never listens to metal," I whisper to Goran as we approach my brother's apartment. The door is ajar. I put my hand on my Glock.

Goran knocks on the doorframe. "Chris?" he calls.

"Fuck. Go, go, go," I say in a harsh whisper.

He unholsters his gun and pushes the door the rest of the way open. He steps through the doorway.

"Christopher!" I yell, pulling my gun and following my partner.

No reply.

"Christopher!" I shout. My voice sounds tight and strained.

An end table is overturned. On the floor beside it is a lamp, and an old photograph of my brother and my sister and me that's been torn in half. Christopher's shattered phone lies a foot away.

Breathe. Breathe. Breathe.

I yank the stereo cord out of the wall just as "Criminally Insane" starts to play. I cross the living room in three strides and lean through the broken window to scan the alley behind his building.

Goran checks the bathroom and the kitchen. "Boyle, he's not here." He gets on the radio and asks for a patrol unit to go behind the building, near the fire escape.

I bite the inside of my cheek until the pain makes my brain work again. I glance at the broken glass on the floor. *Blood. No, no, no.*

"Tom, look at this," I say, squatting to get a closer look. "Where the hell did he go?" My hands start to shake again, so I ball them into fists. *No, please. Not Christopher. Damn it, no. Anything but this.*

We look around but don't find anything to give me a clue as to where my brother is or what's happened to him. Goran keeps asking me questions that I can't answer, things about my brother's girlfriend that I feel I should know but don't.

I pull on a pair of latex gloves and go into the kitchen, where I look through all of the drawers. Nothing. Then I go into his bedroom and look around, but there's nothing there, either. Finally, I go over to yank the cushions off the ratty old couch. Stuffed down into the left side is a black notebook filled with tight, tiny writing, illustrations of me, drawings of my apartment building and car, and weird poems and stories. The latest entry is about that dinner I had with Josh and Julia Becker, complete with sketches of them and a description of the ways in which I might have entertained myself afterward. The whole thing is written in first person, and it's so thoroughly creepy that I bark out a tight laugh in spite of myself.

"What is that?" Goran asks, craning his neck to get a better look.

"Call Fishner. Tell her—fuck. We have to find her. We have to find her," I say. I start to leave, but he stops me with a big hand on my shoulder.

He pulls out his phone and taps the screen. He holds my gaze and sends me some sort of telepathic message about calming down, it'll be fine, that kind of thing. His eyes look sympathetic. When he talks to Fishner, his voice is calm and cool.

I frantically flip through the notebook and notice that the handwriting changes about halfway through. That's where Sarah starts writing in what I guess is her own voice, all about being beaten by her biological mother for being left-handed, and how her aunt Teresa turned her mother in and then refused to take custody of Sarah. As an adult, she tracked down the aunt and watched the whole family, recording their movements in a creepily vivid level of detail. When Elaine Whittle advertised for a nanny, Sarah pushed her friend Allie into applying for the job. Everything, the whole plan, is spelled out here in the woman's own handwriting.

Holy fucking hell. I can feel my heart beating in my throat and a thin line of nausea snaking up from my stomach.

Killing him wasn't part of the plan, though. I read the details of what happened the day of Kevin's kidnapping. Sarah had been watching him so closely, watching Teresa, and jumped at the moment when Graham Whittle left Kevin unattended outside. So the kidnapping was a crime of opportunity. She'd planned to mess with Teresa via Allie and Kevin, but then she caught a lucky break. She told him Allie was in the car and they were going to go to the zoo. She drugged him and kept him in Marnie's basement for several days, plying him with the vodka and sedatives.

Thursday, the day she killed him, she still didn't know what to do with the kidnapped kid and knew she couldn't keep him at Marnie's alone, so she decided to bring a still-drugged Kevin to Cleveland and talk to Sean. But when she got to his house, he wasn't home. She'd started thinking that they could go for ransom, that she could make a little bit of money on messing with her estranged aunt. She was afraid to try to sneak him back into Marnie's house, so she decided to stash him in Sean's garage. While she was trying to tie him up, he woke up, bit her, and ran. Out of Rohypnol— she needed to get more from Sean—she acted in desperation. She grabbed a shovel from the wall of the garage and swung it at him as she chased him. She was trying to knock him down, but one blow landed on the side of his head. He dropped to the ground. She thought she'd killed him, and she was furious: mad at the kid for putting her in that situation and angry with his mother for ruining her life then turning her into a murderer.

From there, the narrative gets weirder and weirder, and I wonder whether she had some kind of psychotic break in the midst of committing these crimes. I scan her description of what she did to Kevin Whittle's body and her baffling list of reasons for her actions. Something hits me. Sarah's mom beat her for being left-handed. I think of Kevin's missing left hand, a hand that we never found: *exsanguination due to severed appendage.* I feel sick. She's obviously completely out of her mind but very smart, which scares me more than anything.

Near the end of the notebook, after a long diatribe about the lack of justice in the world—I skim most of that—she spends about twenty pages obsessing about David Lynch movies. She's got six pages on *Eraserhead*, long ramblings about the woman in the radiator and why psychological horror is "both the best and worst kind" of horror. Her favorite is *Mulholland Drive*, which she calls "the perfect mystery, if you're smart enough to spot the clues." A sharp pain jabs me when I remember Christopher chatting so happily about his new girlfriend and how they bonded over David Lynch movies.

Tucked into a pocket inside the back cover is an article about the Cleveland Film Society putting on a retrospective. She's circled the date, time, and location. I check my watch. *Mulholland Drive* starts in forty-five minutes at Tower City Cinema.

"Call for backup," I tell Goran. "I'm going to arrest this crazy bitch. This is my collar. She's at Tower City. We're going to get her right now. Get me a picture. I need a picture."

"Boyle. Please. Take some deep breaths, or I can't let you do anything with this."

I force myself to breathe. In a nice, calm voice, I ask Goran to call Fishner to get the green light, then we jog to the car. While he's standing outside on the phone, I get in and grip the steering wheel so tightly that my hands start to go numb. As soon as he reaches for the door handle, I start the car.

He plops into the passenger seat. "Boss lady says go get her," he says as he buckles his seat belt. "She's sending us both a picture and calling for backup."

On the way to the theater, I hit the dash lights and siren, the whole deal. I hit about eighty miles an hour at one point on Ontario. The drive to the theater, which would usually take over half an hour, takes eight minutes. A couple of times, Goran tries to remind me that sleet can freeze when it hits pavement and that even though we have all-wheel drive, I need to be careful because there are other people on the road, but I wave him off.

When we get there, I see that patrol has already responded with three zone cars. "Talk to them, Goran. I can't right now. I won't make sense."

He puts his hand on my shoulder. "Breathe, Boyle. We'll get her. Okay? Are you okay? I can't let you—"

I close my eyes for a few seconds then open them. "I'm fine. Thank you. I'm fine."

He hops out of the car and jogs over to the cruisers. I shove my door open then circle around to the trunk for our Kevlar vests. Trying not to imagine what might be happening to my brother, I scan the parking lot for his Cutlass, but I don't see it. *This is my collar. I will put her away.*

Goran comes up beside me, and I hand him his vest. As he's putting it on, he says, "Okay, we've got six uniforms, maybe more on the way from the districts. The first thing we need to do is get in there and get the lay of the land. If memory serves, it's just one long hallway with, like, ten auditoriums. So I'm keeping two on the front door, one on each of the fire exits at the ends, two in the back, and two with us."

I strip off my leather jacket, throw it into the car, and replace it with the vest, which I top with a navy-blue police windbreaker. I slam the trunk lid closed. "*Mulholland Drive* is the movie she came to see," I say as we stride toward the entrance.

"Ten-four, partner. What kind of car does Chris drive?"

"A '99 Cutlass. It's a piece of shit. Green."

Goran radios for more backup and requests that a zone car cruise the parking lot to look for Christopher's car. We slam through the front door of the theater. Two uniforms, a young man and an older woman, enter right after we do and fall in behind me.

I thrust my phone at the guy at the ticket desk. "Do you recognize this woman? Is she in here? Maybe accompanied by a tall blond man?"

The ticket clerk squints at my phone and shakes his head. "No blond guy. But I remember her. She's shown up for every single one of the Lynch films. She seemed out of it today, though. On something, I figure."

"Which auditorium is *Mulholland Drive* playing in?" Goran asks.

"Theater number three," he says. "It's not running for another thirty minutes, but she was early."

"You're sure there was no one with her?" I ask.

He nods. "I'm sure."

We hustle down the hall to theater number three and stop outside the door.

"Here's the plan," Goran says. "Once we're in there, one of us will take each corner." He points at the male uniform. "Baker, you're on the right rear." He turns to the other one. "Moskowitz, you're on the left rear. Boyle will go to the front right, and I'll take the front left. On my signal, one of you in the back flip on the lights. There should be a switch somewhere near the entrance to the auditorium, up on the wall."

The four of us file into the theater and station ourselves as quietly as we can around the edges of the room. Goran raises his hand then lowers it. Seconds later, the lights come on. I squint until my eyes adjust.

Goran steps forward, keeping his voice steady. "Folks, we're sorry to interrupt, but there's an emergency situation. We need to evacuate the theater."

It's a small crowd, maybe only fifteen people, so I scan every face as they get to their feet. One middle-aged guy looks irate. A woman spills her popcorn. A couple of underage kids shove open beer cans back into a bag. They file out of the theater, and I start searching each row.

I call out, "Sarah, this is Liz. Christopher's sister. I know you want to talk to me."

No one responds. I'm standing in a completely empty theater with no brother and no suspect. I sprint to the hallway. Goran and the two unis exit right behind me.

Back in the hallway, two more uniforms join us. "One of you take that end of the hallway, and the other at the other end," I order, suddenly feeling more in control. I turn to Baker and Moskowitz. "Check all of the doors in the hallway. They're probably storerooms, and she could be hiding in there. Slow going in the auditoriums. There are places to hide."

"Do you have a picture?" Moskowitz asks.

I pull out my phone and tap on the photograph from Fishner. I hold out my phone, and the four unis lean in to get a look. They split up and hustle down the hall in opposite directions.

Goran and I start with the two doors closest to the auditorium we just left. They're both locked.

"Hey!" I call to a guy who looks as if he might be the manager. "Will you unlock these doors, please? Don't open them, just unlock them."

He nods and scurries over to unlock them, dropping his keys twice in the process. I motion for him to step to the side. I draw my weapon, and Goran opens one door. Just a storeroom. He opens the next. No perp, no brother.

I holster my weapon and spin around. I point at a door marked Projection Booth. "What's that? Where does that go?" My gut twists. *The projection booth. Playing the director. Running the show.*

"It goes upstairs," the manager replies.

Goran calls to Baker and Moskowitz, telling them to follow us, but I don't wait. I wrench the door open and take the steps two at a time. When I get to the top, I draw my weapon and push through a second door. I hear Goran behind me with the uniforms.

The dimly lit room, which is about a hundred yards long, houses the movie projectors. Almost all of them are running, light flickering through each lens, through a glass porthole, and onto the movie screens.

"Let's start on this end and work our way down," Goran whispers. He turns to the two uniforms. "You two take that side."

We creep around the projectors, weapons drawn.

Baker calls, "Over here," from the far end of the room. "A ladder!"

Goran and I finish clearing our section of the floor and join him down

241

at the far end. Baker shines his flashlight up into the narrow passageway, and the beam disappears against the dark sky.

Shit, really? "It goes to the roof," I say. I point at the unis. "You two, make sure this floor is completely clear. Check those two bathrooms back there, and that office. Radio for at least two more officers to get up here."

Goran goes up the ladder first. "Be careful," he calls down to me. "It's slippery."

When I make it onto the roof, I stand next to Goran and lock my elbows with my thumbs forward on the pistol, matching the way he's holding his own weapon. "That way." I gesture to the right with the Glock.

Goran slides in front of me, his back flat against the back of the large neon sign that bears the name of the theater.

"I'm taking the other side," I whisper.

I half crawl behind a large air-conditioning unit. The rooftop is mostly gravel and stones, probably over rubber or asphalt, and it crunches beneath my boots. The sleet stings my face, but I barely notice. Out of the corner of my eye, I spot movement on my left. Someone is behind another unit.

"Sarah Taylor!" I shout. "This is it! Come out with your hands above your head!" I want to stand up and survey the scene, but I know she's armed. Vests don't protect us from head shots.

A police helicopter circles overhead. *Wow. They've really called in the cavalry for this one.* I say a tiny little thank-you to Fishner. The spotlights swirl around on the roof before coming to a stop behind one of the HVAC units. I know there's a guy up there with a sniper rifle. Through a loudspeaker, they tell her to drop her weapon.

Sarah, bent at the waist in a half crouch, runs toward the roof hatch. If she goes back down there, there's a chance she can take a hostage. I hope patrol cleared the second floor. I drop my left hand, keeping my gun in front of me in my right. I don't like this, but I have to move fast. I bolt toward her.

She pops up from behind another of the HVAC units. She jogs backward toward the ledge, her gun pointed right at my forehead. The spotlight is on her, and I know the sniper is getting ready to shoot. A disembodied man's voice from above tells her to drop her weapon and lie on the ground.

I've got both hands on my Glock now. My finger clenches, putting pressure on the trigger. I've got a clear shot. I'm looking down the barrel at the left center of her chest. Her heart is beating but not for long, because she's going to shoot me, and I have no choice.

Boom!

The shot didn't come from my gun or from hers. It came from above me, registering in my brain under the sound of the helicopter and my own heart beating. She suddenly drops from view.

"Down the hatch! Goran, she's down the fucking hatch!" I scream.

I keep my trigger finger flexed, but I'm no longer squeezing the trigger. One more ounce of pressure, and it would have been my second shooting in three months. There's no way IA would look the other way, and there's no way I would ever get over it.

I don't see Goran, and I'm closer, so I hurry over to the roof hatch. Grabbing the top rung of the ladder, I swing my body over and into the opening. I look down and see Sarah has fallen on the floor of the projection booth. She flails around in the slippery mess from the melting sleet and her own blood, which swirl together on the gray tile like one of those peppermint candies. Her gun is a foot away from her left hand. I can't tell where the wound is, but she's got to be seriously injured. Our snipers are good, and that was quite a drop.

I turn around on the ladder and point my Glock at her. Keeping my weapon trained on her, I awkwardly move down a few rungs. I almost fall once when my other hand slips, but I catch myself.

Sarah manages to get up on all fours then stretches a hand toward her weapon. I have a clear shot to the back of her head, but I'm not in danger now. I won't pull the trigger.

"Freeze! Do not reach for your weapon, or I will shoot you." My voice sounds as though it's coming from someone strong and powerful.

Suddenly, she leaps to her feet and takes off, disappearing from my line of sight. I'm not that far from the ground now, so I release my grip and jump. The impact on my knees is jarring, but I ignore the pain. Her gun is no longer on the floor.

I sprint down the hall. "Freeze!"

I spot her ahead. Her gun is in her right hand. She's not moving very fast, and I overtake her in seconds. I lurch forward and tackle her from behind. On top of her, I try to get my bearings. I've knocked the wind out of both of us, and a sharp pain radiates from my knee. She flails around, trying to get her weapon aimed at me.

"Where the fuck is Christopher?" I growl.

I'm bigger than she is, and she's hurt, but she's strong. I push myself up a little and plant my left knee in her back. I push her right arm down hard into the tile with my left hand. I quickly holster my Glock to free up my other hand so I can cuff her. *Please, Goran. Please be there behind me.* I reach out to pluck the gun from her hand.

Boom!

The sound of the blast deafens me. I realize Sarah managed to pull the trigger.

"*Boyle!* Officer down! Officer down!"

But I'm not down. I'm fine. I don't feel any pain, and it's not my blood. Crimson is oozing from her left shoulder, and more is pooling on the floor beneath her. It's a through-and-through from the sniper rifle. We've got to get her to the hospital, or she's going to bleed out right here.

I reach out and push her gun out of her hand with enough force to send it skittering across the floor. Seeing Goran coming from the direction of the ladder, I yell, "I've got her! Disarmed! She is unarmed! Call an ambulance!"

Baker and Moskowitz burst out of a door down the hall, guns raised and pointed at us.

"I've got her!" I yell again. "I'm fine! I've got her! Don't shoot! Medics! *Now!*"

Goran comes up beside me. "Are you okay?"

I nod. "Yeah, I'm good."

Baker recovers Sarah's gun, a small Smith and Wesson semiautomatic, and hands it to Goran. My partner drops the weapon into an evidence bag then moves over to inspect the wall where the bullet is lodged. Two other uniforms come up through the door that leads downstairs.

I push Sarah's face into the tile with my left forearm against the back of her head. "Where is Christopher?"

"I'm sorry," she whispers.

"We found the car," one of the new arrivals says.

I press her harder into the floor. "Where is Christopher?"

"My job wasn't done yet," she cries. "I wanted you to kill me."

"He's okay," the uniform says. "Shaken up, slowed down, drugged on something, but okay. We got him out of the trunk of the Cutlass. It was parked around back by the dumpster."

I lean forward, getting my mouth inches from her ear. "Your little adventure is over now, psycho." I'm tempted to yank her arms back and cuff her none too gently, but she's fading fast, her blood soaking both of us.

I look down and see that she's smiling. Grinning. She starts to struggle. She's bleeding everywhere. It's not stopping.

"Stop it, or you're going to bleed out. Be still."

"It's nice that you give a shit today, but you were supposed to kill me. You would have, too. You fucking idiot. You've always been so stupid, so selfish." Her voice is spooky because she sounds so calm. Her head falls back against the floor, and her eyelids flutter closed.

I yank off my windbreaker and use it to apply pressure to her shoulder. "Where the fuck are the medics?" I shout.

"It was the last chance," she whispers. "My last chance. That night in that foster home was my last chance at anything like a normal life. And you left me there. I really liked your brother, you know." She takes a labored breath. "Thing is, people like you and me? We can never be in love. We hurt everyone we touch."

I tell her to shut up until she's out of surgery, then she can tell me all about it.

She loses consciousness before I have the chance to Mirandize her.

CHAPTER TWENTY-FIVE

FOR THE FIRST TIME IN months, I don't wake up before my alarm. I'm in a deep sleep when it goes off. As soon as I open my eyes, the cat jumps off the bed and starts meowing for food. "Morning, Ivan."

I grab my phone and see that I have a text message from Julia Becker: *Do you have time this morning for a cup of coffee? I'll be at Gato's by 8.*

Sure, I reply. *I'll see you then.*

She was kind to me the night we apprehended Sarah Taylor. After a shower and a change of clothes, I went back to the station to start the mountain of paperwork. Becker was waiting for me, holding a cup of good coffee with the right amount of cream, her copper-colored hair pulled back into a messy bun. "Are you okay?" she asked.

"I think so. I could use some ice for my knee."

"You want me to stay, in case you want to talk?"

I didn't want to talk, but I thanked her, anyway. She brought me ice for my knee. She was kind.

I get dressed and go out to my car. I notice that the temperature is much warmer than it has been, and I wonder if spring is finally on its way. It still feels like rain, but I'll take it.

I park behind the Justice Center and pull out my phone to text Goran: *Grabbing coffee with Becker. Be in by 9:15.*

I'll buy you breakfast before the big interview, he replies. *Meet me at the diner when you're done with coffee. I'll handle Fishner.*

How that man puts up with me boggles my mind, especially given how I barked orders at him throughout that whole spectacle. I've already apologized, but I'll probably do it again.

I spot Becker at a table in the back corner—the good table this time. I smile and give her a little wave. I try not to limp as I cross the restaurant.

As I slide into a chair across from her, she asks, "Knee still hurts?"

So much for hiding the limp. I shrug. "Not much."

She slides today's *Plain Dealer* across the table and taps on the front page. My stupid picture is there again, but at least it's below the fold this time. You'd think after three days, the media would have something better to report. But no, there I am, drenched in Sarah Taylor's blood, standing next to Christopher's stretcher outside the movie theater. I'm holding my brother's hand while a medic closes a different ambulance door on Taylor in the background. The headline reads: *CDP Special Homicide Well-Known for High Closure Rate.*

I push the paper back to her and stand. "I'm gonna grab a cup of coffee. You want anything?"

She smiles and gestures at her mug. "I'm good. Thanks."

Waiting in line at the counter, I shift my weight off my left leg. I look around at the old man in the corner, the attorneys in the middle, then the mom with three kids struggling to get out the front door. The little girl makes eye contact with me, and we smile at each other. People want to think the city is safe. Even if they hate cops and everything we are, they want to tuck their kids in at night and make sure the door is locked and go to sleep without too much worry, knowing that we put another psychotic asshole away. When it's my turn, I step up to the counter.

The teenager smiles. "What'll it be, Detective? The regular?"

"I'm treating myself today. Double-shot Americano, room for cream."

He calls out the order, and I move down to the end of the counter to wait. People want their realities to match the stories they tell themselves about certainty, about nothing bad happening to them or the people they love. On some level, maybe they even want to put a name and a human face to the people that put the perps in prison, which might explain the stupid newspaper interview Goran and I have to do. Alexis Edwards, the *Plain Dealer* reporter, wants to write another piece on us for next Sunday, something about taking a "more personal angle" and "showing the city that cops are human." Fishner is making us do it. *Whatever.*

Back at the table, Julia is tapping away on her phone.

I take a seat and wait for her to finish. When she looks up, I say, "Taylor woke up yesterday afternoon. I talked to her. She's not denying anything."

She puts her phone back in her bag. "I read your report. Do you really think she wanted you to kill her, or is that another manipulation tactic?"

"She wanted me to kill her. Suicide by cop. She knew I'd never get over it. She knew too much about me." Sarah Taylor isn't happy to be alive. She rambled like a lunatic yesterday when Goran and I were there. "I'm pretty relieved she doesn't have any communicable diseases, after all that blood."

"I'm sure the grand jury will indict her. Her case is scheduled for Monday."

"What about my brother? I'm having dinner with him. Can I tell him he's free and clear of this, beyond having questionable taste in women?"

She chuckles. "Questionable taste, indeed. Yeah, he's off the hook. Taylor's notebook is clear that he wasn't involved, and his alibis still hold."

"Thanks." I take a sip of my coffee. "She'll plead insanity."

"It won't fly. Everything was so methodical, from the abduction to the murders to all the clues she left."

"Yeah, but the abduction itself was opportunistic. I honestly think she did lose her shit after that, had some kind of psychotic break. I'm pretty sure killing the kid wasn't on her original agenda."

She takes a drink of her coffee then looks at me over the rim of her cup. "She killed two innocent people. She left a written confession. She stalked you and Teresa Whittle. She tried to frame your brother. She tried to frame Cox. Craig Phillips. There's no way a judge—or a jury—would go for insanity."

I nod. "Yeah, Heights has good evidence for Allie Cox." A bloody fingerprint on Cox's bathtub was a match for Taylor.

Cora Bosch and I ran into each other in the hospital hallway yesterday, and we were civil to one another. I'm supposed to have a drink with her later this week. We'll see how that goes. I have apologies I need to make to her, too.

"The notebook speaks for itself, Liz, and the physical evidence is hard to beat. You guys did good work."

"Uh-huh." The notebook goes on and on about Teresa Whittle, about me, and about all the ways that Taylor was wronged as a kid. "All of us conspired to fuck her right up."

Becker chuckles. "I know you're not being glib, but it sure sounds that way."

"No, not glib. I mean it. It's possible that the system made her a criminal. All that stuff she wrote about how small the world is, how entwined we all are... it's hard to argue with that. And thinking she's right, even about something as woo-woo as that. It scares me a little."

She gives me a soft smile. "She's still guilty, Liz. It seems like you feel bad for her."

"It's gonna be hard to forget those CFS photos. First her mother, then her foster mother beating the shit out of her... and then being the victim of two sexual assaults." I shake my head. "The system completely failed her."

"Other people have been in that situation, or worse, and not killed anyone, much less a child."

"I know. I really do know." Having a fucked-up, tragic past isn't an excuse. Most people do their best to get through their lives without inflicting their pain and misery on anyone else. "What about Sean Miller?"

"Aiding and abetting."

"The poor dumb shit."

"It's hard to argue with traces of the victim's blood in the trunk of Phillips's car and his fingerprints all over the interior. Your report on your interview with the Whittles was an exercise in brevity. What happened?"

I lean back in my chair and stare out the window before meeting her eyes again. Teresa and Peter both cried and thanked me for coming by, but their grief was so palpable, so real, that it felt like getting kicked in the stomach to witness it. "The look on Teresa's face pretty much said it all. Regret. I started to wonder what would have happened if I'd followed up all those years ago. If I'd asked those kids who was hurting them, if I'd done anything but get in the car and leave." It's out of my mouth before I know what I'm saying. Dr. Shue will be so proud when I tell her.

"You can't blame yourself. That was a long time ago. I'm serious."

I laugh. "I can't believe I'm saying any of this to you." *The universe will reward you for taking risks on its behalf.*

She raises her eyebrows. "Thanks?"

"I'm just not much for sharing. I hope it doesn't make you uncomfortable."

"I'm not uncomfortable, Liz. That's what friends are for." Her phone chirps, and she pulls it out of her bag. "I'm due in court in fifteen minutes. Let's grab a drink after Taylor's grand jury, and I'll fill you in." She stands.

"Sounds good."

As she's walking away, she pauses and puts her hand on my shoulder. "Well done, Detective Boyle."

"Thanks, Counselor." I smile, and I mean it.

ACKNOWLEDGEMENTS

Thanks to my editors, Lynn McNamee and Angela McRae, for filing off the rough edges, with extra-special thanks to Lynn for those interesting phone conversations, for seeing the dark humor in this book, and for laughing with me about things that others might not find funny.

Thanks to the whole staff at Red Adept Publishing for the good work that you do.

Thanks to Claire Anderson-Wheeler, my amazing agent at Regal, Hoffman & Associates, for seeing potential in a very early draft and taking a chance on me. She will never know how much I appreciate her, especially when she was on the other end of those emails during what I call "desperate season," aka heavy-duty revising in the cold, dark Midwestern winter.

Thanks to my parents for instilling a love of dark, demented mystery fiction in me at a very early age and for always encouraging me to follow my heart. I love you. (And seriously: I was reading books about autopsies at the age of about eleven.)

Thanks to my fellow lover-of-the-macabre Jessica L. for the dream sequence that, somehow, brought Liz's character to life for me in the early days of drafting this book. Thanks to my early readers, whose feedback helped me write a better book—Tom, Linda, Suzanne, Megan, Wendy, and Rick, you helped keep me honest. Thanks, too, to my writing buddy KFO, and to Veronica, Em, Danielle, and Hannah. You rock. Now finish those lists.

Special thanks to Deputy Amanda H. for taking time from her own family and law-enforcement career to consult on some of the police work details.

Thanks beyond words to Malia, the love of my life, whose love and support means everything in the world. Writing can be isolating, and writers can be fickle. You make it—and me—less so. It's smaller than a toaster, but only just, and you and I will continue to visit discount stores together and laugh in the aisles as we write scenes for our favorite comedy shows for many, many years to come.

All of the characters and events in this book are figments of my imagination. I am not Elizabeth Boyle any more than you are, though I like to think that she and I have an understanding of sorts. The Cleveland Department of Police does not have a Special Homicide Division. Therefore, the squad room, the ranking system within the unit, and some of the procedural aspects of the book are, like the characters and events, fictional. It was, for example, law until roughly 2005 that CDP officers live in the Cleveland city limits, which makes Liz's apartment in Cleveland Heights a no-go. But for the sake of character, there she is. It's also tremendously likely that I've botched several facets of how real police would investigate this crime, and I've definitely taken creative liberties with the city itself. In short, *none of this really exists or ever did*, and any similarity to actual places, events, or persons, living or dead, is a coincidence.

Any mistakes are my own.

ABOUT THE AUTHOR

Kate Birdsall was born in the heart of the Rust Belt and harbors a hesitant affinity for its grit. She's an existentialist who writes both short and long fiction, and she plays a variety of loud instruments. Kate lives in Michigan's capital city with her partner and at least one too many four-legged creatures.